AMERICAN DREAMS

NORMA KLEIN

AMERICAN DREAMS

E. P. DUTTON | NEW YORK

PUBLISHER'S NOTE: This novel is a work of fiction. Names,
characters, places, and incidents either are the product of the
author's imagination or are used fictitiously, and any resemblance
to actual persons, living or dead, events, or locales is entirely
coincidental.

Published in the United States by
E. P. Dutton, a division of New American Library,
2 Park Avenue, New York, N.Y. 10016.

Library of Congress Cataloging-in-Publication Data
Klein, Norma, 1938–
American dreams.
I. Title.
PS3561.L35A8 1987   813'.54   86-16672
ISBN: 0-525-24487-5

Published simultaneously in Canada by
Fitzhenry & Whiteside Limited, Toronto

COBE

DESIGNED BY MARK O'CONNOR

10 9 8 7 6 5 4 3 2 1

First Edition

In memory of Ibo Silberman

Jay

1963

"**W**hat the fuck are you doing in there?" his sister is screaming, pounding on the bathroom door. "I have a date, I've got to take a shower! If you don't get out in five minutes, I'll break down the door!"

Jay has just been gazing at himself morosely in the ancient glass of his parents' bathroom mirror, hoping to see another face materialize in front of him. Although Marlene can't see him, he makes an ugly expression and yells back, "I'll be out in a minute."

In the background he hears his mother's soft, soothing voice saying, "Dear, he has to get ready. It's a big night for him. He's going to the prom . . . with Xenia."

"What do *I* care who he's going with?" Marlene shrieks back. "How does that impinge on my life? I just want him out! What is he—teasing his hair? Hoping he'll grow?"

"He'll be out in a minute," his mother whispers, fearful he will hear.

How can he not? Since Jay was born, his parents have lived in this two-bedroom walk-up on Barrow Street, for which they still pay an incredibly low rent, all they can afford since his father was blacklisted and forced to quit his job teaching Russian literature at City College. The family subsists on his mother's salary as a librarian at a small private school. Growing up, he and Marlene shared a room until she reached puberty. He was nine when she began her long period of turbulent teen-age angst, an era that, as far as Jay can see, is still going on, although Marlene's been out of college four years. His parents, ever obsequious, eager to sacrifice for "the children," moved into the living room and kept their few possessions in a hall closet. Then came a brief "normal" period when Marlene went away to college. In some ways, Jay reflects, this may have been the highlight of his life so far. His parents reclaimed their bedroom, though they still lived out of the hall closet and felt guilty that the room wasn't kept as a lighted shrine for his sister's possessions. Though Jay continued living at home throughout college, to save money, by then it looked as though at least one of the family's major problems was solved. Turbulent, irascible, brilliant Marlene went on to grad school and not only received a degree in electrical engineering, but even managed to nab a husband, one of her professors, a neat, repressed man twelve years her senior, who always wore bow ties and had a slight twitch around one side of his mouth. "She'll be independent, someone loves her," Jay heard his mother murmur to his father. "I told you if we waited long enough it would all work out."

But last fall, just as Jay started his senior year, Marlene flounced back home again. She is still married to Emery ("they love each other but can't live together"), but she has decided she doesn't want to be an electrical engineer at all; she wants to write science fiction. All day, all night, while Jay has been trying to study, the rat-a-tat-tat of his sister's manual typewriter has issued from his parents' bedroom; his parents are sleeping in the living room again. Occasionally she "allows" him to read one of her productions, but if he says anything other than that it is a masterpiece, she slams out of the room in a huff.

Now, as Jay emerges from the bathroom, he sees Marlene standing in the hallway, her eyes closed. His mother, Sophie, is watching her nervously.

4

"The bathroom's free now," his mother chirps. To Jay she says, "You look lovely, dear."

Marlene's eyes fly open. "I have a migraine. I'm going to call Emery and tell him to sell the tickets."

"Oh, don't do that," his mother says. "It's to the Bolshoi! Your headache will go away. Just take a nice, relaxing, hot shower."

Marlene whirls around. "*You* go with him," she says. "Why don't *you*? You both love each other so much."

"He wants to be with you," Sophie pleads. Turning to Jay, she adds, "He doesn't want to be with a woman in her fifties."

Despite himself—it's the last night in the world he wants to get involved in family quarrels—Jay gives his mother a hug and says, "I bet he'd love to go with you, Ma." Except that probably no, anyone who's signed on with Marlene, even temporarily, wants someone who will dance in high-heeled shoes on his chest, while he writhes at every step.

His sister smiles sarcastically. "Isn't that cute? Mother and child. . . . How come you're going with Xenia? I thought she pitched you."

His mother's memory is selective. She weeds out any events that injure his pride, any prizes he hasn't won. Whereas his sister, with unerring accuracy, remembers every hideous insult that life has dealt him.

"I'm going with Susan," he acknowledges.

"That mousy little one who never speaks? Good luck!" She exits into the bathroom.

"I thought you were going with Xenia," Sophie says, bewildered.

One of the many things Jay hates about living at home is that his private life, meager and uninteresting as it is, is still considered fair game for everyone in the family to discuss, except perhaps his father, who simply doesn't care. The other day he took a walk with his father in the park, a week before his twenty-first birthday. "How old are you going to be?" his father, Eli, asked. "Twenty-one," Jay replied. "Already!" Eli exclaimed in a tone of wonderment, as though the years had somehow slipped through his fingers.

More than almost anything in the world, Jay thinks, he would like a family like other families, a family like Xenia's, or his best friend Conrad's, a family where the father works, or at least earns more than the mother, where everyone has his own room, even his own bathroom! Conrad often complains about the eerie quiet in his parents' home, the precise neatness of the Viennese decor, the small statues from Parke Bernet, the cream-colored walls and Dégas prints. To Jay it seems wonderful, wonderfully un-Jewish, even though Conrad's adopted parents *are* Jewish; but the Viennese element seems predominant, as well as the understated wealth. Conrad's father is a corporation lawyer who came to America in the thirties to escape the Nazis, the same decade in which his own father emigrated from Russia to Germany, to England, and, finally, to New York.

His mother regards his father's life as a tragedy. "A foremost scholar," as she puts it in her respectful tones. "And he can't get a job anywhere. Like a fine jewel just sitting, no one even sees its sparkle, its beauty. What a shame for the world!" But to Jay his father seems perfectly content, reading Chekhov in the original, sauntering over to Washington Square Park for a game of chess with some cronies, taking a two-hour nap every afternoon, occasionally making a pot of borscht or a pot roast so dinner will be prepared when Sophie returns, exhausted, from work. "He was such a fine teacher," Sophie whispers to Jay, often with his father just a few feet away; she is comfortable in the assurance that Eli's increasing deafness makes any chance of overhearing unlikely. "Brilliant!"

Once Jay met someone who had taken his father's classes and who claimed he was a terrible teacher, disorganized, always drifting off into digressions, leaving student exams on the subway. Somehow that image, which seems to fit what he knows of his father, stays with him and casts a shadow over his mother's effusive accounts.

"Ma, I'm not going to the prom with Xenia," he explains patiently, going down the hall to his room. "Xenia and I haven't gone out for three years. She's going with Conrad now. I'm taking Susan."

"But she and Conrad—that doesn't make sense to me." Sophie frowns. "They don't fit somehow. He's your best friend. How could he *do* that to you?"

"It wasn't like that." Jay wishes the evening were not beginning like this. His mother often stumbles onto insights in her probing, relentless way.

"Con didn't *do* anything. Xenia just had some sort of crush on him. She always has. We were just friends, really."

His mother gives him a "do you think I was born yesterday?" look.

6

"You were more than friends. Let me tell you. I've had more experience than you have. I can tell by the way people look when they're together, by their expression. It was love."

"So, it was love," he says impatiently. "Now it's over, okay? Now it's love between Xenia and Conrad. They're thinking of living together. They're even looking at apartments."

"It's not going to last," his mother says. "I'm sorry to cast gloom on your friends' plans. They're not suited."

Jay tries to laugh. "Maybe not, Ma, but *they* think they are."

What he doesn't get was why, if his mother is so psychic about Conrad and Xenia, she doesn't aim that same piercing light on his sister and poor bamboozled Emery, whom Marlene railroaded into getting his doctorate in political science and who calls faithfully every night, sends giant old-fashioned valentines, weeps when Marlene says she isn't sure their marriage is "viable" anymore.

"How about Marlene and Emery?" he says sarcastically. "Is that marriage made in heaven?"

"Your sister is a different story," his mother says. "So sensitive. She's an artist. Artists are a whole other kettle of fish. Look at your father! They're not like you and me. Their makeup is different."

Jay looks at Eli, who is dozing on the couch, the Russian newspaper spread over his face. Where does his mother get this fantasy about his father and sister being artists? On what grounds? Here *he* has won the Columbia journalism award for his series on the civil rights movement, *he* was selected to be in Trilling's advanced writing class; but somehow his mother regards him merely as a bright boy who works hard, period.

"Xenia railroaded you into taking Susan," his mother says, inspecting his gloomy face. "She was afraid her friend wouldn't have a date. I know all about it. The pretty ones, they always have a shy, homely friend. I was like that with my friend, Arlene. *I* was the shy, homely friend."

"I like Susan," he says uneasily.

"You need to draw her out," his mother advises. "Still waters run deep. Those girls are the ones who are the pot of gold at the end of the rainbow. You just need to work harder."

"Sure." The trouble is Susan has no more interest in him than he does in her. She has a crush on Conrad too, the kind of pathetic, hopeless crush girls like that often get on handsome, out-of-reach men. His only identity in Susan's eyes is as Conrad's friend.

"You're the pot at the end of the rainbow too," his mother says. "Some lucky girl will realize that one day. Don't give up."

It's hard for Jay to imagine at times what life has been like for Conrad. While *he* has been living at home from birth until this present moment, Conrad was sent to prep school at thirteen, hasn't *seen* his parents except on vacations since then. God, where is the justice in life? And whereas Jay has spent years trying to excuse his father's lack of success by the fact that he came to America as a foreigner, Conrad's father, Ludwig Zweifach (or Zwieback, as Conrad sometimes calls him behind his back), took the same route. Yet within a decade, Ludwig retook his bar exam, and was comfortably ensconced in a highly reputable law firm. The only sorrow in the Zweifachs' life was their inability to have a child, and even there fate had intervened and brought them a son who, if not Jewish, was tall, blond, charming, affable.

Conrad's father adores Jay. Yet even in that adoration, there is something slightly akin to his mother's identification with him. Sophie sees the two of them as the nonartists in the family, the truckers, the ones who will plod along, earning their daily bread while the luminaries like his father and sister exist, write, think great thoughts that the indifferent world may choose to ignore. One day when Conrad was upstairs working on a paper, Ludwig Zweifach took Jay into his study.

"I want to show you a photo of my best friend, Siegfried Mentz. He was killed by the Nazis. Somehow he has always reminded me of you. If I had had a son, my own son, flesh and blood, he would have looked like you. That's why I think your friendship with Conrad was predestined. I think of you as my son too, do you know that?"

He gave Jay the twinkling, ironical smile that Conrad loves to imitate. Even his slight German accent seemed charming, the kind one might actually attempt to cultivate, not like his own father's Russian-Yiddish accent, which bungles sentences and simply makes him sound like a fool. Ludwig took down a heavy album and pointed to a photo of a gaunt, dark-eyed, haunted young man, a male Anne Frank. Good God, do I look like *that?* Jay thought despairingly.

"He had your spirit, your sensitivity," Mr. Zweifach said. "You are him, come back to life. When I saw you, I knew. God had brought him back to me." Tears glimmered in the middle-aged man's eyes. Jay tried to appreciate the irony that to his own father he was just a grade-grinding drone while to his friends' father he was a Kafka, a dead poet, a Jewish saint!

8

Sophie follows Jay into his room and watches him put on his tie. He's spent an hour trying on different ties and has finally settled on this dark red one with a small paisley pattern.

"What can I say?" his mother says. "You look wonderful. All Conrad has that you don't is height. A few inches. So? Does that make a man a man? Xenia will be sorry someday."

The idea that on a night you are preparing to go to a dance you might want a few moments of privacy, to think, to meditate, to brood, is totally alien to his family's style of communal living. Perhaps that is why he spent an hour in the bathroom, the one room with a lock on the door. He has sometimes wondered if he couldn't live in the bathroom.

"Yeah, Xenia will be sorry, they'll all be sorry." He whirls on his mother, hearing his voice rise and crack in rage. "It's *not* my height. It's nothing that simple. It's my character. It's everything!" Now he's being like his sister, using his mother as a verbal punching bag.

Sophie cringes. "Your character? What's wrong with your character? Who has a better character than you? She's a young girl, a teen-ager. What does she know about character?"

"She's twenty-one." Xenia entered Barnard at seventeen; she skipped a grade in grammar school.

"She's a baby, I'm sorry," his mother says. "I love Xenia, she's a brilliant girl, like your sister, she'll go far. . . . But she looks at Conrad and she sees, forgive me, blue eyes, big muscles, a piece of meat."

Why is he having this discussion? What's *wrong* with him? The one period of peace, potential peace, his sister soaking blissfully in a hot tub.

"Conrad is terrible at sports," Jay finds himself saying. "He has no muscles." The pathetic thing is that he, Jay, *has* the muscles, from weight lifting for six years. Conrad is six feet four and as lanky and uncoordinated as a string bean.

"It's the look," his mother says. "I'm giving you the female viewpoint. At that age women are dazzled by looks. Later they go for character."

"Thanks, Mom," Jay says sarcastically, but sarcasm is such an overused commodity in this house that it usually goes unnoticed.

"Let your father see you before you go," his mother says. "It would give him such pleasure."

"Are you sure you want to wake him up?" His father must sleep fourteen to sixteen hours a day. Jay has thought of entering

9

him in a sleeping contest. He can sleep anywhere, at any time. When his sister was going through a period of insomnia, his father said, "What is that like? You lie down, you close your eyes, you sleep. . . . What is the problem?"

"He's just dozing," Sophie says. She and Jay walk the short distance to the living room, where his father is snoring quietly on the sleep couch, which is his parents' bed at night.

"Eli? It's Jay. He's going to his dance. He wants to say good-bye."

His father starts and blinks, sits up. "You're going to a dance?"

"The senior prom," his mother reminds him. "It's his big night."

"Of course, his big night. . . . We should have a toast, a little schnapps, no?"

His mother brightens. "Yes, only let's wait for Marlene to come out."

"Mom, I promised to pick up Susan at eight-thirty," Jay says, glancing at his watch. It's past seven-thirty, and she lives in Riverdale.

"Okay, we'll start now." Sophie takes out the small rose-tipped glasses and fills each one. "To a wonderful, successful life!" She clinks her glass against Jay's, then her husband's.

Just as they have all swallowed their drinks, Marlene staggers out of the bathroom in her terry cloth robe, her hair in a turban.

"Hey, my headache is gone!" she says triumphantly. "Totally gone."

"Help us toast to Jay," his mother says. "He has to leave now."

Marlene takes a glass and clinks Jay's empty one.

"It's a hard, cruel world out there, baby brother. Be tough!"

"It would be perfect if you and Susan liked each other," Xenia said. "You *ought* to like each other. You're so much alike in so many ways." Xenia's attempting to link him with Susan is like his reminding Ludwig Zweifach of Siegfried Mentz: two losers, two nobodies. The fact is, Jay literally would not have noticed Susan's existence, even though she, like Xenia, was in Russian class at Columbia with him: Barnard girls were permitted to take Russian language classes at Columbia because Barnard didn't offer them. He and Xenia were "friends" by then, through her decision, their ill-fated romance having run its peculiar course in freshman year. Susan and Xenia had gone to grammar and high school together.

Susan had started out at Smith but transferred back to the city in her sophomore year to live with her mother.

Xenia and her shadow. Jay thinks of them that way and that is how they appear in the snapshots he occasionally takes. Xenia—tall and dark with her father's black Hungarian eyes and heavy eyebrows, her coarse braid of hair, vivid embroidered blouses, her explosive laugh, arrogant questions, sometimes infuriating self-assurance and vitality. Susan looks almost like an albino next to her, pale, freckled skin, big light blue eyes cast down, almost invisible eyebrows and eyelashes. She has a whispery, stammering voice and is perpetually slouched over. Whatever Susan wears looks three sizes too big, as though she is trying to disappear inside her clothes. Xenia says Susan always weighs herself fully dressed, carrying *War and Peace,* in hopes of topping one hundred pounds. Whereas Xenia talked a lot in class, kidded with the teacher, asked impertinent, not always relevant questions, Susan only spoke when directly addressed, slunk out of the room as though afraid of being pursued. "Okay, she has an inferiority complex," Xenia blithely explained. "Probably she's the smartest of all of us."

Sitting on the subway, the same A train he rode so many times to Xenia's home, Jay tries not to think of the evening ahead as one in which Xenia and Conrad will be a couple and he and Susan a couple. They are just going as a group, the four of them, four friends. There has been no evidence that Conrad is deeply in love with Xenia. Okay, so they've slept together a bunch of times, but what does that mean? Jay tries to see it as a version of Marlene and Emery: Xenia pounced, somewhat as she had done with Jay freshman year, and Conrad in his amiable, easygoing, genial way succumbed. His mother was probably right: they *weren't* suited. Of course, neither were he and Xenia, but why think of that now?

It was Xenia who approached him one day, one spring afternoon of their freshman year, when their Russian teacher let class out early. They took a picnic lunch to Riverside Park, even bought a bottle of wine. Xenia, flushed, her braid unraveling, confessed, "Can you believe this? I'm still a virgin! I'm a psychiatrist's daughter, I know everything there is to know about repression. Do you think it's that I've been sublimating everything into my work?"

"Probably," Jay said, wondering if she was assuming he was different, more experienced.

"You are too, right?" was her next comment. "You have that look. I recognize it from seeing my face in the mirror. That kind of 'why aren't I getting any? why am I different?' look. But why *should* intellectuals be weirdos?"

"In a manner of speaking," Jay said, trying to hide behind a phrase that might, incorrectly, imply years of almost making it with shy, repressed girls at Bronx Science.

"We could just, you know, do it together." Xenia was flushed. With her bright pink cheeks and round black eyes she looked like one of those peasant girls on his parents' enameled boxes from Leningrad. "We're friends, we like each other, I don't see how it could be hideous, do you? I mean, it's more up to you since you'd have to . . . I'd have to . . . You'd have to find me mildly sexually whatever. Do you think—"

Watching Xenia's self-possession crumble into inarticulateness made Jay courageous.

"Yeah, I think I could," he said slowly. "Sure, it's a good plan. No one but us has to know."

Xenia was yanking up tufts of grass and tossing them nervously into a pile. "I even—God, this will strike you as horrendous, but I actually have this diaphragm which I got about nine months ago, supposedly to be 'prepared.' . . . So, of course, nothing happened, right?"

At that point they were both breathing a little too quickly, and gazing with moronic intensity at the New Jersey skyline across the Hudson. Jay allowed himself to lean over and kiss Xenia, who opened her mouth at once and responded with ego-quickening ardor.

Maybe if they'd done it once and left it at that, Jay thinks now, staring at the ad for hemorrhoids in front of him, he could have emerged unscathed. But Xenia insisted that they do it till they "got it right." She was enjoying it, no mistake, even if orgasms were, she confessed, harder than she'd imagined. And he, for whom they seemed amazingly easy, was falling foolishly and predictably in love. They never even had a falling-out, a fight, a resolution. They simply parted for the summer and when they met in the fall, the beginning of sophomore year, it was clear Xenia assumed their relationship was past history. They were both initiated, they could hold their heads up high. Now they could start looking for "the real thing."

Only the real thing proved, in those remaining three years, to be more elusive than Jay imagined. Occasional girls appeared, seemed tentatively willing, but there was never a moment like the picnic in Riverside Park with its breathless romantic surprise. He planned, pursued, sometimes overcame, but that was all.

Susan lives with her mother in a two-bedroom apartment in a gentile but shabby part of Riverdale. Jay has only been there once or twice. Mrs. Brown is younger, perkier-looking than his own mother, with short fluffy red-blond hair. She is petite, smaller than her daughter, with a slightly frenetic manner. Through Xenia, Jay knows that she was a poor girl who, to support herself through college, got a job housecleaning for a wealthy Egyptian family, got pregnant by the older son, who formally married and divorced her in order that the baby, Susan, would seem legitimate. Under her maiden name, she is a commercial artist, rents rooms to boarders, and, like his parents, sleeps in the living room.

"Hi, Jay." Susan comes to the door in her pale blue prom dress, which looks limp and wrinkled, pulled in at places, unable to conceal her absolute lack of a bosom. Jay thinks how Marlene, who was fat in high school, says she feels a special repugnance for fat people because in them she sees her own former greed. That's how he feels about Susan's shyness, worse than his own, which he's tried, through joining the debating society and being in school plays, to overcome. Try to ignore my existence, my presence, forgive me for being Xenia's friend, and not Xenia, plead Susan's huge pale eyes.

Mrs. Brown waves a fluttery hand at them. She is sitting in the living room, reading, with one of the boarders, an Indian medical student.

"I'm going now, Mommy," Susan calls out.

Mrs. Brown leaps up and comes to the door. "Don't you look handsome, Jay! I love your tie. Is it English? Omar bought all his ties in London. He said they used better material." Omar is the long-lost, now dead Egyptian husband who never remarried after his formal severing from Susan's mother, but whose monthly checks sustained them over the years.

"I get a lot of ties as presents," Jay admits. "Most of them look alike."

"I know, isn't it a pity with men's clothes?" Mrs. Brown rushes on, talking a little too quickly. "They're all the same. Only gay men seem to have any sense of *joie de vivre* or color in the way they dress."

"Mommy, we have to go," Susan whispers. Jay senses she is ashamed of her mother and of the apartment, with its musty, closed-in shabbiness.

"Well, have a *wonderful* time!" Mrs. Brown says expansively. "Don't pay attention to time! This is your big night!"

Outside, Jay and Susan wait for the elevator. Silence, their mutal shyness, envelops and threatens to annihilate both of them.

"She's excited for me," Susan says, looking at the floor. "That's why she talks so fast."

"My mother talks fast too," Jay says.

"She never went to a dance herself. She couldn't afford it," Susan goes on.

"Same with mine. . . . Was the Indian guy a boarder?" He knows he is, but is willing to seize any conversational gambit that enters his head.

"He's a boarder," Susan says. "We have two. The other one is an elderly woman, Mrs. Klotz. She stays in her room a lot. . . . It helps to pay the rent."

"Yeah, I know," Jay says.

"Do you have boarders too?" Susan lifts her eyes momentarily.

Where would they put them? Hanging from the ceiling? But Jay realizes Susan has never seen his parents' apartment.

"No, we just have the four of us."

"Isn't your sister married?" Susan asks, puzzled.

Jay glances at her nails, which are bitten down to the quick.

"Uh, yeah, she is technically, but she and her husband are . . ."

"Getting divorced?"

"No, they're more . . . It's hard to explain. My sister's a little crazy."

Susan's expression becomes alarmed. Her eyes widen. Evidently she thinks his sister has had a breakdown.

"I'm sorry."

"No, it's . . . not really craziness," Jay amends. Why is he talking about his family? "It's more indecision."

"Oh."

They are taking the subway to Xenia's house, where Xenia and Conrad will be waiting. Then, the four of them will drive, or rather Conrad, the only one of them with a driver's license, will drive them to the dance. Xenia's family lives in a mansion. Her father, Igor Szengi, is the director of a large mental hospital; Xenia and her parents live in a manor house on the grounds, set a mile from the facilities of the hospital. "You've got to admit," Xenia has said, "not exactly your typical way to grow up." Jay is looking ahead, wondering if Xenia's parents will be there. He is intimidated by Xenia's father and hates himself for this. Dr. Szengi is not tall and has a hawklike nose, piercing eyes, and a mouth carved in an ironical expression, rarely softened by humor, except when he is caressing Xenia or allowing her to flirt with him. Her mother, Magda, is thin, a former beauty, now ravaged, usually reading silently, smoldering.

Xenia lets them in. She is in a low-cut black velvet dress, her shoulders bare. Her breasts are not large, but in the soft light she looks, to Jay, luminous, gypsylike, burnished, her black hair loose, a little wild, fastened insecurely back with a gold barrette.

"Con isn't here yet. . . . Come on in. It doesn't matter when we get there."

Jay feels an absurd pleasure at Conrad's being late, as always. He knows Xenia is always punctual, and hates lateness.

"You look beautiful," he finds himself stammering. Stupid, unfair to Susan. Did he even compliment Susan on the way she looked? Her dress? He can't remember.

"This is my mother's dress," Xenia says, whirling around so they can admire the full skirt. "It's in perfect condition."

"I haven't been to a dance in years," says Mrs. Szengi in her throaty, world-weary voice. "It would hang on me now. My breasts have disappeared."

Xenia laughs. "Don't be silly, Mooli." She has pet names for her parents.

Jay has a flash of memory of Xenia, naked, on top of him, her broad hips, her large pink nipples coming toward him, the two black hairs under her left breast. "Con is always late," he says.

"He's impossible," Xenia says indulgently, in the same tone she uses with her father, with all men toward whom she is favorably disposed.

Jay hopes Dr. Szengi is away at the hospital, as he often is, but a moment later he appears, dressed more formally than usual in a dark suit, as though he were about to go out for the evening.

"Good evening, Jay, Susan." He nods stiffly. "What a tedious affair!" he says. "Official dinners, trustees . . . Never be a director of an institution," he says to Jay. "They work you into the ground."

"Jay's going to be a journalist," Xenia says. "He won a prize, Poosh, remember? I showed you his articles."

Dr. Szengi lifts one eyebrow disapprovingly. "Yes, yes, we are all writers when we are young—poets, artists. I remember all of us sitting at cafés, our plans to change the world. How naïve we were! As though the world *wanted* to be changed!"

15

"I don't think *we're* naïve," Xenia says, sitting down on the carpeted floor. "Do you, Susan?"

"Probably," Susan says and smiles her half smile.

"You *are* naïve," Mrs. Szengi interjects, and coughs. "If you knew what we know, you wouldn't want to get out of bed in the morning."

"Well, I wouldn't put it quite that strongly," Dr. Szengi says.

"The corruption, the evil, the cruelty . . ." She trails off.

"Do you mean the world?" Susan asks. "Hitler and all of that or just . . . within oneself?"

"All of it," Mrs. Szengi says. "Within, without, it's all the same. The patients here are mad, the world is mad."

Dr. Szengi laughs. "Darling, do you think this is what these charming young people want to listen to on the eve of their graduation?"

"They're not listening," Mrs. Szengi says. "They don't believe a word of it just as we didn't when we were their age."

"I think we're really quite cynical," Xenia says. "Maybe our generation is different. You're talking about before the Second World War, remember."

"I agree," Jay puts in. "I think sometimes we're *too* cynical."

Mrs. Szengi smiles at him. She is fond of him. They've had many long discussions before the fire while Xenia was up in her room, studying.

"No, you're babies. There's no blood on your hands yet."

"But isn't the thing," Susan says, "that one wants to find ways to combat what you say, to fight it, in however small a way." She turns to Dr. Szengi. "The way you're doing with these people who are mentally ill. You're trying to make them better, help their suffering."

Mrs. Szengi snorts derisively, but Dr. Szengi says, "That's beautifully put, Susan. Yes, we can all succumb to cynicism, but we must also try, while there is breath left in us, to help, to clear a path in the forest. . . ."

Xenia and Susan are staring at him admiringly. Jay, glancing away, sees reflected on Mrs. Szengi's face the same contempt he feels for the good doctor, with his self-inflated platitudes and theatrical phrases. "English isn't his native language," Xenia says sometimes to excuse his manner of talking.

Jay thinks of the Nichols-May routine where Dr. Schweitzer comes out with a gun, ready to shoot the tourists who have invaded his territory. Maybe he is just jealous of Dr. Szengi because, despite being a foreigner, he is so self-assured, so successful, so admired by his daughter, whose only wish is to be a psychiatrist like him, to follow in his footsteps. He thinks of his own father, snoozing on the couch, rereading Chekhov, playing chess. "You haven't really had a male role model," his mother remarked sadly one day.

"Where is Conrad?" Dr. Szengi asks, looking around. "The blond young suitor, young Lochinvar, where is he?"

"Poosh, he's always late," Xenia says. "That's just the way he is."

Dr. Szengi smiles. "If you are tall and blond and have beautiful blue eyes, you are allowed all excesses by women. . . . You and I will never know that privilege," he says to Jay, who cringes inadvertently. They are both five feet eight, an inch taller than Xenia.

"Men like that are spoiled," Mrs. Szengi says. "They rot easily."

Xenia laughs. "Mooli! How can you say that of Con? I've never known anyone *less* spoiled! He hardly *has* an ego. It's a problem with him."

"Perhaps he is, how do you say, the exception that proves the rule," Mrs. Szengi offers.

"He doesn't even think he's good-looking," Susan says in awe.

Conrad is my best friend, Jay thinks. Now, maybe always. We will be friends long after Xenia and Susan have passed from our lives. I can't hate him now. I have to fight it. Susan and Xenia are right: Conrad has little ego, no awareness of his looks. He is a pure soul. Xenia says at times he reminds her of Prince Myshkin in *The Idiot*.

"My first lover was like that," Mrs. Szengi says. "Enigmatic, gaunt, spiritual. Nothing much in bed, but his eyes! Burning eyes!" To Susan and Xenia she adds, "I know how you feel."

Jay thinks he is a good lover. Actually, he is proud of his body, which to him looks wiry, sinewy, strong. Maybe he's more proud because it took years of immense self-discipline to transform himself from the pudgy mold in which it seemed all Jewish kids of his generation were formed. It wasn't lack of sexual satisfaction that made Xenia look elsewhere, just restlessness. "There probably isn't anything better than what we have," she admitted once, "but I can't stop looking before I've even begun. Can I?"

"Jay, sit by me," Mrs. Szengi croons. "You look forlorn, off there by yourself. Let these two girls moon over whomever they want. I know the real stuff."

Jay blushes, despite himself. Xenia said her mother used to have lovers, and even though she is not what she once was—he has seen the old photos in which she looks like Garbo, eyes hooded, hats with veils, smoky, beckoning glances—there is still an aura around her.

"Maybe we ought to call Con," he says nervously.

"I'll do it," Xenia says, bounding up the long staircase to her room. She stayed in the dorm at Barnard, but Jay often spent afternoons in that huge bedroom, stretched out on the canopied princesslike bed, caressing, kissing, rolling back and forth.

"That's a lovely dress, Susan," Dr. Szengi says, coming over to her. His voice, speaking to her, is gentle, as though she were a child. Is that how he speaks to his patients? "Very old-fashioned. It suits you."

Susan looks embarrassed. "My mother made it," she confesses.

"You look like a Marie Laurencin painting," the doctor goes on in that same almost condescendingly soft voice. "Doesn't she, Magda?"

"Exquisite," Mrs. Szengi says. "Like *The Glass Menagerie*, come to life."

Jay feels compassion for Susan, who is hunched over, desperate with embarrassment, face flushed, one hand clutching the other.

"I wish—" Susan begins and then stops.

They all look at her, but before she can even finish her thought, her sentence, Xenia sweeps down the stairs again.

"His mother said he left," she says. "Oh, why is Con *like* this? Tonight of all nights!"

"I thought you said it didn't matter," Jay hears himself saying.

At times he hears himself or sees himself as he is sure he appears to Xenia: crabbed, carping, nasty, crippled by envy, like some clerk in one of those nineteenth-century Russian stories his father is always trying to read aloud to the family.

"I just don't see why people can't come on time!" Xenia says. "It doesn't make *sense* to me."

"He probably . . . He must have a reason," Susan whispers.

When Conrad bursts in, about two minutes later, it's like an entrance in a play. He is wearing a bright pink shirt, open at the neck, jeans, a tuxedo jacket, cowboy boots, and his arm is in a cast. Whatever Conrad wears, he looks extravagant simply because of his height, but this getup enrages Jay and, to his delight, Xenia.

"You're wearing that to the *dance?*" she cries, horrified.

"Yeah," Conrad says. "Don't you love it?" He turns around so they all can admire it.

"Look at the sleeves," Xenia says, clutching at him. "They're way too short. . . . Con, they won't let us *in* if you look like that!"

"Why not?" Conrad looks innocently amazed. *"I thought I looked wonderful."*

Jay suddenly feels, though properly clad in a dark, well-fitted suit, like a nobody. The brilliance of Conrad's shocking-pink shirt, the flamboyance of wearing boots; he would *never* have thought of that, and if he had, he would have rejected it at once.

"I think you look great," he says, grinning at Con.

"Like a young god," Mrs. Szengi says dryly.

"I think Xenia has a point, though," Dr. Szengi puts in. "Aren't there rules about dress? What if they don't let you in?"

"Hey, is everyone here such a conformist?" Conrad says. "I don't want to look like a stuffed shirt. The whole thing's idiotic anyway. A senior prom! Come on, Xen, loosen up!"

Jay loves watching Conrad needle Xenia. Her mouth is set in an angry line. Conrad takes out a bouquet of white flowers—he's been holding them, encased in paper—and presents one to Mrs. Szengi, one to Susan, and the rest to Xenia. Damn, I forgot to get Susan flowers, Jay thinks. Xenia's face softens as she buries her nose in the exquisite blooms, white orchids.

"Buttering up the ladies," Dr. Szengi observes.

At that, Conrad snatches another white flower from the bunch and presents it to the doctor. "You need a flower too," he says.

Dr. Szengi bows. "Thank you, Conrad. . . . May I ask what has befallen your arm? Can you drive this way? I had understood you were to convey these fine young people to the dance."

"No problem," Conrad says. "I made it here, I can make it there."

"But what happened?" Xenia asks, coming to his side. "Your poor arm."

"I was roller-skating this afternoon and some little kid crashed into me," Conrad says, adding joshingly: "There goes my career as a concert violinist!"

Xenia is stroking his hand. "Does it hurt? Are you in pain?"

"I'm in psychic pain," Conrad says. "No, don't worry, I'm okay. I may not be able to dance too much, but I'll stand by you."

"Then why are we going," Xenia says, "if you can't dance?"

"We are going," Conrad says, drawing himself up, "because it's a symbol. *The Senior Prom.* We need a symbol of our entrance into the real world."

"I'd just as soon not go," Susan whispers.

"That's silly!" Xenia snaps. "We're all dressed up. . . . Of course we'll go! But it's such a pity. Why were you roller-skating, today of all days?"

"Why not, today of all days?" Conrad says. "I didn't go out *expecting* to break my arm. These little kids are fiends."

"Male hormones," Mrs. Szengi says. "They are uncontrollable."

Conrad goes over and kneels in front of her. "O cruel lady! We're not that bad, are we? We don't *just* crash into things. We create, we paint beautiful pictures, we write poems. . . ."

"You invent nuclear weapons," Mrs. Szengi says, cuffing him.

"I?" Conrad says. "Never! Never touch the stuff."

"I thought you meant man with a capital M," Mrs. Szengi says.

"I'm just a man with a small m," Conrad says. "Hey, Jay, I like your suit. You look like a banker. Real class."

"I feel like a stuffed shirt," Jay says.

"Yeah, you look a little like one too," Conrad says. "I tried to call you this afternoon, but your phone was busy all day."

"It was broken," Jay says. "They didn't fix it until five."

"To tell you about the arm," Conrad says.

"Why didn't you call here?" Xenia asks indignantly. "Why didn't you tell *me?*"

"I didn't want to alarm you," Conrad says cajolingly. "Jay here, he's a man, and men don't get alarmed, right, Jay?"

"Right, we're cool." Alone, Jay and Conrad can go on for hours, joking back and forth on this and many other themes. The "real man" theme is one they both enjoy. Each considers himself a freak who will never fit into the world, but they both get a kind of kick out of joking about it.

"Maybe we should set out, huh?" Conrad says. He goes over and hugs Xenia. "Don't be mad, Xen. I'll dance. It'll be like dancing with a wounded war veteran. It'll be romantic."

Xenia loves dancing. She looks up at Conrad flirtatiously, clearly ready to forgive him. Even though she is tall, he towers above her and manages to make her look petite, delicate, perhaps the way all women want to look. Jay thought he and Xenia were perfect in bed, perfectly suited; their bodies seemed to fit as though made for each other. He has invented for Xenia a desperate promiscuous future in which she charges from man to man, trying in vain to recapture what they once had together, each man, no matter how seemingly "masculine," a pale replica of himself. And someday the revenge: He is walking along Madison Avenue with his current girl friend or mistress, an unconventionally stunning blond (Xenia hates blonds), and Xenia stumbles by with her current lover, an overweight, pompous, spaced-out doctor, and her eyes say to his: I was wrong, I'm miserable, take me back!

Xenia hugs and kisses both her parents. "Perhaps we'll see you later," she says.

"Have a ball, as they say," Dr. Szengi calls. "Dance the night away. . . . And drive carefully, Conrad."

Conrad has taken his father's car, a 1960 Mercury in which he and Jay have taken drives into the country.

I should have learned to drive, Jay thinks. But it never seemed necessary, living in New York. It wasn't like California, or most of the country, where "wheels" are what defined your social life. But maybe they would've eliminated those endless rides on the subway. You didn't have the money, he argues with himself, watching Conrad get in behind the driver's seat.

For some reason Xenia gets in the back with Susan. "You men can go in the front," she says, peremptorily.

Like many of Xenia's decisions, Jay can't figure this one out. Is it a rejection of Conrad? A nudge at him for breaking his arm, for being oddly dressed? Or does she not want Jay and Susan to be stuck dumbly, like two animals about to be sacrificed, in the backseat, the traditional place for making out? Xenia claims she and Susan talk on the phone every day, that they are blood sisters, that their relationship is free of petty envy and backbiting. "We love each other," she said. "Not like you and Con, just horsing around." "It's not just horsing around with me and Con," Jay said. Maybe they do that more in front of the girls. But it's also that even the joshing is like a shorthand language. It's a way of mocking the conventions, mocking who they are, the world. It says more than it seems. Fuck you, Xenia, Jay thinks, getting in beside Conrad.

Conrad gives him a mocking look. "I thought I was taking a beautiful girl to the dance," he says.

"Sorry," Jay says.

Conrad turns around to look at Xenia. "Hey, Xen, what is this? Are you saying you think we're fags? Is that the message?"

"Don't be silly," Xenia says. "I just want to talk to Susan. You can talk about whatever men talk about."

"Oh my God," Conrad says. "What do men talk about?" He looks in mock panic at Jay.

"Search me," Jay says.

"Stop the car," Conrad says. "We have to find a Real Man. Otherwise we won't know what to talk about!"

"Con, I mean it," Xenia says. "Cool it, will you?"

"I am the Prince of Cool," Conrad says. He looks at Jay.

"Where'd you get that shirt?" Jay says. Actually, this is better. He feels a thousand times more at ease with Conrad than he would having to "make conversation" with Susan.

"Just saw it somewhere. I thought: This is the kind of shirt a black guy might wear, a real stud. And yet it has a certain artistic *je ne sais quoi.*"

"You're the artist," Jay says. *"I* look like the banker. . . . Whereas in real life you'll probably be the banker and I'll be the artist."

"And the stud," Conrad adds, oddly.

"I wouldn't go *that* far," Jay says, flattered. He knows Conrad, despite his looks, is sexually insecure.

"I've got it on the outside, you've got it on the inside," Conrad says.

In his secret moments that is what Jay hopes, but now he says, "I'm not sure I have it anywhere."

Con glances at him, a piercing look. "I'm not sure I do either."

This is what they have in common, the ability to josh endlessly and mean more than they say, not having to explain, and the fact that, cutting through the joshing, there are moments of truth where they telegraph to each other that they are both adrift and may always be. Jay never acted that vulnerable with Xenia, the very idea scared him.

It's a warm, overcast night. He opens the window, then glances back. Susan and Xenia are talking quietly, intensely, their heads close.

"Is this too much?" Jay asks.

"It's fine," Susan says. For one second, for whatever reason, her expression is so sweet, so welcoming, that it verges on being sexy. Susan in bed. But her body! No, her body wouldn't be the problem, it would be that sacrificial-lamb quality she has most of the time. But if you were gentle, think how grateful she'd be! No, he won't do it, but who is going to lay Susan? She's the oldest of the four of them, still a virgin at twenty-two. "Don't think she minds," Xenia snapped, after confiding this to him. "Not all women mind. Some are just ultra-discriminating. They want something very, *very* special."

Conrad has a hard time finding a parking space. "Should I just drop you three off and catch up with you?" he asks, but they all chorus, "No!" Jay is curious about what the reaction to Conrad will be when they try to get into the dance.

When they get out of the car, they separate into couples. Xenia takes Conrad's arm and they walk side by side, making a striking, unusual pair. Now that he thinks of it, how many girls will be wearing black velvet in June? Jay wonders. Conrad and Xenia seem well suited, daring, provocative. But no, he and Susan aren't really. He wants to take Susan's arm, but that seems too intimate a gesture. He tries to stand close to her, not to seem standoffish. It's as though they were back in the hall of her apartment house, waiting desperately for the elevator to come.

The girl at the door is someone from their class. She takes the prom tickets and gives Conrad a strange look. Standing behind her is another girl.

"What do you think?" the girl who is standing says.

"Look, I don't care," the other girl says. "Moscowitz is off duty. He looks cute, I think."

Conrad, instead of shooting back a jest, just stands there awkwardly. Xenia sweeps ahead of him, ignoring the girls.

"Go on in," says the first girl. "Whatever."

Jay knows the girl who is standing. He can't remember her name. The sight of her makes him feel guilty. He went out with her the same week Xenia made it clear they were finished. He took her to Riverside Park for a picnic, wanting to reenact what had happened with himself and Xenia. They necked, fooled around; he felt obliged to ask her to the movies, but he knew every second he was using her and never called her again. Maybe she's forgotten him. It was, after all, three years ago. She's had other, maybe worse experiences with guys by now. Maybe he's changed so she doesn't recognize him.

"Why was that girl staring at you?" Xenia says as soon as they enter the dance. "Do you know her?"

"That's Nancy Baum," Susan says. "She was in gym with me. I didn't notice her staring."

"She was staring at *you*, Jay. How come?" Xenia's eyes have a confrontational gleam in them that contrasts oddly with her creamy shoulders and evening dress.

"I broke her heart, I guess," Jay says banteringly.

"You devil." Xenia, for reasons best known only to her, comes up to Jay and looks straight into his eyes. "Seducing and abandoning women! Is *that* all you're good for?"

"I hope not."

"Let's dance, then."

There doesn't seem, to Jay, to be any direct connection between these two remarks. In fact, he thinks she means to dance with Con, but Xenia remains in front of him, lifting her arms to indicate that he should take her in his arms. He can smell her perfume, White Shoulders.

Nervously, Jay glances at Con. "Okay?"

"Sure. Sue and I will discuss the meaning of the universe," Con says good-naturedly.

Taking Xenia in his arms, feeling the pressure of her body, Jay realizes he probably should have asked Susan, not Con, for permission to dance this first dance with Xenia. He whispers, "I don't understand you."

"Don't you?" Xenia says delightedly, taking it as a compliment, which perhaps it is.

They dance.

1968

"Should I get dessert?" Jay asks.

Xenia's eyes are half closed, her cheek resting on her palm.

"Yeah, it's chocolate pudding. It's in those little bowls, covered. . . ." Her voice trails off.

Jay goes into the kitchen of the apartment they have shared for two years. It is not far from Columbia, 110th Street and Broadway, which means that Xenia can take the subway to P and S, where she is an intern in psychiatry and he can take the bus to the *New York Times*, where he is a reporter for the sports page. He was not aiming for sports reporting. It was where the *Times* had an opening when he applied. But now, after four years, he's come to enjoy it. He's stopped apologizing or making jests when people ask him what he does. At first he thought people would think it odd that someone who was rotten at sports would be covering them, but finally he realized no one knows, no one cares. All people heard was *"Times* reporter" and were impressed enough so that what section he was on was unimportant. He has become, for the first time in his life, an enthusiastic and knowledgeable spectator, if not participant.

Today is an important day for Jay. He's waited all day to break the news to Xenia, to tell her that the job offer in Boston finally came through. They want him on TV! To cover sports for a morning news program. Most of the time he will only be shown briefly, but he will write and select his own material. A lot of traveling, twice his present salary. Whether or not he takes it, the offer is the only one he's gotten in his life where *they* came to *him*. Someone noticed his pieces, asked tentatively if he might possibly be interested. Jay knew if he called Xenia at the hospital, her voice would have that spaced-out, exhausted quality it does most of the time. He wants a time when he has her undivided attention, like now. Deep down he worries that accepting the offer could destroy their relationship.

Peering into the refrigerator, Jay sees the bowls of chocolate pudding. Since the Vietnam War started, Xenia has refused to buy Saran Wrap because it's made by Dow Chemical, which also produces napalm. But the wax paper she uses instead has slipped off and the pudding has that thick crust that reminds him of his mother's puddings. He is one man, he notes, to whom the mention of mother's cooking is as likely to produce an upset stomach as a benign smile. Not that Xenia is a whole lot better, but, as she often reminds him, "We're not together for my cooking." True enough. He carries the two bowls into the dining alcove of their small living room and sees with dismay that Xenia is sound asleep at the table, her head flattened on the plastic mat, her arm over her eyes.

"Sweetie?" he cries. "Xen?"

No response. Shit. His big moment, and Xenia is sleeping

through it! Some nights he has carried her into the bedroom, flung her on the bed, covered her with the blanket, and she has slept through till morning. He can't blame her. She has a brutal schedule at the hospital. Medicine does not come easily to her, neither the studying nor the practice. She almost flunked her first year of medical school. Every week Dr. Szengi comes over and tries to help her with what she doesn't understand, draws up lists, charts, suggests articles for her to read. Xenia sits and listens to him like a little girl, her eyes round and frightened. "I don't think I'm cut out to be a doctor," she says all the time. "Nonsense, you'll be a fine doctor," Dr. Szengi assures her. "The best doctors do the worst in their training. A proven fact."

Jay sometimes thinks the "good doctor," as he still likes to call him in his head, may invent some of his little reassuring adages. Maybe he's invented everything, his whole life. There's so much of the charlatan about him. Yet Xenia, who is suspicious of most men, trusts him to the grave and beyond. "Do you really think so, Poosh?" she will say hopefully.

"Xen, I got a job offer today," Jay says quietly. He doesn't want to wake her harshly, by shoving her, because then she will be irritable, red-eyed, exhausted. He wants her eyes to open gently, to take in what he is saying, slowly, wonderingly. He wants to see her expression brighten, to have her suddenly leap up and embrace him and say, "Why didn't you tell me earlier in the day? I would have gotten champagne! I'd have cooked a special meal!"

Another thought. He goes over and puts a record on the phonograph: "I'm So Tired," a Beatles song he especially likes. Nothing obtrusive, but maybe in her sleep-befogged brain the music will penetrate somehow. While waiting for this to happen, Jay eats his pudding. He is still thin and wiry, still prides himself on being in shape. Xenia, on the other hand, has gotten plump since she entered medical school, nothing horrendous, just rounder hips and thighs, even a curved belly, which he loves. Her breasts seem about the same, a pleasing fullness.

I am living with Xenia. She loves me, I love her. We are faithful to each other. Today I have received an excellent job offer. Five years ago these ingredients would have seemed to him to contain all the makings of happiness. Not that he is *un*happy. Just that nothing, once attained, is what it seemed when it was out of reach. Jay has no regrets, no yearnings for another life, but this scene, he morosely eating the pudding, trying to push aside the lumpy parts,

Xenia asleep across from him, seems typical of something in their life together that disturbs him.

For several years after graduation he didn't see Xenia, although they were both in the city. He thought of calling her a few times, but it seemed wrong to try to reawaken the past. He was out in the world, trying to set up a new life, meet new women. Xenia would be a throwback, a security blanket. So Jay reasoned, anyway, and was relieved when he tried to phone her once and she was out; he didn't leave his name. He took her being out as a sign that trying to revive the past would be a mistake.

Then, in the summer of 1966, he saw her in the American Express office in Rome. He was just finishing a three-week vacation, of which Rome was the final stop. It had not been as relaxing as Jay expected, more like a self-conducted tour in which he told himself facts, read books on each area he visited, tried to teach himself the language. His fantasies of beautiful Italian girls, possibly contessas, who would invite him home and murmur to him in velvety but comprehensible Italian, were replaced by the reality of several one-night stands with American girls who were as lonely and searching as he was. He took the phone number of one law student who lived in New York. Another, a red-haired dance instructor, he liked better, but she lived in Minnesota and there wasn't the crazy passion that would have made such a commute even mildly tempting.

When he saw Xenia, he thought she was an Italian girl. She was deeply tanned, her long rope of black hair hanging down her back. She was wearing a white dress and sandals that laced up her sturdy legs. Jay was standing in back of her, mainly looking at her braid, thinking that here, in front of him, was the real McCoy, just such an earthy, luscious Italian beauty he had not managed to lay his hands on. He decided to try his inadequate Italian on her, something simple like "The line is long, isn't it?" By the time he got the sentence perfected in his head, Xenia was at the front of the line. He heard her familiar voice say in distinct English, "Do you have any letters for me? Szengi. . . . Yes, S-z-e-n-g-i. . . ."

When she turned away from the booth, her eyes were downcast. His heart thumping, he called out, "Xenia, it's Jay." The expression on her face was one he had imagined so often that it seemed recognizable, familiar. She looked overjoyed, delighted, her dark eyes sparkled.

"I can't *believe* it," she cried, hugging him, tears actually coming into her eyes. "I was just thinking of you! I was standing there on line, thinking of you."

"I thought you were Italian. You look wonderful, you look incredible." His plans for being cool, detached, vanished so quickly he didn't even notice. "You look like an Italian contessa."

Xenia burst out laughing—her loud, explosive, hearty laugh.

"God, I've missed you, Jay. And here you are. You're right here!" She took his arm with that familiar, possessive warmth, not afraid to show her feelings, to him, to whomever was listening, to the whole world.

Jay was thinking mainly of how incredibly lucky he was: having been stingy in accommodations all through his trip, he had splurged in Rome and was staying at a beautiful little *pensione* with a garden and a huge marble bathroom, a church right outside the window, almost a honeymoon suite, where so far he had just lain, stared at the ceiling, and tried to read Boccaccio in Italian. He would proceed with caution.

"Have you had lunch yet?" he said. It was only eleven-thirty in the morning.

"I'm not that hungry," Xenia admitted.

"Have you been to the Vatican galleries?" Jay went on. "The Raphael frescoes are wonderful."

"Where are you staying?" Xenia asked. She was still holding his arm. "Is it anywhere near here?" Then she burst out laughing again. "Horny Barnard girl attacks former boyfriend in Rome. Sounds like a *National Enquirer* headline, doesn't it?"

"It's actually not that far from here," Jay said. He grinned, stupidly happy, beyond strategy, plans for the future. "I guess lunch can wait, huh?"

That afternoon, of all the many times they were to make love, was a highlight—a first time that was mercifully not a first. No awkward fumbling or insecurity. They knew each other, knew their bodies, their styles of lovemaking, and yet it had been—later Jay figured this out—exactly six years, four months, and four days since the *real* first time. Then they had been seventeen—babies! In retrospect that remaining five days in Rome became like a kind of honeymoon because, after they returned to New York, Xenia had to go rushing back to medical school and Jay returned to his job at the *Times*.

During dull or frustrating moments at work, Jay transports himself back there, to the *pensione*, watches Xenia undress that July afternoon, watches her come toward him, sees the light encircling her. He plays it like a home movie in his head, lyrical or pornographic by turns. Sometimes it seems more real than their actual life together on 110th Street, which has merged into hundreds of afternoons in bed, some great, some perfunctory. Hating himself, he once made love to Xenia while she was asleep.

When he thinks of her these days, it is the way she looks slumped across the table, the Beatles songs making not a dent in her consciousness. Like his father.

Finally he carries her into the bedroom, dumps her unceremoniously on the bed, and goes off to brood in the living room.

In the middle of the night, Xenia wakes up to go to the bathroom and, returning to bed, awakens Jay, who remembers.

"Xen, I got a job offer yesterday," he says as though he were lying awake all night with this sentence on the tip of his tongue.

Xenia buries herself under the covers.

"I never had dessert," she mumbles.

No, that will not do. Jay shakes her.

"I got a job offer. . . . ABC in Boston. I'd be on every day."

"What?" Xenia is still half asleep. "It's five o'clock, Jay. I have to be up in an hour and a half. Let me sleep."

"No, we've got to talk about this," Jay says urgently. "I wanted to tell you earlier. It's in Boston, Xen. Should I take it? It's a great opportunity. If I turn it down, I could hate myself forever."

"Sure, take it," Xenia says, as though hoping to get the conversation over with quickly so she can sleep again. "It sounds terrific."

"But it's Boston. I'll be in Boston, you'll be in New York." Xenia is planning to be a resident at Mount Sinai.

"Well, that's life," Xenia mutters.

Suddenly Jay is furious. Or has he been furious all along, not just since Xenia fell asleep at dinner, but ever since that afternoon in Rome when she just blithely, correctly, assumed he would take her back in his life without a break, never even asked him about what other women he'd been seeing?

"What do you mean, that's life?" he says, his voice rising. "You mean, we're finished, that's that?"

Xenia sits up and yawns. She is still dressed, but Jay has removed her shoes.

"Sure, we'll see each other. There're planes, trains, buses. Why should we stop seeing each other?"

"But what kind of relationship will that be?" Jay asks. "Once a month? I'm too young for that. That's half celibacy."

"So, you'll fuck around on the side and not tell me about it," Xenia says dryly. "Will that suit you better?"

Will he ever love-hate anyone as much as he loves-hates Xenia? Jay hopes not. He would give up this job offer unconditionally if someone would appear and grant that to him.

"Is that what *you're* going to do?" Jay yells. "Fuck around on the side? Is that why you're suggesting it?"

"No, it's no problem for *me*," Xenia says. "Look, I'm working my ass off, I'd sell my *soul* for one blessed night's sleep. And I'm supposed to go scrambling around searching for people to take to bed?"

"How about all those middle-aged doctors who keep grabbing at you?" Jay says. There is one he hates above the others, whom they keep meeting at parties. He is Hungarian, like Xenia's father, and talks to her in Hungarian, which, somehow, even if they are talking shop, sounds endearing, intimate. He is short and fat. Xenia claims she finds him physically repugnant and "not even a good doctor."

"Jay, you know we could be sleeping right now," Xenia says. "Instead we're screaming at each other, and we'll both be wrecks tomorrow. What's this all about? Why now?"

"Because you conked out at dinner! You're *always* conked out!"

"So, what'll you miss going to Boston, then?" She snorts derisively.

Jay tries to get a grip on himself. He hates the image of himself he has in his mind: hysterical, out of control, petulant.

"I want to feel my life is shaping up," he says. "I'm twenty-six! I want to feel I'm going somewhere."

"You are," Xenia says. "This offer proves it. . . . I just never knew you *wanted* to be on TV. I didn't know mass culture, quote unquote, appealed to you."

"I don't know if it does," Jay says, trying not to react to that slighting of "mass culture." "Maybe I *shouldn't* accept the offer. It could be a mistake. That's why I want to have this talk. Tell me what *you* think I should do."

"But why does that *matter?*" Xenia asks. She runs her hands through her thick bristly hair, which is standing out all around her head. "It's your decision. I mean, say you said to me, 'Don't go into psychiatry, go into surgery.' Should I do it just because *you* think it? No! If you want to be a TV star, go for it."

"I don't want to be a TV star," Jay says, furious. "They'll hardly show me. I'll write and edit the segments of the show I'll be on. I'll appear from time to time. If I photograph well, maybe I'll be on more."

"So, how's that so different from the *Times?*" Xenia says. "How's it any better? I thought the *Times* was such a big deal."

"I don't know if it *is* better," Jay says. Suddenly he feels she is right. He feels cold, morose, despairing. Whatever he decides will be the wrong decision—that's the one thing he is sure of.

"How about your short stories?" Xenia says. "Will you have time for those?"

"I don't have time now," Jay says, pleased for the first time in the conversation. His latest rejection was from a small magazine in Nebraska. In a scribbled ballpoint at the bottom of the preprinted form someone had written, "Hit us again, Jay."

"I think your stories are important to you," Xenia says. "You *should* make time for them."

Once again Jay's heart plummets. Important to *you*, she said. Not simply important.

"Aren't they important to *you?*" He hates himself for asking.

Out of a million possible devastating comebacks, Xenia says wearily, "I want you to be happy."

"Okay, wait a minute," Jay says hastily, his adrenaline shooting crazily back and forth. "Let's stop right there. All you want is for me to be happy, right? So if I write stories, fine. Or if I spend my free time jerking off in the bathroom or putting together toy telescopes, equally fine, right? As long as he's happy?"

"Basically." Xenia looks at him uncomprehendingly.

"Don't you see how condescending that is?" Jay yells. "You don't give a damn about anything I do!"

Xenia sighs, clearing her throat. "I'm not an expert on stories. I never read any but yours. I think they're fine, but how can I tell? It's not my field. . . . I don't ask you for advice on my patients."

"Maybe you should," he says sarcastically. "Maybe I'd have more profound insights than all those fucked-up doctors will have in a lifetime. Novelists know more than doctors and always have, always will. Look at Dostoevski!"

"Yeah, maybe they do," Xenia concedes mildly. Jay imagines that her one thought is: I want to go back to sleep. If only he'd shut up. "But they don't cure people. They just describe. We're trying to *cure.*"

"Look at *them*," Jay goes on. "Are *they* cured? They're just a pack of phonies and stupid, crazed big shots. Look at Blumenthal."

Xenia laughs. "You sound like my mother." She gets out of bed and leaves the room.

"Where are you going?" Jay calls, horrified. She's just leaving in the middle of the conversation?

"I'm going," Xenia says distinctly over her shoulder, "to get a drink of water. . . . Do I have your permission to do that? Or do I have to be chained to the bed?"

Jay follows her into the kitchen. She has flipped on the light. Dozens of roaches are crawling around on the countertop.

"Oh shit," he says. "I forgot to put that stuff out."

"Get the Raid!" cries Xenia. "Quick!"

They both grab containers of Raid and start shooting roach spray everywhere. The frightened bugs crawl in every direction, some drowning in the sticky liquid, others staggering off to their invisible homes in the cracks. Jay grew up with roaches. He regards them as an inevitable adjunct of city life. Xenia is appalled by them.

She holds her nose. "We're living in a slum," she says. "Bugs!"

"They don't carry disease," Jay points out.

"But it's so unesthetic. . . . Why is our life *like* this?"

"Roaches have existed for three million years," Jay says. "It's a tribute to their savvy, really, surviving that long."

"I mean our *lives*," Xenia says. "If we love each other, why are we tormenting each other? Why are you waking me up in the middle of the night just to scream at me?"

"You woke up to go to the bathroom," Jay can't refrain from pointing out. He takes a container of orange juice from the refrigerator and drinks from it.

Xenia's face looks haggard. "Just tell me what you want me to say," she answers. "I'll say it. I need my sleep."

Jay thinks. What *does* he want her to say? He's too tired himself to censor what comes out.

"I want you to say, 'I love you madly and insanely and I'll switch my residency to Boston so I can be with you because life without you isn't worth living.' "

Xenia laughs hollowly. "Oh well, I thought it was something big. . . . You just want me to sacrifice my whole career so you can be on TV?"

"No, I—" Jay begins, wishing he could go back and rephrase that idiot sentence.

32

Xenia is beginning to go up in smoke, her eyes glittering. "Look, if that's what you want, Jay, if *that's* your feminine ideal, some lobotomized nonentity who'll just follow you from place to place selflessly, just walk out the door blindfolded and you'll find ten of them in one minute!"

"I want *you*," Jay insists. "I don't want some anonymous person."

"You want me," Xenia rushes on, "but you want to remove everything that *is* me. My career *is* me."

"That's just ambition," Jay says. "How about love?"

"It isn't just ambition!" Xenia looks shocked. "It's wanting to save people's fucking lives! Not just to write little acerbic literary phrases. I want to *help* people. . . . Fuck love! Look at the hospital Poosh runs. All those tormented, insane women who emptied themselves out for men, for 'love,' and now they're deserted. They can't even walk across the room!"

For the last half hour—since he woke up, in fact—Jay has felt a manic clearheaded energy that suddenly deserts him totally. It doesn't fade gradually, it just vanishes. He realizes he is exhausted too. He thinks Xenia is right. Why are they having this conversation now? Why have it at all?

"I want to help people too," is all he says inadequately.

They are silent, both too worn out to know where all this ferocious intensity has come from, knowing the day ahead will be ghastly.

"I didn't mean it about fuck love," Xenia says softly, putting her hand on Jay's shoulder. "Love's important too."

Jay slides his hand under her nightgown and strokes her between the legs. "I want to give you pleasure," he says wryly, "not make you miserable."

Xenia nuzzles his neck, small nibbling kisses. "You do both very well," she says.

They make love and fall asleep for the six and a half minutes left before the alarm goes off. Nothing, Jay realizes, heading for the bathroom, has been decided.

Every other Sunday they visit his parents. Every other Sunday Xenia's parents come to their apartment for dinner. But this Sunday, when they're supposed to visit his parents, Xenia says she is too tired and has to study. He thinks this is some retaliation for their argument the other night, but decides to go alone.

These Sundays with his parents vary. Sometimes he reads aloud a story he has written. The short story is his father's favorite literary form. It's the only thing Jay has ever done in which his father has the slightest interest. Sports reporting is so beyond him that he still really doesn't know what Jay does for a living. When asked, he says, "My son writes short stories." To Jay he says, "My friends don't understand sports. They're European. Jews don't understand sports. . . . Why are you doing this?"

"To earn money," Jay says.

"Money!" His father sighs and shrugs. What can he say about money? It's played as little a role in his life as sports.

For the first time in their lives, his parents are living in comparative luxury. They not only have their own bedroom, but his father has taken over the second bedroom as his study. Marlene, divorced from Emery, is an administrative assistant at the Ford Foundation.

Today, after a meal of oxtail stew that his father has concocted during the week, they sit in the living room and Jay reads his parents a new story he has written. It's about Xenia, but he hasn't shown it to her yet. It's called "I Want to Sleep." It describes a woman who is sleeping her life away. She sleeps with her eyes open, she functions, but her inner soul is deadened. She makes love asleep, cooks asleep. Only at the end of her life does she realize she has not really had one conscious moment in which she took in what was around her, that her husband became an alcoholic and lost his job, that her children have, despite the fact that she is a psychiatrist, gone mad. But, of course, it is too late to change.

"Goodness, how depressing!" Sophie says when he is finished. "Couldn't you end it some other way? Why not have her younger? Give her time to change?"

"I wanted to be unsparing," Jay says wryly.

Why is he *doing* this? What does his mother know? Like Xenia, she hardly reads fiction of any kind, only biographies and letters. "I like to reread the classics," she usually says when pressed.

"Isn't life unsparing enough?" She smiles gently. He is still her baby. He could win the fucking Nobel Prize and she will still smile at him with that indulgent, sweet smile that drives him up the wall.

His father is nodding, eyes half shut, as they always are when he listens to anything, as though visual stimuli of any kind would be too distracting. He says now, "Where did you get this idea, do you know?"

34

"From life," Jay says blithely, not wanting to pin the nail on Xenia, who isn't there.

"No," his father said. "You *think* it's from life, but it's not."

"Eli, he wrote it," his mother says. "If he says it's from life, where else can it be from?"

"From Chekhov!" his father cries. "He, too, wrote a story, and what is it called? 'I Want to Sleep.' What do you think of that?" He looks delighted, for some reason.

"I never read it," Jay says, annoyed. "Can't two people write a story with the same title?"

"You *think* you never read it," Eli says, "but you know this story. It's in your blood."

"Pop. . . ."

But his father won't let him protest. He insists on taking one of the old leather-bound gold-tooled copies of Chekhov down from the shelf and reading the story aloud in Russian. Jay can understand Russian, but not speak it. He listens, exasperated. The apartment is too hot, the radiator is blasting, he has gas from his father's oxtail stew, he wishes Xenia were there. The Chekhov story, as far as he can see, bears no resemblance to his own. It's about a beleaguered servant girl who is kept working around the clock and finally, to get some sleep, smothers a baby she is tending.

"Do you see?" his father says eagerly. His face is alight, as it always is at such times, with unqualified joy. All the things that bring most people pleasure are, for his father, contained in Chekhov.

"It's an interesting story," Jay concedes. "But what is there to see?"

"First, his sympathy for his heroine," Eli says. "He cares for her, he loves her, he absolves her even of murder, because he sees her burden."

Sophie sits forward. "What was the murder?" she asks nervously. "I don't remember a murder."

"At the end she smothers the baby," Jay says.

Sophie is horrified. "She smothers the baby? Why?"

"To get some sleep," Eli says.

"That's crazy! No one would do that! You'd have to be crazy to do that!" Sophie says. "That doesn't make any sense."

Eli ignores Sophie. "Do you see what I say, Jay? His sympathy for the girl?"

"Yes, Pop, I see."

Eli stretches out his hands. "Where is *your* sympathy for *your* heroine? You draw her as a person detached from everyone around her, you extend no pity, you are outside her."

"It's a different story," Jay says impatiently. "I'm not making the same points he is. I'm not living in the nineteenth century, for Christ's sake!"

"He's Hemingway, not Chekhov," Sophie puts in.

"I'm not Hemingway. Shut up, will you?"

But his mother ignores this. "You're yourself. You have your own unique, special gifts. . . ." She turns to his father. "Why is this always Chekhov, Chekhov? Jay has to be himself."

"He has to learn at the feet of the masters," his father says, flipping through to look at other stories.

"Chekhov sat around all day just writing stories," Sophie says. "That's all he had to do. Jay is working, he has a full-time job, a girl friend, demands on his time. . . ."

This time Eli is horrified. "Chekhov was a doctor," he says. "He, too, had pressures on his time."

Sophie snorts. "A doctor! What kind of doctor? What was it to be a doctor then? You gave people a few valerian drops. *I* could be that kind of doctor. And he stopped being a doctor early on. That was in his youth."

Eli is shaking with nervousness. If Jay hadn't seen this happen before, he would think his father was having the onset of an epileptic fit. "He was mortally ill, he was coughing blood," Eli says, wheezing.

Jay puts his hand on his father's shoulder.

"Pop, it's a great story." He shoots a warning glance at his mother. "I'm glad you read it to me."

His father is too exhausted to respond.

"Get us some tea," Jay asks his mother. "He's tired."

"You must be inside and outside of your characters at the same time," Eli says, his voice almost inaudible. "Do you know what I mean?"

"Basically."

Jay resolves on the spot that he will never read another story aloud to his parents. He will send them copies if they're published, and never, even if a gun is put to his head, ask their opinion.

Over tea he says, "I had a job offer this week," and describes it. Sophie is ecstatic.

"Will Xenia go with you? Will you—" She hates even to refer to her fondest wish, that he and Xenia be married. She is certain

Xenia is dying to marry him, that all women loathe the condition of being unwed—as she perceives it, of being potential old maids.

"We aren't joined at the hip," Jay says, using a phrase of Xenia's that normally irritates him.

"You could get married," his mother presses on, evidently afraid he didn't get the point.

"Ma, Xen is in the middle of her studies. She's interning in New York. . . . How could we get married?"

The tea is hot and soothing. His father looks almost normal again, leafing through the stories, letting the idle chatter about "life" proceed unchecked.

"There aren't hospitals in Boston?" Sophie says. "Why can't she go with you?"

It was to avoid hearing such a conversation that Xenia chose to stay home. If she were to hear it, she would say that his mother was treating him like a Jewish prince, assuming women should bend themselves out of shape to serve men. Whose side is he on—his mother's or Xenia's?

"She has her own life," he mumbles disconsolately.

"That's her business life," Sophie says. "How about love?"

Fuck love had been Xenia's words.

"At the moment, I guess, her work comes first."

"Women can't do that," Sophie says. "If they do, they'll suffer. Tell her that."

"You tell her."

"How can I tell her if she's not here? Should I call her up? Should we have a woman-to-woman talk?"

God forbid. "No!" Jay says. "I'll pass on what you said. . . . But it won't do any good."

His mother sighs, glancing at his father.

"Xenia is just like my sister Ella. She never went out, shunned men, all she wanted was to get ahead in her business. So what happened? She got ahead and all the men got married. Then, suddenly, at forty, she changed her mind. 'I want to get married,' she said. What could we say? It was too late. There were no men! Now she's alone, miserable. She's gained twenty pounds in one year. . . . Tell *that* to Xenia."

Jay picks at a thread that is coming loose from the sofa.

"We're a different generation," he says. "Women are different now."

"Nothing changes," Sophie says with a grim kind of satisfaction. "Look at your sister. She had a good man and she threw him aside like a fish! 'He wears bow ties,' she said. 'He's too polite.' Already he's engaged to another woman. Does Marlene care? No."

"Xenia isn't like Marlene. Also, she doesn't shun men. How about me? She has me."

"She won't have you for long if you move to Boston," his mother warns. "There are beautiful girls in Boston, there are beautiful girls everywhere. She should be worried."

Jay sighs. Worry, Xenia, worry. A prize catch is about to swim silently out of sight.

He gets up to go home, taking his story with him. As he puts on his coat, his father's eyes fly open.

"Also, the social commentary," he says.

"What?" Jay says.

"In that story I read," Eli says, " 'I Want to Sleep,' he is making a comment on society. He is saying society is cruel and unjust. You aren't making any comment."

"Pa, we're beyond that," Jay says, feeling hot, both from having his coat on and from irritation. "This is the twentieth century. We have the bomb. We can't get all excited about the plight of poor servant girls."

Eli looks horrified, dumbstruck.

"Don't get him excited again," Sophie whispers, tugging at Jay's coat. "It was a fine story." Aloud, almost shouting, she says to Jay's father, "He has to be himself, Eli."

His father subsides. "True, you have to learn the hard way, make mistakes."

Outside, walking to the subway, Jay thinks there is one thing he has learned. He has to leave New York. He's twenty-six years old and he has never lived away from home, never spent one week of his life out of reach of a phone call from his mother, father, or sister. It's unnatural. How can he discover who he is unless he forges out on his own, away from all of them, even Xenia? Later he will return, the conquering hero, but by then Xenia will have finished her studies and, as his mother says, be love-starved, anxious, realizing "there are no men." What about all the middle-aged doctors? They won't leave their wives; they're fat, pompous, disgusting. Xenia will never do more than flirt with them; they're just father figures. And maybe by then, Jay goes on, embroidering his fantasy, his parents will be worn out too. His father will have come to see that his stories are as complex and interesting as Chekhov's.

His father will bring *his* stories, which by then will be appearing in the *Partisan Review* or the *Sewanee Review*, to Washington Square Park and read them aloud to his friends. "He is becoming a master," his father will say proudly.

The next day, without consulting anyone or asking anyone's advice, Jay calls Boston and tells Mr. Esposito he will accept the job.

"Marvelous!" Esposito calls over the phone. "You've made my day. You sounded so hesitant last week, I was sure I didn't have a chance in the world in luring you here."

"I had to discuss it with my girl friend," Jay says, "my family."

"Of course, of course," Esposito says. "Pulling up roots is hard. But, listen, let me tell you, Boston is quite a city too, some say nicer than New York, more solid, better places to live. Your girl friend'll be happy as a clam here. . . . Or are you going to make an honest woman of her?"

Jay laughs. "When do you want me?"

Esposito explains that the end of the month, six weeks, would be ideal. "You have to tie up loose ends," he says. "I understand that."

Hanging up, Jay wishes for the first time in months that Conrad was in New York. It's not just that he's not in New York, he's in Fairbanks, Alaska, of all incomprehensible places. He started architecture school and dropped out two years ago to paint. But why Alaska? What is there to paint there? Caribou? Jay and Conrad are not letter writers. Occasionally Conrad sends a postcard with an enigmatic brief message, but Jay realizes he knows little about Conrad's life now, and Conrad knows little about his, beyond the fact that Jay and Xenia are together. He seemed unruffled when he heard. "My two favorite people," he said with Conrad-like generosity of spirit. Or did he just not give a damn about Xenia? The fact is that since college Jay has made no men friends like Conrad. He has colleagues he can josh with at work, he plays basketball once a week with a friend; but there is no one like Conrad with whom he can share real things in his life. "You could call him," Xenia has suggested. But call about what? Call long-distance just to chat?

I'm going to Boston, Jay tells Conrad in his head. I'm leaving Xenia. What do you think? Will she wait for me? Will she be faithful?

39

Sure, Conrad says back. Don't worry. Go with the flow.

Jay remembers an argument he and Conrad once had about that phrase, *go with the flow*. Conrad's contention was that the most important things in life happened unplanned, unannounced, that you had to accept them and flow with the tide. Jay contended that life was a matter of structure, that it was insane and self-destructive not to plan. Maybe they were both right, Jay thinks, but he can't live like that, just move to Alaska for no reason, not know where he's heading. Maybe you have to be an artist with a capital A for that. Jay likes to think at such times of Trollope, who worked for the post office but got up every morning and did a prescribed amount of work. Not that Jay does that, but it's more reassuring thinking of Trollope than it is of Hemingway and all those hard-drinking macho types who would only have contempt for someone like himself. The biggest game, the only game he's ever killed is a cockroach.

The following Sunday they go to Xenia's parents' house for dinner. Every Sunday they have prime ribs, which he and Xenia live off for the rest of the week. They stagger home with shopping bags stuffed with rye bread, cakes, sometimes even small jars of caviar. On this particular evening, Dr. Szengi opens a bottle of champagne that the grateful relative of one of his patients has bestowed on him.

"No special occasion," he says. "But why not?"

"Life is a special occasion," Mrs. Szengi says in her throaty voice, raising her glass. In the five years since they graduated, she has aged dramatically. At that time she had frizzy reddish-brown hair, dyed, according to Xenia. Then it became various other colors—blond, even. Now it is snow-white, which makes her black, deep-set, heavily made-up eyes more compelling. She looks ravaged but interestingly so, Jay always feels, compared to his own mother, who has simply aged in a much less dramatic way, her hair going from brown to brownish gray.

"We can drink to my new job," Jay hears himself saying. He had not been planning to announce it. "I just accepted a job in Boston." He keeps his eyes fixed on Dr. and Mrs. Szengi.

"Bravo!" Mrs. Szengi cries. "You didn't even mention it, Xenia."

"I didn't know," Xenia says curtly.

"You knew," Jay fires back.

"I didn't know you were accepting it." She gulps her champagne as though it were medicine.

"I assume they are doubling your salary," Dr. Szengi says with that ironical tone he applies to almost anything.

Why does he assume that? It happens to be true, but his assuming it seems to make the fact less significant.

"It'll involve a certain amount of traveling," Jay says. "But that could be interesting."

"Of course," Dr. Szengi says. "See the world when you're young."

"Just within the United States," Jay amends.

"Don't dismiss the United States," says Dr. Szengi, who has never traveled west of Teaneck, New Jersey, but who goes to Europe every other year. "Beautiful scenery out there, so I've been told."

Jay wonders, as he has countless times, if it's just that whoever Xenia might select would seem to Dr. Szengi unworthy of his magnificent, priceless daughter. Or is it that he, Jay, in particular, seems like an insignificant talentless nobody who is simply taking up space, eating his prime ribs, drinking his champagne until the crown prince appears on the scene?

"I think I need to get away," he tries to explain. "I've never really left home, never really lived anywhere but New York."

"It's never so simple," Mrs. Szengi says. She looks at him with her caressing, intimate smile. "But what about the two of you? You will be parted?"

Jay glances at Xenia, who is still looking grim.

"We'll survive," she says.

"They're young, darling," Dr. Szengi says. "They can't be tied down now, at the beginning of their careers."

Yes, no doubt about it, Jay thinks. The old man is delighted he is leaving. He will crow about it to Xenia on the phone.

"That's what we decided," Jay says smoothly.

Xenia snorts. "We did?"

"And love?" says Mrs. Szengi. "That doesn't count anymore?"

"Absence makes the heart more fond," Dr. Szengi says, not believing a word of it, Jay thinks.

"Or out of sight, out of mind," Xenia inserts.

"You *could* get married," Mrs. Szengi says, smiling. "People still get married these days, so I'm told."

"Mooli!" Xenia says, as though her mother has told a joke in bad taste.

"My wife is old-fashioned," Dr. Szengi says to Jay, who didn't find the remark that weird or offensive. "You have to excuse her. It's part of her charm."

"I have a beautiful veil that I always wanted Xenia to wear," Mrs. Szengi goes on, unperturbed.

"How about this beautiful roast beef?" Dr. Szengi says. "Why is no one appreciating this beautiful roast beef? Enough talk of weddings!"

On the way home Xenia is silent, her mouth still set in the same resentful line. Jay feels pretty cheerful, for some reason, glad he made the decision he did, glad he has announced it publicly.

At home Xenia slings off her winter coat and kicks off her boots.

"Thanks for telling me in such an intimate way," she says, over her shoulder. Her cheeks are bright pink from the cold, her hair electrical.

"Xen, you *want* me to go," Jay says gently. "You don't want me here. You said that. We torment each other. . . . Why not part for a while? It's not the end necessarily." He loves the sound of his own words, so wise, detached, and peaceful.

"What shit!" Xenia says contemptuously. "You just want to go off and fuck nine million girls. It's just an excuse."

"I could do that right here in New York," Jay points out. "I don't have to go to Boston for that."

"Oh, you'll have wider scope," Xenia says. "All that traveling. Lots of delightfully sleazy one-night stands."

"That *is* my main reason for going, actually," Jay says. "The job aspect is really insignificant."

"You want to get away," Xenia says. She is sitting cross-legged on the couch, her arms folded like a Buddha. "Why not just admit that? 'I want to get away!' "

Jay sits down in the ancient wing chair opposite her, a hand-me-down from the Szengis. "Okay, I admit it. *I want to get away.*"

"We're just using each other," Xenia says wearily, twisting her hair around her finger. "You're my security blanket. I'm yours. We don't know how to cope with the real world, so we cling together in this roach-infested apartment."

Are the roaches really that symbolic? Aren't they just a fact of city life? Jay tries to retain his thoughtful, detached mien.

"But, as you pointed out, there are buses, trains, planes. . . . We don't have to lose touch."

" 'As you pointed out,' " Xenia sneers. "You sound like my father."

That, alas, is the straw that dissolves Jay's wonderful detachment, melts it like a snowflake.

"I'm not like your fucking father," he says. "I despise your father! I want to get away from *him* too. From your father and his witty little ironical asides and *my* father and his references to Chekhov, and to *both* mothers. . . . I just want to be myself."

"Good luck," Xenia says.

"What does *that* mean?" Jay asks, wishing he hadn't.

"You'll still be yourself in Boston. . . . So you leave your parents behind? That's incidental." Now she is smug, delighted.

"I want to be on my own," Jay goes on, trying to regain lost ground. "Sure, it'll be painful at first, but that's life."

"Right. . . . To life!" Xenia says, raises an imaginary glass.

Jay just stares at her, at her toes in her red tights, peeping out from her black slacks.

"God, you're a bitch," he says.

"So? There are bitches in Boston," Xenia says.

"Meaning?"

"You'll find one. You like bitches, or what you call bitches. That's your tragedy, kid."

"Christ, no wonder Con didn't want you," Jay says, furious.

"Petty," Xenia retorts. "You don't know why Conrad left. You don't even know him."

"He's my best friend," Jay says. He wishes they could have a pillow fight or, better still, wrestle. He envisions pinning Xenia to the ground, feeling her soft, unathletic body squirm in pain while he twists her arms over her head, her eyes frightened.

"Big best friend," Xenia says. "You never call, never write. . . ."

"Men are different," Jay says.

"Tell me about it," Xenia says. She gets up and stands near Jay. "I'm glad you're going. I wanted you to move out, but I didn't have the courage to ask you. This solves everything."

She is probably lying to save face, but he will never know.

"Same here. I didn't know how to tell you," Jay lies. "I wanted to move out, but I thought the job offer would make it easier."

"So, great, we're both getting what we want," Xenia says tonelessly, looking down at him. The hectic pink of her cheeks has muted, her hair has settled down. She looks tired. The connection between them, whether it's sexual, emotional, or God knows what, sparks, hops like a flea from Xenia to Jay and back again. But neither of them does more than observe it. Let it hop.

Jay moves to Boston. On the day he leaves, one of his stories, "I Want to Sleep," in fact, is accepted by the *Sewanee Review*. This is the first decent magazine that has acknowledged his literary existence. "You have captured all the sordidness and anomie of city life," the editor writes. Sordidness? But he sent the sordid one somewhere else! The sordid one he called "Roaches," and its climactic scene involved a young, intense couple who almost asphyxiated each other with the fumes from the spray with which they intended to kill the roaches in their apartment. Still, who is he to quibble?

Maybe this *is* some kind of beginning. Maybe in Boston he will find himself in more ways than one—beautiful women (as his mother predicted), time to write (while in hotel rooms in Montana, also seeing the country, meeting "real people"), money with which to buy records, a good stereo, decent books, a comfortable reclining chair.

During his first week in Boston, Jay finds a two-room apartment for half the rent he and Xenia were paying in New York. The living room is twice as big, the kitchen clean, the refrigerator new. See! he says to Xenia. See! Except that will not do. He doesn't want an imaginary Xenia perched on his shoulder for the next couple of years, even to sneer at. But in his mind he photographs the apartment and sends the photo to her with a note—No roaches!—scrawled on the back.

Jay discovers one pleasing fact: he photographs well on TV. He looks different, but better, for some reason, rather than worse. He learns to stand up straight, look the imaginary viewer in the eye, learns which is his good side, even grows a moustache. Of course, no one he knows sees him. But that's all to the good. He has no old self dogging his footsteps.

The work is not inordinately difficult. At the *Times* he learned to write quickly, to meet deadlines. He enjoys the group effort, horsing around with the cameramen, even arguing with the producer about how much footage to allow for each segment.

One thing he does not enjoy: traveling. He isn't sure why. Parts of the country are beautiful, true. He meets "real people." But he hates hotels. He tries one-night stands, as he did in Italy, and rediscovers that they are exactly what they were cracked up to be: girls he would normally have no interest in, sex that is no sexier for being transitory. Some of the time he feels the way he did as a kid in the movies when he was afraid he wouldn't get absorbed in the movie, but would just sit there, thinking: I am watching a movie. Now, sometimes, he thinks: I am screwing a girl. He can see, as it were, the edges of the screen. Xenia's words echo: *You'll take yourself wherever you go.*

Okay, so he's not cut out for one-night stands. That doesn't mean he will end up with a bitch. In fact, he doesn't. Jay ends up with the daughter of the copy editor, a thin, quiet girl who works as a receptionist in a veterinarian's office and is thinking possibly, someday, of training to be a vet herself. She has two cats and a dog. Jay is allergic to cats, but that just means they spend more time at his apartment, which he likes better anyway. Her name is Betsy and she grew up in California, but came to Boston when she was a teen-ager. She has a Boston accent and is good at sports. She thinks it's funny that he is terrible, and even says she will teach him to catch so he will do better on the TV softball games. "You're so well coordinated," she says, "in other ways. I just don't get it."

She means in bed, presumably. Jay appreciates her praise. She's only had two other lovers, true, but one of them was, in fact, a fairly well-known basketball player, a black guy who, according to Betsy, wrote poetry in his spare time. "He was this incredibly sensitive person," she says. He still sends her free tickets to all his games, which doesn't bother Jay, who gets free tickets from ABC. Not even the poetry bothers him. Let the guy write sestinas, even, as long as, in Betsy's opinion, Jay is just as good in bed. Perhaps he wouldn't be so prejudiced about this, but Marlene had a black boyfriend in high school and claimed (boasted?) that there was just no comparison, they really *were* that much better.

Betsy's parents have moved back to Point Arena, California. Her only "family" in the Boston area is her brother, Simon, who is a cop. When Jay first heard "cop," he got nervous, imagining a huge, beefy guy who would go bonkers to protect the honor of his sister. But Simon turned out to look like an Italian version of himself—small, wiry, with a thicker black moustache. Also, he is, according to Betsy, gay. "He's not any different from people like us," she tells Jay. "He wants all the things we want: a home, family, kids. He just wants them with another guy."

45

"Kids?" Jay says. "Won't that present problems?"

"They could adopt," Betsy says.

Jay feels nervous at her lumping him with herself in "people like us," but he decides this doesn't represent any predatory impulse. She just means that Jay is "folks" or a *mensh*, as his mother might say. These are the things she assumes all normal people want and she is just saying she takes Jay to be normal. Nor is Simon overbearing with Jay. He's a quiet, shrewd-looking man who comes over sometimes and shares dinner with them. At first Jay feels uncomfortable with him, both because of Betsy and because he doesn't know if Simon knows he knows about his sexual predilections.

One night, when Betsy turns in early (they are at her apartment, the cats are locked in the bathroom), Jay and Simon smoke some pot and ease into what could be called a personal conversation.

"I guess you get a lot of one-night stands," Simon says, "traveling the way you do."

Jay is leaving for Oklahoma City the next day to cover a story about the family of twin girls who are breaststroke champions.

Jay is not sure if Simon is worried for Betsy's sake. He says, truthfully, "That doesn't seem to be my forte."

"Me neither," Simon says. "I've tried it, but . . . I guess at my age you start looking for something more permanent." Simon is thirty-two.

Jay reminds himself that Simon means a guy. He wonders if that could possibly be any harder than finding a girl. "Had any luck?" he says. He feels light-headed and good, enjoying the man-to-manness of their talk, glad Betsy had to go to bed because of her head cold.

"Depends on what you'd call luck," Simon says with a half smile.

"Depends on what you're looking for, I guess," says Jay, who feels a little uneasy avoiding parts of speech.

"I've had *some* luck," Simon says, "but no one where . . . it all came together. I want someone I can share the things that matter to me with, the way you and Betsy share an interest in sports. But I also want someone who's a complement to my personality. I'm kind of a moody person and I want someone who isn't . . . at least to the same extent. I like people who can cheer me up. This one person I lived with a while, it was good, but we were both real moody. That wasn't good."

46

Jay thinks of Xenia. "I had a relationship like that once. You're right, it doesn't work."

"Like you and Bets," Simon goes on, his voice just slightly slurred. "You complement each other. You're kind of cynical and down-to-earth and she's kind of ingenuous and sweet."

Jay inhales and blows the smoke out slowly. "Am I cynical?"

"Oh, I didn't mean it in a bad way," Simon says. "You look at the world and you see what's there. Bets sees what she wants to see. . . . She's that way with guys too." He rolls his eyes. "Some of them have been real doozies."

"The basketball player?" Jay suggests.

"George? No, he was all right. . . . He wrote some real nice poems."

"I heard," Jay says. "I'd like to see some of them one day." Why is he saying that? He doesn't want to see them.

"I may have saved a few," Simon says. "The only thing with George was, well, you had to listen to a lot of stuff about basketball. With me a little of that goes a long way."

"Me too," Jay says.

Simon looks puzzled. "I thought that was your profession."

"It is," Jay admits, "but it's pretty boring a lot of the time. I just lucked into a job on the sports page, and one thing led to another. I have two left hands when it comes to catching a ball."

Simon leans forward, his hands encircling his glass of bourbon. "Now, that's really interesting," he says. "You take me. I'm a cop, law and order, right? That's what people always say. But you want to know something? I don't care tiddledywinks about law and order. I'd abolish all jails if it was up to me. I think our whole criminal system stinks. I think most cops are jerks." He shakes his head. "They'd kill me if I went around saying that, so I never do. I guess I shouldn't even be saying it to you."

"Your secret is safe with me," Jay says gravely. He likes Simon. How great that Betsy has a brother. It's not quite the way it used to be with Conrad, but it's a little like that.

Simon staggers to his feet. "I better go, speaking of work. It's pretty late." Once on his feet, he grabs the walls to steady himself.

"The fact is," he says, "I want what you want. I just want stability, good vibes . . . I even want a kid. Does that strike you as strange?"

Jay gets to his feet too. The room looks a little odd, a little bigger than it did before. Or maybe it's just that some things in it, like the door, look farther away. "Why shouldn't you want a kid?"

"I'm gay," Simon says. "A lot of people think gay guys shouldn't raise kids."

"What do they know?" Jay says.

Simon smiles. He rarely smiles, and this makes his smile more engaging. "Right," he says, slapping Jay on the shoulder. "What do they know?"

"Most people know nothing," Jay says, accompanying him to the door. "That may be cynical, but it's a fact."

"You're right," Simon says. "You're a good guy, Jay. Bets has lucked into a good thing."

Jay hopes this is true. Even stoned, he has severe doubts on the subject. But all he says is, "Thanks. . . . Take care of yourself, Simon."

Life with Betsy, the shared days and evenings and nights, is pleasant but peaceful. One day Jay's story "I Want to Sleep" arrives in the mail. Betsy has never heard of the *Sewanee Review*, and hasn't read a short story since high school. Despite this, she sits right down after dinner and reads "I Want to Sleep" word for word, her lips slightly parted, her head bent. Jay is touched and almost appalled by the amount of intense concentration she is applying. At the end, when she looks up, her eyes are filled with tears. "That woman had such a sad life!" she says.

"I'm glad you liked it," says Jay. He decides to take that as a compliment.

Betsy jumps up from her seat and goes over and hugs him. "You write about such sad things," she murmurs, as though to comfort him. "Is that because you've had a sad life yourself?"

"No, actually my life has been pretty . . ." Jay pauses, searching for the right word. Typical? Crazy? Screwed-up? Boring? "My stories aren't strictly autobiographical," he finishes.

"My mother has insomnia a lot," Betsy confides, sitting close to Jay. "Maybe I'll send her the story."

"I don't have that many copies," Jay says. He has sent one to his parents, to Conrad (does mail arrive in Fairbanks, Alaska?), and (okay, he shouldn't have) to Xenia.

"They should at least give you more copies," Betsy says. "If I wrote a story, I'd want to send it to everyone I ever knew since I was born!" She looks at him seriously. "Did you ever think of writing a story from the point of view of a dog? Or a cat?"

"No, not really," Jay says, stroking her soft, pale brown hair.

"I see all these animals at my job, and you know what sad

lives they've had, left alone all day, and sometimes I think if I were a writer, I'd tell about what it was like to be them, their point of view, I mean."

"That's anthropomorphism," Jay feels obliged to point out.

"What?" Betsy says. Her eyes are getting that foggy, intense look that means she is turned on.

He slips his hand under her angora sweater. She doesn't wear a bra.

"Thinking animals are like people," Jay says.

"Yes," Betsy murmurs. "They are, aren't they?"

The conversation, if it could be termed such, ends, and neither Jay nor Betsy remembers it later. Only as they are lying together, wrapped in the soft plaid blanket from L. L. Bean that Jay has brought from New York, does he say, inwardly to Xenia: Not a bitch, see! Not a bitchy bone in her whole damn body! Xenia just rolls her eyes. Jay isn't going to bother to invent comebacks for her. He'll leave her speechless.

In April he flies up to Missoula, Montana, to do a spot on a family of six Italian brothers who are all wrestlers. Jay likes this kind of assignment because he can interview the other members of the family—the father, who is a stonemason, the only daughter. One afternoon they take him rafting down the Bitterroot River. Back in Boston, it's chilly and windy. Here it's hot, as though it were two or three months further along in the year. He rolls up his jeans, unbuttons his denim skirt, allows himself to flirt in a mild way with the seventeen-year-old daughter, who has sleepy, long-lashed eyes and a jutting chin.

That night, on an impulse, he calls Conrad in Fairbanks, Alaska. He does this not only because he feels lonely and miserable, as he usually does while traveling, whether or not the assignment is interesting, but because he is closer to Alaska, being in Montana, than he would be in Boston. Who knows if Conrad is even there? It's been months since Jay got so much as a postcard. But the response is heartening.

"Hey, Jay!" Conrad says, sounding so close he might be in the next room. "This is terrific. I've been wanting to talk to you, how did you know?"

"I didn't," Jay says. "I'm in Missoula, Montana, so I figured you were . . . pretty close."

"Am I?" Conrad says. "Where's Missoula, Montana? Why are you there?"

Jay explains about his job.

"You're on TV? A TV star?"

Somehow, unlike Xenia, Conrad manages to sound impressed, with a slight shade of humor, as though he and Jay both realize the absurdity of it.

"I'm really impressive," Jay says. "I get fan letters. I grew a moustache."

"You were worse at sports than I was," Conrad says.

"I'm a natural on TV, though," Jay says. "And my girl friend is teaching me how to play softball."

"Xenia?" Conrad sounds amazed. "Xenia doesn't even know what softball is."

"Xenia's in New York. I'm in Boston," Jay says irritably. "We're not living together anymore. We're not together anymore . . . period."

A pause.

"I'm sorry to hear that," Conrad says.

"Why are you sorry?" Jay says. "*You* couldn't live with her. Why should *I* be able to?"

"Oh, that was different," Conrad says. "That was me. I'm fucked-up, Jay. I'm not just kidding around. I mean *truly* fucked-up."

"No, you're not," Jay says. "Who isn't, anyway?"

"No." Conrad hesitates. "There's lots of stuff I haven't told you. I flunked out of architecture school. I didn't 'decide' to leave."

"So? It was all your father's idea anyway," Jay says. "You shouldn't have been there in the first place. You want to paint."

"Yeah, but I'm rotten," Conrad says. "Jay, I'm serious. I'm not pleading for your pity. I'm not trying to be delightfully self-deprecating. My paintings stink."

"Why did you go to Fairbanks, Alaska?" Jay asks.

"Because I'm a jerk! Who in their right mind would go to Fairbanks, Alaska?"

Jay is taken aback. "I thought you had a reason."

"Think again. . . . No, I did want to be far from home." Conrad laughs. "I succeeded there, anyway."

"Do you know people? Is there anyone—"

"Sort of. . . . It's a long story, Jay. Just believe me, I'm not doing well."

"Come home, then."

"Where's home? New York?"

"Yeah."

Jay is uncertain. He's been giving himself the opposite advice, that it's important to get away from home, especially for a young guy in his twenties or thirties.

"And have my fucking parents calling me every day?"

"Go somewhere else, then," Jay says. "Come to Boston, Con. We can room together."

"What about your girl friend?"

"What girl friend?"

"You told me you have a girl friend."

"You mean Betsy?" Jay remembers Betsy. "You'll like Betsy. She's got a nice brother too, Simon. He's a cop."

"I'm scared of cops," Conrad says.

"He's not your average cop," Jay says. "He's gay. Listen, think about it, Con. It'd be great."

"Okay, I'll think about it. . . . How is Xenia? Do you still keep in touch?"

"Not really. . . . She's a bitch. I'm through with bitches."

Conrad laughs. "You think."

Jay tries to preserve his sense of humor. "Whose side are you on, kid? I have Betsy. Who needs Xenia?"

"Betsys are bland," Conrad says. "You need someone spicy, intense."

Jay once told Conrad he wanted a woman who was smarter than he was, taller than he was, but with a crippling neurosis that would make her permanently dependent on him.

" 'Betsys'! This isn't 'Betsys.' This is one particular Betsy. Anyway, why does any girl who's not a bitch have to be bland?"

"I don't know," Conrad says. "But then, I didn't create the world."

"You didn't?"

By the time he hangs up, Jay feels good again. It's as though five minutes had passed since he and Conrad were together in college, not five years. He thought of Conrad when Martin Luther King, Jr., was assassinated, because he and Conrad had marched in a lot of civil rights demonstrations. I should have called him then, Jay thinks now. Why wait to be in Missoula? He wonders if Conrad will really take his suggestion seriously, and come to live in Boston. He sounded strangely desperate and uncertain for Conrad, whom Jay still thinks of as Superman, with his crazy, flamboyant way of dressing. Lying in his motel room, Jay remembers

Conrad appearing at the Szengis on prom night with his broken arm, his cowboy boots, the way he gave each of the women a white orchid. He remembers with a strange kind of twinge walking behind Xenia and Conrad on the way to the dance, the way Xenia clung to Conrad's arm, her black velvet dress, her suddenly turning to Jay and asking him for the first dance.

Jay sits up.

I hope Xenia is really miserable, he thinks savagely. Right this second I hope she is absolutely at rock bottom, her head buried under a pillow. Maybe she's even contemplating suicide, life is so shitty since he left. God, what's wrong with him? Let Xenia be happy. What does it matter? Conrad said: "Betsys are bland." How many Betsys did he know? A hundred? And why was bland bad? Bland could be soothing and peaceful. Jay remembers Betsy curled up on his chest, running her hands through his hair, letting out her small squeaks of pleasure, like one of the cats on her kitchen calendar, entangled in balls of soft blue twine.

In June, Betsy worries that she may be pregnant. She is a lapsed Catholic and is on the pill, so Jay isn't that concerned until she tells him that once before, also on the pill, she got pregnant but miscarried a month later.

"Are you taking the right pill?" he tries to joke. "The birth-control pill?"

Betsy takes about eight pills a day: vitamins, iron, pills for her skin.

"I don't want to worry you," she says. "There are false pregnancies, you know. Like with dogs. Their nipples swell up and they think they're pregnant, but it turns out they're not. They just want to be."

"Do *you* want to be?" Jay asks gently, looking around.

This conversation is taking place in Dr. McClemmy's office, which has late office hours on Thursdays. It is true that the area in which Betsy sits, behind her desk, is walled off by glass from the waiting room, where several disconsolate-looking individuals are sitting with their pets, who are on leashes or in boxes. Still, this doesn't strike Jay as the ideal place to have a conversation like this, something with which he knows Betsy does not agree. Once, when she was discussing something equally intimate in a restaurant and he protested, she said, "But I don't know anyone here. Do you?"

Betsy gives this question her full attention. "I'd like to be if there was a father. I mean, a father who wanted to be one."

There is a pause.

Jay smiles at Betsy, hoping to emulate her ingenuousness.

"I don't think I'm ready to be a father," he says. He tries to suppress even the thought that he doesn't want Betsy as the mother of his children. "I'm pretty young."

"You're twenty-seven," Betsy reminds him. They celebrated his birthday a week ago.

"I think twenty-seven is younger for a man than it is for a woman, when it comes to things like this," Jay says. Trying another tack, he adds, "I'm not even that experienced with women, really."

Betsy leans over and squeezes his hand. "Oh, that doesn't matter. You're experienced enough for me. Do you mean how many girls you've done it with? That's just silly macho stuff."

That isn't exactly what he means. What does he mean? "I think I'm not ready to settle down yet."

"You mean you'd fool around on the side?" Betsy says sternly, poking at her pad with a bent paper clip.

"Nothing that simple," Jay says. He sees a tall, angry-looking woman with an owl on her wrist approaching Betsy's office. "I just think someday I'll be a good husband and father. But not now. The timing is off."

The woman is knocking on the glass partition. Betsy slides it open.

"What can I do for you?" she says angrily.

"I've been waiting half an hour," the woman says. "It's chilly here. He's shivering. . . . When will the doctor take me?"

"You're next, Mrs. Schapper," Betsy says, regaining her poise. "The doctor will be out in a minute. He's operating."

"You said that half an hour ago," Mrs. Schapper says. The owl on her wrist looks asleep, but it's true, its feathers are quivering slightly.

"He can't interrupt an operation," Betsy says. "Shall I turn the heat up?"

"If you would be so kind," Mrs. Schapper snaps, and retreats to her seat.

"Owls are absurd pets," Betsy says severely to Jay, who has no opinions on the subject. Then she adds, "I think you're looking for excuses, Jay. You just don't want to marry me, whether I'm pregnant or not. That's all right. No one said you had to."

Jay feels himself becoming more villainous every second. "Would you, uh, consider an abortion?" he stammers.

"Abortions are against my principles," Betsy says stiffly. "You have to draw the line somewhere. That might not mean so much because you belong to a religion that doesn't care one way or the other."

This is the first reference she has ever made to his being Jewish.

"I don't belong to any religion," he says.

"I thought you were Jewish."

"My parents are Jewish, I'm an agnostic. . . . I never had a bar mitzvah. I've never even been to a synagogue."

Betsy listens to this impassively, unimpressed, as though it were just another attempt to dodge the issue. "I don't know if that counts," she says. "It's your parents that count."

Jay looks at Betsy. She is wearing a soft pink blouse with a bow at the collar, and pearl earrings. Despite being tired and furious, she looks charming and delicate. He wants to rescue her by anything short of committing himself as bounty.

"You could raise the baby with Simon," he suggests suddenly, brilliantly. "You said he'd love a kid."

Betsy's expression softens. "I thought of that, but Simon says it would be, you know, incestuous . . . because of our being brother and sister?"

"Right, there's that," Jay says. He takes both of Betsy's hands and looks up at her. "Bets, I want to do the right thing by you. . . . It's just I also want to do the right thing by *me*, and the two may be incompatible."

Betsy draws in her breath. She looks touchingly plaintive and trembling. Another man, Jay thinks, would sweep her up in his arms and take her away from this office, with its sick owls and feverish cats and dilapidated dogs.

"I'll be all right," she says quaveringly.

A few nights later Jay discovers Betsy's packet of birth-control pills. She always writes the date she started each packet. According to the evidence in front of him, she has not taken a pill for over a week.

"Hey, Bets, you're still taking the pill, aren't you?" he says.

Betsy is in one of her flowered flannel nightgowns and white ankle socks, writing a letter home (not about this). "I can't take them now," she explains. "It might cause birth defects in the baby."

"But you don't know you're pregnant," Jay says, exasperated.

"By the time I know, it could be too late."

Jay tries to be patient. He kneels at her feet.

"Bets, don't you see? What if you're *not* pregnant now? What if your period is just late? You could get pregnant this week by not taking the pill! We've done it three times this week. You could have gotten pregnant *three times!*"

Betsy looks frightened. "You can't get pregnant three times," she says. "Only once."

"Once is all it takes!" Jay sighs. "Please go for the damn test, at least!"

Betsy looks at him, aggrieved. "If you go too early, they just say you're not pregnant. That's what happened last time."

"I thought you weren't pregnant last time either," Jay says.

"No, I was, only I miscarried in the first month."

"Isn't that just a way of saying your period was late?"

"No!"

Jay has a headache. "I think you ought to change your birth-control method, personally. If I'd gotten pregnant twice on a pill, I wouldn't go on taking or not taking that pill!"

"What do you mean, not taking!" asks Betsy indignantly.

"Well, I mean, you haven't taken it for a week," Jay says. "That's what I mean by not taking."

Betsy flings down her letter. "It's none of your business," she cries. "You're not even planning to marry me, so what do you care if I'm pregnant or not?"

Jay takes Betsy in his arms and strokes her, caresses her, tries not to get excited despite the fact that Betsy, in tears, in her flowered nightgown, is, as she must realize, extremely fetching. "Bets, I care, do you believe me?"

He tucks her into bed and calls Simon, saying he has something he has to talk about with him.

"Yeah, she told me about it," Simon says. "You're going to walk, huh?"

His voice is so contemptuous that Jay is taken aback. What has happened to the friendly, engaging Simon of the night they got stoned? He goes over to Simon's apartment, which is not far from Betsy's. Simon has evidently been playing his bassoon—music and the instrument are on the floor. There is a smell of homemade applesauce coming from the kitchen. Simon is more versed in household skills than Betsy will ever be. He will make someone a perfect wife, Jay thinks. He accepts Simon's offer of applesauce and homemade oatmeal cookies.

"I think Betsy's a lovely person," he says cautiously. This is the best applesauce he's ever tasted. He never knew you could actually make applesauce. It really is different.

"Damn right she's a lovely person," Simon growls. "You don't find girls like Betsy growing on trees, not here, not in California, not anywhere." He glares at Jay.

"I agree," Jay says. "It's just—Betsy and I have only known each other a couple of months. That's not very long."

Simon munches on an oatmeal cookie. "You know everything you need to know about someone the first five minutes you meet them."

Unfortunately Jay agrees with this. "I'm also kind of young," he says, "for marriage."

"You're almost thirty," Simon says. "You're plenty old enough."

Is twenty-seven "almost thirty"? Jay thinks that's pushing it a little.

"People mature at different rates," Jay says. "I lived at home throughout college. This is the first time I've ever lived away from home. I think I need more time."

Simon looks disgusted. "You're searching for excuses," he says. "You don't want to marry her. Just admit it. You're just fooling around."

Jay sets down his spoon. It's the lemon that makes the applesauce different. "Okay, it's true I don't want to marry Betsy," he says, "but I'm not just fooling around. I really care for her. Isn't there anything between fooling around and wanting to marry someone?"

Simon looks unrelenting. "Bets thinks you have someone back home."

Jay turns red. "I don't! . . . I once lived with someone, but that's dead, totally finished. We haven't spoken or written since I left New York. She's a bitch."

"Some men like that," Simon says with a half smile.

"I'm not some men!" Jay yells. "I'm me! I *don't* like it. I like women to be nice and friendly and sweet."

"You have Betsy!" Simon yells back. "You won't find anyone nicer or friendlier or sweeter than her."

This is true.

"Okay, I'm a *shmuck*," Jay says, giving up.

Unexpectedly Simon smiles.

"Yeah," he says. "Well, that's over with. Just felt I had to do my brotherly duty. This kind of thing is a bitch. I hate it."

How many times has Betsy gotten pregnant? Has he had to do this many times? Something in his face must reveal what he's thinking because Simon says, "No, I know just how you feel, Jay. I once . . . Someone once was in love with me and I had to end it. It made me feel rotten. He was a nice guy. There was nothing wrong with him." He laughs. "He wasn't even pregnant."

Jay takes a cab home, feeling relieved.

You can't tell how people's lives will work out, Jay thinks. Maybe Betsy will have the baby and meet some guy who's wanted a ready-made family. Maybe some divorced guy who has custody of his baby will see her in the playground and be taken on the spot by the tender, affectionate way she pushes her baby in the swing. One thing will lead to another. In his mind Jay has Betsy married off—the guy could be a banker, maybe a Catholic as well—by the time he gets to his apartment.

For the first time since he got to Boston he is going home. It's been five months. It's almost July now, and Jay decides to take a week off. He'll see his parents. It's his father's sixtieth birthday, and his mother wrote how much they all miss him. "It's as though you were only gone a minute." She even hints they will always be glad to have him back in the apartment if that should appeal to him.

"I think I'll stay at a hotel," he says.

"A hotel?" Sophie is horrified. "But you'll be in New York. We have a guest room. Why a hotel?"

"I just think—" How can he put this? "It might be more private."

"Private for what?" his mother wants to know. "You're bringing a girl?"

"No, I'm not bringing a girl," Jay says.

"We're open-minded, we've always been," his mother says. "Bring a girl. We don't care. We'd like to meet her."

"Ma, I'm *not* bringing a girl, okay?"

"Is she someone you don't want us to meet? She's not Jewish?"

Where does this horrible mental telepathy come from?

"I'm coming alone," Jay says patiently, thinking, I'm leaving my pregnant Catholic girl friend in Boston. "We'll see each other just as much. I've just gotten used to living alone."

His mother hangs up, clearly not believing a word he says. Here every day thousands of Americans hang on his every word.

57

He is successful on the tube—he knows this from the letters he gets—because, as one besotted woman from Newton put it, "there's unmistakable sincerity in every word you utter." But his mother doesn't believe he just wants to be alone!

Jay gets a room at the Biltmore. He's making money. Isn't he entitled to a room at a decent hotel, for God's sake? Back in New York, filthy and horribly hot as it is, he feels a pang of nostalgia. Boston is not New York. No place is New York. Why did he leave? You wanted to get away. Xenia. You *had* to get away. Right, right.

He starts walking all the way from 42nd Street to 110th, drinking in the atmosphere of the city, looking delightedly around him. He takes off his jacket and carries it over one arm, unbuttons his shirt. He is perspiring, it is over ninety degrees out; but he feels buoyant, alive, the conquering hero.

Then, as he is strolling down Broadway at 108th, he sees Xenia and a man walking toward him. On Xenia's face is the expression Jay has imagined so often that for a few seconds he thinks he is just having a familiar fantasy. She looks grim, miserable, her mouth set in a severe line, turned down, her black eyes haunted and despairing. The guy beside her is short and chubby and doesn't look too wonderful either. Xenia doesn't even notice Jay, so immersed is she in her thoughts. She and the man pass by. Jay stops dead in his tracks. His heart thumping, he changes course and follows Xenia and her male companion up Broadway. Xenia is wearing a white dress, somewhat like the dress Jay remembers from Rome, maybe the very same dress. But not sandals, just plain high-heeled shoes. Xenia hates high heels. Why is she wearing them? *She hates her life.* As certainly as he's ever known anything, Jay knows this. He is going to rescue her. He is going to be Superman.

At the corner Xenia kisses her friend good-bye, a perfunctory kiss. It's on the lips, but Jay is not fooled. He knows a perfunctory kiss when he sees one. Xenia doesn't even raise her arms to the guy's shoulders, a dead giveaway. Nor does she turn back to gaze at him. She just walks on, swinging her handbag—she's glad he's gone?—and finally stops at the Cathedral Market, an open fruit and vegetable market on 110th and Broadway, where Jay and Xenia have often shopped together.

Xenia is inspecting peaches, idly; it's not clear if she intends to buy. Jay, about nine feet away, watches her, sees her hand reach down for a peach. Then, not giving himself time to think, he marches over, takes Xenia in his arms, and kisses her passionately, a long—

two-minute? three-minute?—kiss. From the back of the store comes a deep Spanish-accented voice: "Way to go!" A few people actually clap. Although he is not on TV, Jay feels, for the first time in his life, as though he is the hero, not the antihero, not the superfluous man of his father's Russian novels, but the real McCoy.

When they break apart, Xenia starts to laugh. Her face is pink, from embarrassment, from kissing in public, from pleasure. "Where did you come from?"

"You needed me, so I appeared," Jay says, grinning.

Xenia is leaning on him.

"I did," she whispers. "I need you so much."

"Will you marry me?" he hears himself say.

From the back of the store comes the same deep voice. "Marry him, lady! Give the guy a break."

"Yeah," Jay says tenderly, his arm still encircling Xenia's waist. "Give the guy a break, Xen."

"Of course I'll marry you," Xenia says, still breathless, giggling.

"When? Right now?" Jay calls out. "Is there a minister in the house?" Normally self-conscious, he now feels as though everyone in this fruit market, everyone in the world, in fact, is his friend.

From the back of the store the kibbitzer emerges, a huge Puerto Rican man in an undershirt, who embraces Xenia and then Jay. "Congratulations," he says, pumping Jay's hand vigorously. To Xenia he adds, "He'll make a good husband, this guy. You're doing the right thing."

"How do you know?" Xenia asks.

"I seen him. He comes lots of times. Not so much lately, but lots of times in the past. Did you switch your business elsewhere?" he asks Jay.

"No, I—" Jay begins, but the man interrupts.

"You can tell a lot about a guy from the way he buys fruit. The ones who pinch, squeeze, and then wrinkle up their noses. Forget them. They're too fussy. They'll never be pleased. This guy— he's careful, but when he finds what he wants, he looks pleased. Am I right?" he asks Jay.

"I guess," Jay says, delighted.

"You should be a psychiatrist," Xenia says.

"Sure," the man agrees. "I should be a lot of things. But I am what I am. No complaints. . . . Now, do you want those peaches or what?"

59

Both of them have forgotten about the peaches. But, in an orgy of high spirits, they buy, not only two pounds of peaches, but grapes, nectarines, apricots, even a small, fragrant cantaloupe.

"Now get going," the man says, "and don't let me see you back here till you've tied the knot. Okay?"

Arms linked, Jay and Xenia saunter off toward their former apartment. Suddenly Xenia stops dead in her tracks. "Oh dear," she says. "I just remembered something."

Jay feels a sudden sickening pang. There is a guy in Xenia's apartment, someone with whom she's been having a passionate affair. She was looking depressed before not because of the chubby man she was with, but because of this man who is, apart from being a real stud, a cruel, unfeeling lout who is lying drunk, on Xenia's bed, naked, waiting for her to bring him back fresh peaches.

"What's wrong?" Jay asks.

"Susan's in my apartment. . . . She's staying over a couple of days."

Jay's relief is so great he almost feels faint. "Terrific. I love Susan!"

In fact, he's only seen Susan a few times since graduation. She'd become a photographer and lives in Egypt. The few times she came over, when he and Xenia were living together, she was just as shy and uncommunicative as she had been in college. He still feels ill at ease with her, almost as though he and Susan were rivals for Xenia's affection.

"But how can we—" Xenia looks at him, a look of such sweet, embarrassed lustfulness that Jay wishes he could enshrine it in his memory forever.

"I have a hotel room," he says. "We'll just get a cab."

"A hotel room?" Xenia looks puzzled. "Aren't you staying at home?"

"Are you kidding?" Jay can't believe the luck, or is it foresight, of his having a hotel room. He thinks of that time in Rome, the beautiful *pensione*. God often seems out to lunch when it comes to Jay's life, but now and then He does it right.

The next day they get a marriage license, go for a blood test, and end up back at Xenia's apartment, where Susan is waiting with cold beer and pizza from V & T's warming in the oven. The apartment is air-conditioned, wonderfully cool. Susan looks pretty much the same to Jay, still impossibly thin and fragile, with that freckled white skin. Has she gotten laid yet? It's hard to imagine. She smiles at him sweetly and hugs him.

"I'm so glad, Jay. . . . You and Xenia are so right for each other."

Probably, of the three of them, Susan is the only one who feels this unequivocally.

"I'll be the photographer," she says. "You'll want photos, won't you?"

After dinner Xenia goes into the bedroom to make a phone call. There is a sudden silence, as there always is when the two of them are alone.

"Are you going to stay in Egypt?" Jay asks.

"I went over there on an assignment," Susan says, "and I got some more work there. I thought I might just spend a few months, doing some nature photography for *Natural History*, but now . . . I think I'll stay longer. Not forever. It's just . . . a beautiful country. I love the land there, the animals . . ."

"And the people?" Jay asks. It's easier to imagine Susan with animals than people.

"I have some friends," Susan says, looking evasive, as though he were intruding on something too personal. "What I mean is, I have as many friends as I have here. One or two." She laughs quietly. "Most people think I'm weird. There are no single women there. To be unmarried at my age is to be totally weird."

"No singles bars?" Not that Jay can imagine Susan ever going to one.

"No, that's a relief. It's a funny kind of relief being stigmatized that way, like being the town drunk. . . . I'm not preyed upon, the way I would be here. I can live quietly, inexpensively, I can do my work."

As she describes it, Jay can imagine Susan leading that kind of life; he feels guilty about himself and Xenia. But maybe Susan doesn't want that, maybe she doesn't need passion, intensity. It's true, she's always had that eerily self-contained manner. He can imagine her as a photographer, standing for hours, very still, watching.

After they finish the pizza, she shows Jay some of her photographs.

"These are from the region near the Nile Valley," Susan says. She doesn't seem ill at ease having Jay look at her photos the way he is if someone is reading one of his stories in his presence. She sits next to him, pointing out details. Two gazelles drinking from a stream, their huge delicate eyes alert; an eagle soaring against an intensely blue sky; a blur of golden chrysanthemums melting into green grass.

Jay feels a twinge of jealousy. The composition is fine, the sense of color precise. "How did you learn to take photos?" he asks. Even though he knows little about photography, he can sense a sureness his own work lacks.

"I picked it up, really," Susan says. "I guess everything is learning by doing, isn't it?"

"I guess." He is stymied, though, at the professional competence, as well as by the artistic vision. When he thinks of his stories, they seem, by comparison, inept, cramped, self-conscious. "What will you do with them?"

"I don't know," Susan says. Her light eyes look around the room, pensive. "I suppose I should try to arrange a show, but I hate the thought of . . . I guess I want the luxury of just doing it, for myself. And I can manage to live by taking on occasional studio work. Once they're judged and sold, it'll become something different."

"Not necessarily," Jay says. But he knows what she means. He no longer enjoys writing the way he did in college, before he'd begun sending things out.

"Cartier-Bresson said he wanted to always think of himself as an amateur," Susan says. "Meaning doing it for love. I want to do it for love." She blushes. "God, I sound pretentious. Do you know what I mean, though?"

"Sure, I understand," Jay says. It strikes him that this is the only actual conversation he has ever had with Susan in the entire time they've known each other. Even though she speaks haltingly, she seems to know what she wants to say. He wonders if Xenia has left them alone on purpose, so they will become "friends," or get to know each other better. There is still that air of sexual ambiguity to Susan. She could be gay or just celibate or even have a secret lover no one knows about. He becomes aware that Susan is sitting there, studying him, much as he studied her photographs.

"Do you like what you do, Jay?" she asks.

"Pretty much," he says. "I wish I had more time to write." But that's not true—he has plenty of time. He just doesn't use it. He has written only half of one story since leaving New York. "My life doesn't seem settled yet. I feel like I'm—" Maybe Susan's hesitancy has affected him. He can't even say what he means.

"You're still searching," Susan finishes for him. "But now you and Xen are together . . ."

"Yes." He wants her to complete the sentence. Now you will have inner peace, find time to write.

"You belong together," Susan says. "I've always thought that."

At such times Susan reminds Jay of the young girls in those Chekhov stories his father reads, her quaint, naïve way of saying "You belong together," her held-in, gentle, repressed quality, the way she sits with her legs turned to one side.

"Thanks," he says.

Xenia comes back from the bedroom. "That was Harry," she says. To Jay she adds, "The guy I was with when you met me. I told him we were getting married. He had a fit."

Before she has even finished her sentence, a horrible thought occurs to Jay: Betsy. "Shit!" he says, lying down on his back.

Both girls bend over him anxiously.

"What's wrong?" Xenia asks.

Jay hesitates. But he feels this is a time that calls for total honesty. "There's this girl in Boston," he says. "Betsy." He tells them about her.

"Jay, you're really hopeless," Xenia says. "I let you out of my sight for a mere five months and you're knocking up poor, forlorn Catholic girls who don't know how to swallow a pill."

"She's not knocked up," Jay protests. "She just thinks she is."

"Anyhow," Susan says, "it's not Jay's fault. If she didn't take the pill regularly . . ."

"It *is* his fault," Xenia insists. "Picking someone like that. . . . Why, Jay? Was it rebound? You wanted something sweet and guileless because I was too hard-boiled and vicious?"

"Basically," Jay says, and they both laugh.

Susan looks concerned. "You're not hard-boiled and vicious, Xen. How can you say that?"

Xenia looks stern. "Is she in love with you?"

"Not really," Jay says, trying to blank out certain unwanted memories of Betsy breathing soft endearments in his ear. "She may think she is but—"

"This is bad," Xenia says. "You've seduced and abandoned an innocent veterinarian's assistant whose brother is a gay cop. Do you want that on your record?"

"She doesn't sound innocent to *me*," Susan remarks.

"She's tough as nails," Jay says. "She wants a husband. I told her I was too young. I'm only twenty-seven." He suddenly realizes the incongruity of this remark in that he and Xenia are about to be married.

"You're a baby," Xenia says, laughing. "I'm robbing the cradle." To Susan she says, "Did you know he's nine months younger than me?"

"You're both babies," Susan says affectionately.

"If I waited till he's toilet-trained, someone's going to nab him," Xenia says. She looks back at Jay. "So this—what's her name?—Betsy—isn't in love with you, she just wants to marry you and raise a passel of kids?"

"I don't know about a passel," Jay says. "She wants a husband. . . . For a lot of women, men are just means to an end, the end being babies."

"I think the end *is* babies," Xenia says. "For me it would be."

Jay reaches over and hugs her. "Our babies will be different."

"Who says we're having babies?" Xenia says, horrified. *"You* have them. I'm not."

Jay gets down on his knees. "Just one? Just one tiny helpless baby?"

"Jay, what's wrong with you? I thought you were fleeing this dame in Boston just because she was pregnant." Xenia looks bewildered.

"I'm fleeing because I don't love her," Jay says.

"So why were you fucking her?"

Jay is trying to preserve his good humor. "I was supposed to be celibate for the rest of my life just because you booted me?"

"I booted *you*?" Xenia looks amazed. "You walked out! You took the job and walked."

"Some women follow their men," Jay says, furious.

"So, marry 'some women,' " Xenia says.

They glare at each other.

Susan is looking at them in incomprehension. "Hey, guys," she says softly. "What is this? You love each other. You're about to get married."

Jay and Xenia look at each other in dismay.

"It's going to be stormy," Xenia says, frowning.

"Naw," Jay says. "Stormy courtships make for peaceful marriages. Right, Susan?"

"You're both just a little . . . high-strung," Susan says. "But, Jay, I'm worried about Betsy. I think you should call her."

"Damn right," Xenia says. "She's probably knitting little booties. Jay, you can't just go breaking women's hearts so blithely."

Jay sighs. "I haven't broken anyone's heart. . . . No, you're right. I'll call her. Can I use the bedroom phone?" He goes into the bedroom, which is just as it was when he left, the mattress on the floor, books and papers stacked all around the room. Slowly, he dials Betsy's number. It's Saturday and she could be out, shopping. He half hopes she is.

"Oh hi, Jay," Betsy says. "How is it in New York?"

Does she mean the weather? Is he having fun?

"It's . . . fine," Jay says, stumbling. "How are you? How are you feeling?"

There is a small pause.

"A little sad," Betsy says. "I got my period. I know you're probably relieved."

"Well, maybe it's for the best," Jay says gently.

"I've decided you're right, though," Betsy says. "I am going to try a diaphragm. My friend Amy has one and she says they basically work. It's just kind of messy and you can't just . . . You have to get up and—"

"I know," Jay says.

"Oh," says Betsy, as though stunned by Jay's breadth of knowledge about female contraception.

This is not a perfect introduction to the topic, but Jay goes on to explain how a woman he has been in love with since college appeared suddenly in his life again and they've decided to get married.

"It seems sudden, but it really isn't," he concludes, unnerved by the total silence at the other end of the line.

"Is she pregnant?" Betsy asks in a quiet voice.

"No," Jay says. "She's an intern in psychiatry."

"So, she's more sort of a career woman?" Betsy manages to give this phrase a negative glaze.

"In a sense. . . . I'm sorry, Bets. When I came to Boston, Xenia and I had broken up, but I guess, deep down . . ." He can't finish the sentence.

"I hope you'll be very happy," Betsy says stiffly. "Congratulations."

"I hope we will," Jay says uncertainly. "I hope you will too . . . with someone, someday."

Why is everything he says coming out so idiotically?

But Betsy takes it in the best possible way. "That's sweet of you, Jay."

They hang up and Jay feels choked up, sentimental, and relieved.

"She's got her period," he tells Susan and Xenia, who are cleaning up in the kitchen.

"Glory hallelujah," Xenia says, handing Jay a dish towel.

That night, the night before their marriage, Xenia feels they should stay at the apartment, even though Susan is still there.

"I think she'd feel funny otherwise," Xenia says.

"But how can we—the apartment is so small," Jay says, dismayed. He knows he won't be able to make love to Xenia with watchful Susan sleeping or not sleeping in the next room. You can hear someone yawn, the walls are so thin.

"It's one night," Xenia says. "Tomorrow we can go to the hotel and do whatever we want. What's one night? We're going to be married forever." She puts her arms around his waist and rubs her nose against his.

"Yeah, I guess you're right," Jay says, but he feels a sleepless celibate night with Susan in the next room is as far from the ideal as can be imagined. It's not that he doesn't like Susan, it's just that it's been so long since he and Xenia have lived together. He wants to ease into it, somehow, if only to smooth over the precipitancy of their decision.

Before going to sleep, the three of them decide to try and call Conrad.

"Just to tell him," Susan asks, "or do you think he could actually come?"

"He could come," Jay says, dialing, but he feels doubtful that Conrad will. The phone rings and rings. There is no answer.

"Do you know he's actually there?" Xenia asks. "When did you last speak to him or hear from him?"

"A few months ago." Jay remembers Conrad's strange remarks. "He didn't sound that good. He sounded really depressed."

There is a moment of silence.

"I really wish we could get ahold of him," Susan says, frowning.

They try again at half-hour intervals, and then give up.

"He could just be traveling," Jay suggests. "He said he didn't even like living there that much."

"Or he could be out. . . . Or away for the weekend," Susan adds. "I feel worried, though."

"I think he's okay," Xenia says, but not in a very confident voice.

Jay wonders why they are all worried about Conrad. Of the four of them, he seems the most ebullient, relaxed, in touch with the world. Or seemed. Maybe he's changed. Have they all changed already? Jay is overtaken by a mood of restless melancholy that he can't shake off even as he gets into bed with Xenia, who falls instantly and contentedly asleep in his arms. Is it that this apartment has been the scene of so many quarrels, so many passionate make-up sessions? That was our youth, he told Xenia. Now we're seasoned, mature.

He manages to fall asleep, but at three in the morning wakes up with a start. He takes the phone into the bathroom and calls Conrad, but there is still no answer.

Jay gets back into bed, but doesn't lie down, just sits on the edge of the bed, staring at the window, which is protected against robbers by iron gates. He feels Xenia's hand touch him. Her voice says, "Aren't you asleep, sweetie?"

Jay is silent. When he speaks, he says something that he was not aware was on his mind at all. "Do you think Susan's more talented than I am? Do you think her photos are better than my stories?"

Xenia's eyes open. She props herself up in bed. "How can one compare photos to stories? And why does it matter?"

Jay shrugs. The gates look forbidding. In a story they would be symbolic—we are living in a prison—not just a justifiable city dweller's concern for robbers.

"Why are you still like this?" Xenia asks, puzzled. "You're good-looking, you're a TV star, you get fan mail, you had a story in the *Sewanee Review*, I love you, we're about to get married . . . What more do you want?"

"It's not wanting, so much. . . ." But Jay doesn't even know what it is he feels. "Maybe it's Susan being here, even tonight. I want to feel you're all mine, finally."

"I am," Xenia says, bewildered. "But I love Susan too."

"As much as you love me?" Jay demands.

"As much," Xenia says, "but in a different way."

Jay is stunned, dismayed. "How can you love her as much as you love me?"

"Because we've been friends since we were nine years old," Xenia says. "Because we've talked about things I've never talked about with anyone—"

"Things you don't talk about with me?"

"Things you wouldn't care about, just little things: how we used to masturbate, what fantasies we had, how we feel about life—"

"Those aren't little things!" Jay knows he is making too much of this, but he can't turn back. "I don't understand how you can love Susan as much as me."

"Sexual love isn't the only kind of love," Xenia says.

Jay can tell she is babying him, wanting a spoon to put under his tongue so he won't have a fit. He feels an involuntary moment of something like hatred for Susan.

"Her photos *are* better than my stories," he says gloomily.

"They're not." Xenia runs her hand up under his pajama top. "Lie down next to me, Jay. Please. Just love me and don't—don't question everything. Let's try and savor what we have."

She makes love to him as though he were an invalid, coaxing him quietly, gently. Jay lets himself be lulled into it and forgets to wonder if Susan is awake on the other side of the door, listening.

The following morning they go down to city hall. Xenia wears her white dress and Jay wears his summer suit. Susan is in thin slacks of a crinkly Indian material and a soft short-sleeved shirt. She wears a straw hat and big round sunglasses. Jay, looking at her on the subway—she is sitting across from them—feels a moment of contempt for his outburst the night before. He must never discuss anything with Xenia in the middle of the night. This is his first married resolution. At night he becomes a childish, insecure wreck. During the day—well, at least he is seemingly in command. Today, for instance, all those night terrors have vanished so totally it's as though they never existed. Of course, Susan is a good photographer! Why shouldn't she be? And of course you can't compare photos to stories! Why even try? He wishes, even, that he could fix Susan up with someone. If Simon weren't gay? Who would Susan like? Whom could she love?

"This is a silly hat," Susan calls over, taken aback by the intensity of Jay's stare.

"It's a wonderful hat," Jay calls back. "You should always wear hats."

It is Xenia who seems pensive and out of sorts.

"Poor Mooli. . . . She'll hate me forever," she says. "How can I do this to her? Just elope."

"She'll be happy," Susan says. "She's always wanted you to marry Jay."

"She has?" Xenia says. Both she and Jay look surprised at this news.

Susan blushes. "She told me once she hoped . . . But she didn't want to scare you by suggesting it."

"Igor may be less enthralled," Jay says.

"Oh, Daddy loves you too," Xenia says. "He just doesn't show it."

Jay snorts. But today even the specter of Dr. Szengi is not daunting. Xenia is right: from the outside his life looks so full of fine, splendid things. He must try and accept them and not keep turning them over and over, searching for the worm in the apple.

There is a long line of couples outside city hall. Somehow they didn't expect this. None of their friends has gotten married. The couple ahead of them is Hungarian. In a full embroidered dress, her hair in braids, the tiny bride looks as if she were going to a village fair. Her husband is tall and heavyset, with a thick blond moustache—a bricklayer, perhaps. Xenia talks to them in Hungarian and reports back that the bride doesn't know any English. She's just been in the country a week.

"She looks about eleven years old," Jay says. "Is that allowed?"

"It's just her braids," Xenia says. "She's nineteen. . . . He thinks you look Hungarian, Jay. That's a compliment."

"Tell him thanks." He watches Susan, who is taking photos of everyone with her Minolta—not just them, but all the couples in line. Their wedding album is going to look like stills from a documentary of the Lower East Side. In fact, developed the following month, Susan's photos reveal strange little details: a close-up of their hands, Jay looking at the Hungarian teen-age bride's braids, Xenia self-consciously touching her ear as though to make sure her earring is in place, the clerk reading the ceremony, his eyeglasses slipping down his nose.

Behind them is a couple their age who are having a quarrel.

"I just don't want to say 'obey'!" the girl is saying. She is slender, with red hair and a perky manner.

"It's in the ceremony," her partner-to-be says. "Why start off making a fuss over trifles?"

"It's not a trifle," she insists.

Xenia rolls her eyes and leans up against Jay.

"No trouble like that in this quarter," Jay whispers. "We don't countenance that kind of insurrection from *our* womenfolk."

"And since I always obey you slavishly," Xenia says, smiling, "no problem."

Coming out of the official hall, an older couple in their forties offers them champagne. "It's our second time," the man says. "This time we're going to make it."

"Your second time to each other?" Xenia asks nervously, accepting a paper cup.

The woman, a hefty blond in a low-cut white dress, beams. "We were too young before. I was too headstrong."

"I was too pigheaded," the man says, pouring Jay some champagne. It's not bad, some Yugoslavian variety.

As they move on, Xenia laughs. "That surely has no implication for us," she says. "You could search this whole line and not find anyone less headstrong than me *or* less pigheaded than you."

"Oink, oink," Jay says, kissing her forehead.

Susan takes a photo of Jay oinking.

Finally they are at the head of the line. Jay's heart starts thumping in a peculiar way. Why? He is not nervous, there are no relatives, no one's eyes are fixed on them. He thinks of saying jokingly, "Still want to go through with it?" But Xenia looks so solemn that he realizes he doesn't have the heart to joke.

The clerk is a small, bald man who looks at the three of them. "Who is the witness?" he asks.

"I am," Susan says softly.

She stands to the side, looking through her camera, as Jay and Xenia repeat their vows. Xenia's hand trembles as Jay slips on the ring. She puts an identical ring on his finger. They kiss, their lips just barely open.

Outside, the heat is ferocious. Xenia's hair is coming loose, her skin is flushed. She looks vivid and tempestuous, sexy. The line to the wedding bureau is longer than ever.

"All these people," Xenia says. "I wonder if it's like this every day."

"Probably," Susan says. She looks sad.

Xenia kisses her. "When you get married, we'll be your witnesses, won't we, Jay?"

Susan shakes her head. "I'm never getting married."

"Never?" Jay wonders what she would give as her reasons, but he feels it would be impertinent to ask. Tonight they have the hotel room. No Susan, no iron gates, no roaches. Jay squeezes Xenia's hand, letting his finger touch the unfamiliar bump made by the ring.

Susan is looking down into the camera.

"Some people are better off not married," she says. "Look at each other again, the way you were just before."

Jay turns to Xenia. How were they before?

"Did we look happy or anxious or—"

Xenia puts her hand over Jay's mouth. He looks around as though expecting to see someone. Xenia's parents? His own? He realizes, though there was no way it could have happened, that he was still hoping Conrad would have found out about the wedding; that, at the last moment, he would appear, straight from the airport, maybe in some crazy getup, a bottle of champagne under his arm. The wedding seems incomplete with just the three of them.

Hand in hand, Xenia and Jay walk down the steps of city hall. Her camera swinging around her neck, her straw hat tilted, Susan follows them.

Susan

1963

"Of course, if you have other things to do, I'll understand," Carol says. She looks pleadingly at Susan, her head tilted to one side. "It's for moral support, darling. I'm such a coward."

Since her mastectomy two years ago, Carol has hesitated to go shopping, but now she needs a bathing suit for a weekend trip she is going to take with Winthrop Schuler, their family lawyer, recently "booted by his wife," as Carol put it. When she was growing up, Susan took an avid interest in these romances of her mother's. That was how she saw them, "romances." She would sit on her mother's bed, watching her make up in her three-way mirror, entranced by her mother's prettiness, by her descriptions of where she was going dancing. But now Susan realizes that the romance was all in her head. To her mother the various escorts were just that: men to take her places, to keep her from sitting at home feeling sorry for herself. Possibly Winthrop Schuler is under the mistaken impression that he will get further. Susan doubts he will, no matter how good a time Carol has over the weekend. Basically Carol is afraid of men and uncomfortable with them. Her being a widow—this is how she terms herself to strangers—is a convenient excuse.

"Sure, I'll go," Susan says, for, indeed, she has no special plans.

"It's your big night, I know," Carol says. "But we'll get back in plenty of time for you to rest and get ready."

The same romance that she, mistakenly, injected into her mother's life, her mother now injects into hers. Carol knows Susan is going to the dance with Jay and wishes she were going with Conrad, but she has managed to blur all this into her own perception of the coming event as an exciting, fun-filled evening.

Susan sees her mother inspecting Susan's nails, which, as always, are bitten to the quick. There is just a moment of hesitation before Carol says, "You know, I think at Bloomingdale's they sell those plastic nails. You just glue them on. You could take them off tomorrow."

"I don't want to look like some dragon lady." Susan shudders, imagining herself with bloodred talons, clutching Jay's jacket.

"No, they have perfectly nice, ordinary ones, pale pink, peach, nothing extreme. . . . Let's check it out when we get downtown."

Carol is delighted at Susan's agreeing to go shopping with her. She loves shopping, loves it as an end in itself, not as a means to an end. Susan, on the other hand, would be content if today she could order by mail all the clothes she will need from now till the end of her life. Many times over the years Carol has exclaimed how lucky she feels to have a daughter, how since she was a little girl herself, she dreamed of having a daughter. She never adds that she surely hoped for a different kind of daughter, an outgoing, pretty daughter who would love the things *she* loved: dancing, shopping, flirting.

"Okay, we'll see," Susan says. Ever since she transferred from Smith after her freshman year to live at home with her mother, she has been counting the days till she can leave again. That year away, even in a women's dorm, was so free and footloose. Now it's as though she and her mother are rooming together. They both sleep in the living room, though Susan has a six-foot wooden screen behind which she can do her homework late at night, if her mother wants to go to sleep early. Once Xenia suggested they share a room at the dorm, but it seemed to Susan the point of her returning was to help her mother through this period in which, after discovering she had a tumor, she had it removed, and went for chemotherapy to prevent its recurrence. Susan sometimes looks down at her own breasts, which are so small she wonders if a tumor could even take root in them. She knows what a blow the mastectomy is to her mother, who, no matter what she thinks deep down about men, enjoys their attentions.

Does her mother go to bed with men like Winthrop Schuler who pursue her with dinners out, tickets to the opera, weekends at the beach? Susan has never asked, but once, her mother said of a particular man she was seeing at the time, "I told him that for me sex is connected with love. Without love it's just the joining of two animals." One of these would-be suitors was a businessman to whom Carol announced that he would never get very far with her unless he showed some interest in the arts. They were at his apartment at the time, when, Carol reported to Susan, he suddenly took a clarinet out of his closet and, for three hours, played every piece he knew, in hopes that this would lead to passion. Susan could have told him it wouldn't. She could tell poor, wobbly Winthrop Schuler that, no matter how fetching Carol looks in her new bathing suit, no matter how grateful she is to Winthrop for taking care of her financial affairs and her will, his reward will be somewhere other than in bed.

Susan is a virgin, and hates herself for it. She isn't the kind of virgin she reads about in magazines who is "saving herself" for the man she loves, nor the kind who regards her body as a priceless gift to be bestowed only on someone uniquely worthy. At times, Susan thinks she might sleep with anyone, with the Indian boarder, Nulip San, who occasionally gives her what could be interpreted as lustful glances when they meet in the hall on the way to the bathroom. Her virginity is burdensome, annoying, a proof to her, to everyone, that she is what she is. She sees it like a huge V hanging around her neck: virgin. If only there were a do-it-yourself deflowering kit, Susan would buy it immediately and use it. She feels it more keenly now that Xenia is going to bed with Conrad, having already done it with Jay and a few other men as well. Xenia is Susan's best friend and has been since grammar school, but Susan comes as close as she can to hating her when Xenia asks, "Do you think maybe I'm oversexed? It's all I think about some days."

What Susan would like to know is not so much how it feels

physically—she can imagine that from having read *Lady Chatterley's Lover* ten times—but how you can get past the awkwardness of removing your clothes, how you can look into someone's eyes and admit that you are feeling what you have to be feeling to be there in the first place. In book after book, Susan has read the phrase *carried away* and wondered if, even with all the drugs or alcohol in the world, she could ever reach the point of forgetting herself. If she could, she can imagine that alone would be wonderful.

On the subway, Carol, dressed in a scoop-necked, kelly green dress, says to Susan, "I know you'd rather be going with Conrad tonight. . . . But Jay is sweet. I like Jay."

"I wouldn't be going at all if Xenia hadn't forced Jay to ask me," Susan says. She flaunts her humiliation this way because her mother's hopes for her make her so furious.

"Oh, she didn't force him," Carol says, nervous, as always, when Susan does this. "You can't force someone. Jay likes you. I can tell."

"He's in love with Xenia," Susan says, emphasizing "love" savagely.

"That's simply because she allowed him to . . . they were once . . ." Carol says stumblingly.

"That has nothing to do with it," Susan cries in exasperation, though, of course, it does.

Carol's lips are pursed. "You know how fond I am of Xenia," she says. "I just worry sometimes that she . . . You know, men are naturally predatory when it comes to women. It's not their fault. It's hormonal. . . . But in the end, it's the woman who pays."

I hate her, I love her, Susan thinks, sitting beside her mother, plucking the petals of an imaginary daisy. Perhaps if she had two parents she could apportion her love and hate more evenly. Instead, all of it courses toward Carol, who is, as she constantly points out, doing her best as a single mother in a world of couples.

"How does the woman pay?" Susan asks. She takes a perverse enjoyment out of the fact that two girls her own age sitting next to them are listening to their conversation and giggling.

"Well, of course, the obvious way is pregnancy," Carol says. "But that's by far not the only way."

"Her reputation is sullied?" Susan says with what she hopes is only light sarcasm.

"It's hormonal," Carol repeats. "When a man possesses a woman, she is devalued in his eyes. It's the way it is, Suki. I'm only telling you the way it is, not the way it should be."

Xenia has slept with five men: Jay, Conrad, the teacher of her course in Russian literature till the nineteenth century, someone she met one day on a trip to the U.N., and—this is the worst—a former patient of her father's who looked like Robert Mitchum and had tried to kill himself. Five is not a lot, or, perhaps is, depending on how you look at it. How many men do you have to sleep with to be promiscuous? Xenia's contention is that if you enjoy it, you can do it with as many as you like and still not be promiscuous. Susan wishes, more than anything, that she could believe what her mother is saying, that Xenia, at some point—clearly not now!—will have to pay for her "sins." But all Susan can see is that both Jay and Conrad are in love with her. Is that the price?

"Well, no one's begging for my favors," Susan says wryly. "You don't have to worry."

"I'm not worried about you," Carol says. "I never worry about you. It's Xenia I'm worried about. I don't think her mother understands. It's being European. They have different standards. I once tried to talk to her about it and she laughed."

Susan loves Mrs. Szengi and her throaty deep laugh, her chain-smoking, her enigmatic, cynical asides. She can see how it might not be easy having her for a mother, but is anyone easy to have as a mother? Mrs. Szengi gives the impression of having, as she once put it, "drunk life to the dregs," and not really regretting it. Whereas Carol seems more to have sipped, lightly. Dregs would have no appeal for her.

The story Mrs. Szengi tells that Susan loves best is how, as a young woman, she boarded the train to go from Paris to Budapest (at that time a four-day trip). The heat broke down and it was so cold she asked a strange young man to enfold her in his arms each night to keep her warm. The two of them "slept" together for three nights, and then said good-bye at the Budapest station, where he planted a chaste kiss on her brow. A few weeks later she received a letter in which he asked her to marry him.

Carol was a pretty, innocent, naïve American girl. Now she is a just slightly less pretty, innocent, naïve American mother with a teen-age daughter for whom she would like life to turn out better than it has for her. She even turns to Susan as they get off the subway at Fifty-ninth Street and says in anticipation, "It's so much fun to go shopping with you!"

Of all the novels that cause cold shivers of recognition to run down her spine, Susan would put first those about middle-aged spinsters living with their mothers, the mothers in their sixties, the daughters in their forties. Even if her mother comes down with multiple sclerosis, Susan has resolved she will leave home this month and live alone for the rest of her life. She can face anything but the thought of the two of them endlessly shopping into middle age, old age, perhaps even together in an old-age home, allowed out for occasional trips into the city.

"It *is* fun," she says now, to conceal these ungrateful thoughts.

Carol likes a particular style of bathing suit that has never been very popular. It has a skirt and a lightly padded bra. It looks like a ballet tutu. According to her, this style is more "feminine," not just an excuse for displaying flesh. She veers to the side of the floor that has these and paws through them while Susan stares scornfully at the other shoppers.

"You could get one too," Carol says. "You haven't gotten a new suit in ages."

"I don't swim," Susan points out.

"You swim," Carol counters. With her meager savings she sent Susan to summer camp, where, indeed, Susan was given every opportunity to learn to swim. Is the dog paddle swimming? If so, Susan can, in truth, swim.

"Get a suit. You'd look lovely in this color." The suit Carol is holding is pale blue, the color of Susan's eyes.

"I don't like that style," Susan says.

"Then find a style you like," Carol commands. "Meet me in the dressing room."

But I'm not going to swim! Susan thinks. I hate swimming, I hate the sun! Being extremely fair, she can burn just going near the beach, but apart from that she has never understood the pleasure of baking for hours on end, like a roast chicken. She finds two suits in her size and scurries after her mother, who is in booth five.

Carol is wriggling her way into one of the suits, a pink one. She likes the way pink looks with her tinted red-blond hair. But her expression, as she gazes in the three-way mirror, is concerned.

"I think you can tell the difference," she says.

"Between what and what?" Susan asks.

"Between the real one and the other one," Carol says. "Tell me, honestly. Can you tell?"

Susan looks and, honestly, feels that Carol's real breast is less real-looking than the prosthesis, which is firm and perky and round. "I think they look pretty much the same," she says.

"Once they were both like this," Carol says, poking at the

prosthesis, which bounces back. "Not large, but lovely. Men always told me I had lovely breasts. Omar loved petite women. He said he couldn't understand men who lusted after women with breasts like melons."

Why, in a fitting room on a hot June day, does Carol want to talk about her long-dead Egyptian husband?

"I wish I'd known him," Susan says, also feeling melancholy, perhaps due to graduation.

Carol starts taking off the suit. "Oh, but in a way I'm glad you didn't," she says. "He could be . . . Omar was very disturbed. His mother thought he was crazy, like his father. She thought it was hereditary, but I don't think so . . . except perhaps his death."

Omar died two weeks after being released from a mental hospital by asphyxiating himself with a plastic bag. He was forty, the age Carol is now.

"Mental illness isn't hereditary," Susan says.

"I don't think so," Carol says. "But he was very . . . He never had a chance, really. That woman dominated him from the moment he was born to the moment he died."

All Susan knows of Omar is the photo Carol keeps on her bureau: a heavyset brooding man with dark melancholy eyes. Carol only knew Omar for six months before she became pregnant. After their marriage and almost instantaneous divorce, she never saw him, although he lived ten more years. He was forbidden by his mother to see her, Carol claimed. Would he have been happy living with them? In her mind Susan moves Omar in with the Indian boarder and elderly Mrs. Klotz, who is always losing her dentures. But, no, Omar was wealthy. If he had married Carol, the three of them would have lived in splendor, in some palace on Park Avenue, the kind of building Carol stares at longingly when they take a cab. Although she never met him and has never seen a letter from him, Susan can imagine Omar with Carol as she was then, at eighteen. She sees Omar sitting silent, disturbed at the injustices of the world, and perky, ingenuous Carol with her small lovely breasts trying to breathe life into him.

By now Carol is in the second suit, which, to Susan, looks exactly like the first, except it is a darker pink.

"Somehow, in this one, I think I look more the way I used to," Carol observes. "I'm glad I've kept my figure, apart from, you know. . . . Look at my fanny. Not an ounce of fat. You're lucky. You don't have an ounce of fat either."

Xenia has claimed that men actually like her potbelly and her full thighs and hips, that it's all a crock about men wanting gaunt model-like figures. Susan points this out, but Carol says dismissively, "It depends on the man, I suppose. . . . But Xenia will have to be *very* careful her entire life. She could look matronly in no time at all if she isn't careful."

When Susan gets into the first suit she has chosen, Carol looks dismayed before it is even on.

"But you need something on top, sweetie," she says. "You need something to hold it up."

Mockingly, Susan holds up the tie that goes around her neck.

"You know what I mean," Carol says. She looks at the loose folds of material hanging where Susan's breasts are concealed.

"I hate padded bras," Susan says. "They look grotesque. I don't want to look like Jayne Mansfield!"

But imperturbably Carol gets dressed and finds another suit, with, as she says, "gentle padding." Susan hates the suit, hates her body, hates Carol for making her submit to this indignity. But she agrees to buy it just so they will get out of the dressing room. Carol, after paying for both suits, has regained her good humor. "Winthrop said he was dying to see me in a suit," she says with an impish smile.

"Are you going to marry him?" Susan says, wanting to be cruel, but not knowing how.

Carol looks surprised. "I don't know. . . . We only, we've only been dating for a few months."

"But you've known him all your life, for years," Susan persists.

"As Marion's husband," Carol says. "That's different. If a man is someone's husband, you never . . . You don't even have thoughts about him as a man. That can only lead to trouble."

Susan wonders how Winthrop feels, suddenly being transformed from a husband into a man. Maybe it was easier the other way.

At home Carol remembers that they never bought the false nails to glue on and conceal Susan's ragged, bitten ones.

"I'll wear gloves," Susan says sarcastically, but Carol brightens at that.

"I have some lovely lace gloves," she says. "I'll see if I can find them."

As always during the day, as fixed as one of those tableaux behind glass in the Museum of Natural History, Mrs. Klotz is knitting in the dining room.

"Your friend called," she tells Susan.

"A boy or a girl?" Carol asks. She gets irritated when Mrs. Klotz forgets phone messages or gets them bungled. She's told her not to answer the phone, but Mrs. Klotz always forgets. Once she said, "I tried not to answer, but it rang and rang. It seemed cruel not to answer."

"A girl. . . . It's always a girl," Mrs. Klotz says, without rancor. "That same girl, the one with the funny name."

Xenia. Susan goes into the living room to call her back and hears the tail end of the conversation between Carol and Mrs. Klotz.

"We just got some lovely suits, for Susan and me, for the beach."

"You have to be careful not to burn when you're so fair," Mrs. Klotz says. "Don't stay out in the sun too long."

The living room is stuffy. Their air-conditioner has been broken so long that it's like some vestigial organ. Nulip San once poked at it with a screwdriver, but nothing happened.

Xenia's voice on the phone sounds troubled. "You've *got* to come over. . . . Can you?"

"I guess. Is something wrong?" Xenia is always dramatic. She is the play, Susan is the audience. It's always been this way between them.

"I'll tell you when you come."

"Tonight there's a dance," Carol is telling Mrs. Klotz as Susan emerges from the living room. "Susan is going with a lovely young man, a writer. . . . He's going to be a journalist after he graduates."

"That's a good choice," Mrs. Klotz says. It's not clear if she means Susan's choice of Jay, or Jay's choice of a profession. She looks at Susan carefully. "But you're so young!"

"Young for what?" Susan asks. She is fond of Mrs. Klotz, even though all their conversations have a strangely meandering quality.

"You're graduating college already! Going out in the world! Dances, everything!" Mrs. Klotz sighs.

"I'm twenty-two," Susan says. "That isn't so very young." A year older than Xenia and Jay, for instance.

"Twenty-two is very young," Mrs. Klotz, who is eighty-two,

assures her. "At twenty-two I was living at home. They didn't allow me out for coffee, much less to school or with men."

"Well, that was a different era," Carol snaps. "Now young women are very independent. They have many choices, as many as men."

At that Mrs. Klotz rolls up her wool. "No, never like men. . . . Women are not like men."

"I didn't say they were *like* men," Carol says. "I said they aren't tied, the way we were, to having to get married. They can be free."

Mrs. Klotz snorts. "Free!"

"I'm going to visit Xenia," Susan says. "I'll be back later."

"Don't you want to rest a little?" Carol asks anxiously. She has changed into the new bathing suit and is barefoot.

"Oh, and a man called for you," Mrs. Klotz says to Carol. "I forgot to mention that."

Carol turns red. "What man? I told you to write down all messages."

Mrs. Klotz isn't perturbed. "He said not to bother. He said he'd call back."

"Did he leave his name?" Carol stands in front of Mrs. Klotz anxiously.

"I don't believe so," Mrs. Klotz says, frowning.

"Was it Mr. Schuler?"

"I don't remember." Mrs. Klotz looks at Susan, who is about to flee, and then back at Carol. "Look at your mother! A figure like a young girl! No wonder all these men are calling, calling, every minute."

"Were there others?" Carol asks. "Did other men call while we were out?"

"Just the one," Mrs. Klotz says. "I can't remember any but the one."

Emerging into the dusty street, Susan wonders why Carol is so anxious about these calls. What does it matter? To prove she is popular? But who is she proving it to? Never, Susan vows, will she be like that, giving men that power over her life, over her sense of self. If she loves, ever, it will be private. She won't allow her face to get that anxious, frightened expression at the sound of someone's voice. It is too demeaning even to think about.

Always, visiting Xenia, Susan thinks of her father. She wonders what the hospital that he was in was like. Were the doctors like Dr. Szengi, with his dry ironical manner, kindly but European? Why did they let him out if he was so depressed that, two weeks later, he killed himself? Carol managed, somehow, to find out the true story of Omar's death. He was living at home with his mother. Susan has gone over the scene many times in her mind. She sees Omar, as he looks in the photo, waiting till his mother has left the apartment, finding a plastic bag in her kitchen, fastening it over his head. Was it hard to die that way? Didn't you automatically want to breathe as the air gave way? Men in books shoot themselves, choose dramatic, masculine means of self-annihilation. Omar took a plastic bag, something belonging to his mother. Susan knows how he must have felt, knows this choice has to have been deliberate. He never escaped. He made love to Carol when his mother was out and he killed himself when his mother was out. When she was there, he was immobilized, a statue, someone without a will. That's why you have to leave, Susan tells herself, for the millionth time.

Xenia's house is huge and beautiful, but it makes Susan nervous. What if mad patients escaped and broke into the house at night? Dr. Szengi says this is close to impossible, the patients are so well guarded. Still, walking up the long driveway, Susan always looks around herself nervously, starting if there is a rustle in the bushes.

Xenia opens the heavy front door and lets her in. She is wearing shorts and a halter top. Her hair is wet, wrapped in a turban. It takes two hours to dry.

"I'm so glad you came," Xenia says, hugging Susan.

Susan looks at her. Has Xenia been crying? She looks red-eyed and puffy-faced, not pretty, with her hair concealed. Xenia can go rapidly from looking beautiful to almost ugly, whereas Susan feels she always looks the same. "Are you okay?"

"Let's go to my room" Xenia says. They pad up the long stairway to Xenia's room, which is larger than the living room Susan shares with her mother. "I don't think Con loves me," Xenia says intensely, her eyes bright. "I *know* he doesn't. I feel like such a jerk, the way I've been going after him. He doesn't even want to go to the dance tonight. He said so."

"Did you have a fight?" Susan asks. She tries not to feel delighted at this news, knowing it doesn't increase her own chances with Conrad at all.

Xenia is sitting against the windowsill with her knees up. She

85

shakes her hair loose and drops splatter out. One hits Susan's knee.

"We make love, and he just . . . it's like he's not there. Even while we're doing it. It's such an awful feeling."

They have had many such conversations over the years, starting with the early fantasies Xenia described with such vividness when they were nine and ten. She would imagine walking into the bathroom while boys were peeing and insisting on seeing them pee, even touching their penises. She and Susan would scream with laughter at these fantasies, at the imagined terror of the boys in question, who, at school, they ignored totally. But now for Xenia real things are happening and Susan is still just having fantasies, which, over the years, have simply grown more baroque, but are really the same imagined scenes.

"Doesn't he have an erection?" Susan asks, curious.

"Of course!" Xenia looks annoyed. "How could we do it otherwise?"

Susan shrugs.

"He just lies there," Xenia says. "I feel like a whore. It's like he's doing me a favor."

Susan considers this. "Was it better with Jay?"

"The sex was better," Xenia says. "But Jay is just . . . we're too much alike. Conrad is so beautiful. Maybe I shouldn't want more than to just look at him."

Susan thinks that is, literally, all she would like—to look at Conrad naked. Even the awkward, funny way he moves is fascinating to her. "He *is* beautiful."

"He hates it when I say that," Xenia says, smiling.

"I think you and Jay were better suited," Susan says.

Xenia is rubbing her thick black hair furiously. "How can you say that? I used to want to kill Jay! He can get me so mad! He's so cruel sometimes."

"Maybe that was because he liked you."

"It's his character," Xenia says. "He's terminally insecure. We just lost our virginity together, and afterward he tried to make it into a whole big deal, like we'd plighted our troth or something."

Susan leans back against Xenia's bed. "I wish I could lose mine. It seems demeaning to still be a virgin at twenty-two."

Xenia drops the towel. "Do it with Jay tonight! He's good. . . ."

"He's not attracted to me," Susan cries, hating Xenia for being so insensitive. "He's still in love with you."

"Just flirt with him," Xenia says. "He doesn't know you're interested in him. You act like he's just a friend. Come on a little."

"I don't know how."

"You just do it. Vamp it up."

"What if I bleed like a stuck pig?"

"Nobody does. . . . Jay likes you, Susan. He'd be perfect. He's very . . . caring."

"I thought you said he had so much hair all over his body."

"He has a great body," Xenia says. "He's in terrific shape, much better than Con."

"You do it with him, then!" Susan says. "You sound like you're still attracted to him."

"Jay and I are like brother and sister," Xenia says. "By objective standards I think he's a good lover, but . . . we just have horrible fights. With Con it's the opposite. He's gentle, vague, like I'm not there. If you could only mix them up together!"

Susan begins imagining an orgy, the four of them: Susan, Xenia, Conrad, and Jay. But immediately it turns into a nightmarish fantasy in which both men are falling all over Xenia, and Susan is curled up alone on one side of the bed.

"What was it like with the man who was in the hospital?" she asks. She thinks anything Xenia says about this man may apply to Omar.

Xenia shudders. "That was so stupid, so dangerous!"

"Is that why you did it?" Susan doesn't mean to be needling—she's really curious.

"I really don't think so," Xenia says. "We met at a party and it only came out afterward that he had been a patient here. . . . No, maybe he said it earlier. What was it? He was almost thirty, he had a great body. He'd been a—what do you call those men who do things with boats?"

"A sailor?"

"A longshoreman," Xenia remembers. "He had such muscles! I remember his saying, 'Feel my muscles,' right there, at the party. And he was a born-again Christian. He said he'd actually *seen* God." She laughs. "He was pretty scary, actually."

"I didn't think longshoremen had nervous breakdowns," Susan says.

"No, neither did I. You'd think it would just be overeducated, neurasthenic people who had time to think about things. . . . Of course, he did say he'd been unemployed. Maybe that gave him time to think."

In Susan's mind a movie is unrolling of Xenia with a large muscular man—with tattoos on his arm? "Did that make it sexier?"

she says. "The longshoreman part? His being so different, cultur-
ally?"

"Yes, definitely." Xenia makes a face. "He drove me somewhere and it was cold and dark and I thought: Jesus, this guy
could kill me! I felt so scared that I couldn't even really enjoy the
sex. I just wanted it to be over."

Will I ever do scary, exciting, forbidden things? Susan wonders. "Maybe I *will* try and seduce Jay," she says, smiling faintly.

"You should," Xenia says. Her hair is dry and stands out like
a burnished, bristling mass. "What harm can it do?"

Susan knows she won't seduce Jay, but it's fun to sit and talk
with Xenia like this, as though it were a possibility. "I wonder if
Carol ever goes to bed with anyone," she says.

"I thought that lawyer wanted to marry her."

"Lots of men do. . . . But I think she holds them at arm's
length. I think she thinks sex is messy and uncouth." Susan remembers Carol as last seen, in her tutu-styled bathing suit and
bare feet, her slender, girlish, one-breasted body.

"It could be her breast," Xenia suggests. "Not having both, I
mean."

Susan stands up. "She was always like that, even with two of
them."

That evening, Susan, Carol, Mrs. Klotz, and Nulip San have dinner together. Nulip San does the cooking on Tuesday and Saturday. He is an excellent cook. His are the only meals worth eating,
in Susan's opinion. He always uses fresh vegetables, everything is
lightly spiced, but aromatic. He is a Sikh and wears his hair in a
turban. Just before dinner he gives Susan a white gardenia. "For
the prom," he says. His accent is very light, more English than
Indian.

Susan doesn't know what to do with the flower, it's so unexpected. She just takes it and smiles, embarrassed.

"What a lovely gesture!" Carol cries. "Thank you, Nulip."

"I heard it is traditional, before a dance." He brings the pan
of shrimp and vegetables in from the kitchen.

Mrs. Klotz looks bewildered. "You are going to the dance?"
she asks Nulip.

"No, no, *I* am not going," he says. He hands Mrs. Klotz a
plate. She never eats the vegetables, always eats around them, so
they leave a strange design on the plate.

"Susan is going to the dance with *Jay*," Carol says, speaking too distinctly, as she always does when she is annoyed with Mrs. Klotz.

"He's the one who writes stories," Susan says, wishing she didn't have to eat anything. She doesn't want to hurt Nulip San's feelings, but she has no appetite. "I once showed you one of his stories."

"Yes, I remember," Mrs. Klotz says. "He's very talented." She beams unexpectedly at Nulip San. "You should go to the dance too."

"I cannot dance," Nulip San says, serving Carol.

"Nulip isn't graduating," Carol explains in the same tone of voice. "This is a *graduation dance*."

They eat their shrimp and vegetables in the hot, stuffy room. Susan feels grotesque in her pale blue dress, her pearls. Not knowing what else to do with the flower, she sticks it in the glass of water in front of her and then realizes she can't drink from the glass.

In the middle of dinner the phone rings. Carol springs up to answer it. "Oh hi, Win. . . . No, we're almost finished. Did you? I heard someone had called, but you know what she's like. . . . Of course, I thought it must be you, but I wasn't sure." Carol takes the long cord of the phone and winds her way into the kitchen.

Mrs. Klotz smiles, abashed. "My memory is not what it once was," she says to Nulip and Susan. "It's very annoying. I don't blame Carol for getting angry at me. She has so many calls!"

"I, too, forget," Nulip San says.

"Some things I remember very well," Mrs. Klotz says, "but not names." She glances at Susan. "This is the man who wants to marry her?"

Susan nods. Even though Carol can't hear, she is afraid she might.

"But she doesn't love him," Mrs. Klotz concludes. "That's the way it always is. A loves B, who loves C, who loves D. . . ."

"You are a pessimist," Nulip San says to her, smiling, as though it were a compliment.

"No, I've just lived too long," Mrs. Klotz says. "You and Susan will find happiness, I'm sure."

There is a deadly moment of silence. Does Mrs. Klotz think Susan and Nulip San are a couple? Or does she mean they will find happiness separately? After this month I will never live here again, Susan thinks. I will never live with any person again.

Over the years, especially when Carol wasn't dating anyone

special, she and Susan watched dozens of old movies on TV. Susan remembers these times as among the nicest of her childhood, the two of them snuggled under the quilt, both in nightgowns, eating popcorn, drinking hot chocolate, and watching lives that turned out the way theirs were supposed to have turned out. Susan remembers movies in which the daughter of the family is going to her senior prom. She comes down the stairs in her full-skirted dress, a half smile on her face, tentative, though she is as beautiful as Elizabeth Taylor (usually because she *is* Elizabeth Taylor), and her folksy but urbane Spencer Tracyish father tells her how lovely she looks and hugs her, her slightly bratty but cute younger brother says something teasing, her little sister lies on her bed and squirts perfume on herself, and finally a handsome, square-jawed, dark-haired young man pulls into the driveway and walks slowly up to the door.

Okay, so that was a fantasy, everyone knows movies are fantasies, but it seems to Susan too cruelly distant from that to be sitting with Nulip San and Mrs. Klotz in a un-air-conditioned dining room while her mother drifts around the kitchen, murmuring half endearments to her family lawyer and would-be lover.

The three of them eat silently while Carol's conversation and laughter occasionally waft in at them like background music. For some reason Susan remembers how once there was a fire in the building in the middle of the night and Nulip San rushed out without his turban and Mrs. Klotz rushed out without her wig. Susan had never seen either of them that way before—they looked de-sexed, Mrs. Klotz with her balding, round, white head, and Nulip San with his thick curly black hair, just like his beard.

For dessert, Nulip San says, he has a surprise. By this point, Carol has come back to the table, apologized for her absence, and eaten the rest of her food quickly.

"A surprise?" Carol says. "How thoughtful!"

They all wait in silence and then Nulip comes in, carrying an ice-cream cake with icing over the top, spelling out Happiness to Susan! He has stuck one candle in the middle, which Susan blows out. "Thanks," she says.

"We're having a party," Mrs. Klotz says, delighted. "A real party." She loves sweets, and she and Carol have had arguments about her habit of sneaking in at night and polishing off half pints of butter-pecan ice cream.

Carol is watching Susan anxiously. "Be careful with your dress," she says.

"It *is* lovely," Nulip San says, giving Susan the first piece.

"I hope the young man is worthy of it," Mrs. Klotz says.

Carol looks irritated. "It's Jay. . . . You've met him, he writes stories. . . ."

"But is he worthy?" Mrs. Klotz goes on, happily spooning up her ice cream and cake.

"He has to be or Susan wouldn't be going to the dance with him," Nulip observes.

Carol takes a small bite of her cake. "Well, he may be worthy, but he's late. . . ."

"He lives in the Village," Susan says, apologizing for Jay. "It's a long trip."

After dinner they move into the living room. Nulip San turns on some music on the radio. Carol brightens.

"Oh, I love that," she cries. "I used to dance to that. I love South American dances. That was my specialty—the samba, the rhumba." She gets up and, alone, starts dancing around the living room.

Susan, sunk in the wing chair, feels a mortification so extreme she is surprised she's not blasted out of her seat, watching her mother shake her hips and sing quietly under her breath.

"I want to learn to rhumba," Nulip San says, watching Carol, his arms crossed.

Susan is sure Carol will make a snooty remark, but she just flashes Nulip San a delighted smile and takes his hand.

"It's easy," she says. "Anyone can learn. . . . You too, Suki. Come on, learn the rhumba! Those dances never fade. They're sexy. It's all in the hips."

Susan gets reluctantly to her feet. "I don't have hips," she says dryly.

Carol ignores this. "Sway gently," she says. "Just a little come-hither wiggle. That's it. . . . Nulip, you're good! You're really good. Watch him, Suki. See how he moves. You're too stiff."

In fact, Susan thinks Nulip and her mother look good to-gether. They dance around the room, wiggling, swaying, and it seems to Susan that they make a much better couple than Carol and Winthrop Schuler, who is ten times stiffer, even, than Susan. Is it true that if you can dance well, you will be good in bed? Would Nulip San be good in bed?

At that point, mercifully, the doorbell rings. It is Jay. Susan rushes to the door, not so much overjoyed to see Jay as to escape. "Hi, Jay."

He looks earnest, attractive, but awkward, his hair, which is usually bushy, like Xenia's, flattened down with water. "Sorry I'm late."

On the way to Szengis' Susan realizes that, of course, she has just escaped from one awkward situation into another. At least nothing she could ever do in front of Nulip San, her mother, or Mrs. Klotz would disturb them. Whereas she is sure Jay is thinking every second: Why isn't she Xenia? Why did I agree to take her out? She remembers a horrible moment in high school when Xenia asked a boy who had a crush on her to take Susan out for a soda. "I told him how much fun you were once you relaxed," Xenia said. Susan uttered not one word the entire time. At the end of the half hour the boy said, "Now, tell Xenia I was a good boy, okay?"

Men are just people. This is a theory Xenia has sometimes propounded. Try to imagine they're women, she has advised Susan. They have fears and doubts. They're not, basically, all that different from us.

Yes, they are! Susan cries inwardly. Okay, sure, she knows Jay is probably feeling awkward and uncomfortable, but there's a sense, even so, that he's in command of the situation. They are nearing the Szengis' house, having walked the six blocks from the subway. Well, here goes. Pretend he's a woman.

"I would feel funny living so close to a mental hospital," Susan says.

"Me too," says Jay. "Xenia says you get used to it, though."

"My father was in one once," Susan says.

"I didn't know you had a father," Jay says. "I mean, I thought your mother was divorced."

"Well, he killed himself many years ago by putting a plastic bag over his head," Susan says, "but they never lived together. He just helped support us."

This is great small talk en route to a dance! But Jay says, "Gosh, I'm sorry to hear that . . . about your father. Had he been depressed a long time?"

"All his life, evidently," Susan says. "He lived with his mother . . . which is why I don't want to." Even though she is trying to pretend Jay is a woman, it isn't working. Every remark she makes seems peculiar and abrupt. She has the feeling she is Carol, forcing herself, as Susan, to talk.

"Yeah, I can't wait to get away either," Jay says. "I've lived at home all my life, all through college, for financial reasons. It's the pits."

"Right," Susan says.

Jay sighs. "I didn't even have my own room till my sister was a teen-ager. I think privacy is just about the most important thing in the world."

"Does that mean you never want to get married?" Susan asks. Oh, why did she say that? Will he think she's proposing to him?

"No, I want to get married someday," Jay says. "When I . . . find the right woman and when I can afford to support her. . . ." His voice trails off sadly.

Is he thinking that he has met the right woman, Xenia, and she likes his best friend better? Is he thinking that to support a woman like Xenia in the style to which she's accustomed will take quite a bit of money? "I'm never getting married," Susan says. That, too, seems to her overly vehement. No one's going to ask you, so don't worry, she imagines Jay thinking.

"Not even if you fall in love with someone?"

Susan thinks of saying, "I'm not going to fall in love with someone," but then he'll have to say, "Sure you will," so she just says flatly, "No."

Jay rings the doorbell.

Susan is filled with dismay when she sees Xenia, who has flung open the door and is hugging both of them—dismay not just at Xenia's easy physicality, but at the fact that her hair, which was bristly and wild several hours ago, is now arranged beautifully with delicate wisps around her ears. Her eyes are no longer red and accusing, but limpid and moist. She looks like a Middle Eastern princess. I want to be Xenia, Susan thinks for one second, and then has to correct herself because she really doesn't. For whatever odd reason, she really would rather be herself, just a better, more self-assured version.

Even though she is here, at the Szengis', and they both like her, Susan suddenly, unexpectedly wishes she were at home, learning the rhumba from Carol, dancing and eating ice cream with Nulip San and Mrs. Klotz. A few times the four of them have even played bridge at a level so rudimentary that it could hardly be called "beginning." Mrs. Klotz forgot the trump suit every time.

When Conrad finally arrives late, everyone's mood changes. Even though his arm is broken and Xenia is angry with him, suddenly it seems like a party and Susan is glad the four of them are going together. She is touched that Conrad thought to bring a flower for her. She didn't really expect a formal corsage because she felt Jay was only taking her as a favor to Xenia.

Squeezed next to Xenia in the backseat of Conrad's father's car, with the warm summer air blowing in on them, she feels happy.

"Is everything okay now?" she asks Xenia softly, alluding to her afternoon mood.

"Oh yes," Xenia says. "It was just a mood. . . . Maybe it's the idea of graduating. Even though I've been looking forward to it, it's scary."

Why should it be scary for Xenia, who has been accepted at P and S Medical School and has the next four years of her life totally planned out? "I know what you mean," Susan says. Even though Conrad and Jay are in the front seat, it's almost as though she and Xenia are sitting in her room, talking.

"Remember how we used to talk about rooming together, getting an apartment in Paris," Xenia says, "traveling around the world? I wish we still could."

"I want to travel," Susan says. "I'm going to work till I can save some money and just take off."

"Lucky you." Xenia sighs. "I'll be slogging away. The first year of med school is supposed to be murder. I'm so un-cut-out for it. All that memorizing!"

"You'll be a good doctor, though," Susan assures her.

"I think so. . . . But will I make it?"

Susan wishes the whole evening could be like this, just chatting comfortably with Xenia about things they have discussed hundreds of times. She isn't sure what is different, trying to talk to Jay. Maybe it's that with Xenia she doesn't have to *pretend* she's a woman, she *is* one. But what does that mean? A woman is someone who isn't judging you and finding you wanting, who likes you just as you are. Does Xenia feel that when she is with men?

Now they are out of the car and Xenia and Conrad are walking ahead. They look relaxed, joking around. Xenia has taken his arm so naturally.

Susan looks up at Jay, who is again stiff and silent at her side. Should she bring up her father's suicide again? That seemed to be the one topic that got him going. But instead she just walks ahead, hoping that once inside, with all the noise and music, it will be easier.

Susan doesn't know anyone at the dance except Xenia, Jay,

and Conrad. Because she was a transfer and lived at home, she doesn't even know many Barnard girls, and since she always studied at the Barnard library, she never met any Columbia boys, except the ones in her Russian class. Instead of feeling relaxed, she is overwhelmed by a wave of panic as they enter the room. Why am I here? Why did I let Xenia talk me into this? Susan remembers that she can't dance, she doesn't know how to talk to men. In a daze she watches Xenia and Jay dance off together.

"I guess I wouldn't be a very good partner for you with this arm," Conrad says, looking down at Susan.

"Oh, that's okay," Susan says. "I don't know how to dance, really."

Conrad laughs. "Neither do I. . . . Xenia can't believe how clumsy I am. It's the same with sports. People always assume I'll be great at basketball because I'm so tall, but I can't get the ball in the basket."

"Does that bother you?" Susan asks. She can't imagine Conrad being bothered by anything.

"It used to. . . . People expect your looks and your personality to go together, somehow. Mine never did, especially at prep school. The guys who looked like me all came from these WASP families in Connecticut, fathers who drank, mothers who were on the social register. No one could believe I was Jewish."

"Are you?" Susan has never thought of Conrad as Jewish either, even though she knows his parents are. He is so blond and clean-cut-looking, his body is so lean and long-boned.

"Sure. . . . What else could I be? I don't mean I'm religious or anything, but I was bar mitzvahed . . . just to please the old man."

Conrad's father *is* an old man. Susan has met him a few times and he looks almost like a grandfather. Xenia told her that he was forty-four when they adopted Conrad.

Both of them stand side by side looking around the room at the dancing couples. For some reason Susan feels at ease with Conrad. He is so gentle, the way very large dogs often are.

"Xenia and Jay make a good couple," he says amiably. "Don't you think?"

What can he mean by that? That he and Xenia *don't* make a good couple?

"Yes, I do," Susan says. Without stopping to censor, she adds, "I think Jay still likes her."

"Yeah," Conrad says. "Sometimes I get that feeling myself."

This remark puzzles Susan. He and Jay are best friends. Don't they talk about such things, the way she and Xenia do? She keeps thinking of Xenia's remarks in the afternoon, how passive and detached Conrad is in bed. *Does he have erections? Of course, how could we do it otherwise?* Maybe sex is like a sport, requiring some innate grace and ease that Conrad, despite his looks, doesn't have. Jay has it. It's funny. Watching him on the dance floor, Susan sees how bouncy and energetic he is. *Why don't you seduce Jay tonight? He's good.*

At that moment the dance ends and Xenia and Jay return to Conrad and Susan.

"Why aren't you dancing?" Xenia demands.

Conrad points to his arm.

"Oh, that's an excuse! You can't just stand there all night!"

"Okay." Conrad turns to Susan. "Can you put up with this?"

He is doing this, of course, to make up for Xenia and Jay taking the first dance together. Nonetheless, Susan is stunned. "It's fine with me," she says, glancing at Xenia to see if she is annoyed.

The music is fast and lively. "We'll dance to our own drummer," Conrad says, enfolding Susan awkwardly, like a giant stork taking a starling under its wing.

In fact, it is awkward dancing with Conrad, not only because of his broken arm, but because he is a foot taller than Susan. And yet it is also wonderful, romantic, thrilling. Susan fantasizes that sometime in the future Conrad will be horribly injured in some way and need someone to take care of him, like Mr. Rochester in *Jane Eyre.* Not blindness. It seems too cruel, even in a fantasy, to wish that on Conrad, who loves art and is planning to go to architecture school.

"My mother was trying to teach me to rhumba," she says, feeling suddenly lighthearted and happy.

"Let's pray they don't try anything like that. . . . Am I stepping on your feet? Am I okay?"

"You're fine," Susan says. She wants to add, "You're wonderful," and to her own surprise, she does.

Conrad smiles down on her with his lazy, warm smile. "We're not a bad combination," he says, not realizing he is giving Susan fantasy material to last a decade with this one casual remark. They pass by Xenia and Jay, who are talking intensely, and Conrad waves. Xenia, catching Susan's eye, winks.

96

1973

It is early October. In two weeks Susan is returning to America on a visit. Now, at five in the morning, she is standing in a remote part of the Nile Valley. It is dark, not dawn yet; she has been standing motionless for hours.

Susan learned of the area in the summer of 1967, when she was in the New York office of the Egyptian Conservation Fund. She told the director that she wanted to take photos of anything connected with nature: landscape, animals, birds. "Are you doing this for yourself or for us?" he said with a smile.

"I'm not sure." She hadn't thought of it that way.

"Even if it is for yourself, it will end up being for us." He wished her good luck.

Three times a week she does studio photography at a small firm in Alexandria, not far from where she lives. But the man who runs the studio allows her to choose her own hours, so long as she puts in the requisite number each day.

She's found that she can stand for hours, even in the rain, waiting for the birds to settle. At times she has the sense that she has disappeared and become part of what she sees through her camera: a monarch butterfly, a pelican diving into the gray-black water, a family of Nubian ibex with their whimsically curved horns, gazing straight ahead with benign expressions.

She has been living in Egypt for six years now. Every month a letter arrives from Carol, who has married Winthrop Schuler, asking when Susan will return. Egypt frightens Carol—it's so far away, so close to a war zone. "I miss you all the time," she writes, as though they were lovers, parted through fate. In most of her letters Carol uses the pronoun "we" so frequently that Susan sometimes thinks that is why she got married. But when she is writing about wanting Susan at home, or, at the very least, just back in America, she says "I." "You don't have to settle in New York," she writes. "I know how important your independence is to you. Settle anywhere. Just come home. *We* have beautiful landscapes too."

This is true. Susan has traveled in Colorado and Montana and seen landscapes just as dramatic and intensely outlined. In fact, often scenes here remind her of the American West—the rocky areas in the Sinai Mountains with mountain goats leaping from rock to rock, the herds of shaggy sheep in the Western Desert, the eagles soaring against an improbably blue cloudless sky.

Then why *is* she here? She is lonely most of the time. Except by now the loneliness has so woven itself into the texture of her life that it is no longer a negative thing. Perhaps she wants the freedom connected with that loneliness. If she were anywhere in America, her mother could call; she would feel connected. She might stand, as she is now, watching a bird settle into its nest, but she wouldn't be invisible, even to herself. "Someday I'll return," she writes to Carol, meaning it, knowing it's a dodge.

"When?" Carol writes back.

"When I've done all I can do here."

Carol has tried to entice Susan with the idea of having a show in New York. Winthrop has connections, she claims. At least, after six years of such hard work, all those photographs, someone should see them, more people than see the occasional work she's done for magazines. If no one sees them, to Carol it's as though they don't exist; it has all been a waste. Whereas to Susan it's as though once they *are* seen, they won't be hers anymore. All those moments, standing there, feeling at one with the land and sky and animals, will have been simply to give people a numbered catalogue they can glance through, toss away. "I'd like a show someday," Susan writes. "I'm just not ready yet."

In fact, her one friend in Alexandria, Ariane, an Egyptian woman educated in America, has a small art gallery, and has persuaded Susan to show some of her photographs there. "Not for you," she says. "I want to attract customers. I want them to know something about their own country. Most of them know nothing. They have no curiosity. If they have money to travel, they go to America or Europe. They don't realize it's all here."

Susan enlarges, crops, and mats twenty of her favorite photos. She and Ariane hang them, quietly discussing which order would be best.

"You like families," Ariane observes. She is divorced and, like Susan, lives alone.

"Do I?" Susan asks. "Why do you say that?"

"You usually show animals in family groups." Ariane points to the stork couple sitting on their massive nest.

"That's Harry and Mabel," Susan says. "They come back every year, to the exact same place, the very same tree. He comes to inspect the nest in February, fixes it up, and then, just as spring is beginning, they come back together. . . . Storks mate for life."

Ariane smiles. "Does that appeal to you?"

"You mean, for me or for them?"

"For you."

"I've never had a real family, so I don't know. . . . No, not for me. I can't imagine myself in a family. Can you? With children and a husband who returned every night at a certain time? It's not that I have contempt for it, I just can't imagine myself living that way."

"It's pretty deadly," Ariane agrees. "I tried it. . . . I'm not like you. I come from a big, bustling happy family, and I wanted to set it up again. But—needless to say—I'm not my mother. All the things that come naturally to her—the noise, the constant demands on her time—drive me mad. And we didn't even have kids."

Susan looks at the storks and at the gazelles, a couple also, drinking from the stream. She has never thought of what Ariane has suggested—that these animals appeal to her not just because of their natural beauty and grace, but because they seem to come together with an ease that isn't possible for humans. "I don't want kids either," she says. "But I can imagine a relationship with a man, not in marriage necessarily. Just a friendship, both of us doing our thing."

Ariane is looking at her skeptically. She is short and heavyset, with tilted dark eyes and waist-length black hair. "Is this based on an actual man you knew or know, or just fantasy?"

Susan laughs. "Oh, fantasy, of course. . . . I don't know any actual men."

Ariane is having an affair with an engineer who lives in Cairo. She hasn't confided much about him, but says now, "Fantasies are better. Stick to that."

In the ten years since graduating from college, Susan has managed to lose her virginity. But that is really about all, she thinks. She hasn't gained anything. She doesn't understand much more about why men and women come together, for love or passion or families, than she did as a teen-ager, giggling with Xenia. It all seems a mystery. Sometimes she sees couples walking down the street and they seem to mesh, they have a closeness that is not just holding hands or touching even, but a centeredness. Susan half believes that achieving this is possible, if rare, but she doesn't hope for it for herself. She likes the fact that in Egypt, where everyone marries in their early twenties, she is an "old maid." Even that old-fashioned pejorative term appeals to her. In New York, anywhere in America, she would be fixed up constantly by well-meaning friends, by Carol. Winthrop, she knows, has cousins, nephews, sons of colleagues. Here there are no singles bars, no parties except ones composed of couples meeting for a glass of wine, parties to which Susan is usually not invited but, if she is, no one bothers her. Even the common thing in America, the lonely or predatory married man, seems an extinct species.

"This is my favorite," Ariane says. "These hyacinths."

"They've been growing there for hundreds of thousands of years," Susan says. "At least since the third century B.C."

"You know so much more about my country than I do," Ariane says. "It's funny."

"I don't know anything about America." Susan wonders if the photo of the hyacinths is too deliberately an imitation of Monet, the softness of the blue blossoms against the water.

"What we learn in school, we forget," Ariane says. "What we learn by just living is burned into us. I sometimes wish it were the other way around."

Susan's apartment is small, two rooms. She has a dog and a cat who coexist peacefully. Carol has only been over once to visit. She offered money for Susan to move to a larger place, but Susan declined. "It's quiet here," she explained.

"Do you have friends?" Carol asked. "Aren't you lonely sometimes?"

"I have friends." Susan was evasive. "I'm not lonely."

Carol, at fifty, is still slender, perky. She seems younger than me, Susan often thinks now. Maybe it's that hopeful, genuinely wide-eyed expression on Carol's face—as though she is still waiting for something wonderful to happen. Susan has no special feelings about Winthrop Schuler. He hardly ever speaks and, when silent, he has a melancholy, vague expression. "I thought I could make him happy," Carol once said. "But now I'm not sure. Are men ever happy?"

"I'm hardly an expert," Susan said wryly. "You better ask someone else."

Now, having finished hanging the photos, Susan and Ariane have a cigarette. Ariane has a luncheon appointment, and Susan has promised to sit in the gallery till she returns. There has been as announcement in the newspaper about the show, but Ariane doesn't expect anyone to appear until evening, after work. "But you can't tell," she says, sweeping up her cloth bag. "See you soon."

Alone in the gallery, Susan lets herself look carefully at each print, wondering if this is the best selection she could have made. She remembers prints she chose not to include—a mongoose, a pair of quail, a rock formation near the Red Sea. Is Ariane right? Is she preoccupied with family groups? Perhaps there's something in it. Xenia, now a psychoanalyst (she writes Susan, is eager to see her again), would undoubtedly think so. That's another thing Susan likes about Egypt—no shrinks, no one to analyze why you do this or don't do that. It's very comforting.

Xenia and Jay are evidently going through a bad time. Xenia doesn't go into details in her letters. Susan hopes it is just another of their endless explosions, which are followed by lulls of passionate closeness. This seems to have been their pattern from the beginning, one that Susan finds frightening, but also, in some way, admires.

A bell tinkles, and the door to the gallery is pushed open by a tall, overweight, bearded man with wild grayish-black hair. He is perspiring heavily. "Is it open yet?" he asks in English.

Susan explains that it is open. Most people know at once that she's a foreigner, but they don't always guess which country she is from. Several have suggested she might be Dutch or Swedish, but she knows that's because of her fair skin and light hair. Also, she doesn't have the sleek, prosperous, assertive look they assume to be typically American.

The man walks around the room, looking at Susan's photos. She realizes this is the first time she has ever been present when someone looked at her work this way. It makes her nervous and she wishes she could leave. Why is he here? Ariane's gallery is small and out of the way. Susan pretends to read the newspaper open in front of her and sneaks glances at the man. He stares long and hard at each photo, coming close, backing away. Susan feels as though it is she he is examining with that intense, intimidating stare. She hopes he will just leave without speaking.

He approaches her desk.

"I want to know something about the person who took these photographs," he says.

The name attached to the show is just S. Brown.

"It's a photographer," Susan says guardedly.

"From Alexandria?"

"No, she . . . she's from America, but she's lived here for six years."

The man frowns. "Curious. America? Are you sure?"

"I'm sure," Susan says. After a second she asks, "Why are you surprised?"

"She knows the land here so well. I've been to many of these places. I'm an amateur conservationist, but I have never seen any of this. I saw, but I didn't see so deeply . . . so religiously."

"Religiously?" Susan is puzzled.

"Yes. There is such a sense of the inner harmony and beauty of life. This is what she is trying to express. We are trying to become a modern country, but all around us is history, life and earth woven together. This is what the Psalms are all about, after all." He pauses. "I'm a professor of religious history here, born in America, but I've lived here twenty years."

"The photographer isn't religious," Susan says. She feels angry at his inflating and embroidering her prosaic visions in this manner.

"She *is*," the professor insists. "I can tell you that. She is religious—more than I am, perhaps."

Susan tries not to laugh. He is so large, looming over the desk like some Old Testament prophet. "How do you know so much about her?"

He makes a sweeping gesture at the photos. "It's all there. . . . I take photographs myself. I can tell you—you don't just set up the camera and click the way many people think. It comes from inside. It comes from the soul."

Susan finds herself staring at him. He has a slightly mesmerizing quality—the emphatic way he speaks, his largeness, like a water buffalo. "Well," she says laconically, "I'll tell her."

"Does she live here?" he asks. "In Alexandria?"

"I'm not permitted to give out her home address."

"But she lives here?" he persists.

"Yes, she lives here."

"Will she come here, to the gallery?"

"Maybe."

The professor gives Susan a strange glance. He walks away and begins a tour of the room again. After five minutes, he returns. "She *is* religious," he says.

Susan just shrugs. She stares back at him, trying to appear arrogant, if only just to counter his self-assurance.

The professor starts to leave, but at the door he turns. "You are the photographer?" he asks.

She has no compunction about lying and has many times, but Susan finds herself saying, "Yes."

The professor looks delighted at his discovery. He comes back to her desk, his face wreathed in smiles. "Are you angry?" he asks.

"Why should I be angry?"

"That I know you better than you know yourself?"

Susan can't help laughing. "Don't you think that's a little presumptuous?"

"One of your parents was religious," he informs her.

"My father," Susan says, "but that doesn't make me religious. Anyway, why does it matter? I've never believed in formal ceremonies."

"You don't have to," the professor says. "You have been there in spirit. You want to sing the praises of the Almighty. That is what you have done here."

It strikes her as funny, his imposing his own structure of the world on hers. He is so insistent, so convinced, she almost begins to wonder if he isn't right. "I just don't know," she says awkwardly.

"Has your father seen these photos?"

"He's no longer living."

"I'm sorry—for him. They would give him such pleasure."

Would they have? Susan thinks fleetingly of Omar. "I'm a stranger here," she says. "But I do love the land and the animals. I don't think that it's made me religious."

"Perhaps I'm intuitive," the professor says. "Maybe I have insights into people, the way you do with your camera. Will you grant that possibility?"

"Yes," Susan says.

He looks again at the wall of photos. "You are fond of birds," he says, not so much as a question, but a statement. "I, too. I had a small aviary as a boy. Every day after school I tended them."

"They're so graceful," Susan says, deciding that, for the moment, she has no choice but to accept him, even with his insistent questions.

"Yes, even when not moving, they are graceful." The professor points to a photo of two bulbuls, one resting its head on the other's shoulder. " 'For, lo, the winter is past . . . the time of singing is come.' "

Susan smiles shyly. "The Song of Songs."

"Aha!" He looks delighted. "You said you weren't religious."

"I've studied the Bible at school. It can be seen as a literary, cultural document, not just religious."

He comes over to her desk again. "And your father? You say he *was* religious? Are you rebelling against that?"

"I'm not a rebel," Susan says. "At least not in the way you think." She has a moment of realizing she could cut this conversation short by telling him she has to go, but by admitting she took the photographs, she feels she has given him the right to question her. Or is she pleased that, for the first time in her six years here, someone has taken such an intense interest in her? "My father committed suicide when I was young. I don't really know much about him."

For some reason, the professor's face darkens. "Yes," he says.

What does he mean by "yes"? Yes, he understands? Yes, it explains Susan's photos?

"We all are tempted by such thoughts occasionally, all of us . . . ," he adds.

Are men ever happy? Carol wanted to know. The professor looks unhappy.

"There is so much despair," he goes on, almost to himself. "One wonders . . ." Then he catches himself. "But in your photos there is joy. That is why I love them. You see the natural world and you rejoice. 'Rejoice, greatly, O Daughter of Zion. Shout, O Daughter of Jerusalem. Behold thy king cometh unto thee.' "

Susan can't resist finishing, " 'He is triumphant and victorious, lowly and riding upon an ass, even upon a colt, the foal of an ass.' "

The look of pleasure on the professor's face is so great it's almost absurd. "You see, you are not what you seem. You want to fool me."

"I *don't* want to fool you," Susan says. "I love the Bible, but I don't believe in God. I love nature, I just . . . have doubts about mankind."

He shrugs. "We all have doubts."

"If I believed in God," Susan goes on nervously, "I'd have to hate him because I see so much evil and stupidity in the world. But since I don't, I can just view it as a series of mistakes, biological mistakes."

The professor points to the bulbuls. "They are also a mistake?"

"No, animals, birds, seem to inhabit another kind of reality. That's why I like photographing them. Not so much to have the photos, but to feel I'm a part of that world."

The professor is standing in front of Susan. "You are a strange, wonderful person," he declares. "I think I am falling in love with you."

"Go right ahead," Susan says wryly. "Be my guest." He is such a strange mixture of buffoonishness and intensity, she can't decide what she thinks of him.

He sits on a chair next to her. "I am married, of course—unhappily married. But perhaps you are right. That, too, was simply a mistake. A biological mistake."

"In what way?" Susan asks. She wonders if he ever combs his hair. His hair and his beard are like a great tangled growth spreading out in all directions. They remind her of the Lear limerick about the old man who had birds nesting in his beard.

"She is beautiful." Suddenly he leans forward, grabs Susan's hands in his powerful grip. "I know, you hate men who are attracted by the beauty of women. You think they are traitors, stupid. . . . And you're right. But we pay for our stupidity. I am paying. Does that please you?"

"Why should it please me?" Susan says. She hates her nervous, embarrassed laugh, which seems something like a stammer. She adds, probably unnecessarily, "I'm not married. I don't know why people marry."

"You love living alone," he says. He has let go of her hands, as though surprised at the gesture.

"No, not love. . . . But I like my life here." The topic is too huge to be encompassed in a few sentences.

"You are here permanently?"

"No."

"When do you return?"

"Oh, I'm just going back for a few weeks, but my mother would like me to return for good. She feels it's not safe."

"She's right."

"I feel . . . safe here," Susan says. "Though I know what she

105

means. But here no one is watching me. My life is my own. In New York that wouldn't be true."

"What about children? Do you want them?"

"No." She decides not to varnish this with any disclaimers.

"You live for your art?"

Suddenly, almost absurdly, Susan gets angry. "Stop doing that!" she cries.

The professor looks bewildered. "What am I doing?"

"You keep categorizing me, trying to interpret me to myself. . . . I'm leading a simple life. None of those platitudes apply to me. There's nothing interesting about me! Fall in love with someone else if you're bored by your wife!"

The professor looks overwhelmed by her outburst, and Susan herself is horrified at how strongly she has spoken.

"I'm *not* bored with my wife," he says softly, looking away. "She angers me. I don't understand her. . . . It's *not* boredom." He points to the photo of the bulbuls again. "It should be like that, but it's not."

"No," Susan says wistfully. "It rarely is." After a moment she adds, "In the spring, when they're nesting, they sing so beautifully."

There is a long moment of silence.

"You are also misinterpreting *me*," he says. "I am in love with you . . . with your spirit, not your body. I am not making a pass."

Susan laughs. "Thanks," she says sardonically.

"No doubt you have a wonderful body," the professor goes on, "but lust is . . . too complicated for me. I'm almost forty, middle-aged. . . . Do you have a lover?"

Susan shakes her head. "I'm not looking for one either."

"That's obvious. . . . I, too, am not looking."

Even if she were looking, Susan thinks, this bearded wild-looking man would not be for her. He would invade her apartment, her life, the same way he has invaded the gallery.

"Unlike you," he goes on, "I love children. I would like to be a father. But my wife . . . We have had troubles there."

"You could adopt," Susan suggests. Actually, it's easier to imagine him as a father than as a husband, with six children clambering over him, begging for stories.

"Maybe eventually. It's not so easy."

Since he has been so intrusive about her life, she asks, "Does your wife work?"

The professor shakes his head. "No, she is not like you. She has no art, no work. She wants life to make her happy."

"Dangerous," Susan says.

"Of course. . . . But everything is dangerous, no? The two of us in this room. Danger is everywhere. I like that. It adds to one's sense of life."

In her mind Susan is on the airplane flying back to America, trying to decide what she thinks of this man. Right now, with him in front of her, she has too many feelings and opinions to sort them out.

"I am tiring you," the professor says, looking troubled.

"No. . . . I was up late last night, thinking about going home."

He hesitates. "I would like to see you again. Would you permit that?"

Any answer would be all right. Susan knows she is under no obligation to see him again and feels no compunction to be polite. But she finds herself writing down her name and address on a slip of paper.

The professor takes the paper. "Susan . . . Susannah. You have a biblical name. I am Whitley Lewis." Upon leaving, he bends down, holds her by the shoulders, and kisses her chastely on the forehead.

Jesus, Susan thinks. And now where will he go? Home to his beautiful, bored, angry wife? Back to the university? In the fifteen minutes before Ariane returns, she runs through a variety of scenarios in her mind. In one, his wife dies in childbirth and Susan helps him raise his child, a little boy. But, no, she doesn't want children and certainly not another woman's child. Perhaps she just dies in childbirth. . . . You don't know her. You are allowed to kill her off in fantasy. . . . In the ten years since graduating from Barnard, Conrad, whom Susan hasn't seen and never corresponded with, has been her masculine ideal. His beauty, his gentle grace, his antic sense of humor, his confusion about himself. She's never been certain if she's even attracted to him sexually. He's just the one man with whom she's ever felt a peculiar kind of rapport. Not like what just happened with the professor. Conrad would never intrude that way on anyone. He has an innate courtesy, as though he had been born a prince and raised among commoners. This man, this professor, is sloppy, fat—yes, fat, not overweight—boorish, ridiculous, as far from a sexual ideal as she can imagine.

But in her mind he undresses; they drink wine; they roam

through beautiful sunlit fields, looking at birds; he reads poetry to her; she becomes religious; they convert each other and are happy. What a perfect fantasy. Never see him again, she advises herself. Don't spoil it. Ariane is right. Why did she give him her address? *I'm sure you have a wonderful body.* No, I don't. I don't have a wonderful body. I'm flat-chested, freckled, pale, bony, impossibly shy, awkward. Lust after my wonderful spirit, my soul. Leave my body to its own devices.

Xenia used to say, "God, I felt so wild today in class! I don't even think that teacher is cute, but he really turns me on. Or maybe it's just sheer horniness." Sheer horniness. Is that all I'm feeling now? Despite her love of imputing ugly motives to her own behavior, Susan feels she has to reject this hypothesis. He crashed through her defenses. In the abstract, she hates people who do this; she has even, at times, wanted to kill people like him. But maybe it's that sitting here before he appeared, it seemed to her that all she was was these photos, not a person, just a seeing eye. It seemed too barren and ghastly, though at other moments she can dress it up more appealingly. Exhausted, she lays her head on the desk and closes her eyes.

"You must be starved," Ariane says, returning. "How'd it go? Anyone come in?"

Susan shakes her head, startled. In her dream he was thin, she was religious, they lit candles. "I'll call you when I get back."

Why didn't she tell Ariane about the professor? She and Ariane are friends, but it isn't as equitable as it used to be with Xenia. Susan is more the listener. Xenia talked, but she listened too. More important, Xenia knew all of Susan's life, whereas no one here knows or can even understand what it was like growing up in New York City in the fifties. Everyone's image of America is so distorted that Susan no longer even tries to explain. They assume everyone voted for whoever was president at the time, everyone loved Eisenhower, everyone listened to Elvis Presley, everyone was rich. Susan can't explain the world she grew up in, in which most of her friends had European parents, where the high school she attended considered Adlai Stevenson right-wing, where she did her term paper on Sacco and Vanzetti and the graduation play was *Watch on the Rhine* and the principal of the school was called up before the House Un-American Activities Committee. Cheerleaders she read about in adulthood—as alien as headhunters in the Congo. This America is too special and peculiar to make sense to an Egyptian, and she has long ago stopped trying. Yet everything she is, at some bottom level, is influenced by how she grew up. Could Ariane even understand how she felt about the professor without knowing about Con? Susan feels she is not good at filling in gaps, describing her past. Here in Alexandria she has no past, which is both a blessing and a deprivation, just as her living alone is.

On the plane flying home to America, she sits next to an American rabbi, who gets on at a stopover in Rome. He is a young, handsome, blond man who is reading about the Watergate hearings. Susan, of course, knows about what is happening, but one benefit of living so far away is that the news seems remote.

"They're really going to nail him," the rabbi says with satisfaction. "Boy, I can't wait!"

He is beaming with goodwill, self-satisfaction. He has been in Rome to visit his sister, who married a foreign service officer, but he's glad to be going home.

"They're crazy over there," he says. "The way they drive, they're maniacs. . . . Maybe they need to be to live that way."

"Is your sister happy?" Susan asks.

The rabbi laughs. "My sister? What a question. Sure, she's happy. Her husband's rich, they have four kids, two Saint Bernards. . . . What more does anyone want? It's Forest Hills transplanted a few thousand miles away. He cheats on her, she cheats on him, the kids are gorgeous and eat too much. . . . How about *your* sister?"

"I don't have a sister."

"A brother? A husband? Kids?"

"Just my mother."

"I thought you were coming home to get married," he says. "How're you going to find anyone over there? Everyone's married."

"I'm not looking," Susan says. She is having her second Bloody Mary. Each year, for her return home, she does this, not from fear of flying but to anesthetize herself for the journey. She gets drunk quickly. Often one drink is enough.

"Sure you are, a cute kid like you. I'll introduce you to my cousin Jamie. A little fucked-up, but a good kid. An engineer. Only he lives in Salt Lake City. Could you hack that? *I* couldn't."

"I . . ." Where does she start? "I'm not a cute kid, I don't want to meet your cousin Jamie, I couldn't hack Salt Lake City, I—"

"My cousin Hy? He's right in Brooklyn, real estate, just pitched his second wife, a real ball breaker." Suddenly he looks embarrassed. "You're not gay?"

"No." She touches her boyishly short hair self-consciously.

"His first wife left him for another woman. I just don't want to get him ensnared in anything like that again."

"Actually," Susan says, emboldened by the giddiness of being drunk, "I'm in love with a married professor who lives in Alexandria."

The rabbi whistles. "Oh boy. Trouble. As my mother would say: Stop right there."

"We haven't started yet," Susan says. The delight of exchanging confidences on a plane is making her euphoric.

"Don't!" He shakes his head. "Can I give you some advice? Don't! For *his* sake. I know. This is from the horse's mouth. The guy has a wife, right? Pretty, maybe, but not what she once was."

"Beautiful," Susan interjects, imagining long dark hair, a swanlike neck, a pouting full mouth.

"Did he say beautiful? No, she was *once* beautiful. Now she's unhappy, dissatisfied, the kids nudge her, she gave up her job—"

"They don't have kids. She doesn't work."

He whistles. "This is even worse. She's miserable, she goads him from morning till night. 'Kids, kids, give me kids.' What can he do? He's trying. His sperm have conked out. Or maybe it's her. She's frigid because she hates him."

Susan, drunk, is getting alarmed. "It's not that bad . . . I don't think."

"Listen, what's your name?"

"Susan."

"Susan, let me tell you. I don't just think. I *know. I'm* married. I have a wife, I have kids, the whole *geschmear*. . . . I met a sweet little girl like you once, big blue eyes, not Jewish—of course!— sensitive, lovely, she blew glass, that was her . . . profession."

The stewardess is collecting their trays.

Susan says, "But it didn't work out?"

"How could it? I broke her heart, for starters. I'd come home, look at my wife, who is good-looking. . . . Did I show you her picture?" He takes out a photo of an attractive woman, with fluffy brown hair and pale pink lipstick, standing in front of a modern house. "I'd look at my wife and I'd think: Why are you dark, not blond? Why loud, not gentle? Why Jewish? I'm a rabbi and I'm asking, Why Jewish? Do you get my point? Don't do it!"

"Okay, I won't," Susan says. "You convinced me."

"You had me worried," the rabbi says. "I know more about this man than you do. He's thinking about you morning, noon, and night. You don't mean to, but you're wrecking his life, his peace of mind. . . ."

"No," Susan cries. "We've never even slept together."

"That's worse. The beginning stage is the worst. All those fantasies. Once you really do it, it starts to fade a little. Save this man's life. Your own too. Things'll work out with his wife. It's temporary, it's a stage. . . . You don't really want to marry him, do you?"

Susan thinks of Whitley Lewis's wild gray beard. "No," she says firmly.

"Give the guy a break." He has become melancholy, dreamy, having had a double Scotch on the rocks. "He needs you as a fantasy, something to think about during the day, an oasis of calm, unconnected to the rest of his life. That's all. It masquerades as lust."

Susan feels melancholy too. "I don't know anything about lust," she says. She starts thinking about the woman the rabbi was involved with. She blew glass. Always, it seems, people have commented on Susan's resemblance, physical, in personality, to the heroine of *The Glass Menagerie*, and always Susan has hated those people and has cringed at the suggestion. She thinks of the rabbi's sister, married to a foreign service officer, with children who are becoming part of a foreign culture. She vows not to disturb the peace of mind of Whitley Lewis.

Susan has insisted that Carol not meet her at the airport. She takes a cab to the apartment Carol now lives in with Winthrop Schuler, a six-room duplex in the east seventies. Carol is now living the life she used to envy with such intensity, but, like all realized dreams, it is not what she expected. This, at any rate, is what Susan surmises. She even refers to the "old days" in Riverdale with tender nostalgia. Nulip San is now married, a pediatrician—he and his wife have a joint practice in Phoenix, Arizona, and send Carol a Christmas card every year. "They have two cars, everything they ever wanted," Carol says. "The American dream come true." Mrs. Klotz died a few years earlier in an old-age home, but every month until her death Carol went to the Bronx and visited her, even after Mrs. Klotz stopped recognizing anyone. "They say that, but you never know," Carol said. "I think it cheered her up. . . . I told her all about you. She remembered. Her face lit up. She adored you, Suki. She always said, 'When she gets married, send me a photo.' "

The apartment is in a quietly elegant neighborhood, there is a doorman; but once in the apartment Susan feels she could be back in Riverdale. Carol has thrown out none of her old furniture. It sits, consorting oddly with Winthrop's antiques, but perhaps no more oddly than Carol consorts with Winthrop Schuler.

When Susan enters the apartment, Carol hugs and kisses her, then steps back for a close examination. "You have nice color," she concludes. "But Suki, look at you!"

She means Susan's clothes: a denim shirt, jeans, and espadrilles. But in a way Carol is almost glad of Susan's shabbiness. It means a whole day, several days, lie ahead in which they can go from store to store buying up a storm; underwear, dresses, belts. Like those make-over sessions she loves in women's magazines. "We can afford the finer things now," Carol says, but still her eye is drawn by a bargain glimpsed from the corner of one eye.

When they return from their first foray, Winthrop, who is retired now, though he, like Carol, does volunteer work at Sloan-Kettering, is immersed in the Watergate hearings.

Winthrop admires Richard Nixon, whom he once socialized with when they were both lawyers. "He's a man of integrity," he says at dinner. "It's all a great tragedy."

"I thought everyone hates him," Susan remarks. Despite everything, she cannot envision Winthrop as other than another boarder, someone whom Carol has been kind enough to let live with them for a small sum.

"People are quick to judge," Winthrop says. "Who are we to cast the first stone? He was concerned with the safety of his country. He's a scrupulous man."

To the extent Carol has political allegiances, they are Democratic, but she lets Winthrop proceed unchecked. "I don't find it fascinating, though," she says. "Do you, Suki?"

"Fascinating?" Susan asks, poking at her asparagus in hollandaise sauce.

"The whole thing—power, men in high places doing weird, possibly evil things. . . . It just doesn't seem very interesting."

Winthrop smiles indulgently. "Power not interesting? Darling!"

Carol looks abashed, but not undermined. "They go on and on in such detail. It's like those soap operas Mrs. Klotz used to watch, only it's mainly about men."

"Soap operas!" Winthrop shakes his head and sips his seltzer. He was once an alcoholic and joined Alcoholics Anonymous a decade earlier. At times he has said, with the closest thing to passion Susan has ever heard from him, "I would give my soul for a dry martini!"

Carol has a housekeeper now who comes in, fixes dinner, and leaves it on the stove with last-minute instructions. As always, Susan finds she doesn't have much appetite, but accepts a small helping of everything.

"Well, the Israelis must be feeling proud of themselves," Winthrop says. "They certainly showed the Egyptians what was what."

"I guess so," Susan says. She picks at her macaroni and cheese.

Carol turns to Susan. "That's why we want you home, sweetie. We think of you day and night. I can't sleep anymore. I wake up and think of you, over there, so far away."

This discussion is a set piece. They have to have it at least once every visit.

"I'm planning to come home," Susan says.

Carol's eyes widen. "When? In a few months?"

"I have to work it out."

Later in the evening Winthrop disappears into his study. Carol asks Susan tentatively if there is anything keeping her in Egypt. "I mean, with men. . . . Is there anyone?"

"No one special," Susan quickly says.

Carol hesitates. It's as though Susan is inside Carol's head, hearing what she doesn't dare ask. "It's good to have someone special," Carol suggests timorously. "Someone who really cares for you."

Susan just says, "Yes."

"I won't be around forever," Carol goes on. "I hope I can die knowing there's someone around to care for you."

"A professor thinks he's in love with me," Susan offers mockingly.

Carol, as expected, looks alarmed. "A professor? Is he American?"

"Yes, but he's married," Susan adds, "unhappily."

"Oh, Suki!" Carol is so dismayed she seems unable to speak.

"That doesn't sound like the man for you. You need someone special."

They sit in silence, thinking of who this might be.

Suddenly Carol exclaims, "I was sorry to hear about Xenia and Jay! They always seemed so happy. . . . Are you going to see her?"

Susan nods. From Xenia's letters, she has not understood the reason for the split, but it gave her a pang. She yawns. "I think I'll turn in . . . I'm getting sleepy."

It isn't until the next morning over breakfast that Carol comes in and hands Susan a letter.

"This came last week," she says. "I think it's from that boy you went to college with."

Susan looks at the letter: Conrad Zweifach. No return address.

"Why didn't you give it to me right away?" she cries angrily.

"I forgot, I was so excited seeing you again," Carol says. "I figured it could wait."

Susan takes the letter into her room, sits down on the bed, and opens it. She has not corresponded with Conrad, and has only heard bits and pieces about him from Xenia over the years, that he was trying to paint, was having some problems, is not married yet.

> Dear Susan,
>
> I'm writing this letter, knowing it may not reach you. I know you aren't living in America, but that you sometimes return on a visit. We've been out of touch so long—I hope this letter doesn't seem like an imposition.
>
> To get to the point, I've been sick, I've had a nervous breakdown and I'm now incarcerated in a mental hospital. It would mean a lot to me if you could visit me. When you are here, I could explain my life and all that has happened. If you can't come, I understand.
>
> Could you please not mention receiving this letter to anyone?
>
> Love,
> Conrad

The letter is handwritten in an even, steady script. Below is the address of the hospital. Staring at it, Susan feels a strange, giddy sense of excitement, as though the contents of the letter were quite different—a proposition, a proposal. *Could you please not mention receiving this letter to anyone?* Does that mean he has told no one?

Does even Xenia not know? It thrills Susan that of all people Conrad chose her to write to, but it frightens her also. She has never been to a mental hospital, except the grounds of the one Dr. Szengi worked at. She never even studied Freud in college. Nor does she have any special interest in mental illness. If she thought about it, she would say that she herself seems so strange, life itself seems so strange that it's hard for her to imagine what particular kind of strangeness it is that would cause people to be locked up.

Susan comes out of her room with her face grim, her mouth dry. Carol looks up from rinsing a teacup in the kitchen and says, "I hope he's fine, Conrad. Such a sweet boy. He wrote so well."

"That was Jay," Susan says.

"Oh, of course. . . . Conrad was the beautiful one. You had such a crush on him, Suki! Do you remember?"

"No," Susan says dryly. "I don't remember."

"Not that I blamed you. . . . But handsome men are sometimes . . . Well, of course, life spoils them, women spoil them. What does he want?"

Susan wonders how other adult children assert to their parents that they are no longer children, that they are entitled to certain kinds of privacy. "He wants to see me," she says.

Carol almost drops the saucer, she is so delighted. "I'm so glad we got that blue dress!" she says. "It makes your eyes so blue. If I had your eyes, I would wear blue from morning till night."

"It's not a formal occasion," Susan says. "We're just . . . meeting."

Carol smiles impishly. "You never can tell. . . . Winthrop proposed to me when we were walking to the dentist. Anything can happen at any moment!"

Later that afternoon Susan changes into the blue dress because not to change into it would cause an uproar not worth considering. And in some ways it soothes her to try to regard this occasion as Carol is regarding it. An old friend, a man she had a crush on ten years earlier, wants to see her, to talk, to reveal his soul, to catch up on old times. Why is Conrad sick? It seems unfair to Susan. Not that it's ever fair with anyone, but he seemed so balanced, so wryly sure of himself, so humorous in the face of Jay's intensity and Xenia's volatility and her own impossible shyness. Susan remembers dancing with him at the senior prom, his broken arm, the awkward way he enfolded her.

She drives to the hospital in Carol's car, a Chevy. Susan feels self-conscious driving this sleek, expensive car, with its deeply cushioned seats, a token of Carol's new life.

The mental hospital is a set of brick buildings, not unlike a small college. At the admissions desk, Susan signs in. The woman behind the desk looks up Conrad's name.

"Are you related?"

"No," Susan stammers.

"A friend of the family?"

"Yes."

"Well, he's allowed off the grounds, but he must be back by four. Just a little outing, if he feels like it; nothing stimulating. Try to avoid discussing anything depressing."

"Okay, sure," Susan says brightly.

"You can go up those stairs," the woman says.

Susan, in her blue dress and new sandals, climbs the stairs with a sense of foreboding. Perhaps, though, if Conrad is allowed off the grounds, he is almost well, about to leave. She is frightened that he will look different in some way. Did he try to kill himself? Is that why he's here?

She sees him sitting in a chair, reading. Other patients are watching TV. As the door swings open, Susan and several other visitors stream into the room. Conrad doesn't look up.

Susan approaches him quietly. "Con?" she says softly.

His expression when he sees her is so strange, totally bewildered. Has he forgotten he wrote to her? "Susan."

"I'm sorry I didn't come earlier," she said. "I've been in Egypt. I just got your letter today."

"I'm sorry I wrote you," he says. "It was unforgivable, stupid."

He looks different and yet the same to her. His hair is quite long, almost shoulder-length, and his face looks thinner, almost gaunt, his blue eyes sunken and vivid.

Conrad is sitting, Susan is standing, like two children frozen in a game of statues.

"I—I thought we might take a drive," she says. "I brought my mother's car. . . . It's a lovely day."

For a second Conrad's face gets a familiar, almost impish expression. "I'd love to go for a drive," he says. "I'm so glad you came. I never thought you would. It was like putting a note in a bottle. . . . Just wait here. I'll get my jacket."

He is dressed shabbily, in jeans and a wrinkled shirt, an old

116

denim jacket, but no more shabbily than Susan was before Carol took her shopping.

Just the same, he looks at Susan and says, "I'm sorry . . . for the way I look, for my clothes. You must have hardly recognized me."

"You just look a little thin," Susan says. She touches her dress self-consciously. "My mother made me buy this."

They walk outside into the radiant October sunlight. In the car Susan says, "Where shall we go?"

"Far away," Conrad says. "Far away from here."

"We could go around the Cloisters," Susan says. "I know how to get there. . . . I'm not a very good driver."

"Do you want me to drive?"

Susan hesitates. She isn't sure if that's allowed.

Conrad, seeming to sense this, says, "You drive, Sue. . . . I'll just sit back and rest."

No one else has ever called her Sue. Susan grips the wheel and heads off. Once she glances at Conrad. His eyes are closed, his long body stretched out. Is he asleep?

"This is wonderful," he says, not opening his eyes.

"How . . . how long have you been there?" Susan asks. Everything she says seems inappropriate. *Don't talk about anything depressing.*

"Six months." He laughs bitterly.

"That's such a long time."

"It's hell."

Does he mean being sick or the hospital itself?

"What made you decide to go there?" Susan asks. "Or would you rather not talk about it?"

"I didn't 'decide,'" Conrad says with that same bitter tone. "It was decided for me. By my father, actually. . . . For my own good, of course. It's a nightmare. It's beyond anything I can describe to you. They drug you from morning till night. Your only company is total loonies, people who think weird little purple men are coming out of the sky. . . . The so-called therapy sessions are a total farce. It makes *One Flew over the Cuckoo's Nest* seem like a TV sitcom."

"Then you should get out!" Susan cries.

Just then a car darts in front of her and she loses control of the Chevy for just a moment, then swerves it back into place. Her heart is beating frantically.

"I'm upsetting you," Conrad says, turning to her.

"No, I'm just a very bad driver." Susan glances at him. Her hands are shaking. "Do you mind—is it all right if we pull over? I think we're near the park."

At the Cloisters she finds a parking space and immediately takes a cigarette out of her purse, offering one to Conrad. He takes one. They remain sitting in the car.

"I've given them up," he says.

"Me too," Susan says. "Except in times of . . ."

"Absolute need," Conrad finishes. He laughs. He turns to Susan. "Tell me about your life. You're an Egyptian citizen now? Are you married?"

"Oh no, I just . . ." Susan tries to explain to him about her life there, her photography. "I'm always on the verge of coming home. Maybe that's an excuse for never having to put down real roots."

"I know all about that," Conrad says.

"Don't you have real roots?"

"No, not here, nowhere. . . . I tried Alaska. I wanted someplace far away, but it didn't work. I never, as my father would say, 'found myself.' I'm an impostor, Sue. I always have been."

"In what way?" To Susan, Conrad has always seemed so unlike an impostor, so at ease in the upper-middle-class Manhattan world she only watched from afar.

"You know, my parents wanted a Jewish kid, when they couldn't have one of their own. But they couldn't find one. And I came along through the agency and my mother—she'd waited so long, she was delighted. . . . But I think I never fit; they never really felt I was theirs. It's nothing specific, even. They sent me to boarding school when I was thirteen. . . . I always envied those kids who had something specific to rebel against: broken homes, vicious parents. With mine it was nothing that precise. I just didn't belong."

Susan hesitates. "But we all felt that, in one way or another."

"Did we? Did you?"

"I've never left home," Susan is amazed to hear herself say.

"How can you say that?"

Susan tries to think of what she means. "I mean, I'm always there. Everything I do is in relation to Carol. I could go to the moon and that thread would be there, connecting us. Maybe it's because I've never had a family, or even a lover in a permanent way."

"Are you gay?"

Susan laughs. "Nothing that simple. . . . No, I just . . . I don't know how to act with men. I'm too silent. I don't know how to talk to them." It doesn't strike her as a contradiction that she is talking to Conrad so easily.

"I'm a man."

"You're . . . different. A part of my past."

Conrad looks ahead. "It's the same with me. I have no family, no girl friends, but I don't know if I want one. I don't know what I want."

"How about your painting?"

"I'm no good. . . . I kept at it for years, determined to prove my father was wrong, that I could make it as an artist. But it isn't just lacking talent. I don't have that . . . whatever it is—vision. I'm afraid I have nothing inside. I—" His voice cracks.

Susan touches him. "Can I do something? I want to help."

Conrad is shaking slightly. "Yes," he says. "You can do something." Suddenly he opens the car door. "Let's get out of here."

Outside it is a perfect autumn day, slightly cool with a bright sun. Conrad stands looking around at the sky, the trees. "It isn't the world's fault," he says.

"What do you mean?" Susan asks, glad they are out of the car, with its claustrophobic closeness.

"When you feel the way I do, you can blame yourself or the world. Blaming yourself is shit, it's endless. But blaming the world—" He breaks off. He is walking briskly into Fort Tryon Park, and Susan has to hurry to keep up with him. "I'm free," he says as though to himself. "I'm out of there. I really feel free."

"But you have to go back," Susan says timorously. "Don't you?"

"No, I'm not going back. Never."

"Is that allowed?" Susan feels frightened.

"No, it's illegal. . . . But patients do it all the time. It's called AMA—Against Medical Advice."

"Won't your parents get upset?"

"Fuck my parents!" He looks furious. "Who put me in there? I've been living like a criminal for six months. I've been subjected to drugs, harassed by these crazy doctors."

"No, but I mean . . . where will you go?"

He hesitates. "I have a place to go."

"Where?"

"I can't tell you. . . . When they find out I'm gone, they may question you. You have to lie. Say I just disappeared, that you went to the ladies' room and when you returned, I was gone."

"You mean, go back to the hospital and tell them that?"

"No, not if you don't want. . . . Just go home. They may not get in touch with you."

Susan is breathing quickly, her side aches as though she's been running too fast. They are in the woods now. It's cool and dark. "I can't do that. You're asking me to break the law."

"I thought you said you wanted to help."

"What if they—" She doesn't even know how to finish the sentence.

"Don't you know how to lie?"

"Sure."

"Then lie, Sue! Please—lie for me. It's my life. I was dying in there, I was going crazy. . . . I'll find my way now."

"But how?"

"I'm not crystal-clear about everything, but I'm a different person. I'm not . . . I value my life now."

Susan is afraid she could be having a breakdown herself. Everything around them is whirling crazily. She feels overwhelmed with dread and despair. "You're going to kill yourself. That's why you want to escape."

"No." Conrad grabs Susan and holds her hands tightly. "I swear to you I won't."

Susan stares into Conrad's eyes. "Do you swear? Really? Absolutely?"

"Absolutely. . . . I wouldn't do that to you, for one thing. But, look, you can kill yourself in the hospital, if you want to. You're not really that well guarded. I'm not escaping for that."

"But did you try, before? Is that one reason your parents put you in?"

"Yes. . . . But it was . . . You've never felt that way yourself?"

"No. . . . I mean, I've been depressed, but never to that extent." Susan laughs. "I'm too much of a coward, I think."

"Well, here's one thing I know now," Conrad says. "One reason they lock you up, supposedly, is you may do harm to yourself or others. But no one is in that place because they wanted to die. Anyone who wants to die can just jump out of a window. They're there because they hate their life. They don't need to be locked up. That's just a form of humiliation. That's how those doctors get their bucks. It has nothing to do with saving lives."

The world has begun to settle down. Susan and Conrad are standing in the woods, under a large oak tree. Susan sits down. "My father—" she begins.

"Yes, I know," Conrad says softly. "Xenia told me."

After a second Susan looks up. "Why did you write me, Con? Why not Xenia? Or Jay?"

Conrad's mouth twists sardonically. "This is Xenia's world. Look how she grew up, how she worshiped her father, still does. She believes in all this mumbo jumbo. She thinks it's real. If she'd come to see me, she'd have been sympathetic, but she would have tried to talk me into staying, 'for my own good.' She's a part of the establishment. And she's a fucking coward."

"*I'm* a coward," Susan says wryly.

He looks down at her. "You're a different kind of coward. . . . You're like me. You haven't found a way to fit in. I don't think you put people into boxes or try to categorize them. Maybe it makes life hard for you."

"And Jay?"

"Jay's in Europe. And he's so close to Xenia, I just thought he would—"

"They may get divorced, Xenia wrote."

"I know, but they still . . . They could get back together. It's always been like that with them—horrible fights, making up. They're joined at the hip." Conrad gives Susan an inquisitive glance. "Are you sorry I wrote you?"

"No." Susan thinks fleetingly of her old fantasy of rescuing Conrad. This wasn't exactly what she meant: like all fantasies come true, it's a parody.

"Why are you smiling?" He sits down beside her.

She tries to tell him. "You always seemed so . . . perfect. I guess I wanted . . . I thought if you had some injury I could . . . you could need me."

"I do need you," Conrad says. "But not that way. . . . I'm gay, Sue. Didn't you know that?"

"No." But like all supposedly hidden things, as soon as he says it, it makes sense.

"I'm the worst kind of gay. I'm not proud of it. I hate it in a way. I've tried every form of gay life. I thought maybe being bisexual would be the best. A marriage to an understanding woman, lovers on the side. Nothing works. It's like whatever way I do it, part of me stands by mocking, self-hating. Not out of . . . What I mean is, I respect gay men who can live with it openly. I just haven't been able to. I've had men friends like Jay whom I've felt really close to, and women I've loved, quote unquote, men lovers whom I've been bowled over by sexually, emotionally. . . . But it never comes together. My despair was thinking it never would."

"What do you think now?"

"I think I have to stop trying to figure it out. Just say maybe that's my lot, and there are worse ones. Maybe if I stop trying, it'll happen."

Susan leans forward and takes his hand. "I hope so, Con."

They sit together, in each other's arms, the blue sky above them, the wide tree against their backs. Susan can feel that Conrad is aroused, but she knows it isn't because of her, or not in any simple sense. "If you want to make love, I will," she whispers, with great effort.

"I want to physically because I'm so damn horny," Conrad says with a laugh. "The only sex I've had in six months was with some aide who used to take me into the isolation room. . . . But it wouldn't be fair, would it?"

Susan wants Conrad in the same way she always has. She is still attracted to the strange mixture of his charm, his peculiarity, his aloofness, which is always there, even now when he has poured out his soul, when he is being intimate. "I want to," she whispers.

They are in a part of the park that is deserted, but still they do it quickly, furtively, without much sensual pleasure. Despite this, Susan remembers it all her life, as some crazed moment of fusing with another person. She doesn't come, and when Conrad does, it's anguished, almost, with a single cry that resembles pain more than pleasure. I'm a conspirator, she thinks. This is something I'll never be able to tell anyone.

"You see—I'm not a great lover," Conrad says. "Maybe you were better off with your fantasy."

"It was . . ." She doesn't know what to say to him that won't embarrass or scare both him and herself.

"Will you be seeing Xenia this trip?" Conrad has one arm locked under his head, the other around Susan.

"Yes."

"Don't tell her anything, not even that you know I was in the hospital."

"I won't." Suddenly she thinks of a practicality. "Do you have money? I can lend you some."

"Lend me thirty dollars, if you have it. . . . I'll mail it back to you."

"Can't you tell me where you're going? Just to set my mind at ease."

"A friend. . . . He used to live in Alaska. He doesn't know about the hospital. I haven't been in touch with him for a while. But he'll let me stay with him for a few weeks. I won't tell him where I've been."

Susan keeps thinking of Omar, his despair hidden, then reappearing. She trusts Conrad. She has to. She can't believe he would be capable of betraying her. "You'll be all right? You really will be?"

"I will. I promise. Look, I'll write you a month from now in Alexandria. Will you be back by then?"

Susan drives Conrad to the bus station, and there in the noisy city they say good-bye. They embrace, holding each other tightly.

"Take care," he says gently.

The world they were in before—the forest, his confessions, their coming together—seems a thousand years away, another life.

"You too." She drives off, not looking back. Take care, Con.

When she gets home, Susan lies down and sleeps. Carol and Winthrop are both out. She has a nightmare about the hospital; they are trying to lock her up. She screams, running down endless dark corridors. When she wakes up, she is drenched in sweat. The phone is ringing.

"Is S. Brown there?" the voice at the other end demands.

"No, I'm sorry, she's not," Susan says, knowing it's the hospital.

"When will she be back?"

"She's en route to Alexandria. . . . She left a few hours ago."

"I see. . . . Is this a friend of hers?"

"Yes."

"Do you know where she went this afternoon?"

"No, I don't. I work and . . . I just got back."

"She didn't say anything about visiting someone in a mental hospital, a friend of the family?"

"No, she didn't."

"You've never heard her mention the name Conrad Zweifach?"

"No, I haven't."

123

"And you say she's on the plane right now?"

"Yes."

"Thank you. . . . If you should hear from her in the next week, could you have her call this number?"

Despite her fear, Susan feels a peculiar kind of exhilaration, almost happiness. *Don't betray me, Con. Be safe.* She looks into her eyes in the mirror and wills this message into thin air. Just then the door opens. It's Winthrop and Carol, who've been to an opening at the Museum of Modern Art. Carol is in a black dress, looking elegant, looking like someone she isn't, someone who lives in a Park Avenue duplex and takes winter vacations in the Caribbean.

"Did you have fun?" she asks brightly.

"What?"

"With Conrad. . . . Did you have a good time?" Carol looks hopeful.

"Yes, we had a lovely time," Susan says quietly.

"Conrad is a charming young man Susan went to college with," Carol explains to Winthrop.

"A former beau?" Winthrop asks teasingly.

"No, just a friend," Susan says.

"That can be dangerous." They all go into the dining room, where the housekeeper has set out dinner.

"Did he like your blue dress?" Carol asks, going into the kitchen.

"Yes, he loved it," Susan says mockingly.

"He must have noticed how different you look now, how sophisticated. . . . What did you do?"

"We went to the Cloisters," Susan says. Why is she getting a mocking satisfaction out of this conversation, so like a parody of a million such conversations she has had with Carol over the years?

"What a perfect day for it!" Carol exclaims. "I love the Cloisters in the fall! . . . Did you walk in the park?"

"Yes."

Carol hands Susan a bowl of vegetables.

"And so?" she says flirtatiously, her head to one side.

"And so?" Susan mimics, taking the bowl.

"Is he available?"

"Not really."

Carol brings the roast pork into the dining room. Winthrop is sitting at the table.

"Now, sweetie, Susan has a right to a private life, you know," he says. "She's thirty-two."

This statement, simple as it is, causes Carol alarm. "Oh, I didn't mean . . . Of course she does! But Conrad is an old friend."

Winthrop begins carving the meat. "I'm sure when Susan becomes engaged, she will invite us to the wedding. Until then, we should let her live her life as she wishes."

"I didn't mean it that way," Carol says crisply. "You don't understand. Susan and I are friends, not just mother and daughter. We've always shared things."

"I rest my case," Winthrop says. His eyes are twinkling as he asks Susan, "One slice or two?"

In bed Susan thinks of Conrad's tormented face, his bright blue eyes, which looked beyond despair, their furtive exchange that, although brief and a total failure from any possible sexual standpoint, was, for her, like the way astronauts must feel stepping out of their space capsule into air. Right now Conrad is with his friend, inventing an explanation for his sudden appearance, lying, but feeling free. I freed him, Susan thinks joyfully. I rescued him.

Xenia's office is on Eighty-fifth and Park. She shares it with another psychoanalyst. Susan stops in front of the polished brass plaque that reads DR. XENIA SZENGI, DR. ARTHUR THOMPSON. Even though she has known Xenia is a doctor, it really hasn't sunk in until this moment, seeing her official title on the brass plaque. Susan enters the waiting room. There are two chairs, a table with some old magazines, prints on the walls. Xenia's last patient gets out at 5:40. It's 5:34.

This is Xenia's world. . . . She thinks it's real. . . . She's a part of the establishment. To Susan, Xenia has always been just a friend. But after the time she spent with Conrad the day before, she wishes in a way they weren't going to meet in Xenia's office. She knows Xenia asked her to come here because she is proud that she finally made it, proud of all the things Conrad regards with such scorn. Any world, to fit into any world, is so hard, Susan tried to explain to Conrad. She picks up a copy of *Natural History* magazine lying on the table. It's the one she sent to Xenia. It has some of her photos in it. Has Xenia put it out especially, knowing Susan would come here? The issue is six months old, but then many of the other magazines—*M.D., Scientific American*—are out of date too.

The door opens and a tiny, dour-looking man walks out of the office. He takes his coat from the coat rack and leaves. A moment later Xenia opens the door to her office.

"Hi," she says. She looks delighted to see Susan and rushes over to hug her. Susan feels a pang of guilt. She's never consciously concealed anything from Xenia. She's afraid that she will think about Conrad all the time and Xenia will notice.

"Come in and see my office," Xenia says proudly, ushering Susan in.

It's an office like any other office; a dark carpet, a desk, a couch, a large Picasso reproduction on the wall.

"I want to get one of your photos for over the couch," Xenia says. "That print is so corny. I want something different."

She looks, if not like a doctor, then certainly like someone who belongs in this room, not an impostor. Her hair, still long, is drawn back into a bun; she's wearing a gray suit and low-heeled, sensible shoes.

Catching Susan's expression, Xenia says apologetically, "It's on purpose. Everyone kept saying I looked so young and girlish with my braid. I couldn't bear to cut it off. And you want patients to somehow think of you as an authority figure."

"You could grow a gray beard," Susan suggests.

"I think I look just right," Xenia says, turning this way and that. "What do you think? A little matronly and dull, but thoughtful."

"I guess I like you the other way." Has Xenia really become what she looks like?

"Let's just wait here a few minutes," Xenia says, glancing at her watch. "I'm expecting a call. Then we can go out and eat. . . . You look so pretty! Is the dress new?"

"I went shopping with Carol the second I stepped off the plane."

"Of course. I like it, that color blue." Xenia is sitting at her desk near the phone. She gestures to the couch. "Sit down or lie down or whatever. Are you tired?"

In fact, Susan hardly slept the night before, thinking of Conrad, worrying if he is safe. She wishes she had asked him to call her today. "Okay, I'll lie down," she says. The couch is covered with mattress ticking.

"Do they tell you about their dreams?"

"Sometimes, if they can remember. . . . Lots of people can't."

"I dream almost every night," Susan says. "I guess I'd be a good candidate for analysis."

"You let it out in your work. You don't need it."

Susan is silent. "Probably I do as much as anyone. But you have to believe in it as a system for it to work, don't you?"

"Not really. Some people come as total skeptics, seeming skeptics, but if you can get past that—" The phone rings. "Oh yes, hello, Mrs. Bernstein. I was expecting your call. . . . No, I don't think you have to worry about that. I think the drugs are working. . . . Why? That's simply not true. I'm checking the levels in his bloodstream very carefully. There's no chance of that. I— He's doing very well. You'll have to trust me. Can you do that? . . . Whenever you want. Naturally. Please feel free to call anytime." When she hangs up, Xenia whistles. "Parents!"

"Tell me about it," Susan says. It's comfortable and soothing, lying on the couch, her eyes closed.

"I've finally found a drug that works on her son. He's doing terribly well and suddenly she's anxious. Before, when he was suicidal, unable to leave the house, she wasn't at all worried because he was completely in her control."

Susan half sits up and turns so she can see Xenia.

"That's why I don't ever want to have kids. I think it goes with the territory."

Suddenly Xenia looks grim. "I don't either. Certainly not now."

"Why not now?"

"I had an abortion last week." Xenia looks away. "I didn't tell Jay. I'm not going to. Do you think I should?"

Susan is puzzled. "I thought you were getting divorced."

"We are! He's in Europe, and when he comes back he's moving to California, San Francisco. But if he knew, he'd probably . . . Jay's always wanted kids. He'd say, 'Let's start over, let's . . .' It's over! That's all there is to it. Don't try to convince me to try again."

Susan sits up, frowning. "I wasn't going to. How could I?"

"I'm so *angry* at Jay!" Xenia says, staring out the window. "I feel he's been so dishonest about so many things. He's seen other women. He's lied. I don't think I have any responsibility to him."

Susan thinks of how Conrad said, "They're joined at the hip."

"You've had fights before, though."

"Susan, you don't understand." Xenia looks angry, her eyes are large and bright. "You've never been married. You've never even lived with a man. You can be friends at the beginning, but the second you're the wife, quote unquote, there's all this sickening garbage that they dump on you. I never want to be anyone's wife again! Never!"

127

Xenia is still Xenia. Her cheeks are flushed, she looks ready to explode. Susan feels more at ease with her than she did with the composed lady doctor in the gray suit whose name is engraved on the brass plaque outside the door. "How about men?" she asks. "What will you do about men?"

"I'll have lovers. I like sex. . . . I enjoy the company of men. I like talking to them. But not in that forced way."

"I don't . . ." Susan begins, and then stops.

"You don't need men the way I do," Xenia says, in that way they had years ago of finishing each other's thoughts and sentences. "You're lucky. You're more sufficient unto yourself. I admire that so much! I just can't *be* like that."

Susan wants to tell Xenia about the professor. But she just says evasively, "How do you feel about married men?"

Xenia laughs. "A taboo, on feminist grounds, et cetera, et cetera. . . . But sure. I've decided—forget the rules. You don't steal anyone who isn't ready to be stolen. Why not me rather than some kooky single girl who'll pressure him to marry her? I'm harmless, relatively speaking. I keep him off the streets."

"Who's 'he'? Or were you speaking metaphorically?"

"Another shrink. They all fuck around. They're all a bit *meshuggeneh*. . . . His wife is an airhead, your standard Jewish princess for whom the whole thing didn't work. She 'allows' him to pounce on her every couple of weeks. It's all power plays, Susan. Marriage is power plays. *I* was like that with Jay. Attacks, counterattacks . . . I know he doesn't love this creature in the Midwest that he's been putting it to on his trips. He wants to get at me. Why leave clues around? Just for the fun of seeing me fly into a tearing rage?"

Susan stands up. "You sound a bit cynical."

"Shouldn't I be? Am I wrong? Is the world really a wonderful place? Do *you* know dozens of happy couples?"

"What I mean is, how do you tell the people who come in here how to live, if *you* feel so . . ."

"I help them, I help some of them." Xenia looks challengingly at Susan. "I believe in what I'm doing. I think there is real suffering in the world and this is my way of trying to help. My private life is different."

Susan is sure Xenia would be understanding if she told about Conrad, but she remembers how urgent he looked when he made her promise not to say anything. "Let's go out and eat," she says. "I never had lunch, I just remembered."

They walk along Park Avenue. It's started to rain and Xenia has a big black umbrella, which they share. Susan likes this, their walking arm in arm, companionably.

"I love rain," she says, holding out her hand to feel it. She remembers washing their hair in the rain when they were eleven, screaming with excitement on the lawn of the Szengis' summer house in Croton.

After a moment Xenia looks at her. "Conrad's in a hospital," she says. "He had a breakdown. I ran into his mother a few weeks ago."

"Have you . . . been to see him?"

"I wondered if I should. Con was so private. He might think of it as an intrusion."

"Why do you think he's there?"

Xenia is silent a moment. "Con was always . . . He had sexual problems, identity problems. I love him, but I think he's very fragile."

"He always seemed so composed to me."

"Not to me. It's skin-deep. He's so beautiful. Everyone thinks that ought to make a difference, but it doesn't. . . . Remember what a crush we had on him?"

Susan nods, feeling sad and constricted again. The rain is heavy but soft.

"I'm so glad you're here!" Xenia's face is moist and shining. "I wish you could stay. So many times, there's something I want to tell you but it doesn't seem important enough to put in a letter. So I tell you in my mind."

"I do that to you too, sometimes," Susan says shyly.

"Are you still happy there? Don't you miss America sometimes?"

"I miss . . . not America exactly. I miss feeling a part of the culture, the way you feel you can hate it or love it if it's your own country. There's that sense of familiarity. I miss you, I miss specific things or people. . . ."

Xenia squeezes Susan's arm. "Come home, then!"

"Someday I will."

At dinner, they catch up on the rest of their lives, their parents, friends. Xenia's life sounds so different from Susan's, always busy; meetings, projects, she's learning to ice-skate, she plays in a chamber-music group every Thursday.

"I'd hate myself if I weren't me," Xenia admits, chewing on a sparerib bone. "But I need the structure. . . . Oh Christ."

Susan frowns. "What?"

Xenia grimaces. "My friend, the man I mentioned earlier—"

"The married one?"

"He's over there with his wife and sons. Damn, I thought tonight he had to work late. . . . We sometimes come here together. Look at him, but do it so he doesn't notice."

"I'll go to the bathroom so I can walk past their table," Susan says with a sly smile.

She gets up and walks slowly across the room. As she passes the table, she looks at the family. The sons are teen-agers, loud, gawky. The man is heavyset, graying, with a moustache and glasses. As Susan passes, he glances up at her and then away. He looks bored and tired.

When Susan returns and sits down, Xenia says, "What'd you think?"

"I didn't see her. . . . He's . . . intelligent-looking. He's a lot older than you, isn't he?"

"Fifteen years. Is that a lot? Yeah, it's a bit of a father-figure thing. I bring light and pep into his dreary, exhausted life. He's a really fine doctor. He's written some excellent books. I do still lust after men's minds."

Susan teases her. "Not bodies?"

"Not especially. . . . Oh look, she's going to the ladies' room. I'm going too. Wait here."

"Xen—" Susan grabs her arm, but Xenia wrenches her arm away and follows the small, dark-haired woman into the ladies' room.

The waiter approaches their table. "Are you finished?"

"Yes, I think so," Susan says. "Maybe we'll have dessert, though. Could you wait for my friend to come back?"

A few minutes later Xenia returns with a gloomy expression.

"God, that is *so* typical," she says.

"What?"

"She's beautiful! She's prettier than me! He goes on like she's some wrung-out, sexless blob. She has a terrific figure, *huge* breasts. What is *wrong* with men? Why do they all lie?"

Susan shrugs. "Hey, want dessert?"

"Hey yourself! Of course I want dessert! I should go over there and thump him on the head. You should have *seen* her figure. If you took both of us . . . Oh, forget it."

They order chocolate cake and coffee.

"So, will you still see him?" Susan asks.

"Yeah, I guess. I hate being alone. How do you hack that? Don't you feel lonely a lot of the time?"

Susan nods.

"But?"

"I wouldn't know how to live with another person." Susan looks across at Xenia, into her dark, velvety eyes. "Was the abortion awful?"

"I lay there and every time I felt pain, I thought: Jay would hate me if he knew I'm killing his child. And that got me through it, some kind of vengeful satisfaction. . . . Then I got out and I suddenly thought: It was me too. I killed part of *me*. . . . But no regrets, really."

The doctor and his wife and sons leave the restaurant. As they walk out, Xenia says, "I'm such a fool. So he wrote a few good books. So what? . . . Susan, let's visit Con. Do you want to?"

Susan touches the tips of her fingers together. "I don't think we should."

"He's probably out of touch, but maybe it would do him good."

"No!" Susan cries. "I don't want to."

Her tone is so extreme that Xenia stares at her, concerned. "You still care for him, don't you? Is that it?"

"It's something else," Susan says. "Someday I'll tell you about it, but not now. Okay?"

Xenia looks puzzled. "Something about you and Con?"

Susan nods. Where is Con now? With his friend? Alive? If he isn't alive, will she have killed him? "Do you think the patients in those hospitals are really suicidal?"

"Of course," Xenia says. "Why else would they be there?"

"But if they really wanted to kill themselves, couldn't they just do it?"

"But it doesn't always work, like anything. A lot of them almost succeed."

"They let my father out and then he died two weeks later," Susan says. "Maybe they don't know what they're doing."

"They're not infallible," Xenia says. "They let your father out too soon."

A feeling of dread creeps over Susan. Con is dead, she's killed him. If it weren't for her, he'd be safe, taken care of. "Do you think Con is suicidal?" she asks.

Xenia nods. "Remember that time we tried to reach him in Alaska for the wedding? He'd taken an overdose. He told Jay about it."

Susan buries her face in her hands and starts to cry.

"What's wrong?" Xenia goes over and sits next to her, strokes her hair. "Sweetie, don't. Tell me. . . . Is it a man?"

"I've done something terribly wrong," Susan says. "I can't tell you."

"You're just judging yourself too severely," Xenia says soothingly.

"What if I killed someone?"

"Did you?"

"I don't know, I don't think so. . . . Oh Xen, I just . . . I didn't mean to. I swear to you!"

"Please don't be upset," Xenia says. "I've known you forever. . . . You might hurt yourself, but you'd never hurt anyone else. You're just upset." Xenia's arms are around Susan.

"This is something for which I'd never forgive myself," Susan says. "Never."

"Is it something that happened or that you fear may have happened?"

"That I fear may have happened."

Xenia takes Susan's hand. "It didn't happen. . . . Do you believe me? *It didn't happen.*"

Xenia has become the doctor, Susan the patient. And in the middle of her despair Susan can imagine Xenia as a good doctor, her soothing, steady voice. Of course Xenia can't know it didn't happen, but Susan allows her words to flow around her. When Susan was a child, Carol was never the kind of mother you read about—plump, comforting, maternal. She was always nervous herself. Perhaps because of this, it's especially nice to have someone take care of her, play mommy as well as doctor.

"You know what?" Xenia says. "Come back with me. Stay at my place for a week. We'll have a chance to really be together, to talk, not just in bits and pieces. I have a sleep couch. Do come, Susan."

"How about your life? All those things you were mentioning? Won't I get in the way?"

"You can come with me to them or not, whatever you want. . . . Like with the chamber-music group, they wouldn't mind if you came. But you don't *have* to. You can just do whatever you like during the day and then at night we'll meet and have dinner, maybe see some movies. . . ."

"Carol?" Susan tries to mock her own anxiety about this.

"You have to decide about that. . . . Tell her it's for me. She'll understand. Or should *I* tell her?"

"Would you?" Susan feels craven, not being able to face Carol on the phone, at least not this particular night.

She goes back to Xenia's one-bedroom apartment and together they fix up the sleep couch. Xenia gets a comforter out of the closet, fresh sheets. She brings Susan a drink of warm milk and brandy and has one herself.

"Daddy used to make this for me when I had my period. Isn't it wonderful?"

"Do you still think of him as Daddy?" Susan says.

"Isn't that terrible? But how can you suddenly change? I mean, you call Carol by her real name, but she still treats you like a child. So do names really mean that much?"

"Maybe not," Susan agrees.

"I see him as a person now," Xenia says. "But only up to a point. Jay always went at me about that, my being too attached to him, having to decide everything by talking it out with him. It wasn't that. Daddy just knows so much, he's in the same field, he's helped me so much. . . . What does Jay know?"

Just as Susan thought or hoped she had rescued Conrad, so now she feels Xenia has rescued her. She puts the half-finished drink down on the floor and yawns.

"Sleep well," Xenia says, tucking her in. "No more guilt attacks, okay?"

"I promise," Susan says. And sure enough, she sleeps soundly and wakes up with a knowledge that Conrad is safe, which, three weeks later, when she returns to Alexandria, turns out to be the case.

In the two weeks she stays with Xenia, Susan does as Xenia prescribed. During the day, Xenia sees her patients and goes to her meetings. Susan takes walks in Central Park, brings her camera, visits photography and art shows, becomes a tourist in her own city. Somewhere midway in her visit she starts feeling a tremendous pang of homesickness for Egypt. Xenia seems so involved and basically happy in the world in which she has chosen to live. Maybe this is because it's a world that has the approval of her father. It's like inheriting a throne, except she had to work to get there; but the outlines of the world were established for her. Susan thinks, as she walks through the park, of Conrad's remark that he has always felt like an impostor. She thinks of her own feeling that she is a tourist in her native city, and a stranger in Alexandria, where she has lived six years. Xenia could feel similar contradictions, but evidently she's chosen not to. She could, if she had a different personality, be bowed down by the irony of telling other people how to live, how to improve their marriages, when her own has broken up, when she claims most of the psychiatrists she knows are miserably married. But she has chosen not to regard this as a problem. She still feels she can help people. Perhaps it is all, then, a question of choice. Either you focus on the ironies and discrepancies to the point where the world looks like a jigsaw puzzle with most of the pieces missing or you don't think of it as a puzzle at all, just as a painting, a photo, a scene to be enjoyed, savored. Even the pain, if you could look at it that way, would be a part of it.

Could this have been my life? Susan wonders. Xenia still has dinner with her parents every Sunday night, for instance. Susan imagines a life where she works for a museum or as an assistant to a photographer, has dinner with Carol and Winthrop once a week—once a week!—does what she has been doing during this month's visit as a regular schedule—keeping up on art shows, current movies—furnishes a charming, small apartment with objects from Bloomingdale's, which Carol would delightedly charge on her gold credit card. Susan has no real contempt for this world, but she knows that for her it wouldn't work. She wouldn't feel a part of it. Perhaps that's why she is homesick now for her apartment in Alexandria, where no one expects her to fit in, where her apartment is bare and simple, her needs minimal, her life peculiar but her own. Or is it just that wherever she is, she will imagine that somewhere else she would fit in?

Living with Xenia is like their old fantasy of rooming together, but of course it's different. Susan is a boarder in Xenia's apartment. Still, at night, when they are talking, fixing dinner, laughing together, it does have some of the relaxed magic of the old times, a sense of comfortable sharing and jokes that go back to before they were even teen-agers. Susan loves it. One night Xenia says she is going out with Ralph Blumenthal, the married psychoanalyst Susan glimpsed at the restaurant.

"He'll just come up for a moment. . . . He belongs to my chamber-music group. You're sure you don't want to come?"

Susan is sure. She enjoys an occasional evening at home alone, something she would never have had at Carol's.

Ralph Blumenthal looks less bored and tired than he did when glimpsed in the restaurant, but Susan still doesn't like him. She doesn't think this has anything to do with the morality of the situation. She has always felt that any human arrangements that make sense to the two people involved are their own justification. But Blumenthal seems irascible, condescending.

"I understand you are a photographer," he says to Susan while Xenia is in the bedroom, getting ready.

"Yes," Susan replies.

"I've visited Alexandria. A beautiful city, but I could never live there. . . . Your father was Egyptian, I understand."

Susan is angry at Xenia for having told this man anything about her. It seems an invasion of her privacy. "I'm not there for that reason," she says stiffly.

"Just wanted to escape from home?" he says dryly.

"Partly."

"You can't do that by running away. Sooner or later it will catch up with you."

Susan shrugs. She hates men like this. How can Xenia make love with him? He has pudgy hands and wears a thick wedding ring. So he's written memorable books. So what?

"We all run, of course," he goes on, as though she had replied, "but our unconscious is keeping track. It knows *why* we are doing what we are doing. It waits patiently, but then it leaps."

"I don't really believe in the unconscious," Susan says. This is only half true, but she wants to annoy him.

"Is it a matter of belief? Do you believe we are in this room? That the world is round?"

"No, I think the world is flat."

At that moment, Xenia, in a pretty red dress and dangling gold earrings, enters the room, perfumed, bright-eyed. "Ready?"

"Of course *I* am ready," Blumenthal says. "But I'm worried about your little friend. There is a lot of denial going on."

"Ralph, come on," Xenia says, but she says it affectionately. She winks at Susan. "He can't stop even in off hours."

"I won't send you a bill," Blumenthal says waggishly, waving a finger at Susan.

After they leave, Susan feels restless and irritated. She feels she allowed Blumenthal to bait her and she is angry at herself for that, and is angry at them. Xenia, how can you run your hands over that pudgy body? Does he analyze their lovemaking? Susan has always thought that, not having had a father, she would be an ideal candidate for a romance with a "father figure," but so far at least, older men usually annoy her. It seems to her that, with younger women, their urbanity is always a glaze over a kind of contemptuous or at least condescending outlook. Even his flaunting that thick gold wedding ring seems slightly obscene to her, almost more dishonest than if he were the sort of man who didn't wear one at all. Xenia claims he is wonderful in bed, a master at oral sex. . . . Well, what do I know? Susan thinks.

She goes for a walk, but when she returns at ten, the apartment is still silent. Xenia has said that sometimes, after the chamber-music session, they go to his office to make love. Susan is startled when the buzzer rings from downstairs. She presses the intercom and the doorman's muffled voice says, "Visitor coming up."

Xenia has said nothing about a visitor. But would the doorman let just anyone up at night? Nervously Susan peers through the seeing eye.

"Who is it?"

"It's me." A male voice.

"I'm sorry," Susan says. "I can't see that well. Who is it?"

"Jay."

Susan opens the door, terrified but excited. Jay looks startled at seeing her.

"Xenia's out," she says. Should she have let him in? Xenia has said nothing to indicate Jay would be returning from Europe. "I'm just—I'm staying here for a few weeks."

If it were not for her fear that she shouldn't have let him in, Susan would be delighted to see Jay. He looks different—tan, more self-possessed, wearing a trench coat, like a journalist in a movie, his hair rumpled.

"It's good to see you, Susan. . . . Could I have a drink while we wait for Xenia? I assume she'll be back."

"I guess I'm afraid she'll be mad that I let you in," Susan confesses, giving him some Scotch. "Should I have?"

"Why not? We're still married."

"But aren't you—"

"Yes, but what is Xenia afraid of? That I'll cause a scene? Scream and rant? Rape her?" He looks bitter.

"She may not think anything," Susan says. "I just wasn't sure."

There is a moment of silence. Always with Jay, Susan feels awkward. She's not sure why, since he always tries to be nice to her. But she feels he regards her as a sexual neuter, a non-Xenia, and this humiliates her.

"How's Alexandria?" he asks.

"Fine."

"Still taking photos?"

She nods.

He looks restlessly around the room. "Where *is* Xenia?"

"She has a chamber-music group," Susan says warily.

Jay laughs. "Oh right. . . . Is Blumenthal still in it?"

It seems pointless to lie, though Susan is not sure what he knows about Blumenthal. "Yes."

"They're still at it?"

She hesitates, then nods.

"Did you meet him?"

"Yes. . . . I didn't like him."

Jay shakes his head. "God, why does Xenia see him? Will you explain it to me? Of all the pretentious, pompous fools in that whole damn institute, and believe me, he's got lots of competition, he is the most—"

"I assume they have a good sex life," Susan says wryly, picking up a pillow and putting it on her knees.

Jay laughs. "Oh right. . . . Sex. Xenia doesn't care about sex! She just lies there and thinks about the unconscious."

Susan hates this. She knows Jay has to be bitter, just as Xenia is, but she doesn't want to be caught in a crossfire. Perhaps something of her inner conflict shows because Jay says, "Sorry, Susan. . . . It's not your . . . What did you think that day we got married? Did you think we'd make it? Did you think we'd be happy?" His face suddenly looks so boyish and vulnerable that Susan is touched.

"I thought it would be stormy, but I thought you'd make it."

He smiles sadly. "I did too."

Susan feels conscious that her basic loyalty is to Xenia, whether or not she feels momentarily sorry for Jay. "Xenia says you have a girl friend in the Midwest."

"Oh bullshit! . . . She knows that's not true."

"You don't?"

"It's someone I used to know in Boston. Betsy. She's unhappily married. It's not love, it's not even sex. . . . She thinks I'm terrific. She doesn't give a fuck if I was ever analyzed. She never heard of Jung. That's it, period."

"So, would you . . . would you like to get back with Xenia?"

He shakes his head. "I just wanted to get a few books I didn't have time to pack when I moved out." He looks around the living room. "A nice little bachelorette apartment. Very chic. Very charming."

"I don't know where the books might be," Susan says. "Most of them are in the bedroom. Do you want to look?"

"Sure." He gulps down the rest of the Scotch.

While Jay is in the bedroom looking for his books, the key turns in the lock. It is Xenia, her violin under her arm. She looks happy. "You didn't like him, right?" she says.

"No, I just . . . Xen—"

"He can be a pain, but he's a sweetie underneath. And he is so different when we're alone. He can be so tender. . . ." She yawns and heads into the bedroom.

A second later Susan hears a shout from Jay. "Of course it's my book! What are you talking about?"

"Look at the sticker," Xenia yells back. "Why does it have my sticker in it, then?"

"How should I know why you put your fucking sticker in it? I brought this book to college. I've had it since I was fifteen."

"My father gave it to me for my birthday. . . . Do you want me to call him?"

"Fuck your father. . . . Maybe he gave you another copy. *This* copy is mine!"

Susan gets up and stands in the doorway. "Hey, kids . . ." she says jokingly. She hates the way both of them seem so totally unaware of her presence.

They both turn on her, furious.

"Why did you let him in?" Xenia yells.

"I didn't know," Susan says, bewildered at how childishly they are both acting.

"Susan, for some strange reason, regards me as a sane human being who was coming here with a perfectly reasonable claim," Jay says.

Xenia rushes out of the bedroom and comes back with a large art book. "Do you want the Matisse too? Take it."

"Of course I don't," Jay says. "I gave it to you as a present."

"So? It's your money. Why don't you give it to your next wife?"

"Please. . . . If you think I'm going to get married again after this . . ."

Xenia taunts him. "You'll be married next year."

"Okay, we can have a joint wedding," Jay says in the same tone. "You and fatso, once he strangles his wife. . . ."

"Ralph is one of the most respected psychoanalysts in this city," Xenia says.

"Does he perform oral sex on all his female patients and then charge them forty bucks an hour?"

"What would *you* know about oral sex?"

Suddenly Susan steps in between them. All through their petulant, angry exchange, she has felt like a voyeur. Is this always to be her role in life, watching other people fight, make love, break up, to be no more a part of the action than a lamp or a table? She wonders if, while they are fighting, they are truly unaware of her existence or if, in the same perverse way she enjoys watching them, they enjoy having an audience. "Hey, cut it out, both of you. . . . This is ridiculous."

"You've never been married," Xenia says. "What do *you* know?"

Jay suddenly grins. "Yeah, we hate each other. Leave us alone. If I can't hate her, who *can* I hate?"

There is a sudden silence. The hate, with its flickering excitement and sexual intensity, vanishes and sadness remains. For some reason Xenia walks over and hands Jay the book. "It doesn't matter whose it is," she says. "You take it."

Jay takes the book. "Well, thanks. . . . There were a few others. . . ."

"Look for them. It's okay."

Xenia walks out of the bedroom, Susan following her. With an exhausted, melancholy expression, Xenia lies down on the couch, her arm over her eyes. Susan looks at her. Her anger at Xenia vanishes. There is complete silence in the apartment. Finally Jay emerges with several books. Xenia sits up, yawning. "I'll get you a shopping bag."

"I'm going to San Francisco," he says to Susan, making conversation.

"I've heard it's a beautiful city," Susan says.

"I wanted a change." He takes the shopping bag Xenia hands him, puts in the books. The shopping bag breaks open and the books fall to the floor. "That's okay," he says, stooping and gathering up the books. "I'll just carry them." Jay walks to the door. "So long," he says in a general way to the two of them. Waving, he departs.

Xenia doesn't say anything after he leaves. She goes in to the bathroom, takes a shower, and soon emerges shiny-faced, her hair loose down her back, wearing a long pink nightgown. Susan, still stunned by the encounter between them, is sitting on the couch, not reading. She was always jealous of what Jay and Xenia had together, but also felt a part of it because the three of them had been friends since they were teen-agers. There is something so final and ugly about what has taken place that Susan feels a black curtain falling over what she thought of as a romantic part of their shared youth. The end. No more reprieves.

"Well," Xenia says, "that's marriage for you, in case you were thinking of trying it."

"I wasn't," Susan says.

"You take two people who were really good friends, who laughed at each other's jokes, who shared common ideals, and you wave a little wand over them called marriage and suddenly they're at each other's throats, they hate each other. . . . I wanted so much to tell him about my abortion! I could hardly hold myself back."

"Why?" Susan is genuinely puzzled.

"I wanted to hurt him," Xenia says, frowning. "The way he's hurt me. . . . I know it's childish. I know! . . . Anyhow, I didn't do it."

Susan gets up. "I don't think I've ever loved or hated anyone that much."

Xenia goes into the kitchen and pours herself some juice.

"You think Ralph is a prick, and he is in a way, but what I like is, we'll never be that close, we're giving each other something in a very limited way. He doesn't love me and I don't love him. Sometimes it seems like love but he's onto his second wife, he's seen a lot of things die a natural or unnatural death. I like his burnt-out quality. It's a relief after Jay. Jay cares so much about everything."

Susan follows her into the kitchen. "I like Jay, but I never know what to say to him."

"That's what he feels about you." Xenia stares into space. "Sometimes I hate the way I'm becoming. Maybe it's maturity, but I hate it! So many compromises. . . . I think of you, and your life seems so pure, so undivided."

"It isn't," Susan says without her customary vehemence on this topic. "I think it's just that everyone else's life seems easier or, just as you said, more undivided. That's the way I've felt about you. You have your meetings, your chamber-music group, your colleagues. It seems like there wouldn't even be *time* for self-doubt."

Xenia laughs. "There's always time for self-doubt." She hugs Susan. "I'm so glad you've been here, though. It's helped."

When she returns to Egypt, Conrad's letter is waiting for her.

> *Dear Susan,*
>
> *It's two weeks since we were together, but I feel as though it were a thousand years ago. You can't imagine what it's like to be out of the hospital, to be in control of my own life. Sometimes scary, but basically exciting and good. Let me know how you are doing. You can write me care of this address. Thank you for what you did. I will always remember it.*
>
> *Love,*
> *Con*

There is a knock at the door. The professor is beaming, his hair even looks slightly brushed. He is holding an enormous bunch of calla lilies. "Welcome," he says.

They embrace gravely, solemnly, as though they were old friends who had been parted by war.

"Welcome," Susan whispers.

Conrad

1963

"Conrad, where are you going?" His mother looks alarmed as Conrad attempts to sneak out of the apartment, his roller skates over his shoulder.

"Just want to get a little exercise," he calls breezily. "I'll be back later." Because she has materialized in front of him, he bends down and kisses her on the nose.

Lotte Zweifach is tiny, five feet tall, just two inches shorter than Conrad's father, Ludwig. Once, when Conrad was young, he read a story about a dwarf couple who gave birth to a normal child but had to give it away. At six feet four he feels like that child. Everything in his parents' apartment is delicate, from the two-inch Chinese ivory horses his father collects to his mother's exquisite, hand-painted bone china. The apartment could have been moved, in toto, from nineteenth-century Vienna—the cream-colored walls, the paintings with their heavy gold frames, the lace-covered dining-room table. Conrad always feels, literally, like a bull in a china shop.

"But tonight is the dance," Lotte says, still anxious. In her sixties, she is still delicately pretty, her hair white. She has soft skin and lovely violet-blue eyes and almost always wears a shade of blue. She still has a slight Viennese accent.

Conrad gathers what she means is that the dance should be enough exercise. She is always worried about his being overactive physically. To distract her he takes a deep breath. "Wow, what's cooking? It smells great."

"Dobos torte." Her face changes expression, beams. "The *Times* is coming in half an hour to interview me. I'm so excited! Do I look all right?"

"Gorgeous." Lotte has been working on a Viennese cookbook ever since Conrad was born. He's amazed it ever got published.

"She might like to meet you, the reporter," Lotte says.

"What for?"

"To find out how you like my cooking. To get a quote."

"Tell her everything you cook is delicious. That's why I'm so fat." It's a family joke that to his mother he is gaunt, horribly thin, and she is afraid all her friends will think it's because she's been starving him.

"Don't stay out too long," Lotte says. "It's supposed to get hot." When he was a boy, every day when he left for school she would say anxiously, "It may rain," or "It may get colder," as though any possible change in the weather was frightening.

His mother was forty when he was adopted, his father forty-four. In all the many ways in which Conrad finds his background hard to explain to people—his parents are Jewish, Viennese, elderly—the most peculiar is that his father fought in the First World War. The stories his parents tell about the way they grew up are so alien to anything most American kids have heard that he never repeats them. Maybe that's why Jay is his best friend, and why he feels at ease with Xenia. Their families are almost as strange, though not quite. Though he knows his parents have been as good and devoted to him as parents can be, Conrad can't help imagining what it would have been like if his real parents, who were high school students, had been able to marry, had *wanted* to marry. What a totally different childhood he could have had! If his real parents had married, they would now be only thirty-seven and thirty-nine.

He used to have fantasies about them when he was young. He would imagine a brawny, tall father who would play baseball with him in the yard, a vivacious mother who would look like a big sister and have an explosive laugh. But for some reason he no longer thinks about them. In fact, he has no desire to try to locate his real parents, no curiosity, even, about their lives. For some reason he's sure his father, in particular, has become some kind of bum, is probably always getting fired, maybe drinks too much. He doesn't have such sharp images of his real mother—but she, too, probably is on to her third husband, plays Bingo, has swollen ankles.

Sometimes, to amuse himself, Conrad imagines the two sets of parents getting together for dinner: his real parents and Lotte and Ludwig. His real father—Bill, probably, or Hank—will be tall, blond, the kind of guy for whom life was easy through high school, successful with women, a noncommitter. Would he feel some bond just on a genetic basis? Or would his father—"Dad"—just strike him as a jerk, the kind of guy who watches sports on TV all weekend, who talks about scoring with women, who never even reads the newspaper? Even though Conrad feels Ludwig quite often regards him with incomprehension, he has the feeling his real father, "Hank," would regard him with exactly the same feeling, based on different standards. Ludwig can't understand, for instance, Conrad's inability to speak any foreign language, since he speaks four flawlessly, two others fairly well, and can read Hungarian. Nor can he comprehend Conrad's inability to master any musical instrument or to love classical music. "Try and explain to me what your problem is," he said when Conrad got a C-minus in French. "Is it the grammar? Is it the word structure?" Conrad couldn't explain.

"Hank" probably barely speaks English, talks in monosyllables. Conrad, sitting at this imaginary dinner, imagines he would, without wanting to, feel scornful toward "Hank." "Hank" would knock over the gravy boat, tell dirty jokes that no one would get. But then Conrad realizes that even in fantasy he is imagining his real parents together as a couple, whereas, of course, they have gone their separate ways years ago. If his real mother, "Jan," remembers "Hank" at all, it's probably as some smooth-talking bozo who got her into bed against her will. Did they even have fun? Was the sex at least good? Probably not. Probably he used up all his energy persuading her and then came in one second and she felt some sticky stuff dribbling down her leg and wondered why she'd let herself be carried away.

In the park images of both sets of parents fade. He is just himself, Conrad. It's a beautiful day, the trees are fully green and open. There are mothers with baby carriages, couples making out on the grass, a man in a business suit flying a kite. Conrad straps on his roller skates and takes off. He loves roller-skating. If only it had counted as a sport! He sails along, feeling like a huge graceful bird. Conrad, the flying stork.

He doesn't even see the little boy coming at him. Suddenly Conrad is flat on his back, his arm bent backward, a feeling of excruciating pain darting through his body. The little boy, who is seven or eight, doesn't run away. He stands in front of Conrad, looking worried.

"Hey, mister, are you okay? You didn't stop when I came across the path. I didn't mean it. . . . Are you hurt?"

He looks so terrified that Conrad tries to murmur, "I—I'm fine."

"Can you get up?"

"I'm not sure." Conrad tries to raise himself with his good arm. The pain is almost laughably intense. What can have happened to his arm to cause such pain?

"Maybe you broke it," the little boy says.

Just then a girl, maybe three years older than the boy, skates up. "Where'd you go?" she says to the boy, probably her brother.

"I ran into this man," the boy says nervously.

The girl looks scared too. "What do you mean you ran into him?"

"I think I broke his arm. . . . He can't get up."

Both of them stare at Conrad, who is trying to ignore the pain and reassure them somehow.

The girl, who is freckled and skinny with frizzy red hair, kneels down to Conrad. "Should I get a doctor?" she asks.

"Where would you get one?"

"I don't know. . . . Our father is a doctor."

"What good does that do?" the boy says. "He's at the hospital."

"We could take him there. . . . Do you want us to?"

"Sure. . . . Could you help me take off my skates?" Conrad asks.

They each remove a skate from one of his feet, and without

the skates Conrad manages to stagger to his feet. The pain is not so much lessened. It's just that by now it seems a part of his being.

"Can you make it to Central Park West?" the girl says. "We'll go with you." To her brother she says, "Boy, you could be put in jail for this! What's *wrong* with you? You're such a jerk!"

"I know," the boy says so gloomily that Conrad puts his good arm around him.

"I'll be okay," Conrad says. "It's just—I have to go to a dance tonight."

"Are you a dancer?" the girl asks excitedly. "A ballet dancer?"

"No, I'm a student. . . . I'm graduating college."

"Which one?" the girl asks eagerly.

"Columbia."

"Our father went there," the boy says, excited. "Did you know him?"

The girl turns on her brother. "How could he? Daddy graduated years ago! *He's* graduating *now*." To Conrad she says, "Right?"

"Right."

They are at Central Park West now. Conrad wonders what to do. If he goes home, Lotte will be hysterical and her interview about the cookbook will be wrecked. Why not go to the hospital and have his arm set and put in a cast or whatever? He waits passively with the boy while the girl darts out and flags down a cab.

"Mount Sinai," she says importantly to the driver. They sit on either side of Conrad, watching him anxiously. "I'm Molly and he's Seth," the girl says. "We're brother and sister."

"Our father's a doctor," the boy adds.

"He *knows* that," Molly says, exasperated. "We told him." To Conrad she says, "He's just seven."

"And a half," Seth adds.

"How old are you?" Molly wants to know.

"I'm twenty-one and a half," Conrad says. The pain is slightly diminished if neither of them touches him. The smallest touch sets off a crazy spiral of pain.

"Maybe we have the same birthday," Seth says. "I'm December twenty-second."

"I'm December twenty-sixth," Conrad says.

They both look grave.

"That's the worst birthday anyone can have," Molly says. "That's even worse than my friend, Sheila, who has one on December twenty-fourth."

"It's not *so* bad," Conrad says.

"Do you get the regular amount of parents, I mean presents?" Seth asks.

"Yeah, he gets eight sets of parents," Molly says scornfully, "all wrapped up in gold paper." To Conrad she adds, "Don't mind him."

"Actually, my parents are Jewish," Conrad says, "so I don't get Christmas presents. I get Hannukah presents."

"That's just like Sheila!" Molly exclaims. "She's Jewish too."

"Maybe he knows her," Seth suggests.

Again Molly looks exasperated. "Just because they're both Jewish? There are *millions* of Jewish people in New York! . . . Do you like being Jewish?"

Conrad considers this. Their constant battery of questions distracts him from the pain. He likes them, even though they may have wrecked his graduation dance. "The thing is, my parents are Jewish, but I'm adopted, so my real parents weren't."

Seth looks confused. "So what happened to your real parents? Didn't they want you?"

Molly reaches behind Conrad and socks Seth. "How can you be so rude? They probably wanted him, but they were too young or too poor. . . . Right? What's your name?"

"Conrad Zweifach."

"That's a funny name," Seth says. "Is that your real name or your adopted name?"

"My parents who adopted me gave it to me," Conrad says. "They're German."

"I don't think it's such a good name," Seth says. "Conrad isn't so bad, but I don't like the rest of it."

"No one asked you!" Molly snaps. "It was just his parents' name! What can they do about it? . . . Is your father a doctor too?"

"He's a lawyer."

Suddenly Seth looks anxious. "Will he sue us?"

"No, he won't sue you," Conrad says. "Don't worry about it."

"I didn't mean to run into you," Seth says.

"Well, you did," Molly says. Looking at Conrad, she adds, "He never looks where he's going."

They are at the hospital now. Conrad has a few dollars in his pocket with which he pays for the cab. Molly helps him out. The two kids prop him up and steady him as he walks into the building.

It takes about an hour to have his arm set and put in a cast.

150

Conrad isn't sure if they will be there when he emerges, but they are—sitting quietly, looking through magazines. They are impressed by his cast.

"Boy, I guess you really broke your arm," Seth says. "I mean, *I* broke it."

"Can I write my name on your cast?" Molly asks.

She and Seth borrow a ballpoint pen from someone in the waiting room and inscribe their names.

"Then when it comes off, you can save it," Seth tells him.

"As a precious memory," Molly says ironically.

They live not far from the hospital and decide to take a cab home.

"Do you have money?" Conrad asks. He's all out himself.

"The doorman pays," Molly says.

By the time Conrad gets home it's late afternoon. His father is already back from work. Ludwig opens the door and says dryly, "Back from the wars?"

Lotte rushes out, horrified. "What happened? You were gone so long. . . . Were you hit by a car?"

Conrad explains.

His parents are grim. "Why do they let children act like that?" Lotte asks. "In Europe someone would be with them, someone would watch them. Here they run loose like wild beasts!"

"It was really an accident," Conrad says. "They were good kids. They took me to the hospital."

"Did you get their names?" his father asks.

"No."

Lotte is shaking her head in that anxious, trembling way she has. "Tonight is the dance! What will you do?"

With his good arm, Conrad pats his mother on the shoulder.

"I'll go to the dance. It's my left arm. . . . I'm not a very good dancer anyway."

"I sometimes think this is a country of barbarians," Lotte says.

"And Europe is not a country of barbarians?" says Ludwig.

"Not in the same way," says Lotte. "Here it's everyone, little children, housewives, all pushing, shoving, loud. . . ."

To get her off the track, Conrad asks, "How did the interview go?"

His mother looks sad. "She never came. . . . I got the day wrong."

Conrad wonders if he should call Xenia. But she'll only get

upset and probably assume, as he thinks his mother does, that in some way it's his fault.

Lying on his bed before dinner, Conrad wishes tonight were not about to happen. In some unexplained way he feels breaking his arm could have been half deliberate. He should not be going to the dance as Xenia's partner, her lover. They are not a true couple. There's something false about them. Xenia has assured him dozens of times that she and Jay were never more than temporary partners, friends, and Jay has never denied this. But Conrad knows he and Xenia are not right together. Sexually she takes the lead and is so enthusiastic and ardent that at times it is catching, but he always feels his passion isn't real. He isn't that involved. When he was in prep school, he felt basically the same about the girls he slept with then, but with them he felt less guilty because they were girls he hardly knew. At that time he felt that this might be the problem. Now he knows it's not.

He doesn't want to be gay. In fact, he's never allowed himself to consummate any of the feelings he's had for men. Up till now he's assumed it was something he could control by his will. Women like him, he would have a choice if he wanted. But the relationship with Xenia has made him see it won't work. He could marry, father children, but would always be trapped in a pseudo-life with guilt feelings toward whomever he chose as his wife. Maybe some form of celibacy, close friendships with men that, for him, could be tinged with other feelings. Would that work? Only once has another man ever approached him sexually, a student at Deerfield. He pretended not to understand and spent the rest of the year avoiding him.

He wonders now how his father would react. His mother would, of course, be hysterical. But his father, on the surface anyway, is urbane, sophisticated, not at all moralistic. A few times his father referred to a friend as though he were gay. His mother seemed to accept it too, but Conrad knows that if it was *her* son, she would feel differently. She would assume it was bad genes, something passed on by his real father. Could that be true? If there's one reason he would like to meet his real father someday, it's because he wonders about that. He's read of families where all the brothers are gay. It would be comforting to think it was genetic, or at least partly so, something he had simply inherited, like his height or his blue eyes.

At dinner, Lotte becomes nostalgic about the first time she met

Ludwig. "At that dance," she says. Looking at Conrad, she adds, "I didn't know English well at the time."

"She said to me, 'Are you a criminal?' " Ludwig smiles.

"I meant, 'Are you a soldier?' He was in uniform. You should have saved that uniform, darling. You looked so dashing in it."

"I hated it," Ludwig says. "I hate all military things. Never join the army, Conrad."

"Don't worry."

"They tear your soul out. No matter what they say they're fighting for, it's all the same."

Before he sets out, Conrad gets mildly stoned, just enough to get a slight distance from the dance, the pain in his arm, all the mixed feelings he has about starting architecture school, finally being about to move into the real world. He's put off thinking about it and he and Jay only josh about it, but he's scared. He would like to spend the rest of his life roller-skating in the park, doing useless things for which he'll never be judged. He wishes he could spend the evening with Molly and Seth.

Xenia and Conrad are dancing, to the extent they can with his arm in a cast. Her hand is on his neck, resting lightly, caressingly. For brief moments like this, Conrad feels it could work, that he could become the person he wants to be, and there would not be much psychic pain.

"It was nice of you to dance with Susan," Xenia says.

"I like Susan."

"We both had such a crush on you freshman year." Xenia looks up at him. "Did you notice? We used to take turns staring at you in Russian class."

"I was too busy trying to learn the Russian alphabet."

"We wrote stories about you, awful, corny pornographic stories. We even thought of sending them in to magazines."

"What did I do in the stories?" He smiles down at her, at her upturned lovely face.

"It's too embarrassing to tell."

He's made up stories like that too, of course, but involving men. He wonders how Xenia and Susan would define "pornographic." But anyway, they too had an inner life that had nothing to do with reality. Except that they shared it with each other. Sometimes, when Jay is earnestly confiding his hopes and fears about the future, Conrad feels so close to him that it seems that he

153

could tell him. It's absolutely not a question of fearing Jay's being judgmental. It's only a fear that it would somehow spoil their friendship, that Jay would take it to mean that Conrad has been lusting after him all these years under the guise of friendship. Which isn't true. His closeness to Jay isn't sexual. He feels pretty sure of that. But it means too much to him to chance spoiling it. Or maybe Jay knows or suspects and is being tactful in never raising the topic. Sometimes Conrad has imagined that in the coming year, if they are living in separate cities, he will write to Jay about it. It might be easier to do it in writing.

He and Xenia join Jay and Susan at the punch table. It's an alcoholic punch. Conrad is reluctant to drink on top of being stoned. He's tried that a couple of times with disastrous effects. Jay has had a few glasses and looks funny, pale.

"Jay, don't overdo," Xenia says, taking his hand. "That's silly."

"Don't play mother," Jay snaps. "I'm fine."

"You look peculiar."

"That's because I am."

Susan and Xenia go off to the ladies' room.

"I'm stoned, or I'd join you," Conrad says, indicating the punch bowl.

"Xenia gives me a pain," Jay says.

"Maybe she's in love with you," Conrad suggests, meaning to be consoling and also thinking it's half true.

Jay's face darkens. "Bullshit. . . . She's been drooling over you for years."

"Well, it'll all be over soon," Conrad says.

Jay laughs. "What will? Life on earth? College? You and Xen?"

"Right, all of it."

"I thought you were thinking of living together."

"It won't work," Conrad says. It's in conversations like these that he feels he could almost tell Jay.

Jay looks concerned. "Have you told her yet?"

"I'm a coward."

"Tell her. It's cruel not to. You're right—I don't think you're suited."

Conrad's heart starts ricocheting. "Why?"

"She'd boss you around. . . . You need someone more ethereal."

"Like Susan?"

"Not *that* ethereal. . . . Maybe an older woman. Listen, we're both young. Why should we tie ourselves down?"

"I agree." Conrad has a sense, largely of relief, of their having navigated past dangerous territory. "Don't say anything tonight, though."

"Of course not." Jay is looking to where Xenia and Susan are coming toward them. "My lips are sealed."

At midnight they decide to leave the dance.

"Let's go back to my place," Xenia says. "My parents'll be asleep."

No one objects.

"How's your arm holding up?" Jay asks.

"It's okay," Conrad says. Actually, it's beginning to hurt again. He wishes he'd brought some pot. The feeling of being stoned has completely worn off now and everything has a sharp, unambiguous quality. He hates himself, his life.

"Can you drive?" Susan asks softly.

"Sure."

Conrad drives slowly, but he has the feeling the car isn't totally in his control. Xenia, sitting next to him, is watching him nervously. As he makes a turn, the car goes momentarily off course, but he brings it back in time.

"You're going to kill us!" Xenia cries. "Let's get out right here!"

"We're right in the middle of the West Side Highway," Jay says. "Are you okay, Con?"

"Well, actually I do feel a little shaky," Conrad admits.

"Let's pull off for a minute," Xenia says.

Conrad wishes he hadn't brought the car. He wishes he were home, that it was tomorrow or a year from now, or a year ago. He doesn't want to be here in the car with all of them. He manages to pull the car off to a grassy spot on the side of the highway.

They sit in silence.

"I should have taken drivers' ed," Xenia says.

"Never depend on men," Jay says, with a laugh.

Xenia wheels around. "That's *not* what I meant!"

"I can drive," Susan says suddenly.

They all stare at her.

"When did you learn?" Xenia asks.

"My mother taught me one summer at the Cape. . . . But I don't have a license."

"Still," Xenia says. "Can you really drive? Would you be able to drive us to my parents' house?"

"I'd have to go very slowly," Susan says.

Conrad is immensely relieved. The pain and the feeling of anxiety make him afraid he may pass out. He leans over and kisses Susan.

"I'm going to lie down in the back."

Susan goes in front with Xenia and starts the car. Conrad slumps over toward the window. His arm feels like a leaden weight. "Oh Jesus," he moans.

"Are you really okay?" Jay whispers, concerned.

"Semi-okay." Conrad closes his eyes. Maybe Susan will kill all of them. It'll be one of those stories you read about in the *Daily News. Four kids with everything to live for perish in a car accident on the night of their graduation dance.* If Susan did it, it wouldn't be his fault. Kill us, Susan. Just drive off the road, into the river. His eyes closed, Conrad sees the car rising into the air, then spinning downward into the dark cold water. Instant death, no pain. No more worries, decisions, disappointing people, pretending. Sweet instant death.

But Susan drives with creepy, slow steadiness to Xenia's parents' home. As they pull up the driveway, Jay says to Conrad, "I think I had too much to drink."

"I think I didn't have enough." Conrad, emerging from the car, feels he would sell his soul for some strong, excellent grass.

"How are you feeling?" Xenia and Susan crowd around him with worried faces. "Is your arm any better?"

Of course! His arm. In fact, his arm is giving him no pain at all, it's completely numb; but, grateful for the excuse, Conrad says, "Maybe I better lie down. It's hurting quite a bit."

Liar, pretender, fool.

Xenia leads Conrad up to her room, where he sprawls out on the bed, shucking his jacket.

"Listen, I have these painkillers that Daddy gives me for when I have my period," Xenia says. "Would you like one or two? They really work. You'd be out like a light."

Conrad is beyond pretending. "I'd love one."

He is flooded with such a sense of gratitude that the evening, for him, is over, that no more will be expected of him, that it seems almost like desire. Impulsively he reaches for and kisses Xenia's hand. "You're wonderful."

Her face alters, she looks touched by what seems like the romantic intensity of his tone. "You are too," she whispers.

Will women always be so easily fooled by him? How can they

156

be? Why don't they see through him? He takes the two large red pills Xenia gives him along with a glass of water.

"Is it all right if I sleep here? Your parents won't mind?"

"No, why should they? They adore you. . . . Mooli always says, if she were ten years younger, she'd run off with you."

Sinking back on the pillow, Conrad laughs hollowly. "I think she could do better."

"No, she couldn't." Xenia kisses him tenderly on the forehead. "I love you."

"I love you too." He wishes this lie were harder for him. It's absurdly easy. It isn't even totally untrue. He means: I love you for not seeing through me, for giving me these pills, for accepting me, even if on false pretenses.

Alone in the dark room, Conrad feels a sense of peace and happiness that is almost like what he was imagining in the car. In a minute he will fall into a deep sleep. Everyone—Jay, Xenia, Susan—believes he is entitled to this because of his arm. Thank you, Seth. You saved my evening. Or should he thank his own clumsiness? Or the benevolent god who knew he would need this? As he sinks into sleep, Conrad looks back on the day just past like a graph—the moment of joy and release as he started roller-skating, the pain when he fell, the fun of going with Seth and Molly to the hospital, and then, from the moment he returned home, that familiar feeling of constriction, everything narrowing down. At the dance he was fine, he became what he was supposed to be, and, though there was a distant sense of unease, as long as the effects of the grass lasted it all seemed to be happening to someone else. Some other tall, blond, blue-eyed, handsome man was dancing with a lovely girl in a black velvet dress who thought she was his lover. No one pointed at them in derision or cried: Who are you kidding? And now he's safe, he's falling. . . .

In the middle of the night, or perhaps later, he hears Xenia enter the room. It's as though he were still asleep; that feeling of safety still has possession of him. He watches her undress in the semi-darkness, the outline of her body, her full breasts. Then she slips into bed next to him. Without thinking he reaches over and touches her hair. "Xen? What time is it?"

"Oh it's late, we stayed up talking, it's almost four. . . . How do you feel?"

"Wonderful. Those are great pills."

Conrad lets Xenia make love to him. She takes his clothes off, kisses his body, touches him everywhere he wants to be touched. It's *A Farewell to Arms*. He's the soldier in the hospital, she's the nurse giving him solace. In his fantasy it was a male nurse, but for the moment in the dark he feels only that someone is giving his body tremendous pleasure and is asking nothing in return. Xenia has claimed this is a turn-on for her, that sometimes just the knowledge that she is in bed with him can make her come. "You must have a great imagination," he once said jokingly.

"You have such a beautiful body," she says as they lie entwined afterward.

"Forgive me," he murmurs.

"There's nothing to forgive," Xenia says. "Let's go to sleep."

Where are Jay and Susan? They must be staying over too, probably in the guest room or the living room. Poor Jay. He should be here with Xenia. They would make love all night. He would make love to her, not just lie here like an inert object. If Jay is awake, he is hating Conrad, envying him. Forgive me, Jay. Only to Susan does he feel no complex tangle of emotions, just gratitude that she got them there. Thanks, Sue. Sleep tight.

In the morning Conrad wakes up at eight and finding Xenia still asleep, goes into the Szengis' kitchen. Jay is making coffee.

"Sleep well?" Jay asks.

How is he asking that? Does he mean he sees through the whole thing? Is he asking if Conrad and Xenia made love? "Like a log," Conrad says. "Xenia gave me some painkillers that could've felled a water buffalo."

"Her father gets everything free, as samples."

"I feel fine now." It's true. The dance in some way was a kind of test and now it's over. Pass-Fail. He passed, or anyway, passed out. "What did you do last night?"

"Had an orgy," Jay says, smiling. "Too bad you missed it."

"Even Susan?" He lowers his voice in case she's awake, though the door is closed.

"What do you mean, even Susan? She couldn't get enough. I was exhausted. . . . No, actually, we played Monopoly and got sloshed. I was so drunk, I was kind of beyond drunkenness. Have you ever had that feeling?"

"Who won?"

"What?" Jay is watching the coffee pot to see if it's stopped perking.

"In Monopoly."

"Oh. . . . Well, of course we didn't finish. I was ahead."

They take their coffee out on the lawn. It's quiet and still, the grass is wet.

"Thank God last night is over!" Conrad says.

"I know," Jay says.

What does he mean? Conrad glances at him. He wants to tell Jay everything, about being gay, about the way he felt the night before, even about thinking: Kill us, Susan. He says, "My arm wasn't really bothering me last night. I just pretended it was. I took the painkillers just because I couldn't face the rest of the evening."

"Yeah," Jay says.

"Were you feeling the same way?"

"I've been looking forward to this for so long," Jay says, staring up at the trees, "leaving home, getting out on my own. You probably can't understand that. You haven't lived at home since you were thirteen. I'm twenty-one and I can't go to the bathroom without three people asking me where I'm going!"

Conrad laughs. "But you have a home."

"So do you."

"Not really, not in the same way. I think they feel awkward when I'm around. I remember this story I read when I was in first grade about this little girl who had a dog who was much too small, so she wished for it to get bigger. It kept getting bigger and bigger. Finally it was bigger than the house! They didn't know what to do with it, it was the size of a dinosaur."

"Listen, I'm sorry," Jay says, "but I can only sympathize up to a point with your problems being tall. Want to trade? Would you rather be five eight?"

"It's just a symbol of feeling out of it," Conrad says apologetically.

"Girls love tall guys," Jay says bitterly. "Look at Xenia. She's only five feet seven, but she thinks I'm a shrimp."

"No, she doesn't."

"She does so! She told me that. She said any guy under six feet can't hold her undivided attention."

"That's absurd."

"Okay, it's absurd, but probably nine-tenths of the women in the world share it."

"You're plenty tall enough. Why worry about it?"

Jay is exasperated. "You said it's a symbol. I'm just saying so is everything. I wish I were taller, you wish you were shorter. What we're saying is we wish we fit in, that the world, which we're about to go into, the great unknown, will take us in."

"You'll be fine," Conrad says. "You have nothing to worry about."

"Why should I be fine?" Jay is getting angry. "I want to write, but who says I have any talent? I want a terrific woman to love me passionately. Who says she'll exist? Who says I won't have to settle for some dumpy, dilapidated leftover?"

"You know what you want," Conrad says. "That's the main thing."

"So I know. If I know what I want and I can't get it, how does that make me happy?"

Conrad says nothing. "It's better than not knowing." They are so close. Why can't he say what he's feeling? He wants Jay to intuit it, to make some mental leap. But Jay doesn't.

Just then, Dr. Szengi marches out of the house, in a suit, carrying a briefcase. "How was the dance?" he says.

"Great," Jay says.

"I assume you all turned in at the wee hours. . . . Or have you not been to bed at all?"

"We've been to bed," Jay says arrogantly, almost contemptuously.

"And the ladies? Still asleep?"

Jay looks at Conrad. "I don't know. Have you seen any ladies?"

"They're asleep," Conrad says to Dr. Szengi. "I hope it's all right that we stayed over. My arm started bothering me and no one knew how to drive."

"I would have been insulted if you hadn't." He walks off, waving. "Have a good day."

As the car pulls away, Jay says, "How can you do that?"

"What'd I do?" Conrad says, bewildered.

"You're so fucking polite. God, I hate him! Whenever I used to come over here, he'd give me these cold stares like I was some worm that had crawled into the house."

"It's your imagination."

"I wish I'd said to him, 'We were up all night fucking your daughter, you Magyar creep.' " He laughs curtly. "Only it was only true for one of us."

"I was out cold," Conrad says.

"All night?"

Why is Jay like this? He's like a terrier sometimes when he gets that intense look. "Most of the night," Conrad says.

"Did you fuck her or not?"

"We made love once."

"I thought you were out cold."

"I woke up when she came in. . . . It wasn't anything, Jay. Don't get so excited. She made love to me. I was half asleep."

Jay looks savagely away. "If you weren't my best friend, I'd hate your guts."

"What do you hate?" Conrad says. "I don't love Xenia, she doesn't love me. . . ."

"She does so. She spent half the night talking about you, about how wonderful you are, so sensitive. . . . I almost threw up."

"She knows nothing about me." Why can't he tell Jay? It seems absurd to be having this talk, which keeps skirting the truth and then backing away. Jay will have contempt for him if he knows. He wants the cloak of everyone not knowing. He can't give it up.

"No one made love to *me*," Jay says wryly, looking suddenly, unpredictably, in a better mood.

Conrad suddenly feels an immense relief that he has not told Jay anything. Their friendship is special, perfect as it is. What would be gained by a confession? Awkwardness. It would be stupid. Jay would feel he had to say some consoling words, would probably suggest he see a shrink. "God I'm starving," Conrad says, leaping up. "Let's fix some breakfast!"

"We can bring them breakfast in bed," Jay says. "Xen loves my scrambled eggs. You have to add vermouth at the last minute."

Conrad fries the bacon, Jay fixes the eggs, they heat some sweet rolls in the oven, and then carry the tray up the long winding staircase. Jay carries the tray, Conrad follows with the coffee and cream. Xenia is still in bed. Suddenly Conrad remembers that she's naked. She stretches, yawns, and looks up in delight.

"How wonderful! I was just lying here thinking of food." She gets out of bed, naked, and says easily, "Let me make myself decent."

Jay turns red and sets down the tray. When Xenia closes the bathroom door, he looks at Conrad and rolls his eyes. Conrad laughs. He feels as differently from the night before as anyone could feel. Jay is his best friend, Xenia loves him or thinks she does, they're about to eat a terrific breakfast, his favorite meal. Xenia comes back in an Oriental silk bathrobe, tied with a sash around her waist.

"This is like that play," she says. "Did you ever read that? *Design for Living.* One woman, and two men. Maybe we should do that. The three of us live together." She reaches for a platter of eggs and bacon. "Is Susan still asleep?"

"I'll get her," Conrad offers. He wants to leave Xenia and Jay alone. He wants to give Xenia to Jay.

He goes downstairs and finds Susan still asleep, curled up to one side. "Sue? We're having breakfast."

She opens her eyes with a start. "Is it terribly late?"

"Around eleven. . . . Come on up to Xenia's room when you're ready. We're having it up there."

When he returns, Xenia and Jay are comfortably ensconced on the bed, eating, looking relaxed and happy.

"Your parents are amazing," Jay says to Xenia. "Letting all of us sleep over. . . . Mine would have a fit. I can't even imagine it."

"Mommy never gets up before noon," Xenia says. "No, you're right. Daddy says conventional morality is all nonsense, that we have to create our own lives."

At this moment that seems possible to all of them. Conrad envisions some future in which he will introduce Xenia and Jay to his male lover and they will like and accept him; he will be an architect, designing marvelous buildings.

Seeing Xenia and Jay side by side, looking so natural together, Conrad says without thinking, "You two should get back together. You belong together."

Xenia turns pale. "What do you mean?"

Jay is furious. "That's so condescending."

Conrad tries to apologize to Jay without saying anything. He knows Jay feels this is a betrayal of what they were talking about on the lawn, Jay's passion for Xenia. Maybe it is. Where *do* his loyalties lie? He truly feels he wants both of them to be happy and wants, also, to be let off the hook.

While they are sitting there, silently, trying to recapture the good spirits of a moment earlier, Susan comes in. She is wearing her prom dress. "I didn't have anything else to put on," she explains.

Conrad takes her hand. "May I have this dance?" He gives a low bow.

"Sure." She lets him whirl her sedately around the room while Jay and Xenia watch. "How are you, Con? Recovered?"

"Right as rain," Conrad says.

"He was just pulling a fast one," Jay says. "His arm was fine. He didn't feel like playing Monopoly with us. He knows we're friends."

Conrad lets this one get by, knowing Jay is still miffed at him. "Those pills of your father's are superb," he says to Xenia. "If I had a father who was a doctor, I'd be a junkie."

"Would you?" Xenia asks, concerned.

"There are times when you just want to block everything out," Conrad says.

"But why last night?" Xenia asks. "With all of us? We're your friends. You don't have to pretend about anything with us."

"Sure I do," Conrad says.

Xenia looks puzzled. "Why? We don't pretend with you. . . . Do we?"

"I guess he means we all pretend some of the time," Jay says. "No matter who we're with."

"I don't think *I* do," Xenia says. "Do *you*, Susan?"

Susan is quiet a moment. "Yes, I do," she says.

Xenia sets down her coffee. "This is so fascinating! What do you pretend *about*?"

She is looking at Conrad, but Jay says, "Everyone has secrets, Xen. . . . Otherwise we'd all be . . . naked. Just like people wear clothes because their bodies aren't perfect. It's the same with our personalities. We try to cover up things we don't like about ourselves."

"I can see what you mean for outsiders, but not for friends. Isn't that what friends are for, people you can reveal anything to?"

"Not everyone wants to *be* that revealing," Jay says.

Conrad wonders if this conversation between the two of them means that Jay knows more than Conrad suspects. Or does he mean something about himself?

"Civilization and its discontents," Xenia says, reaching for another strip of bacon.

"Spare us," Jay says. "It's too early in the morning."

Xenia throws a pillow at him. Jay throws one back. Conrad takes the breakfast tray off the bed while Xenia and Jay run around the room, pelting each other with pillows.

"Freud is dead!" Jay yells. He twists Xenia's arm behind her back. "Say it, say it."

"Jay, stop," Xenia cries. "You're hurting me."

"Say it."

"Freud is dead," Xenia says. The second he lets go, she says, "And you're as neurotic as he was."

Jay laughs. "Is that a compliment? Are you saying I'm a genius?"

"No, I'm saying you're completely fucked-up *and* you almost broke my arm."

Jay comes over to Xenia and becomes mockingly consoling, stroking her arm.

"I'm sorry, I'm just a brutish male. Those hormones your mother is always talking about."

Susan gets up. "Let me take your pictures, all of you . . . Do you have your camera, Xen?"

"It's in the closet. I don't know if it has film in it."

Susan returns with the camera and says, "It does. . . . Okay, all of you, get into bed the way you were before."

"Dirty pictures?" Jay says. "How much flesh do you want?"

"Do whatever you feel like," Susan says, angling in on the three of them. Xenia is in the middle, Conrad and Jay on either side. Jay leans over and kisses Xenia on the mouth. Susan clicks.

"What were you doing?" Xenia says, her eyes wide.

"She said do whatever I felt like," Jay says. He stands on his head. Susan clicks.

"Con, look at me," Susan says, moving to one side and coming closer to him.

Conrad hates being photographed. He wishes she would just take more shots of Xenia and Jay. He straightens his shoulders.

"Don't be scared," Susan says. "Look to the side, near the window. Right."

Conrad has never seen Susan acting so authoritative. She tells them where to move, gets them in funny poses on the floor, peeking behind each other.

"But you should have done this last night, when we were beautiful," Xenia says.

Jay takes Xenia's prom dress out of the closet and holds it up in front of him. "Do I look beautiful?"

Susan clicks.

"You're just wasting film," Xenia says. "Take one of us looking normal."

"Okay," Susan says. "Look normal."

Jay mugs. "I don't know how. I'm a hopeless neurotic. How do normal people look?"

Conrad strikes a pose, his head thrown back. "Like this."

"That's normal?" Jay says. He takes Xenia's prom dress and puts it around his head so it covers his face up to his eyes.

"Jay, that's a beautiful old dress that my mother lent me," Xenia says. "Please be careful."

At that moment, Mrs. Szengi peers into the room. "You children are up already?"

"It's noon," Conrad says.

"We always slept all day the night after a dance." She is in a long black bathrobe, her voice throaty. "Did you all have a wonderful, exciting, romantic time?"

Xenia comes over and hugs her. "We did, Mooli."

"Oh, to be young again!" Mrs. Szengi says. "The heartache! The passion! The absurdity!" Then she marches briskly over and says, "Here, the coffee is cold. Let me make you some fresh."

1978

To celebrate Ludwig's eightieth birthday, the Zewifachs are taking a European vacation: Vienna, for the opera, perhaps Prague, and finally Paris, to see their son. "It may be our last trip," Lotte writes Conrad. "We want to do it while we can."

It amazes everyone in Paris that Conrad, who is just thirty-seven, has parents who are so old. In France they imagine that all Americans marry at sixteen and have children immediately. "Many do," Conrad explains, and tells the story of how he was adopted, the peculiarity of a Jewish couple being able to adopt only a non-Jewish child. That, too, doesn't make sense to anyone here. They don't think of Americans as being Jewish. They imagine all Americans look, at their best, like Conrad—tall, athletic (so they assume), and good-natured in (they assume) an uncomplicated way. Though he has settled in Paris to escape being classified, Conrad sees that here, too, he is classified, but in a different way.

It's hard for him to imagine that his father is eighty. He has seemed elderly for so long—not that he's been weak or feeble; but he's had that detached, gently ironic manner, his hair has been gray and thin since Conrad was in high school. Only the last time he visited them was Conrad aware of the way his father's hand shook just slightly, reaching for a book. Of his parents, his mother's health is worse: she seemed on the verge of blindness a year earlier, and then a cataract operation restored most of the sight in one of her eyes. For Lotte, to whom reading is all-important, it was a miracle. The year before that, in 1976, Ludwig had a stroke. He, too, had seemed on the verge of, if not death, total debilitation, but then he slowly recovered. In his father Conrad senses an iron, indestructible will. Occasionally he will pause before speaking, but when he does speak, it is with perfect intellectual mastery. When he was younger, it appeared effortless. Now the effort shows, but Conrad doesn't care. He would be horrified to see his father decline mentally, lose his memory. Even though he's always hated the screen his father erects between himself and the world, he would not like to see him without it.

When Conrad returns home, as he does about once a year, his mother tells him her worries about his father, and his father tells him his worries about her. "He fell once and he couldn't get up," Lotte says with a frown, and Ludwig, when Lotte is absent, murmurs, "I was so relieved she can read again. She would have gone mad without reading." The day his father fell, their housekeeper wasn't present and his mother was herself too weak to pull him to his feet. Finally, they called the super and he gently lifted Ludwig up and set him down on the couch. Conrad imagines the scene: the burly Cuban super lifting this tiny, immaculately groomed, but fragile man, who probably seemed to the super like a human doll.

It was on his last visit home that Conrad told them about Dale. Or at least he thinks he did. He hesitated—not, he feels, for the usual reasons. His parents think he has finally "found himself." He is running an art gallery in Paris. They believe that it is doing well, that he has friends, seems sure of himself, pulled together, that the depressions dogging his adolescence and early adulthood have been put aside. All this is close enough to the truth so that he hesitates to disturb it in any way. What would be the point? His parents are at the end of their lives. His mother no longer even asks if he has met any nice American girls over in Paris. She informs friends he is enjoying his freedom.

He spent the week at home, wondering if he should tell, and finally chose an evening when his parents' friend Serge Sherwin, an oboist whom Conrad has always assumed might be gay, was coming for dinner. It wasn't even that deliberate. It was simply that at dinner, with Serge there, Conrad began describing his friend, Dale, who works for a travel agency in Paris.

"Another expatriate?" his father asked. He turned to Serge. "Isn't it curious? Here we worked so hard to get *out* of Europe, to escape to America, the land of opportunity, of dreams fulfilled, and now they go back there. What does it mean?"

"You can fulfill dreams elsewhere than in America," Serge said. A foot taller than Mr. Zweifach, he is a stooped man with a small goatee, who suffers from asthma.

"Things have changed," Lotte said. "Hitler is gone. Europe isn't what it was. Who says America is so wonderful? Conrad wants culture, friends who are more sophisticated, people who love art, who appreciate it. . . ."

"Is that what it is?" his father asked.

"Partly," Conrad said uncomfortably. "People settle there for different reasons."

"And your friend, Dale," Serge asked. "What's *his* reason?"

Conrad wasn't sure why or how he meant that question but, looking just at Serge, he said, "He's gay and he feels his family might find that hard to accept."

"Of course," Serge said smoothly. "Families usually do."

"Where is he from?" his mother asked after what seemed like a pause, though Conrad wasn't sure if it was just that the whole conversation seemed strangely stilted.

"He's from Iowa," Conrad said, taking a sip of wine.

"Well, of course in Iowa, I imagine anyone who deviates in any way is an outcast," his father said. "We would all be outcasts there."

Lotte looked puzzled. "Why would *we* be outcasts?"

"Just being Jewish. . . ."

"Dale is Jewish," Conrad said. "Or his father was."

"That *would* be difficult," Serge said. "To be Jewish and gay in Iowa! . . . Is he an artist also?"

"Well, he used to paint, but, like me, he came to the conclusion that he didn't really have what it takes."

"You just didn't have self-confidence," Lotte protested. "You did beautiful things." To Serge she said, "The painting in the hall is one that Conrad did in Alaska. I think it's wonderful. There's such a sense of peace."

"Still, I think you did the right thing," Serge said. "You are connected to art, you help others. In a way that is contributing to the art world just as much as if you were a practitioner."

Conrad smiled. "That's a nice way of looking at it."

"Was your friend Dale sorry?" Serge asked. "Or is he philosophical like you?"

"He's philosophical," Conrad said. Why is only Serge asking him about Dale?

"It's nice you have a good friend, over there," Lotte said. "I was afraid that would be difficult, the way it's been for me. . . . I've never had friends here the way I did in Vienna. American women are different. French men must be different."

Conrad took a deep breath. "We're thinking of living together," he said. "His lease is about to run out and I have an extra bedroom. It would help with the rent and he's interested in the gallery."

"Sounds very practical," his father said. Their eyes met. Had Conrad just told them he is gay or hadn't he? Who at that table knew?

Lotte looked concerned. "Friendships can be ruined that way," she said. "Some friends you can live with, some not. It's a matter of compatibility, like marriage."

Serge has lived with his married sister and her husband for most of his adult life.

"I've never found that with anyone," he remarked calmly. "I have many friends, but none with whom I'd care to live on an everyday basis."

"But it's different with you, Serge," Lotte said. "You don't want a family. That's the main reason people live together."

"Not if they're of the same sex." Serge looked up as the housekeeper came to remove his plate.

"Conrad needs someone to talk to," Lotte explained to Serge, as though he was questioning why Dale was moving in. "It isn't easy living in a country where you're a foreigner and they never let you forget it. You need someone who you can unwind with, who knows your roots."

"Iowa is a foreign country," his father remarked. "Corn, oats, horses . . . Why is Paris more foreign than that?"

Maybe his own real parents were from Iowa originally. Doubtful, but sometimes Conrad fantasizes about this to explain the sense of kinship he feels with Dale, a kinship that seems strange to both of them, as though they had grown up together.

Dale is ten years younger than Conrad, but by now that hardly seems to matter. There are moments when Conrad will refer to a song or a political event that was taking place when he was in high school or college and will realize that to Dale those events are "history." But in manner and character Dale seems mature, much more than he was at that age. Maybe it's a question of having come to terms with his sexual identity earlier. As Dale describes it, his sense of being an outcast was so great that he left home permanently at sixteen and hasn't been back since. I didn't have anything that extreme to break away from, Conrad thinks. Understanding parents, enough money even for therapy, if that would prove to be the answer.

If there is a taboo subject with his parents, it is the autumn he escaped from the mental hospital without their knowledge or consent. Conrad thinks of this as the true beginning of his adult life. He's amazed, when he thinks back on it, that in the state he was in then—confused, agonized, uncertain of everything, including whether to live or die—he mustered the energy to break away. "When you have nothing left to lose, you're free," Dale said.

His parents were horrified, not just because they feared for his life, but because they had grown up in a world where obeying the rules was usually rewarded. Neither of them had ever been to a psychoanalyst, but many of their friends had, or were psychoanalysts themselves. They regarded it like art or literature, as a way of organizing life that could provide answers.

A week before his parents are due to arrive, Dale and Conrad discuss how to handle it.

"Do you really want me around while they're here?" Dale asks.

Conrad isn't sure if he's sensitive about Conrad's feelings or just insecure about the impression he may make. "Sure, I want you around," Conrad says. "I want them to know."

"Why?"

"They're my parents."

They've been over this, without agreeing. Dale claims there is such a gap between his parents' view of the world and his own that he owes them nothing. Conrad feels he owes his parents, if not everything, a great deal. He knows he is a coward, but doesn't want his parents to die not knowing who he really is.

"So, tell me what you want me to do. How should I act?" Dale has a wry, humorous face, dark hair, greenish eyes, a long aquiline nose. "Am I the close friend, the lover, the roommate, the farmer's son who's passing through Paris . . . ?"

"Just be yourself," Conrad says. "Don't make a big deal of it."

"Look, to *me* it's not a big deal, but you've been talking about it for the last two months. What if I fail the test? I've never met anyone like them before."

"It's *not* a test," Conrad says. He hopes this doesn't sound falsely ingenuous, because, of course, he knows what Dale is feeling. "They're not like your parents. They're European, they're sophisticated. And, I think they know already."

Dale has heard the story of the evening with Serge.

"Con, they don't know. You didn't tell them."

Conrad smiles. "I think I all but told them."

"Okay, you all but told them . . . but that's not actually *telling* them. There's a big difference."

"You don't have to dot every *i*, or cross every *t*."

"With parents you do."

Conrad sighs. "Look, if it's going to make you too uncomfortable, don't be here. Really. I can handle it on my own."

"Do you want me here?"

"Yeah."

Dale grins. "Okay, so I'll be here. No sweat."

Their apartment is small, right above the gallery, in a courtyard off the rue Corneille. There is a large living room, two bedrooms, and a small garden in the back where they often eat on summer evenings. Conrad knows his parents will like the apartment. The furniture is not unlike theirs, though it's more spare and the artwork is contemporary. But it's tasteful and beautiful. His mother will appreciate the garden. How different would he be feeling if he'd fallen in love with a Catholic French girl whom they were about to meet? Clash of religion, of culture. Dale is half-Jewish, American, not unlike friends he had in college. Not, in some ways, that different from Jay. And anyhow, there is not going to be any public declaration. This will be *Dinner with Serge*, act 1, scene 2, only Serge won't be there. Conrad just doesn't want to hide Dale away, but he has no intention of saying, "Meet my lover," or making any revealing physical gestures. Why be provocative? His aim isn't to hurt or shock them, just to have them accept part of who he is.

"It sounds great on paper," Dale says when Conrad tries to

articulate some of this. "It's just based on the assumption that parents are people and—"

"They've accepted so much about me that wasn't what they wanted," Conrad says. "Why not this?"

"You tell *me*."

When his parents finally appear, Conrad is shocked at how elderly and frail they look. His father, especially, seems to have shrunk. Always thin, his face now looks almost skeletal, and he carries a cane. His mother still looks beautiful, her white hair simply done, her blue silk dress graceful. He feels a pang of pity and protectiveness as they edge into the apartment; his anxiety washes away.

"What a lovely neighborhood!" his mother says. "It's just beautiful."

His father sits down at once, as though he might collapse. He pats his face with a handkerchief. "Well, we made it," he says with a smile.

"Mother, Dad, I'd like you to meet my friend Dale," Conrad says. Dale is hovering in the doorway just behind them. "He lives with me."

Lotte turns. "We're so glad to meet you."

Dale edges forward with unexpected shyness and mumbles something almost unintelligible.

"You're an artist?" Lotte asks. "Like Conrad?"

She still thinks of Conrad as being an artist, though he hasn't painted for years.

"I— Well, I have painted. I paint sometimes, but I'm not . . . I work in a travel agency."

Conrad looks nervously at his father. He is sitting still, as though he were an inanimate object. "The opera in Vienna was wonderful," he says suddenly. "Worth the whole trip. *Così fan Tutte.* . . . Do you know it?" he asks Dale.

"I've heard of it," Dale says. "It's by Mozart, isn't it?"

For the first time, Conrad wishes this meeting was not happening. Not because of Dale or his parents, but because he wishes Dale either knew the opera or wasn't self-conscious enough to say, "It's by Mozart, isn't it?," which he is sure will strike his father like "An orange? That's a fruit, isn't it?" He didn't think he would judge Dale in any way, just his parents, and is horrified that he *is* judging him.

"It's so rare," his father goes on, seeming unperturbed, "to

171

find wonderful singing, wonderful acting, and people who look right for the parts. Here you had it all."

"But we're exhausted," Lotte says ruefully. "We're not what we once were."

"You *look* wonderful," Conrad lies, or half lies. They do look wonderful for people their age. "Let's go into the garden. I thought we'd have lunch there."

He fixed something in the morning, something simple because of his father's low-salt, low-cholesterol diet: poached fish, asparagus, rice. He's chilled some wine because his mother still drinks wine.

Dale follows silently, looking dazed. Conrad knows his parents must seem strange to him. It's one thing to explain them, another to have them right here.

"This is all so beautiful," Lotte says, accepting the plate Dale offers her. "You're lucky to have such a nice apartment. . . . Is it close to where you work?"

She is addressing this question to Dale, who still seems slightly spaced out. But, looking up, he says, "It's over the gallery. It's pretty near where I live, I mean work. I take a bus."

"Paris is still the most beautiful city," Lotte says. "I feel unfaithful to Vienna, saying that, but the buildings, the atmosphere, the people! If I were young, I would live here, like both of you. *Especially* if I were an artist."

Dale sits down opposite her. "I hear you used to be an actress," he says.

"Oh, years ago, *centuries* ago," Lotte says. "I gave it all up . . . for love." She glances at Ludwig. "No regrets. I wasn't that talented. I just loved the world of the theater."

"I do too," Dale says. "I used to act in college. I wasn't too great, but it was fun, I miss it."

"The older I get, the more I think fun is the most important thing in life," Lotte observes. She smiles playfully. "I hope that doesn't sound hedonistic. I didn't mean it that way."

"They know that," Ludwig observes dryly.

Conrad wishes he could shut off his inner monitor, which is regarding every sentence that his parents or Dale utters as though it was something to be translated into a foreign language. Sometimes he is Dale, scrutinizing his parents, sometimes his parents, scrutinizing Dale. "Dale used to be a painter also," he says. "Like me."

"I told them that already," Dale says with a half smile at Conrad, as though to say: Don't be so nervous, it'll be okay.

"But you are still an artist," Lotte says. "You have an artistic spirit. That's what counts."

Ludwig has been eating his fish quietly, as though he were on another planet. His silence isn't rejecting, just self-absorbed.

Suddenly he says, "I still can't forgive the Viennese. No, it's still there. . . ."

"For what?" Dale asks.

"For giving in to the Nazis, for becoming worse, even. . . . A city based on such culture, such beauty! How could it happen?"

No one has an answer.

"Such brutality, such ugliness," his father goes on. "Right beneath the surface. But who would have known?"

Dale is drinking more wine than he normally would, Conrad observes. He says, "My father was Jewish. He told me how during the Second World War, neighbors thought he was a spy because he used to go up hunting in the hills by himself."

"Human nature is savage!" Ludwig says, his eyes dark and hollow.

Lotte looks alarmed. "But Paris is different. Here you can live any way you want and no one cares."

"That's what I like about it," Dale says. "Once I got here, I felt like I could breathe easily for the first time in my life."

"Conrad feels that way too," Lotte says. "Don't you, dear?"

"Yes, I do," Conrad says. He has a fear that Dale will do something overt like take his hand or put his arm on Conrad's shoulder, some physical gesture that will destroy what seems to be a perfect equilibrium. Even when they are with friends, Dale is more physically affectionate and open than Conrad. Conrad half likes it and half minds it. Yet, it's been true of everyone he has ever liked sexually or as a friend—Xenia, Jay—that ease with physical gestures, that lack of inhibition.

"See, I come from a *really* small town," Dale says. His tone seems to Conrad overly relaxed, too at ease. "We're not talking New York and sophistication. We're talking beans and horses and cows. I spent my childhood thinking I was an alien who'd been beamed down from another planet. That was what got me through it."

"How dreadful!" Lotte says. "It must have been terrible for you."

Dale polishes off his wine. "Maybe it helped. Seriously, I think sometimes if you have it too easy growing up, you rot inside. I had to find out who I was when I was young, like six or seven, and I did. I feel kind of proud of that."

Lotte is staring with absolute fascination at Dale. She has that manner with men, a kind of natural flirtatiousness that never bothered Conrad when it was directed to someone of her generation. "You know, I think I still don't know. Here I am, going on eighty, and I still don't know really who I am. I suppose it's too late now." She smiles.

"I think you *do* know," Dale says, equally playful. "Deep down."

Conrad is horrified at his ingratiating, intimate tone. How can he talk like that to a woman his mother's age whom he's just met? But Lotte seems uperturbed.

"You're right. I know deep down, but I never let it out."

"Still," Dale says, "you know. That's what counts. Right?" As he finishes the sentence, he looks up at Conrad and freezes at the sight of his expression.

Conrad is ashamed of his inner judgmental feelings—how different is he, at bottom, from his father, who has hardly spoken?

In the pause that follows, Lotte stands and says, "Do you mind if I smoke? My husband hates me to, but I seem to need one after a meal."

"Go right ahead," Dale says.

Lotte gets up, as she always does, to smoke a few feet from Ludwig, who waggles a finger at her. "Lack of discipline," he says, as he has said a million times over the years.

Dale raises his glass. "To lack of discipline," he says. "Long may she wave."

Ludwig's face darkens. "I hope that isn't the guiding principle in your life, young man," he says.

"I wish it could afford to be," Dale says lightly. "Unfortunately, I have to eat."

Ludwig gives him a long, even stare. "And if you didn't?"

"Then I'd probably just bum around with Con, lie on beaches, paint, and live the good life."

Conrad feels like the moderator in a debate. He feels Dale and his father are behaving badly—his father by being so totally humorless and dry, Dale by deliberately baiting him. As though to up the ante a few more points, Dale stands up and puts his hand on Conrad's shoulder.

174

"What's for dessert?" he says to Conrad in a soft voice, with a hint of a challenge in it.

Conrad tries not to flinch when Dale touches him.

"Just some fruit. Can you get it?"

He sits rigidly while Dale clears. Lotte returns from her smoke and joins them.

"If only we'd bought that brownstone," she says to Ludwig. "We could have had a garden."

"And burglars," his father points out.

"These lovely summer evenings," Lotte says. "I'm glad you found such a lovely spot. . . . Do you have any of Dale's paintings? I'd love to see some."

This is the opposite of what Conrad expected. He thought his father, in his dry, detached way, would be the accepting one, that his mother would be hysterical and thrown off guard. He shows her two of Dale's paintings, which are hung in their bedroom.

"Yes, I think he's very talented," she says.

As they return to the garden, she says to Dale, "I like your sense of color."

"Thanks. . . . I should paint again. I think for a while it was almost punitive—like, if I couldn't earn my living that way, I didn't have a right to do it at all." He peels a peach and offers it to her.

"Oh no," Lotte says. "You should do it for *you*. . . . And maybe—who knows?—someday, they will sell. I wish Conrad would take it up again also."

"Maybe we both will," Dale says.

Conrad watches Dale and his mother eat their peaches, the way they both let the juice spill over their fingers and lick it off unselfconsciously. He sees them as a couple, as though they were the same age, and sees himself and his father, both silent, unable to communicate. But his father, at eighty, is entitled to be that way. What is *his* excuse?

After lunch they get up and say they must return to the hotel for their nap.

"I'll go get you a cab," Conrad says, and accompanies them into the courtyard and then into the street. His mother holds on to his arm, his father inches along with his cane.

"That was such a lovely lunch," Lotte says. "I like your friend, Dale. Thank you for introducing us."

Conrad mumbles something. He is relieved to escape into the effort of finding a cab for them, which he does. He helps them both into the cab and gives the driver the address. The one thing he is pleased with is his fluency in French.

When he returns to the apartment, Dale is sitting in the garden, having another glass of wine, into which he has sliced a peach. "This is fantastic wine," he says. "I'm going to get bombed."

"I thought you already were," Conrad says.

Dale raises an eyebrow. "Oh come now, was it that bad? Loosen up, kid. You survived, they survived, I survived. . . ."

"At least you hit it off with my mother," Conrad says, sitting down. He feels appallingly sane and clearheaded and doesn't feel like drinking.

"Your mother's a sweetie," Dale says. "Does she really always ask his permission to smoke, even now?"

"It's just a routine they go through."

"Well, I congratulate you for getting through a childhood with Ludwig," Dale says. "Too bad he was Jewish. He would have made a great Nazi general."

"That's stupid," Conrad says, hating the heavy Germanic accent Dale gives to Ludwig. "He's a very cultured, urbane person. He was brought up in another era. You have to make allowances."

"I do?" Dale laughs. "Why do I? He's not *my* father. . . . God, I'd love to have him meet George sometime. They'd really hit it off."

Dale has described his father as a large, silent, macho man with huge hands and feet, whose main love in life is hunting.

Conrad is silent. He wants not to say anything, but he can't hold back.

"Why bait him, though? What was the point?"

"How was I baiting him?"

Conrad lifts an empty glass. " 'To lack of discipline.' "

"I was just kidding around. . . . He's so grim. I wanted to get him to relax a little."

"He's eighty," Conrad says defensively. He feels Dale, by being high, has an edge over him.

"So, he's a hundred and ten. If I live to be eighty, I won't be like that because I'm not that way *now*. And I'll bet anything he was the same at our age."

This is true. "It's also being European," Conrad adds, looking away.

Dale stares at him. "I don't get this. . . . Who cares *what* it is? He's an uptight, self-absorbed stiff! Do I hear any counter-suggestions?"

"He's still my father."

"Meaning?"

"Meaning I love him in a way, and I want to . . ." Conrad can't finish the sentence.

"I want to please him," Dale says in a baby voice. "I want to do nothing to upset him. I feel so scared he might possibly get the feeling that my roommate isn't my roommate but is—ta-da!—my lover, that I'm just going to hide under the table and not open my mouth for a whole hour."

"He knows I'm gay," Conrad says.

"He does not."

"I told him. . . . I told you that."

Dale shakes his head. "Con, you never told him."

"How can you *say* that? You weren't there!"

"You never told *him*. You never told *her*. . . . Neither of them know. They don't know right now. They'll never know."

Conrad is furious, but tries to hold his anger in. "They're not like *your* parents. They don't have to have everything spelled out that way. These aren't people who lip-read and count on their fingers. They don't hunt animals with guns and skin them alive!"

"I can't believe this," Dale says. "You just don't have the guts to tell them and you can't even admit it."

"It's understood," Conrad says coldly.

Dale looks at him for a long moment. "No wonder you're so uptight. Jesus! Look, I'm saying I understand, having met them, why you're the way you are. I forgive them for screwing you up, okay? That's generous of me. Think how much easier life would be for me if you weren't that way."

"Thanks a lot," Conrad says wryly, but feels wounded because so much of this sounds true.

"They're like little dolls," Dale goes on. "I think that's why Ludwig has that authoritarian streak, actually. Napoleon was a little guy too. They can't swagger, so they have to diminish people verbally."

"My mother's small."

"It doesn't count with women. They can be one inch high. That's considered charming. But they must have felt weird going places with you, this giant son."

"*I* felt weird," Conrad says. The tension is disappearing.

Dale gets up and embraces him. "My parents are weird too," he says. "Everyone's parents are weird."

"Not like this," Conrad says. He knows they will make love,

that the afternoon will dissolve into something good. In his mind his parents go back into their tiny carved wooden house.

"Worse," Dale says, caressing him. "Wait till you meet George. . . . You're in for a real treat."

When his father dies six months later, he wonders if he should have been more open. But there was so much that he and his father never talked about. He wonders if his father ever told his mother much about his own life before meeting her. Yet evidently she accepted that. He flies home for the funeral.

It feels strange, being home, living in the same apartment where he grew up, where nothing has been moved or altered in over thirty years. From a practical standpoint his mother should move to a smaller apartment, but Conrad is glad she doesn't want to.

"I don't think I could make a change at this point," she says gently one evening when the guests have gone. "This is my home."

"You won't be too lonely?" he asks. Of course, he is going to continue living in Paris, and of course she is going to continue living in New York.

"As long as my eyesight holds up," she says. "I have my friends, I can walk in the park. I don't want to marry again, I don't think."

Conrad is startled. It had never occurred to him that she would marry again, that she even thought of this as an option. Marry who? Aren't all the men her age dead?

"Serge was very sweet to think of it," she says. "Now that Helga is dead—his sister died last year, did you know?—I think he's lonely and of course I love him, he's a lovely man; but I don't think it would be for the best. We can go to concerts together, plays. . . ."

Conrad is stunned. "I guess I . . . always assumed he was gay," he says.

"Serge?" His mother's blue eyes widen. "What made you think that?"

Conrad shrugs.

"He was very attached to Helga, but he had his women friends—usually married, of course, so there wouldn't be any fuss about his having to marry them."

Is she saying that *she* was one of these women friends? Conrad doesn't want to ask or even to know, but his mother smiles.

"He's very charming, Serge. Women like him. . . . But I think men like that can be a little bit spoiled, don't you?"

"I guess," Conrad says.

"I used to worry that you would become spoiled," Lotte says. "But you have a fine character, and that has prevented it."

Conrad touches his hair, which is turning gray. "I'm not so great-looking anymore," he says ironically.

"Yes, you are," she says. "Because you have suffered, and one sees that in your eyes. You suffered, but you came through."

Conrad looks out the window. It's gray and bleak outside, but inside there's a feeling of warmth and charm in the apartment, as there always was. At this particular moment he feels he could accept anything—that his mother had lovers, that Serge was one of them. He has a fleeting sense of his mother as a person who could have led a different life, had other children, become an actress, returned to Vienna after the war. Other people seem so fixed in their identities, it's hard to think they had choices. His parents seemed so married, despite their differences in personality, that he finds it impossible to think of the life—perhaps happier? more relaxed?—that his mother could have had with another man.

He helps his mother with the obituary for the *New York Times*. Evidently Ludwig wrote a version he wanted to be used, but it has to be brought up to date, things have to be altered. When they finally finish with it, Lotte seems pleased. Conrad thinks how, in a way, all he knows of his father is contained in this two-paragraph statement. A few facts, a few publications. What did he feel about his life? Did he consider it a success? Going over his father's papers, Conrad half hoped he might find some old love letters, some private diary, something where he revealed what he felt about Conrad, but there was nothing. He kept a diary or journal many years back, but it was concerned exclusively with his work and took note of the weather each day.

Although his mother doesn't seem to notice he is gay, Conrad feels that everyone else in New York does. He hasn't been back for this long—several weeks—in years and probably he didn't notice before. What about him could be different? He thinks he dresses and looks the same. Does he look at men more closely in the street? He is trying not to, but enough men approach him so that he is aware something is different. He doesn't have sex with anyone. He isn't sure if it's living at home with his mother—not just the literal fact that he couldn't bring someone back there. It's more that in New York he is a different person. This is the city of his youth, and while here he becomes that person again. That person would not have picked people up in the street. Not that he does it in Paris either. He tried it briefly and it didn't work. He is ready to believe it's his fault, Ludwig's legacy, as it were, though inwardly he believes he is still not a casual person. Dale is, according to the verbal agreement they have, entitled to do what he wants and Conrad knows he sees other men sometimes, but—is this strange of him?—it doesn't make him jealous. An affair in any complex sense would. A pickup, no matter how good the sex, he feels he can accept. Once or twice Dale tried to goad him into being jealous, and he got angry and it ceased. He is willing, even, to see his lack of jealousy as his own problem, holding everything in. But he's almost forty; too late to change that.

On impulse he calls Jay's parents. He knows Jay is living in San Francisco, but he feels like finding out more than he's been able to from Jay's occasional postcards and brief letters. Always, though it seems they have lost touch to some extent, Conrad thinks of Jay as his best friend. He wouldn't even tell Dale that, because he means it in a way that doesn't totally make sense to him. Maybe it's that at the age they were really close—in their teens and early twenties—Conrad felt he was vulnerable in a way he isn't anymore. He is relieved not to be. For him that kind of vulnerability is too painful. But he connects Jay with something about himself that he mourns, without really wanting it back.

A woman's voice answers.

"Mrs. Aronson?" Conrad says. "This is Conrad Zweifach. Jay and I were friends in college. I was just—"

"Oh Con, hi. This is Marlene," the other voice breaks in. "I'm just over for a visit. This is such a funny coincidence. Jay just called. Are you in town for long?"

"Just another week. My—my father died."

"Oh, I'm sorry. Ours did too, last year. Ma's still at home, but she has a nurse come in and check on her. How's *your* mother?"

"She's very well."

Marlene's voice is startlingly like Jay's in its intonations and rhythms.

"Why don't you come on down? I can't stay on the phone, but I'd love to see you, catch up. . . . Are you living in Paris still?"

Conrad agrees to come down for coffee later that afternoon. He wishes Jay were there, but he has a sudden feeling of nostalgia, wanting to be in Jay's parents' apartment again. Like his own parents, the Aronsons never moved. It's the same brownstone on Barrow Street, but the surrounding neighborhood is much more elegant now than in the sixties: a children's clothing store, a small French restaurant, an Italian bakery.

He never knew Marlene well, except as a temperamental older sister who bossed Jay around and made life miserable for him. He isn't even sure he knows what her profession is or whether she's married.

The woman who opens the door is small, like Jay, with short curly red-brown hair and a bright purple jumpsuit. With her skinniness and big eyes, her slightly frenetic quality, she looks like an actress or dancer. "Con? Hi, how terrific you could come down! I'm just getting Ma settled. Helen, the nurse, will take over soon and we can go out for coffee. Would you come in and say hello to her?"

Conrad is led into a stuffy bedroom where an elderly, stout, gray-haired woman is half sitting, half lying in bed. He is shocked. She looks not only completely unlike the woman he remembers as Jay's mother, but about twenty years older than his own mother. She stares at him uncomprehendingly.

"Ma, this is Conrad, Jay's friend. Remember I told you he might stop down? He's in New York, visiting." Marlene talks brightly and cheerfully.

The elderly woman frowns. "I'm not sure," she says. "My son is in San Francisco. You knew him?"

"They were best friends," Marlene says. "Con's father just died. He was a lawyer. They were from Germany. Lotte and Ludwig."

Mrs. Aronson smiles helplessly. "I don't remember." Then she adds, "Thank you for coming."

The nurse arrives. Marlene talks to her briefly, and then takes a sheepskin coat from the closet. "There's a place right around the corner," she says.

"I don't think she knew who I was," Conrad says as they walk out onto the street. There's a biting wind.

"Well, some days are better than others. Since Pa died, she's gone downhill pretty quickly. . . . Your mother is okay, you say?"

"Amazingly well." Conrad feels almost guilty when he thinks of his own elegant, perceptive, alert mother.

"It's all physical," Marlene says. Her coat has a hood that almost conceals her face. "Something just snaps, or doesn't, and once it starts, there's not much you can do."

They find a small table at the back of the coffee shop. Marlene keeps her coat on, shivering. Close up, Conrad sees she looks older, more tired. "How's Jay?" he asks. "He doesn't write much so I—"

"Oh, he never writes," Marlene says. "He's impossible. He's fine, really. He teaches now, did you know? He left journalism. Says he wants to get married again, but the proof of the pudding is in the eating, and I think he's still basically just fucking around. No great romances. Maybe I've made up for him. I just left Mel, my third husband, last month."

Conrad stirs his espresso. "I didn't know you were married . . . again," he adds, though he isn't sure he knew she was ever married.

"Oh yeah. . . . The kids—my daughters—are from Ira. I have two, two teen-agers. Mel had two also, joint custody. All the usual confusion. At least we didn't have any together! No, it's pretty amicable, as these things go. . . . I think Jay may have the right idea. Just because you have a yen for someone, why make it legal? Why live with them? I guess, despite seeing myself as a rebel, I've just been your garden-variety middle-class Jewish girl. How about you?"

"I've never married," Conrad says. Her staccato conversation is so New York that its rhythms have an unfamiliar ring to him.

"Do you have a lover? I guess I always assumed you were gay." Marlene reaches for some cakes that the waiter has placed in the center of the table.

Conrad is taken aback. Always? How could Marlene, whom he hardly remembers, have "assumed" that? Did Jay tell her?

"I do have a lover," he says. "He's American." He tells her about the gallery, about Dale's background. Then, hesitating, he says, "When you say you always knew, do you mean you knew when Jay and I were in college?"

Marlene looks embarrassed. "Well, yeah, I'm sorry, was I not supposed to know? Jay never mentioned it. Maybe because a lot of my friends were, I just took it for granted."

Conrad smiles. "It's taken me a lot longer to take it for granted. I'm not sure I do, even now."

Marlene's face has become flushed and younger-looking. She takes off her coat. "I was bi for a while," she says. "Do you ever try that? I figured—this was right after Ira made off with this cutie pie of three and a half, and I thought: God, who needs men? I've always had close women friends and I thought: Well, I'll add sex and everything'll be perfect. . . . Only it wasn't." She laughs. "Have you ever made it with women? Sorry if I shouldn't be asking. Feel free not to answer."

"I used to have occasional girl friends," Conrad says, "through my twenties, but they were just . . . It wasn't what you describe. They were women who I was fond of. But there was no—"

"Passion?" Marlene finishes for him. She dumps three packets of sugar into her cappuccino.

"Maybe that's the word. . . . Or maybe there was passion on their side, but I always felt I was a sham."

He wishes he were having this conversation with Jay, though he knows he never could, even if Jay were there. He likes Marlene up to a point, but he knows he'll probably never see her again. Is he hoping she'll pass this information on to Jay? Is it a way of telling him indirectly?

"You can't force it," Marlene says. "I still think men are impossible, but two weeks without one and I'm climbing the walls. I don't mean just sex. I mean, maybe I need their rough edges, their thickheadedness to make me see who I am. . . . With Angela— my friend, lover, or what have you—it was too smooth, maybe; like you said, a sham."

"Did your parents know?" Conrad asks. The eternal question.

Marlene laughs. Her laugh reminds him of Xenia, the way it booms out so that people at adjoining tables turn around. "They would have died! They're not sophisticated like your parents, Con. Those things weren't done. You shot people like us. We were a menace to society. When I was in my teen-age rebel phase, I brought home people you wouldn't believe—transvestites, you name it— and Ma just thought that was the way people in the arts dressed. 'Your arty friends,' she used to call them. . . . At least they had Jay. He was always the good little boy. Only now—typical!—the good little boy lives conveniently three thousand miles away and *I'm* the one who comes over once a week to check on Ma. But what the heck. We all make our choices. I don't regret mine."

Conrad never thought of Jay as "the good little boy." "You think Jay won't remarry?" he asks. "I always thought he would."

Marlene shrugs. "I always thought he was carrying a torch for Xenia . . . for years. But, look, as a man he can make his mind up at sixty and there'll still be tons of females waiting eagerly. He's not exactly sitting home putting stamps in his album. But he never lives with them."

"One-night stands?" Conrad wishes he weren't so pleased to hear all this.

"Not really. . . . Oh sure, he did that for a while, I guess. No, I think he sees various women more or less steadily, but there's always a reason it can't get serious. Like they're married or whatever. He wants limits. I never wanted limits! We're opposites in that way. Maybe he's more of a realist. . . . Listen, call him. He'd love to hear from you. He still talks about you a lot. He admired you so much, Con! He still does. Call him while you're in this country."

"I don't have anything to say, exactly," Conrad says.

He waits for an evening when his mother goes out to dinner with some friends. Then he calls Jay's number. For some reason his heart is thumping rapidly. Out of what? Fear? Excitement?

Jay says, "Hello?"

"Jay? Hi, it's Con. . . . I'm in New York and I ran into your sister the other day. She . . . suggested I call you."

There's a slight pause. Conrad's heart sinks. Jay is wishing he hadn't called.

"Is this a bad time to have called?"

"It's not that good." Jay lowers his voice. "Someone's here. . . . Can I call you back?"

"Sure, I'll be in all evening."

For the rest of the evening Conrad tries to read, watches some TV, but feels bored and then angry. He called Jay at seven. It's now eleven. Finally, at 11:10, Jay calls back.

"Sorry about that," he says in his more familiar voice.

"A girl?"

"If they're over fourteen, they're women," Jay says. "You've been out of the country too long. Hasn't feminism hit Paris yet?"

"Not as much as here," Conrad says.

"Anyway, she went happily home to her husband and kiddies, so I'm as free as a bird."

"Who is 'she'?"

"Someone," Jay says. After a second, he changes the subject. "So, how are things in Paris? I may come over there in a few months. I was thinking of writing you. Could you put me up for a few days?"

"Sure," Conrad says. Of course, he should at this point mention Dale, but Jay's cursory "someone" has taken away any desire to confide. "I'd love to see you again."

"Did Marlene lunge at you?" Jay asks. "She always thought you were, as she put it, impossibly gorgeous."

"I guess my appeal has dimmed with age," Conrad says. "We had a nice talk, though."

"You heard all about Emery, Ira, and Mel, I trust?"

"Who's Emery?"

"The first one. That was so long ago, she's probably forgotten. Oh listen, Marlene's okay. She's been a good mother. She's good with Ma."

"I'm living with a friend in Paris. He'll be there. I just thought you should know."

"Oh sure, no problem, as long as you don't mind." Jay says this so easily that Conrad doesn't know if it means that, like Marlene, he's always known Conrad is gay, or still doesn't know.

After Conrad hangs up, he goes into the living room and finds his mother and Serge sipping Grand Marnier and listening to a Schubert trio.

"Now listen to the difference," Serge says. "You have to have played together as a group for *years* to get that kind of tone."

"I suppose you're right," Lotte says. "I'm not that musical. I just can't tell the difference."

"You sing so beautifully," Serge says. "Of course you're musical!"

Conrad tells them about Marlene and Mrs. Aronson. "I'm not sure she recognized me," he says.

"Goodness." Lotte's face darkens. "She can't be much older than I am, can she? Or younger, perhaps."

Serge pats her hand comfortingly. "You'll never be like that, Lottishka."

"I think that's the most frightening thing of all," Lotte says, "losing one's mind that way gradually, imperceptibly. Worse than losing one's looks, one's health. . . ."

"How about gaining?" Serge says with a smile. "Gaining wisdom, maturity, insight, seeing things more clearly than when one was a mere lad like this fellow here."

His intonations are startlingly like Ludwig's. Were they always? Conrad remembers how, when he was little, his parents always called him, or any other child, a "little chap," an expression they'd picked up in England, where they'd lived two years before coming to America. They used it for girls as well as boys.

"I don't see things very clearly," Conrad says. "I feel as though things get less clear the older I get."

Serge sips his Grand Marnier. "Ah, yes, true, but suddenly you will find the fuzziness vanishes. And you know when that happens? When you stop trying to figure it all out and make sense of it. When you just accept."

"I've never tried to make sense of it," Lotte says.

Serge again touches her hand. "That's your secret, dear."

Conrad is not sure how he feels about this. It seems to him that Serge has not only taken his father's place, he has become his father. The same little compliments, tiny gestures of affection; the same Schubert trios, sips of Grand Marnier. Of course, basically he is glad. How much easier to go back to Paris, knowing he isn't leaving his mother alone, especially at her age. But despite this, it is a little disquieting how suddenly and perfectly Serge has stepped into this role, as though he had been dress-rehearsing for it all his life.

Conrad has never thought of himself as perceptive about people. But he thinks later: It's the little things one notices, the tiny gestures, that open the door to sudden revelations.

The next show he is planning for the gallery is a photography show. He does photography shows sometimes, and this photographer, Gideon Kimmer, an Israeli who now lives in the south of France, is amazingly good. He does abstracts mainly: doorways, aerial views, almost like Mondrian in their subdued absence of color and severe, unusual angles. You can always tell what he is photographing, but the object becomes, through a deliberate lack of perspective, both what it is and something else. Dale said he would help set up the show. He's good at that. Conrad trusts his judgment implicitly—more than his own, in fact. He feels that he himself has an affinity for the business side of the gallery, for knowing what he wants to exhibit, but Dale has a better sense of how to present the work, how to display it for maximum effect.

They are walking around the gallery, the three of them, so that Conrad can get an overall feel of how it looks, when Gideon says, "You had a successful trip?" and, seemingly unconsciously, touches Dale's shoulder as they pause in front of a large gray photo of the edge of a flight of stairs. It is not so much the touch as the way Dale flinches guiltily and steps several feet backward. Conrad glances at him questioningly. Dale is staring too fixedly at another photograph.

"Yes, it was successful," Conrad says coldly.

After Gideon leaves, Conrad sits down at his desk and starts opening the mail that has been marked "important." Dale walks in with his hands up.

"Can I plea-bargain?" he says, with the rueful smile Conrad usually finds charming.

"There's nothing to say," Conrad says flatly. "I hope it was mutually enjoyable."

"No, it was a drag," Dale says with a half smile. "Hey, Con, be human for a couple of seconds, okay?"

Conrad hates being this angry. He knows he doesn't know how to express it, "let it out," and it seems demeaning to want to kill someone over something this trifling. But he also hates Dale for knowing him well enough to pick up on small expressions. Otherwise he could pretend he was feeling nothing. "I don't know how," he says, opening a letter.

"Sure you do. It's easy." Dale comes closer. His voice softens. "Probably I shouldn't have because he's connected with the gallery. I know that's one of the rules. But you were away the better part of a month, and—"

"The better part of a month?" Conrad mimics savagely. "People have been faithful to each other for years . . . and I'm away 'the better part of one month.' . . ."

Dale is still trying to joke about it. "Look, sometimes you're hard to take. You know that, right? I love you, but you can be hard to take. Sometimes I feel like having fun. . . . Like your mother said. Just plain simple fun. Not love. Just fun. . . . Does that make me a monster?"

"Of course not." Conrad opens another letter. He tries to keep his hands from trembling. "Have as much 'fun' as you want. . . . Is this continuing now that I'm back, or have you satisfied that urge for the moment?"

"God, I hate it when you're like this!" Dale says. "I forgive you for being the way you are. . . . Why can't you forgive me for being the way I am?"

"What have *I* done that needs forgiveness?" Conrad says dryly.

"Okay, maybe 'forgiveness' is the wrong word. But do you think you're fun to live with? Is it incomprehensible to you that you would get on a lot of people's nerves a lot of the time?"

"That's outside the issue of morality," Conrad says. He has a sudden horrible thought that, now that his father is dead, he has swallowed him, he has become his father.

Dale rolls his eyes. "Jesus, donnez-moi un break, will you? Judge, jury . . ." he acts as though the photos are alive, watching them. "What do you say? Should I be punished or do I deserve the fucking Nobel prize for living with this guy and trying to find all his hangups charming?"

"You can live anywhere and with whomever you want," Conrad says.

"Well, he's gone back to get his stuff."

"What?"

Dale hesitates. "He's been staying at our place. He didn't have a place to stay. Now he's found a friend's place, and—"

"He's been staying at *my* apartment?"

"Con, you're showing the guy's work in your gallery. *You* think he's a genius, not me. I think his stuff is sterile, empty shit, frankly. So why can't he stay at your apartment?"

"I want him gone by noon," Conrad says. He tries to annihilate Dale with his expression.

"He's probably gone already," Dale says. He is flushed and finally openly angry. "And I'll be gone sooner than that so don't worry." He wheels out of the gallery, slamming the door.

Conrad has always been glad that he is thin and has low blood pressure. He feels he is precisely the type who could acquire high blood pressure, but for whatever reason he doesn't have it. What he does have at moments like this is a feeling that his heart is flipping around like an acrobat on speed. How much of this kind of foolery can a heart take and not give way? The next day he goes to the hospital to have his heart thoroughly tested. He comes through with flying colors. "It's stress," the doctor informs him. "Nothing to worry about on the physical level."

And on the psychological level? He no longer believes in psychiatry, and he's never cared about meditation or Eastern religions. He had thought, ever since his last horrible depression, that he had found both the cause and the solution. The cause was trying to deny his homosexuality. The cure would be accepting it, finding a permanent partner, a friend and lover who would—how absurd these words sound now!—love him for what he was. Was that so ridiculous a goal? Don't many people attain it every day with members of their own sex, the opposite sex? Conrad feels he has tried everything—women, men, many partners, one. And the idea of settling, at not yet forty, into a dessicated celibacy enrages him. Find someone else. There are other people.

But it seemed so close to perfect, so close to what he wanted. No, more than that, it seemed what he did want. Why should he care about this idiot photographer who, he feels even now, is more talented than Dale realizes, maybe a major talent? "You were away the better part of a month." Maybe a month seemed more like a year. Maybe Conrad has played "the father" so much that he's forced Dale to act the child. If he had set no rules? But that would be dishonest. He felt allowing an occasional fling was stretching his own sense of morality as far as it would go. It wasn't infinitely stretchable.

His apartment seems huge, empty, absurdly neat. He eats out every night. A month after his return to Paris, a letter comes from Jay saying he will be in Paris in a few weeks and hopes it will still be all right to stay at Conrad's apartment. Of course, it's all right. Conrad writes back that he's really looking forward to it, but he isn't. He's dreading it. He feels as though in his mind he's been staging this meeting with Jay for years. And with Dale there it might have been awkward, but it would also have been what Conrad wanted. He wanted to show Jay that he had finally settled down, had a permanent lover, was successful at his work. Now there's nothing to show, only that nothing has changed, that he's still searching, confused, a mess. He thinks of giving an excuse, saying he won't be in Paris at that time. But he still wants to see Jay.

Gideon's show opens, but Dale doesn't come to the opening. Gideon, of course, arrives with many friends, but Conrad knows that Dale's nonappearance means nothing. Dale was too ashamed to come? Or Gideon told him not to?

Conrad takes Jay to the gallery the day he arrives to show him what it's like. Maybe it's jet lag, but Jay keeps yawning and finally confesses he can't understand why this is supposed to be art.

"It's so abstract," he says, "so bleak. . . ."

"That's the point," Conrad says, annoyed. Jay seems very American to him—a certain way he has of talking, of standing, a certain abruptness. He looks older, his hair is thinner, but he is still wiry, quick, his eyes observant, often melancholy. It is hard for Conrad to know how to act with Jay. Despite all the years they've been friends, their lives have diverged so sharply that the friendship seems more an idea than a reality. Conrad finds himself looking at the calendar, wishing Jay were staying less than a week.

Despite his inner feelings, he tries to be the perfect host. The first night he takes Jay to an excellent restaurant and on the second cooks a delicious meal at home.

Jay stays in the kitchen watching him. "I usually just open a can of hash," he says. "Do you do this all the time?"

"I like to cook," Conrad says. "It's hard to live in Paris without some of that rubbing off."

Jay picks up a shallot and rolls it along the counter. "Wasn't some guy living here with you?" he asks. "I thought you said—"

"Oh, right, Dale." Conrad busies himself with watching the butter melt in the copper pan. "He used to. He . . . doesn't anymore."

One thing about Jay hasn't changed. He may not like to cook, but he loves food and throughout dinner exclaims constantly, "God, this is fantastic! What a meal!" When Conrad brings out the Grand Marnier soufflé, he even makes that time-honored joke, "You'd make someone a great wife."

Conrad hesitates. "Do you ever think of getting married again?"

"Are you proposing?" Jay says, grinning.

"I don't think I'm the marriageable type," Conrad says.

"I want kids," Jay says. "That's always been something that—"

"But are you seeing anyone special?"

Jay nods. "It's a bit complicated."

"What's the complication?"

Jay finishes his wine. "She's black. . . . And she's been married before. She has two kids, fifteen and seventeen."

"Which is the complication?" Conrad asks, feeling absurdly disappointed.

"I suppose everything. If there was only one problem, I'd feel confident that love would overcome, but it's all so . . . Her first husband was white too. I don't think that matters so much to her *or* to the kids. But I just wonder how much of a father you can be to someone else's kids."

"Would she want some with you?"

"Maybe. We've talked about it. . . . She's a year older than me, thirty-seven, so we wouldn't have a lot of time." Jay touches the candle in front of him, pressing the soft wax. "We've broken up and stayed apart for a year or two. When I first met her, she was still married. It's just—" He looks up at Conrad. "We seem to mesh in a way. I can't describe it exactly. She loves me the way I've always wanted someone to. We don't fight. It isn't like with

Xenia—all storms and making up and the next day chaos again. Maybe I've changed, or maybe it's just that with some people . . . Have you ever felt that?"

"Met anyone with whom I've had that kind of rapport?"

Jay nods.

Without allowing himself to wait long enough to censor the reply, Conrad says, "Dale. . . . He and I were together two years."

"Maybe he'll come back," Jay says. "Do you want him to?"

Conrad nods. "He can be a pain, but, yeah, I would like him back."

"Tell him."

Conrad tries to smile. "How about pride?"

"Not worth much."

"Morality? Fidelity?"

Jay shrugs. "I've cheated. . . . I used to want to kill Allegra when she'd do it with her husband, and she'd say, 'We're married,' and I'd say, 'I don't give a fuck.' I was really childish. I'm very jealous. . . . But I'm not proud of it. It has nothing to do with morality."

"So, you're not planning to be faithful to her if you marry?"

"Sure I am. . . . But I won't leave her if I'm not and I won't leave if she isn't faithful to me. What I mean is, life is too short."

Conrad explodes. "I hate that expression! Life is too short to get out of bed in the morning! It's such an excuse! Why can't people restrain themselves? We all have urges, but why not hold back?"

"I don't want to live in a straitjacket, that's why. Fidelity can be deadly. If it's done of free will, fine."

Conrad wonders if Jay and Dale would have gotten along. "Dale is a little like you," he says. "Not in any specific way, but he's American. . . ."

Jay is silent, looking at the candle. "I never knew you were gay."

"Marlene says she always knew."

"You always seemed so . . . in control," Jay says. "God, I envied that. I still do."

Jay is so calmly accepting, so unruffled by what Conrad was certain would be a major, earth-shaking disclosure that he's almost disappointed. Does this mean that they could have had this conversation years earlier, that all his anxieties about Jay's possible reaction were pointless? Dale would appreciate the irony of this; Conrad isn't sure he can, quite yet.

Suddenly the stiffness and awkwardness he felt earlier with Jay has vanished. They are back in college again, with that inexplicable closeness he's never felt with anyone else. Maybe once sex enters in, it changes something. "Marry her," he says.

Jay looks startled. He's been staring off into the dark room, a brooding expression on his face. "What?"

"Allegra. Is that her name? Marry her. . . . I don't think one gets that more than once, what we were talking about, that kind of closeness."

"Why not?" Jay asks.

"I don't know. . . . I've just found it to be rare."

"How many people have you had sex with?"

"Ten, fifteen, maybe. . . . I wasn't good at one-night stands."

"I was." Jay grins. "I'm not boasting. It's just I really did enjoy some of them, maybe a third. But I would think it would be easier with men. There wouldn't be that need for explanations in the morning."

Conrad laughs. "*I* was the one who wanted explanations."

"I don't regret it," Jay says. "I needed to get it out of my system. I felt demoralized after my marriage to Xenia broke up. We didn't have what I have with Allegra, but when things were good, they were so good! It was electrical, like we were inside each other's minds. Only it never lasted. I felt like she was married to her father, and that whole New York psychiatric scene made me so sick."

"Don't you believe in it?" Conrad wonders if Jay knows about his having been in the hospital.

"Maybe it works sometimes. But no more than swallowing six green candies every morning. No, I think what upset me the most was we'd go to parties and meet these supposed luminaries and they were all irascible, egocentric little men who treated their wives like shit and fucked anything that moved, including their patients. It seemed such a farce! And Xenia was willing to spend her life trying to fit into that world. Probably she's married one of them and they sit around analyzing their sex life. Probably she's as happy as a clam." He sounds bitter by the end of this tirade.

Conrad listens to Jay's outburst with some relief. He was afraid Jay had found inner peace and true love. Now he seems like the old Jay, flying off the handle, exaggerating, too intense. "I think you should have a family," he says. "I think you'd be a good father."

Jay looks touched. "Yeah? Do you? I wonder. . . . I really would like that. Isn't that something you . . ."

Conrad shakes his head. "If you lived in Paris, I'd love to get to know your kids, play uncle. That's about all. I like quiet and order. Maybe if they could be born at sixteen . . . or twenty."

They start getting ready for bed. "You can use the bathroom first," Conrad says. He doesn't think he is attracted to Jay, but two months of being alone, the release of being able to talk intimately with someone translates into something akin to desire. It makes him acutely uncomfortable. When Jay comes out of the bathroom Conrad glances at him guiltily and says, "See you in the morning."

As he lies in bed, trying to fall asleep, fantasies of Jay mingle with ones of Dale. He knows it's Dale he's missing and that Jay, just in a few small ways, reminds him of Dale—his unabashed openness, his humor. There's more of the observer in Jay, the quiet, thoughtful way he listens. Dale is more impulsive, even childish at times. But the thought of Jay about to marry a woman he loves casts a shadow over Conrad's soul. He wants it because he loves Jay and wants him to be happy. But he wishes Jay were alone, like him, that nothing had quite worked, that the future looked bleak and uncertain. He hates self-pity and simply watches his own, monitors it.

Three months later a photo arrives from America. Jay and Allegra are getting married. Conrad studies the photo. Allegra *is* beautiful—almost as tall as Jay, slim, perfect posture, a little like a dancer, with dark hair pulled back in a severe style, a warm smile. Her kids are standing awkwardly to one side, a plump curly-haired daughter and a handsome, older-looking son, who resembles her. Now baby announcements will come thick and fast. She's almost forty. They won't wait long. Conrad feels the ark moving off to sea. He hates the solitude of his apartment, hates even the ease with which he's adapted to it, the solitary meals, bringing a book to his favorite restaurant. He sees himself from the outside, distinguished, graying, well dressed, impenetrable. Once a German tourist started speaking to him in German and he was horrified. Ludwig's legacy again? He thought he looked like a Parisien. His blond hair?

One evening Dale rings the bell. Conrad has just returned from dinner. He is both calm and unprepared. His heart does its familiar jumps and turns, rolls through hoops.

"Can I come in?" Dale asks.

"Sure. . . . How've you been?"

"Rotten. . . . So have you. You look lousy. Why do you keep eating at Chez Albert?"

Conrad flushes. "How do you know?"

"I've been following you. You never noticed?"

Conrad shakes his head. "Why?"

Dale smiles. "Look, I'm not good at this. Should I come back or not? If you want me to, I will. I'm not different. I'll probably still do stupid, irritating things. . . . I don't want to change. I don't want to hurt you, but I don't want to change. Is that acceptable?"

There are many answers to that, but Conrad just says, "Yes." He walks over and puts his arms around Dale, who is trembling.

"I've missed you ridiculously," Dale says.

"Me too."

In bed, after they make love, Dale says, "I waited for you to make the first move, and then I said to myself: He can't. That's his problem. I knew you'd die of misery and grief and loneliness, but you'd never make the first move. . . . How can you *be* like that?"

Conrad sighs. In his mind he takes a photo of himself and Dale intertwined, and sends it to Jay. He feels so happy, the room actually looks different to him. But it's a calm kind of happiness. "Maybe it's because I'm an only child," he says, half joking.

"Donnez-moi un break," says Dale.

They decide to vacation in Egypt in the fall. Neither Dale nor Conrad has ever been to the Middle East. They book a two-week trip with a travel agent. It isn't until they are in Alexandria that Conrad thinks of Susan. Despite his gratitude to her for having gotten him out of the hospital, she's someone who fades from his mind when she is out of sight. There's something so quiet and elusive about her. He can't even remember exactly what she looks like. But since they have a free afternoon, he looks her up in the phone book and finds her number.

"An old girl friend?" Dale teases.

"Never. . . . If you see her, you'll understand."

He's never told Dale about the hospital. He's mentioned that there were times in his life when he was depressed and saw a psychiatrist, but he thinks the rest would seem too strange to someone brought up the way Dale was.

Susan is away. Someone answers her phone and says she is on a trip near the Fayum taking photographs. It's a man's voice, but who is it? A lover? A husband? Susan can't have gotten married. Conrad finds the idea peculiar, but realizes he doesn't know Susan that well. When Xenia was around, Susan was always so quiet. Xenia's shadow, Jay used to call her. They decide to visit her there.

He and Dale find her in a thicket of rushes. She's hidden behind some rocks and is standing so motionless that she looks like a statue. Her pale red-blond hair is loose, she's wearing faded jeans, a white shirt.

"Susan?" Conrad calls softly, not wanting to disturb her, she seems so intense.

Her eyes light up with undisguised delight. "Con! . . . Wait just a sec. Stay where you are, okay?"

He and Dale stay back and watch as a large white bird alights on a nearby tree. Then Susan moves away from her equipment and runs toward them. She is tanned, healthier-looking than when he saw her in New York; but her voice still has that tentative quality.

"This is my friend, Dale," Conrad says. He explains how he tried to reach her in Alexandria. "Someone answered and told us where you were. I wasn't sure if you were still living there."

"I'm going home," Susan says, happily. "Finally! I went back for some job interviews and I got accepted as a photographer for the San Diego Zoo. I figure California can't be more alien than this has been."

"How long have you lived here?" Dale asks.

Susan thinks. "Twelve years. . . . God, that *is* a long time, isn't it? I came over just for a month's stay and that became two months and then a year."

"Couldn't you have stayed permanently?" Conrad asks.

"I don't think I belong here," Susan says. "I love the land and the animals and . . . a few people, but it's a foreign country. Really foreign. I've never fit in. They don't have single women here, except widows. They never knew what to make of me."

Conrad hesitates. The glaring sun is over her shoulder, so that it's hard to look directly at her. He didn't bring sunglasses; Dale did.

"I thought perhaps the man who answered . . ."

"He's a friend," Susan says in her quick, shy way.

"An Egyptian?"

"No. . . . an American who settled here, but . . . well. . . . Can you wait? I'll gather my stuff up and we can go for a drink somewhere. I haven't had lunch. You have to stay here for hours if you want to catch them."

They help her with her equipment and load it into the back of her car.

"I'd like to see your photos," Conrad says. "Now that I have a gallery."

"I'll send you some slides." Susan grimaces. "I guess that's what returning to the States will mean, having to set up shows, be a professional. I sort of dread it."

He wonders if she's any good. "I'd love to see them."

Dale seems at ease with Susan, more than he usually is with women he hasn't met before. She still has an androgynous quality, unassertive, her pale blue eyes with their questioning expression.

"I didn't know you were living in Paris," Susan says. "Xenia's the only one I keep in touch with and I don't think she mentioned it."

"I haven't seen Xenia in years," Conrad says. "Is she okay?"

Susan hesitates. "I think she's fine. She never married—re-married, I mean."

"Jay did." He mentions Jay's visit.

"I always wished they would get back together," Susan says softly.

"Jay's the one you mentioned?" Dale asks. "The one from college?"

Conrad nods. Susan is gazing at him intently. Though he hasn't thought of it for years, he suddenly remembers that walk in the woods near the Cloisters, that terrible, furtive lovemaking.

"Have you been all right?" Susan asks tentatively.

Knowing she is referring to that time in his life, Conrad says, "Fine, yes, that's all . . . over."

"I worried about you for years," she goes on.

"I've always been grateful for what you did."

"You looked so frightened."

"Maybe it's just being young," Conrad says. "Everything seems so important, wanting answers."

There is a moment's pause.

Suddenly Dale says, "What are you both talking about? I don't get it."

"It's nothing," Conrad says quickly. He hates feeling so

ashamed. "I was once in a hospital and Susan visited me, helped me escape. . . ."

Dale stares at him. "What kind of hospital?"

"A mental hospital." Conrad is furious at Dale's denseness. "I was depressed, my parents had me locked up. Okay?"

Dale looks startled. "It's just . . . you never mentioned it."

"Why should I? Do you tell me everything that's ever happened to you?" Conrad hates his own tone, which is absurdly high-keyed. For the first time since it happened, Conrad feels acutely ashamed—not only of having been in the hospital, but of having made love to Susan, who he knew loved him in her quiet, strange way for so many years. Was he trying to buy her silence once he escaped? He has always thought of himself as essentially kind, thoughtful. And yet here is Susan, not very changed, having found a world into which she fits, a world of animals and nature. She has clearly forgiven him.

They don't discuss it for the rest of the trip. Both of them are caught up in traveling, which they love, and Conrad is relieved. He is always more frightened at glimpses of his own temper than of anyone else's, as though his surface calm is a deception and he could easily become childishly violent, screaming. He sees himself as a possible cartoon figure, turning bright red or purple, his eyes bulging, his heart finally going totally haywire.

One Saturday—a few weeks after their return to Paris—they go bicycle riding in the country. It's a perfect fall day, slightly cool, a faint sun. Conrad hates the extremes of both summer and winter. He loves bicycling along the quiet road, the thought that they can make love in some field, unseen by anyone. For some reason Dale hates making love out of doors. Conrad thought he would be at ease in nature, having grown up in the country; but he has a terror of someone appearing and seeing them. Also, he hates bugs of all kinds, even ants and beetles. Conrad loves seeing Dale act silly and nervous.

"I think bugs are fascinating," he says, teasing, plucking one off Dale's shoulder and holding it in the palm of his hand. "I could have become an entomologist, actually."

"Con, come on, throw it away. . . . You don't know. It could be deadly."

"It's a beetle."

"French beetles could be different."

Conrad tosses it into the field. He says, "Susan would like it here, the birds, the stillness."

For some reason—is he still angry about the beetle?—Dale sits up, naked except for the blanket that he wraps around his shoulders.

"Why were you such a fucker that day?"

"What?" At this moment that day seems truly far away to Conrad.

"So you were locked up? So what?"

"Have you ever been?"

"I was in jail once."

"For how long?"

"Two days."

"This was six months."

Dale hesitates. "Okay, so I bet it was lousy. I'm just saying—"

"You know nothing about what it was like," Conrad says coldly. He begins dressing. The sun is going down, it's becoming chilly. "What do you know about mental hospitals?"

"Nothing. . . . I'm just a half-wit from the Midwest, remember?"

"Don't pull that." Conrad looks at him. "It was a horrible experience. I don't want to think about it or talk about it, or—"

"What good does it do to pretend it never happened?"

"I didn't say that."

"You think I'm going to look down on you or something?" Dale touches Conrad's shoulder. "A lot of us go crazy and keep right on walking around. That's ninety percent of humanity, you know?"

"Not ninety percent," Conrad says, but is touched at the intent behind the exaggeration.

"Sure, maybe ninety-nine. . . . Where you grew up, people went to shrinks or, if they got out of hand, they got tossed in mental hospitals. Where I grew up, you stole cars, drank yourself sick, maybe beat up some guy in a bar. . . . What's the difference?"

Conrad smiles grimly. "Your way sounds better."

"Try it sometime," Dale says.

It's a time of day Conrad loves, just before twilight, a kind of soft, subdued sunlight.

"It was everything. . . . My parents coming to see me once a week, sitting there tensely, silently, hating me for not being the kid they thought they'd adopted, blaming the adoption agency for having landed them with someone weird, not even Jewish—"

"That was all in your head, probably. . . . Did they ever say that?"

"Parents don't have to say anything. I saw it in their eyes. Their disappointment, rage."

"So?"

"And the doctors, the endless tests. It was so incredibly humiliating. I've always done badly on IQ tests. That's one reason I had less of a choice for college than I should've. I can't count backwards from ten."

Dale smiles. "Too bad. It's fun. Whenever I have a spare moment, I count backwards from ten."

"The doctors told my parents I might have brain damage, though there wasn't any evidence. But they couldn't understand how I could do so badly otherwise. My father was petrified. I was so devastated. Brain-damaged!" Conrad turns away and lowers his head, closes his eyes. What had seemed far away, dealt with, suddenly looms up with scary intensity.

"But it wasn't *true!*" Dale says. "So why does it matter now?"

"It was as though it were true. . . . I felt maybe it *was* true."

Dale holds him. "Con, you know you're not brain-damaged."

Conrad looks down. "I haven't changed. They should've kept me locked up. I talked Susan into helping me escape because she had a crush on me, because she was so gentle, malleable. I got her involved."

"I'd have helped you escape, if I'd known you then."

"Would you?" Conrad looks into Dale's eyes, knowing the conversation doesn't mean anything. How can Dale know what he would have done in a situation he's never been in?

"Of course I would! Anyone would. . . . Those guys should be shot. If they were here right now, I'd kill them, for doing that to you."

"I wanted to kill them," Conrad admits. "That's why sometimes now, when I start to get angry, it scares me, as though if I let it out, I'll just go berserk."

"Con, you're a pussycat, I hate to tell you. . . . You're not going to kill anyone. Your parents were wrong. Your father was an uptight prick and your mother was too scared of him to say anything. I bet she wanted to get you out."

"Maybe." Sometimes, looking back, Conrad has thought that that could be true.

"For Susan it was probably one of the highlights of her life. She still thinks you're terrific."

"I was using her, trading on her feelings for me."

"I'm using you, you're using me. . . . There's nothing wrong with that."

"I shouldn't have had sex with her, though," Conrad says.

It's almost dark as they bicycle back, one behind the other. The avenue of trees arcs above them, stately, like the arcs in a cathedral. There's a smell of new grass, field flowers. Conrad feels emptied out, hollow. He wonders if you ever do tell anyone everything or even if it's necessary. If someone loves you, they know more than you can tell. Dale knew about the hospital in a way. He knew, but he also idealizes Conrad and so he'll never know how strong that feeling of worthlessness and self-hatred was. And Conrad is glad of that.

"Only if there's room," Conrad says. He's calling Jay long-distance because he and Dale will be in San Francisco to meet several artists for whom Conrad is arranging exhibits. Jay and Allegra have only been married for a few months. Won't it be an intrusion?

Jay insists it won't. They are still living in the house in which Allegra lived with her first husband. He's moved into Berkeley to be near the physics center where he does research.

"We have four bedrooms. Space is no problem," Jay insists.

If they were true honeymooners, Conrad might not even have thought of it. But Jay has said they've known each other several years, and her children evidently go back and forth between her husband's new house and their present one. Conrad feels indirectly responsible for Jay's marriage. He was the one who said, "Marry her." Perhaps if he hadn't, Jay would still be a bachelor, running back and forth between women, trying endlessly to make up his mind.

"Why don't I stay at a hotel and you stay with them?" Dale suggests.

"What sense does *that* make? I *want* you to meet Jay. That's part of the point."

"I don't like the sound of it. He has his little wifey, so you drag me out like, 'Look, I have one too.' "

"That's absurd. . . . You're a part of my life. Jay would've met you last summer, only he didn't."

"There's something uncomfortably pat about it," Dale says. "The two couples, everyone being terribly polite and accepting. I hate it already."

"Look, she's black. They must've had to do their share of feeling uncomfortable, apologetic—"

"Apologetic?" Dale leaps on the word, horrified.

"Not apologetic. She doesn't feel apologetic for being black any more than we do for being gay."

"I hate this kind of analogy, Con. . . . I hate the sound of this whole thing."

Conrad is annoyed. "Stay at a hotel, then."

"No, I'll come, but I want to know the rules. Do I go in the kitchen and talk about recipes with her while the two of you reminisce about old times?"

"Don't be a jerk. . . . You're making it into a production. Jay's my friend, period. Maybe she'll be a bitch or unpleasant or God knows what. I doubt it, but I have no idea."

"What if I hate him?" Dale goes on, his voice rising. "He's your best friend, quote unquote. What if I think *he's* a bigoted, narrow prick?"

"What if our plane explodes in midair? What if World War Three starts tomorrow? Come on, you can think whatever you want of Jay. Just act human, to the extent that's possible."

Dale rolls his eyes.

They live in a sprawling two-level house in the Berkeley Hills, cool, large eucalyptus trees shading everything, almost junglelike. Allegra is quiet, allowing Jay to do most of the talking. She seems ill at ease, stiff in her off-white dress. Conrad wonders if Jay and Allegra had a discussion similar to his and Dale's before they arrived.

One thing he is determined not to do: judge Dale's behavior. If he's quiet, fine. If he talks, fine. Jay is jokey, outgoing. Now that he sees them together, Conrad wonders why he thought Dale and Jay were alike. Jay has that verbal, Jewish, sometimes relentless manner, picking up on things everyone says. Dale seems shyer, younger. Conrad is aware of the ten years' difference between Dale and the rest of them. Dale's not even thirty yet, a baby.

Allegra's seventeen-year-old son, Peter, seems to like Dale. "I'm going to France this summer," he tells them at dinner. "I wish it could be Paris, but this group, they just place you somewhere. It could be anywhere."

"All of France is beautiful," Con says. It's impossible not to be struck by Peter's physical beauty, his lean body, high cheekbones.

"I want to go there to study," Peter says, "but these people don't think it's such a good idea." He shoots an amused, condescending glance at Allegra and Jay. There is a setup; Dale (twenty-eight) and Peter (seventeen) versus "the grown-ups," Allegra, Jay, and Conrad, all in their late thirties.

" 'These people' just think you should get a good, well-rounded education first," Allegra says dryly, helping Conrad to some fish and snow peas.

Peter laughs. "Well-rounded! Mom, no one is well-rounded anymore. That's from the sixties. You find what you want to do and you do it. What else is life all about? Right?" He looks at Dale for confirmation.

"It's great, knowing what you want so young," Dale says.

Conrad senses Dale is attracted to Peter and is trying desperately to conceal this from Conrad.

"But you can know and then change," Allegra says. "I was sure I wanted to be a ballet dancer until I was eighteen and I realized I didn't. So I went into philosophy. . . . How can you know at seventeen or sixteen?"

"*I* know," Peter says coolly. He has brown skin and closely cropped black hair, an American Indian look. "Some know, some don't."

"I didn't know anything at that age," Conrad says. "I just wanted to do what would make my parents happy."

"Me too," Jay says.

"But you had your writing," Conrad says. "You always knew you wanted to write."

"So, how come you don't do it?" Peter says. His manner is self-possessed to the point of arrogance.

Jay turns red. "I still write . . . sometimes."

"Your stories were wonderful," Conrad says, feeling sorry for him, understanding Jay isn't ready yet to be the stepfather of a contemptuous son.

"You never acknowledged receiving them." Jay holds his glass of wine, suspended.

"I should have. I didn't know what to say." Their eyes meet.

There's a pause. Peter's sister, Joan, who's been quiet until now, says shyly, "I write stories"

"Joanie's terrific," Jay says, relieved to get away from the topic of his own writing.

"I think your stories are good," Joan says to him. "I *love* your stories. You should send them out."

"They don't have endings," Jay says. His glance at her is affectionate, warm, with none of the combativeness he seems to have with Peter.

"That doesn't matter," Joan says earnestly. "I can write the endings for you. I'm good at endings."

Allegra is expecting a child. Conrad would not have noticed—she looks slim and wears a dress that conceals her waist—but after dinner she keeps yawning and finally explains the reason she is tired. Conrad glances at Jay, who is beaming.

"That's marvelous," Conrad says politely.

Allegra stretches. "I'm going to turn in, hon." When she moves, Conrad can see the years of ballet training, the graceful, effortless way she stoops to pick up a newspaper that has dropped on the floor. With her tilted, almond-shaped black eyes, she reminds him of Maria Tallchief.

The three men are left alone. Jay offers them brandy. Conrad accepts, but Dale says he'll just have bourbon. Conrad has the feeling Dale wants to be in Peter's room, getting stoned. Stop. No judgments. What Dale's feeling is his own business.

"It's going to be twins," Jay says. "We had amniocentesis, since Ali's in her late thirties."

"Father of four," Conrad says, joking but slightly horrified. He remembers Dale's remark: You'll both have your little wifey. He doesn't feel that, but has a sense that from now on he and Jay will never be that close, that Jay is becoming the kind of person Conrad shies away from instinctively: the doting, gregarious father showing photos of his kids.

"I like Allegra's children," Jay says, "but they're not mine, really. They see their father a lot. They accept me, but . . . It's different from raising your own, watching them grow. I don't know. Maybe it's just some primitive male thing of wanting to pass on one's genes."

"I don't want to pass on *my* genes," Dale says. His words are slightly slurred.

"I suppose not everyone . . ." Jay falters, as though "remembering" Dale and Conrad are gay.

"I've never even met my real parents," Conrad says. "It doesn't mean anything to me."

"I hate babies," Dale says. "We had to take in my aunt's two when she died, on top of my three younger sisters and brothers. I heard enough screaming to last me a lifetime."

"Maybe if they were born at sixteen," Conrad says, "when you can talk to them."

"Like Peter," Dale says. "He's terrific."

Conrad shoots him a warning glance.

Jay looks surprised. "You want Peter? God, I feel like killing him most of the time. He's so incredibly arrogant. We weren't like that, were we?"

"It's all show," Dale says. "It's cute. *I* was like that."

"If I say red, he says blue," Jay says. "I guess it's just testing me, maybe resentment at my making off with his mom, but it gets to be a real pain. . . . He has girls calling him every second. We finally had to get him a separate phone number—the line was always tied up."

"Does he like girls yet?" Dale asks.

Dale, Jesus. What's wrong with him?

"No one special," Jay says. "I doubt he's a virgin, but he's not in love the way I was at that age."

"He's definitely not a virgin," Dale says. "If he were, what a waste."

All of Conrad's good intentions vanish with this remark. Why is Dale doing this? "Young people today are different," Conrad says, looking at Jay. "I think we took relationships more seriously."

Dale gives a hoot of laughter. "Young people today! Hey, Con, I'm twenty-eight. I'm not exactly in an old-age home yet."

Conrad wants to say: Then act your age. But he just looks at him sternly.

"You're right," Jay says. He sounds mellow, relaxed. Maybe all this is going over his head. "I used to want to kill you when Xenia started liking you. Remember graduation night? The way the two of you disappeared?"

"But we didn't make love," Conrad says. He can hardly remember, except for having broken his arm that afternoon.

"Sure you did," Jay says good-naturedly. "You told me. When we were sitting on the lawn. You *admitted* it."

Conrad sets down his glass of brandy. It's first-rate. He's feeling a little more mellow himself, keeping Dale out of his line of vision. "If I admitted it, then it must have happened."

"You really don't remember?"

"No."

"God, that's so strange!" Jay looks at Dale, who's listening with a puzzled expression. "I was in love with this girl in our class and she dumped me for Con. What made it worse was we remained friends and I used to have to listen to her rant on about all his virtues. It drove me nuts."

"Still, *you* got her in the end," Conrad says. "Not me."

"Did I?" Jay gets that bitter expression that still appears when he thinks back on his marriage to Xenia. "I think maybe you won that one."

Dale holds up his glass. "Is there any more?"

"Only a little, I'm afraid." Jay refills the glass halfway.

Settling back in his chair, Dale says, "I had a thing sort of like that in high school. This girl, I forget her name, had a crush on my best friend, Tom. She didn't know we were making it together. She kept trying to bribe me to get access to him, and I had to pretend to take the bribes, knowing it was useless. She was such an idiot!"

"That has nothing to do with what we were talking about," Conrad says, furious.

"No? I thought you two were best friends," Dale says with an innocent expression.

"We weren't lovers," Jay says unbelligerently. "We were just friends."

"Yeah?" Dale smiles a little. "Well, it's a fine line."

"It's *not* a fine line," Conrad snaps. He knows Dale thinks everyone is bisexual deep down; they've argued about this dozens of times.

"Well, you're lucky in one way," Dale says, yawning.

"How?" Jay asks.

"I'd go crazy living in a house with a kid like Peter," Dale says. "He's so . . ."

Jay grins. "I *do* go crazy, but not in the way you mean. . . . Anyway, he's my child. Wouldn't that make it taboo?"

"More tempting, maybe," Dale suggests.

"Dale, shut up, okay?" Conrad says. "We get the point. Act your age."

Dale smiles at him tauntingly. "But I'm just a kid, remember?

A mere kid. You've got to make allowances. . . . Do *you* make allowances, Jay? I'm not even thirty."

Conrad knows Jay senses his discomfort. Instead of replying, Jay says, "Peter looks very much like Allegra. . . . It's too bad for Joanie. She looks just like her father."

"I don't even know if I'd want to be that gorgeous," Dale says. "Think of all the options you'd have. It could be exhausting." He stretches out on the couch and closes his eyes.

"Do you want to go to sleep?" Conrad says, wishing he would.

"No, I'll just lie here, if that's okay." Dale opens one eye. "Is that okay with you guys?"

"Sure," Jay says, glancing at Conrad.

There is a moment's pause. Is Dale really asleep or just feigning so he can try to overhear the rest of the conversation? Either way, Conrad feels fed up. "Let's go for a walk," he says.

They leave Dale and walk outside. It's a dark, cloudy night. There are no lights except those of the city below. They walk along the road in silence.

"I don't know why he's acting like that," Conrad says.

"He must feel uncomfortable," Jay says. "Afraid I'm going to judge him, maybe."

Conrad's eyes are becoming used to the dark. Jay is walking alongside him, his hands linked behind his back.

"I love him . . . but he can be an incredible pain."

"So can Allegra," Jay says. "Her reaction to feeling she's on show is to shut up, but sometimes she puts on this snobby former-ballet-dancer thing, almost an English accent. . . . I hate it! I hate ballet dancers."

"To love is to forgive?" Conrad asks wryly.

"What other choice is there? If you want someone permanently in your life, half the time they're going to drive you crazy. But if the other half is good enough, it's worth it. I didn't ask to be a father of four. I wanted one kid, that's all. Just one. Twins don't run in *my* fucking family."

Conrad hears the eucalyptus leaves crunching under his feet. "That's a good way of putting it. 'If the other half is good enough . . .' "

"You like Dale because he's more spontaneous than you are," Jay says. "The flip side is his acting *too* spontaneous. . . . I like Allegra because she's poised and detached, but the flip side is she can be cold, like I'm some guy she's hired to give her another batch of kids, help her with her own."

"That sounds unfair," Conrad says, delighted by it, nonetheless, by the conspiratorial closeness between them that excludes pregnant wives, lovers, everyone.

"That's my point," Jay says. "The closer you get to someone, the more everything about them becomes magnified—all the good things, all the bad."

Conrad glances at him. "*We* don't have that," he says. "Yet we're close."

"Friendship's different. . . . If sex didn't matter, friendship would be fine."

"There are times when I wonder if it matters enough to make up for all the *tsuris* it brings," Conrad says.

"And then," Jay says, grinning, "there are times when it's *so* good, you don't even ask."

Conrad loves Jay for the way he took the evening, for his easy, nonjudgmental manner. He knows Dale would regard this conversation as a kind of betrayal, and he's glad. He wants to get back at him.

When they return to the house, it's quiet. Dale is no longer on the couch.

"I guess he went to bed," Conrad says. "He must have really been tired. I thought he was just bluffing."

"See you in the morning," Jay says.

But Dale isn't in bed, nor in the bathroom. Did he go for a walk by himself? Was he really so angry he just left and—but, where could he go? Anyway, his stuff is still here, unpacked, in the corner of the room. When Conrad figures out where Dale probably is, he thinks: This is it. The hell with all of Jay's pronouncements about forgiveness and understanding. If Dale's in Peter's room, making it with him or trying to, I'll never see him again. Period. The question is, which is more dignified: to go look or to go to bed? Conrad decides to forget dignity. He goes down the stairs to Peter's room, which is on the lower level, by itself.

Loud rock music is coming from the room. That's why they gave him the lower level, Jay said. Conrad pushes open the door, steeling himself. Dale is sitting cross-legged on the floor, next to the phonograph, and Peter is sitting on the bed. They are fully dressed in the same clothes they were wearing earlier in the evening.

"Was it on too loud?" Peter says. "Did Jay pitch a fit?"

"No, he's gone to bed," Conrad says. They look like two kids after school, sharing the latest albums.

"Peter has a great record collection," Dale says, with such seeming innocence and enthusiasm that Conrad is amazed. "God, I wish I could get a copy of this." He holds up a Rolling Stones album.

"Want to pull up a seat?" Peter says, indicating an imaginary chair.

Conrad stands tentatively. He hates this kind of music. Could the Beatles have sounded like this to his father? Probably.

"No, I'm turning in," he says, looking meaningfully at Dale, who just waves casually and even calls out, "Sleep tight."

Back in his room, Conrad decides he's entitled to take two Valiums. That, combined with the brandy, will render him unconscious, which is all he wants. It works so quickly that he doesn't have time to unwind the strands of his feelings. They just dissolve into midair.

Sometime later he wakes up as Dale eases himself into bed next to him. "What time is it?" he asks.

"Late," Dale whispers. "Are you mad?"

Conrad just closes his eyes and pretends to be asleep.

Dale starts making love to him. "Nothing happened, okay? He's just a cute kid. We had fun. I didn't feel like being one of the grown-ups."

With his body, which is more forgiving than his head, Conrad forgives him, accepts him again, loves him, decides that Jay is right: if the other fifty percent is good enough . . .

In the morning Dale is up first, splashing his face with cold water, shaving. "These are great beds," he says enthusiastically. "I slept like a log. How about you?"

Conrad thinks of the massive argument they could have, the jabs and counterthrusts, the biting retorts. For what? They've done that before and will again. Right now, he wants to see the world as Dale does. Last night is over. This morning, a beautiful, clear sunny morning, is here.

When they return to Paris, Conrad opens his mail and finds a note from Susan. It contains a dozen slides of her work.

> Dear Con,
>   Look at them first, not as nature photos, but as patterns of color and texture. They're closeups of the Australian blue-gum eucalyptus

trees. The color of the bark keeps changing. I feel like I could never run out of new ways of seeing them. . . .

Dale is in the studio and Conrad calls him in.

"God, these are incredible," Dale says. "Who did them?"

In one slide the vivid turquoise blue creates the shape of a head, a huge dark eye staring outward. In others, patches of orange intersect with grays and greens, as though an artist had taken infinite care to apply layer upon layer of paint, yet kept it delicate, with the fine-grained feeling of lace.

Conrad is stunned by the beauty and simplicity of the slides. Susan never talked much about her work. He's always thought of her as a drifter, someone who lacked the tenacity of vision to become an artist. It's as though everything he knows of her has to be rethought. Has he ever really known anything of Susan?

He calls her number in Alexandria. The male voice who answered once before sounds brusque, angry. "Why are you calling?" he says angrily. "I told you to stop bothering me!"

"I haven't called before," Conrad says. "I wanted to speak to Susan Brown. It's about her slides."

"Susan is dead. She was murdered!" the voice shouts. "Don't you read the papers? Don't you know anything? What's wrong with you?"

Conrad is silent, hoping this may be a madman who has broken into the apartment.

"I didn't know. Please tell me what happened."

"'She was on the beach, photographing birds. She just wanted to go back one final time. Some Moslem Brotherhood terrorists landed and stopped to ask her the way to a nearby village. She told them and they shot her."

"But . . . I don't understand," Conrad stammers, his throat contracting. He knows this man loved Susan: it's clear in his voice. "Why did they shoot her if she gave them the directions?"

"Tell me why," the man cries. "Tell me!"

Conrad has an insane, desperate feeling he can change what he has just heard by rephrasing it verbally. Meanwhile, the room is whirling around him. He places one palm flat on the desk to steady himself. "She was about to go home," Conrad says. "If only someone had tried to stop her from going back to the beach that final time."

"How could anyone have known? Did *you* know? Did *I* know? They killed her because she was there—that's all."

"I was her friend," Conrad says, trying to keep his voice steady. "I knew her from college. My name's Conrad Zweifach."

"She sent you slides," the man says more quietly. "They are very beautiful."

"Yes," Conrad manages to say. "They are. They're wonderful. I'm so sorry."

"I was her friend also," the man says after a long pause. "This is a crazy country, dangerous. She should never have come here."

But then you wouldn't have known her, she never would have found her subject. "What shall I do with her slides?" Conrad asks. "Shall I return them to you?"

"Do as you like," the man says. "Nothing matters anymore."

Xenia

_____

1963

In Xenia's dream, Jay is making love to her. She is excited, but she knows that outside her door are Conrad; Dudley Shenk, her Russian literature professor; Mark Hoskins, the boy she met at the U.N. in her sophomore year; Keir Hunt, the former mental patient and longshoreman. They are all waiting to make love to her, and are also discussing her. She can't hear exactly what they're saying. Some of the phrases sound flattering, others contemptuous. "She has too much hair between her legs," one of them says. "I never did it with a Jewess," says Mark, who was from New Hampshire. "Are they different?" "I felt like killing her," says Keir. "I would have given her an A-plus, but I was afraid people would notice," says Dudley, who was married. Then her father appears and explains to all of them that Xenia is going to be a psychiatrist, and from now on will devote herself to her studies. "You may leave by the front door, if you're quiet," he says in his Hungarian accent. "We mustn't disturb them." "But why him?" one of the men asks. "Why is *he* allowed to be with her?" Her father is angry. "Xenia is at Barnard, she is graduating today." "No, she's in there, fucking." Her father starts to rattle the door. Xenia tries to push Jay off. "They're going to break in. Jay, stop!" But Jay is just about to come, he doesn't hear, or doesn't want to hear. Xenia is frightened. In a second all of them, including her father, will break in and denounce her, beat her, maybe even kill her. "Jay, please!"

She wakes up so abruptly that for a few seconds she feels she is still in her dream and glances at the door, which is closed. Quietly Xenia tiptoes across the room and opens the door. There is no one there.

"I think the unconscious is boring," Jay has often said. "What does it teach you that you don't already know?"

Xenia has tried to argue this with Jay, but now she just collapses on her bed, trying to pick apart her dream and rob it of its scary power. You feel guilty. You've done it with too many men. (How many is too many? The eternal question.) You're afraid that may be a pattern—picking forbidden people: married men, the mental patient, men who could kill you. You're afraid of acting too impulsively, like with Mark. You hardly knew him. He turned out to be fine, but you didn't know that. You just went with him to the hotel, and he could have been the Boston Strangler. No, he couldn't. He was a sweet, preppy guy from New Hampshire. But remember the gold cross around his neck, the way his eyes were two different colors. So? He wasn't dangerous, he was mild, he had trouble getting an erection. Like Con. You pick men who are either gentle to the point of collapse or excitable, scary. . . .

But that's all over, Xenia argues with herself. Five men isn't a lot. From now on she'll live with Con, she'll love him and make him more sure of himself. . . . No, it isn't going to work with Con. She knows that already, maybe knew it all along. I should call Susan and tell her we should do it the other way. She can go with Con, I'll go with Jay.

Xenia picks up the phone and gets the boarder, Mrs. Klotz. "Is Susan there?"

"You want Susan?"

"Yes. I would like Susan." Xenia has had conversations with

Mrs. Klotz before. She knows you have to be patient and repeat everything.

"She went shopping with her mother."

"When will they be back?"

"They are shopping. . . . They'll be back later."

"Did they say when?"

"I don't think so. . . . Should I tell them who called?"

"Tell them Xenia. Remember me, Mrs. Klotz? We've met lots of times. I'm Susan's friend."

"Susan's friend. . . . You want Susan to call you?"

"Yes, can you remember?"

Mrs. Klotz chuckles quietly. "I can try."

By now it's nearly eleven, and the dream has almost vanished. It's like a jigsaw puzzle with many pieces left on the table. Xenia takes a long shower and goes downstairs for breakfast. Her mother never gets up before twelve or one. Her father is sitting in the living room, reading the paper. She bends down and kisses him.

"Not at work?"

"My conference isn't until one. . . . Today's the big day?"

Xenia yawns. "I suppose. . . . I just realized I did something stupid."

Dr. Szengi gives his daughter a fond look. "Not stupid, surely."

"I insisted that Jay take Susan to the dance and he really wants to go with me, and I should go with him . . . just for old times' sake. I feel I've been throwing myself at Con. He doesn't want me."

"Of course he wants you," Dr. Szengi says. "How can he not want you?"

Xenia pours herself some coffee. "He doesn't, Poosh." She loves these morning talks with her father while her mother is sleeping. Pulling her robe around her, she sits at the end of the couch, her knees up. "I had such a terrible dream. Can I tell you?"

"For a small fee," Dr. Szengi says. "A cup of coffee, perhaps."

She brings it to him and he sits, with a slightly mocking attentiveness, listening. Xenia tells him about her dream, but instead of detailing the men, she says, "The four men I've ever slept with." But she feels she has to tell her father that he was there, that he was a part of her dream. Otherwise, how can he analyze it for her?

"You are moving on," he says, "out of my life. I am, in a sense, one of these abandoned lovers whom you must cast aside in order to lead an adult life. But you are afraid I, like the others, will be angry with you, will try and hold you back."

He has made himself, as it were, the star of the dream. Was he? Xenia can't remember it so well anymore. "I'm not going to cast you aside," she says gently. "You're the one I *don't* have to cast aside."

"But you want to," Dr. Szengi says. "You want to move on, to reject me. . . . That's who these other men are. They are versions of me and with all of them you offer yourself, and then you see they are not suitable in one way or another. As I, being your father, cannot be suitable as your lover."

Xenia frowns. "I don't know. That doesn't sound right. I don't think it's about incest."

"It's about the forbidden. You are behind a locked door and I cannot enter. You exclude me, just as, when you were a child, I excluded you when I made love with your mother, and you wondered what was going on in the dark, silent room."

Is this true? Despite, or perhaps because of being a psychiatrist's child, Xenia's memories of her childhood are spotty, vague, no clearer than the dream she had an hour or so earlier. "I don't think I want to exclude you," she says.

"But you see, you don't. You have to tell them that from now on you will be a psychiatrist, like me. Therefore we will be joined. The two of us will exclude the rest of *them*. This is the part of you that wants the childhood bond to continue into adult life."

Jay would agree with that, Xenia thinks wryly, much as he hates her father. "But why is it Jay?" she asks, genuinely curious. "We broke up so long ago. I don't want him anymore."

"But he wants you. And the intensity of his feeling is compelling. He is the only one of four suitors who will fight to keep you."

Four suitors. That sounds so quaintly old-fashioned. "They weren't suitors exactly," Xenia murmurs.

"Why four?" Dr. Szengi asks. "What do you think is the significance of the number four?"

"There were five," Xenia says.

"But you only mentioned four."

She hesitates. "There was a fifth. He was in the dream too."

"Then why leave him out?"

"I was afraid you'd be angry."

Dr. Szengi smiles. "Angry that you have lovers? That you are no longer a child?"

"That he was a former mental patient, here. He might have been your patient." She feels both excited at her boldness in finally telling him of Keir Hunt and curious as to how her father will react.

"He was the best lover?" Dr. Szengi says, sitting forward intently.

Xenia thinks back. Yes, he was. How did her father know that?

"Because it was the most forbidden," her father says, seeming to read her thoughts. "Because you were afraid I would mind."

"Not because of his body?" Xenia says playfully. "He'd been a longshoreman. He had wonderful muscles."

"Muscles!" Her father smiles.

Xenia sets down her coffee. "In the dream it is as though I'm a whore with all of them. The men, like customers, waiting. . . . Does that mean I want to be one?"

"All women do," he says dismissively. "It's a common fantasy."

"To be degraded?"

"It's like a rape fantasy. Not *real* rape. You want to be wanted. You see, in the dream you are keeping all of them waiting, *you* have the power over them, over me. . . ."

Xenia stretches out, her feet in her father's lap. "It seems pretty tawdry," she says. "I wish I had more original dreams."

Dr. Szengi touches each of her toes. This is a game they used to play when she was younger, where he would pretend he was very hungry and going to eat her toes. "Still very tempting . . ." he says.

"I think I pick the wrong men," she muses, her eyes closed, feeling drowsy again. "Almost on purpose."

"Wrong in what way?"

"Too weak. . . . Men who are divided, connected to other women. Dudley was married, the guy from New Hampshire had a girl friend in his hometown, even Keir was separated from I think it was his second wife."

"You can't ever really have them," Dr. Szengi says, a little smugly. "Like me."

"I think I *do* have you," Xenia counters, wiggling her toes. "Don't I?"

He hesitates. "Possibly too much. . . . But I think we have navigated safely through the shark-infested waters."

"Sharks?" Xenia giggles and sits up. "Who are the sharks?"

"Your mother, the women I might love or make love to . . ."

217

"Do you think women are sharks?" She looks at him teasingly. "*Very* interesting. . . . Castration anxieties. Is it our teeth?" She bares her white, even teeth.

Dr. Szengi gets up. "Yes, all women are dangerous, even daughters."

"I *want* to be dangerous," Xenia says. "I don't think I am, really."

Her father leaves to go into his study. She thinks of his interpretation of her dream. Is he right—that it's really about him, about having to give up her childhood life? Xenia has always felt that there was an erotic bond between herself and her father, but it always seemed intellectual, playful, something they were both conscious of, at least for as long as she can remember. It doesn't seem to have anything to do with stories she's read about evil fathers sneaking into their daughters' rooms at night, and trying literally to seduce them. Her father would die rather than do that. In fact, physically he is a little distant with her, and she's glad.

When her mother wanders down at twelve-thirty, her hair disheveled, Xenia is sitting on the lawn, sunning herself, wondering when she should wash her hair.

"I thought I heard the phone ringing," her mother says. "Did you get it?"

"Poosh must have," Xenia calls out lazily. "He's in his study."

She has no desire to tell her mother about her dream or even to confide in her. When Susan tells of the long, cozy evenings she and Carol share, the way Carol tells Susan everything about the men she dates, Xenia feels envious. Her mother tells her very little, even though she seems to have had an interesting life. What if I told her my dream? Her mother thinks psychiatry is nonsense, and it's become a private link between Xenia and her father.

Xenia dozes in the sun. As she enters the house, finally, her father is leaving. He waves.

"Five lovers!" he says cheerfully. "Think of the number five."

Sometimes her father irritates her. There is no significance to the number five except that she has slept with five men!

"What lovers are these?" her mother asks. "I don't see five lovers."

"It was a dream," Susan says loftily. "We were trying to analyze it."

"Five is an odd number," Mrs. Szengi says. "Too few to be significant. I don't like the number five."

Xenia looks at her mother. She always looks somewhere between beautiful and terrible. Her cheekbones are prominent and she wears eye makeup even to bed, so that in the morning her eyes are smudged and raccoonlike. She starts smoking before she gets up, but told Xenia once that her voice was always so hoarse, even when she was a child, that they wanted her to play boys' roles or animal roles in school plays.

"I'm just twenty-one," Xenia says, not knowing how she means that. Obviously her mother knows how old she is.

"Oh well, twenty-one is different now," her mother says, going back to the kitchen. She always makes espresso for breakfast, hates regular coffee and tea. "We all married so young, everything was speeded up. . . . It must be so dull to be young nowadays. Everything is allowed. Sex, romance must be terribly dull."

Xenia gets annoyed when her mother takes this world-weary, European attitude toward everything.

"If the man is exciting, why should it be dull?"

"If the man is exciting. . . ." Mrs. Szengi butters a slice of toast. "How many exciting men are there in the world? One? Maybe two? Surely not five."

"How many did you have?" Xenia asks archly. "How many exciting ones?"

"One," Mrs. Szengi says, biting into her toast.

"Who was he?"

Her mother smiles. "Oh well, I need my secrets just as you do, darling."

Xenia feels angry when her mother hints at some tantalizing past, involving exciting men. She has the feeling maybe it's all invented, they never existed. She feels as though she's spent her childhood trying to understand her parents' marriage, why they are still together. They rarely fight, unlike her friends' parents, but they are distant with each other, like two people who happen to find themselves on the same ship or island, and are trying to be sophisticated and cordial about it. Yet surely they could have gotten divorced. They don't live in circles where divorce is taboo. Xenia assumes they are both unfaithful or have been. Once a huge bouquet of flowers arrived for her mother, and her father simply smiled and said, "You see, I'm not jealous. Not at all." It's hard to tell who her father could love. He is flirtatious with women, but in such a stylized way, kissing their hands, paying elaborate compliments. But it all seems general, his manner.

Xenia thinks of his interpretation of her dream, how he referred to her waiting outside the bedroom as a child, while they made love. Did this happen? She doesn't remember. What strikes her is the implication that they did do it at one time. Perhaps they still do. Now that she's leaving home, she wants them to be happy, in their own peculiar way. She is afraid that she is the glue that has held them together.

"Susan says her mother is dating someone who wants to marry her," Xenia says.

"Does Carol like men?" Mrs. Szengi asks, licking jam off the knife.

"Well, sure. . . . I mean, she's not gay."

"Perhaps for the financial security," Mrs. Szengi says.

What does she mean? That there is no reason to marry other than that? Or is she talking just about Carol and her economic situation, having had to raise a daughter without a husband? "She's really young," Xenia says to goad her mother. "Only forty." Her own mother is forty-six.

"Yes, Americans do everything early," Mrs. Szengi says. "That's why so many of them are all washed up at forty."

"This happens to be a very nice man," Xenia says, wondering why she is quarreling with her mother, and what about. "A lawyer. His wife divorced him recently."

"Lawyers!" Mrs. Szengi half smiles. "I sometimes think they are as boring as psychiatrists, if that's possible."

"Why do you think psychiatrists are boring?" Xenia asks.

"Wanting everything in boxes!" Mrs. Szengi says. "Wanting to categorize. Poets know more than doctors."

"That's what Jay thinks," Xenia says thoughtfully.

Her mother looks at her. "Jay is lovely. You made a mistake with Jay, darling."

"It's my life!" Xenia flares up.

"Of course it is." Her mother refuses to even get into a fight. "Motherly advice is usually idiotic. I always wanted to kill my mother when she gave me advice."

Xenia leaves her mother in the kitchen and goes up to dress, just in shorts and a halter top. When she returns to the downstairs part of the house, her mother seems to have gone also. Today is a day the housekeeper doesn't come in. Xenia is glad. She loves having the house to herself, the quietness. Sometimes she pretends she is an eccentric old lady living in a huge mansion.

She wanders into her father's office. It gets no direct sunlight and is dark and gloomy except for the array of plants near the window. On his desk are papers, things he is writing, articles submitted to him as the editor of a psychoanalytic journal. Sometimes Xenia reads them and gives her opinion on whether they are well written. Most of them aren't. She sits at her father's desk, thinking that someday she will have such a desk and will, perhaps, be editing such a journal herself.

The front doorbell rings, Xenia answers it. A tall, thin, correctly dressed man with an appealing, angular face is standing there, looking ill at ease.

"Is . . . Dr. Szengi home?"

"No, he's not," Xenia says.

He looks flustered. "I thought we had an appointment."

"Was it here? At his home? He usually has his appointments at his office."

"Yes, he said specifically to come to his home, since it was Saturday." He has an English accent.

"What was it in reference to?" Xenia asks.

"A paper I wrote for *The Psychoanalytic Quarterly*. He wanted to discuss some points."

"What's your name?"

"Beverley Bowan."

Xenia tries to remember his paper, if she read it, what her father had to say about it. "Why don't you come in for a moment?" she asks. "I'll see if he left a note about it."

She ushers Beverley Bowan into the study.

"I'm terribly sorry to be so much trouble," he says.

"Oh, it's no trouble," Xenia says. She looks among her father's papers and finds "B. Bowan." "It's in the pile that he feels are publishable. . . . Perhaps he just wants a few small changes."

His face lights up. "I'm so glad. . . . I wasn't sure if my style would be appropriate."

Xenia looks right at him. He's handsome in a stuffy, slightly uptight kind of way. "I'm sure it'll be all right. . . . Maybe he'll be back soon. Would you like some tea or a drink or whatever?" She knows her father won't be back for hours.

"Perhaps a tonic, if that wouldn't be too much trouble."

They go into the kitchen. Xenia wonders if he finds her attractive. She thinks of her dream. As she pours the tonic, she imagines taking him upstairs to her bedroom while her parents are gone.

"Are you English?" she asks, handing him the glass.

"Yes, I've just been over a comparatively short time." He takes a long swallow of the drink. "Thanks, this is excellent." He smiles at her. "You look very much like my daughter. You have a very English face."

"Really?" Xenia feels insulted. "I thought most English girls were blond and pale-skinned."

"Not in the Midlands, where I come from. . . . Are you a student?"

"I just graduated college." Xenia studies him. "In the fall I start medical school."

"Going into the family business?" he asks wryly.

"Yes, I think so. . . . Is your daughter over here with you?"

Beverley Bowan sets down his glass. "No, she's back in England with her mother. We're . . . separated for the moment."

"You mean, just geographically, or the other way as well?"

He has blue eyes that regard her with steady, but detached interest.

"The other way. The old story, I suppose. In my wife's words: one can treat other people's problems, but is hopeless at one's own."

"That's one reason I'm not sure I'll marry," Xenia says. "Psychiatrists seem to make such a mess of their personal lives."

"Surely not all."

"A lot." She feels he is flirting with her in a decorous kind of way and it's enjoyable, not really dangerous, just fun.

"You'll be an exception," he says. "After all, you've grown up with all this wisdom around you. Or perhaps you're like my daughter. She doesn't want to marry at all, just have many lovers and take life as it comes. I may be misquoting her, but I think that's the general idea."

"Do you think that works for women?" Xenia says intensely. She is conscious of being underdressed and he overdressed, like a milder version of Manet's *Déjeuner sur l'herbe*.

"Oh yes, why not? I don't think women are that different nowadays."

"My father does," Xenia says. "He thinks women suffer if they're promiscuous, that they take it more seriously, biologically as well as psychologically."

Bowan raises his eyebrows. "That sounds a bit old-fashioned."

"He is."

He looks away a moment. "I want my daughter to be happy. I think she sees the conventional life of a woman didn't 'work,' as she might put it, for my wife, so she wants to try something else. . . . Why not, really?"

"Does she have lovers already?" Xenia asks. "Or is this just a plan for the future?"

"Oh, I think she's no longer a virgin. Is that what you meant? We never discuss it, really. I don't think daughters much want their fathers' input in such things, especially if their fathers are psychiatrists. . . . It becomes terribly sticky and overbearing. I'm sure she'd feel I was interpreting everything she told me."

Impulsively, Xenia tells him how she describes dreams to her father and how he interprets them for her. She even tells him the dream she actually had and what her father said about it.

"How extraordinary!" Bowan says with a wonderful English mildness.

Xenia smiles. She knows she is flirting with him, but so what? Nothing will happen. "What's so extraordinary about it?"

"Having the freedom to talk about things like that with your father. You don't feel it has, well, not to be heavy-handed about it, slightly incestuous connotations?"

Xenia laughs. "Probably. . . . But is that so bad, as long as it's just verbal?"

There's a moment of silence. Xenia feels extremely attracted to him and doesn't know what to do. Impulsively she asks, "Do you think I've been flirting with you?"

"No more than vice versa. . . . Needless to say, I'm flattered. I assume I'm a father figure, or that you like older men."

"Not especially," Xenia says only half truthfully. She feels very nervous, as though part of her were pushing forward, the other drawing back. "If you knew my father wouldn't be back for several hours, would you want to make love to me?"

"Would I want to, or would I allow myself to?"

"Either."

"I would consider it unethical and unwise in any number of ways."

"Because of my father?"

"That, and my position. . . . And my daughter, curiously."

"Why should *she* matter?"

"You'd be a stand-in for her. I would feel my wife were watching disapprovingly."

Xenia feels hurt. It's not going to happen. She isn't positive she wanted it to, but she feels as though he's rejected her.

In a very gentle, sweet way Bowan says, "I've never *been*

propositioned, actually. It's a wonderful thing to happen at forty."

"Oh, it'll happen again," Xenia says, smiling. "Rapacious American women."

"What a pleasant thought." He moves to the door. "Tell your father I'm so sorry. I'm sure the mistake was mine."

After he leaves, Xenia feels a burst of anger and disappointment. Am I going to get into serious trouble with men? Why do I do this? It's just flirting. Nothing happened. He was a perfectly respectable person. He flirted back. What am I doing, though? Picking men like my father who will respond as he doesn't? For a few moments Xenia remembers making love with Jay, and feels a burst of longing so acute she feels dizzy. I should be going with Jay tonight. I wish I was. I wish I could rearrange it. It was stupid trying to fix up Susan and Jay. Manipulative. Cruel. Why do I do things like that?

When Susan finally calls, Xenia is so relieved she cries, "Come on over, right away, can you?"

As they drive back from the prom, Xenia feels relieved that Susan is at the wheel. Conrad's unsteadiness while driving, his anxiety attack, alarmed her. It isn't the way she thinks of him. He's always seemed wry and in control. At the dance they mostly danced without talking, but she felt a bond with him and all her turmoil earlier in the day seemed silly. So he broke his arm. Anyone can break an arm.

Upstairs, back at the house, she and Susan go to the bathroom. They go in together. Susan sits down on the toilet to pee while Xenia examines herself in the mirror and applies powder to her flushed shiny face.

"Why did I wear black velvet?" she says grimacing. "I look like something out of Charles Addams."

"It's such a lovely dress," Susan says. She gets up and flushes the toilet. "Still. . . . Thank heaven the dance is over!"

"Yes, it was silly, even going, wasn't it? I feel like if it hadn't been for me, no one would have gone. We could have just stayed here and talked."

Susan is washing her hands. "I'm worried about Con," she says.

"You mean the thing with the car?"

"Yes. I think something's bothering him."

Xenia looks at Susan in the mirror. "I don't ever feel I can ask.

With Jay or you I feel I can say anything or ask anything, and somehow you take it the right way. But I never know if Con wants anyone to break through."

"I know," Susan says. "I wouldn't dare ask him anything either. I suddenly was afraid he really wanted to kill himself."

"And all of us?" Xenia sucks in her breath.

"No, not all of us."

When they come downstairs, Conrad says he needs to go to bed. Xenia brings him up to her room. She stands quietly by the bed while he takes the pills.

"Con, are you okay?"

"Sure," he murmurs. "I'll be fine. Just tired, that's all."

"Nothing's seriously wrong, then?"

"Not a thing. . . . Just couldn't handle it all."

If he were Susan or Jay, Xenia feels, she could probe further. What does "handle it all" mean? But she just kisses him lightly on the forehead.

"Sleep well," she says.

When she goes downstairs, she finds that Jay and Susan have set up the Monopoly board.

"I think he's just tired," she says.

Susan looks at Jay. "Do you ever discuss personal things with him?"

"Sure." Jay is counting out the paper money.

"We think Con's really upset about something," Susan says.

"He's fine," Jay says. "Don't worry about it."

"You always want to sweep everything under the rug!" Xenia snaps.

"And you want to make everything into a melodrama," Jay snaps back. "Cool it, Xen. . . . Do you want to play Monopoly with us, or do you want to brood?"

Xenia feels wounded, as she always does when Jay attacks her, though she hates the fact that he still has such power over her. "We were going to live together after graduation," she says. "Now I just don't know. I don't know if I'm right for Con. Maybe he needs someone more . . . stable."

"You're stable," Susan says soothingly.

"No, I'm not," Xenia says. "I keep doing stupid, impulsive things."

"Such as?" Jay says mockingly.

"None of your business," Xenia says.

225

He lies down and looks at her with his taunting black eyes. "Tell us, Xen. Come on. You're among friends. You made it with your father, finally? You plighted your truth?"

"My truth?" Xenia says, pouncing. "Very interesting slip."

Jay flushes but continues. "Come on. Tell us how it was. Was it all you'd dreamed of after all these years? Or can't he get it up anymore?"

Xenia sits up straight, glaring at him. "My father and I share many things—intellectual companionship, friendship. It's a very special relationship which you just don't understand."

"Sure I understand," Jay says. "My heart belongs to Daddy. Isn't that how the song goes?" He gets up and starts singing, out of tune.

"Why do you care anyway?" Xenia says. "You're just acting jealous and stupid."

Jay keeps dancing around. "The jealous, rejected lover, despondent, having spied his intended in the garden with her father, falls, silent and forlorn, to the ground." He collapses on the rug.

"Who rejected who?" Xenia says. "You want to make everything my fault."

Susan reaches out and touches her arm. "Why don't we just play?"

"Because he upsets me!" Xenia says, afraid she's going to cry. "You tease about everything, Jay. There's Con upstairs, maybe seriously upset about something. I feel . . . whatever, and to you it's all a joke."

At this, Jay becomes serious. "I'm sorry. . . . Forgive?"

Xenia stares at him, hesitates. "Yes."

They play for two hours, but their conversation is just lighthearted, revolving around the game. Susan and Jay keep alternately winning and then reversing their positions. Xenia can't concentrate on the game. She worries about Conrad, asleep upstairs, about whether they should live together, whether she should live with anyone.

"I wonder if I'll ever feel as close to anyone as I do to both of you," she says, looking at the two of them. "Even someone I marry."

"I won't," Susan says. "I know that. . . . But I'm never going to marry."

"Really?" Xenia says. "I think you will. Maybe late, maybe someone older, someone very kind and artistic."

Jay sits back and stretches. "How about me? Who will I marry?"

"Oh, you'll marry some blond airline stewardess from Eugene, Oregon," Xenia says, "and have four towheaded sons and she'll adore your books, though she never reads them, and you'll cheat on her and live happily ever after."

Jay laughs. "Wow, what a future." He looks at Susan. "Do you agree? Is that whom I'm going to marry?"

Susan smiles. "No, I think you'll marry a dark-haired, very intelligent cellist, and you'll have two daughters and they'll both be very brilliant and sensitive."

"When am I going to win the National Book Award?" Jay says.

Susan considers. "At thirty-four."

"And will thousands of intense, exciting women throw themselves at my feet?"

"Yes," Susan says, "but you'll be faithful to your cellist wife."

Jay grimaces. "I will? God, I hope not! Is she a soloist or with a small symphony or what?"

"An all-women's quartet," Susan says.

"Only," Xenia puts in, "she finally runs off with someone who teaches medieval history at Brown, leaving *you* with custody of your two preteen daughters."

"What happened to my four sons?" Jay says.

"This is Susan's fantasy. . . . I'm just finishing it."

"Do I take to the bottle?" Jay asks. "Do I sink into the slough of despond?"

"Well, you have a writing block for the better part of a decade," Xenia goes on, "but—"

"Finally you pull out of it and write a brilliant novel," Susan finishes, "and the cellist, having realized what a mistake she made, returns."

"I hope I throw her out," Jay says.

"No," Susan says. "You forgive everything and live happily ever after."

Jay rolls over flat on his back.

"Jesus . . . what if you're both right? What if I have six kids, four towheaded sons from the stewardess, two from the cellist. . . ."

"How about me?" Xenia says. "Tell me *my* future."

Jay sits up and pretends to rub an imaginary crystal ball.

"Let me see. It's foggy. No, now it's becoming clearer. . . . You will marry a tall, distinguished psychoanalyst who is, sadly, terrible in bed and can only see out of one eye."

Xenia reaches over and kicks him. "I give you a blond stewardess! Why do I get a half-blind impotent shrink?"

"Because you deserve it," Jay says.

Xenia reaches over and kicks him again. "Okay, well I'm taking back the stewardess."

"You never said she was any good in bed," Jay says. "I assume she just lay there like a lump."

"No, worse," Xenia says. "She shakes all over and grinds her teeth. . . . So, do I stay with the good doctor, or do I move on?"

"You move on, of course," Jay says. "He is the first of . . . four equally brilliant fucked-up men who grovel piteously at your feet. But you only care about your work, put up with their neurotic obsessions for you . . . but ultimately retire to the country and write a four-volume tome on the Oedipus complex rediscovered."

Xenia looks at Susan plaintively. "Is that what *you* think?"

Susan shakes her head. "No, I think you'll do what you said I would do. You'll marry late, someone older, kind, maybe not a psychoanalyst, maybe a lawyer who does idealistic things but doesn't earn much money."

"Will we have kids?" Xenia asks. With Susan she is serious, as though she thinks it will be an accurate prediction.

"I think just one," Susan says, "a very quiet, intense boy with big, dark eyes. No, wait. I think maybe your husband will be a physicist. Is that okay?"

"Sure," Xenia says. She glances at Jay, who is gazing glumly off into the corner of the room. "How about Con?"

There's a moment of silence.

"I don't think Con will marry," Susan says.

"Really?" Xenia asks. "Why not?"

"I don't know. . . . I see him as a sort of loner. He might live with someone."

"What do you think, Jay?" Susan asks.

"I'm so tired, I can't think."

"Just tell me what you think about Jay—I mean, about Con."

"I don't know," Jay says. "I agree with Susan. It's hard to imagine him in a regular family."

"Maybe he'll marry an older woman who already has children," Xenia suggests. For some reason she wants their imaginary fates sealed. She doesn't want ambiguity, even in fantasy.

"Sure, that sounds good."

They leave the Monopoly board open on the floor. Xenia gets out blankets and sheets and shows Susan where there are fresh towels. As she passes through the darkened living room, Jay is standing near the window, not yet undressed. She comes up to him and kisses him quickly.

"Sleep tight."

"Yes," Jay says in a soft, intimate voice. "You too, darling."

Darling? Did he mean to say that? The "darling" encircles Xenia as she goes up the stairs. In her mind it is Conrad who is downstairs, and Jay awaiting her in bed. Conrad seems to be asleep. With the moonlight coming in the window, Xenia studies him, his thoughtful face, the pale hair. He looks peaceful, though, and she feels reassured. It was just the pain from his arm. He'll be all right.

He wakes up as she slides naked into bed.

They slip into each other's arms. Slowly, carefully, Xenia takes Conrad's clothes off. He seems half asleep, although he lets her stroke his body and kiss him, responding, but seemingly totally passive, as though he wanted only to be made love to. This is a turn-on for Xenia. It's exciting lying on top of Conrad, moving as fast or as slowly as she wants. Toward the very end, as she is about to come, he fades out of her mind and other people enter: the English psychoanalyst sipping his tonic and gazing at her with his thoughtful blue eyes; Keir Hunt, who grasped her arm so tightly she cried; Jay, touching her in the dark.

Does anyone ever make love to just one person? Or is it always all the people one has actually loved or been attracted to? Do they all live on in that secret part of one's mind, coexisting as if in a dream? Fragments of her father's "interpretations" come back to her: *you want power over them . . . you want to leave me . . . shark-infested waters . . .* And her mother's *Are there five exciting men? . . . I need my secrets. . . . Would I want to or would I allow myself to? . . . Who rejected who? You want to make everything my fault. . . .*

The house is finally quiet. Everyone is asleep. Xenia puts her arms around Con and allows the many voices in her head to swim silently away.

Susan puts her camera back in the closet and she and Xenia go down to the kitchen to help Mrs. Szengi with the dishes. Jay and Conrad are going to use the bathroom first.

Mrs. Szengi surveys the kitchen—pans on the stove, a low fire left burning under one of them, butter melting in a dish, cupboards ajar. "Men in the kitchen!" she exclaims.

"Still, they fixed a wonderful breakfast," Xenia says. She looks at Susan, who looks oddly formal in her prom dress, like an Alice in Wonderland with somewhat disheveled hair. "Wasn't it good?"

"I never have breakfast," Susan says. "But it was good."

"All Americans think about is food," Mrs. Szengi says. "Supermarkets as big as museums. Stuffing, stuffing. I tell you, I see these babies and they are ringed in fat, they can hardly *move* and still the mothers are saying, eat, eat. . . . How about food for the soul, the spirit? You are like me, Susan. You need spiritual food."

"I've always been too thin," Susan says. "Carol worries." She indicates her figure in a self-deprecating way. "We went shopping for bathing suits today, and everything looked awful. I looked like a bean pole."

Mrs. Szengi is loading dishes into the dishwasher. "Just wait," she says, "wait till you're forty and all those svelte, big-bosomed prom queens will have gone to fat and you'll be as slim as a girl. I promise you."

Xenia loves to eat and knows keeping her weight down will be a lifelong problem. "Do you mean me?" she says archly.

Her mother looks at her. Xenia is in her bathrobe, barefooted. "Men like zaftig women," she says. "They like flesh. You have nothing to worry about."

How does this square with what she just said about svelte prom queens going to seed? Xenia is always annoyed at this kind of conversation with her mother, which never follows any logical sequence. She knows her mother feels that she has the soul of an artist, and that Xenia and her father are dull, scientific types, though sometimes she links herself and Xenia as both having feminine intuition, as opposed to masculine reason.

Susan goes into the spare room to get her things together. Xenia climbs the stairs to her room. She feels tired and sad. Somehow the evening was not what she had imagined it would be like. Of course, she hadn't thought about Conrad's broken arm or the fact that he would fall asleep the minute they came back from the prom. She thinks of making love to him the night before. Does he enjoy it or just tolerate it?

Conrad is lying on her bed, staring pensively out the window. "Hi," he says.

Xenia sits down next to him. "Where's Jay?"

"Taking a shower. . . . I couldn't because of my arm."

The room is still half cast in shadows because the blinds haven't been raised fully.

Xenia says, "I think maybe we shouldn't live together, Con. Do you? Do you still really want to?" Her heart is thumping as she says this. She isn't sure what she wants him to say.

"You're right," Conrad says. "It would've been a mistake. It was a nice thought, though."

What if she hadn't said this? Would they still be going to do it? Sometimes Conrad's passivity enrages as well as bewilders Xenia. "Will you find your own apartment?"

"Something," he says.

He is lying there so still, his blue eyes focused on the window, so self-contained it's almost scary. "I would have liked to be what you wanted me to," he says. "I wanted that too."

"I didn't want anything special," Xenia says. The sound of his voice is so melancholy and soft, it touches her. "I just wanted us to be two friends who made love sometimes."

He shrugs. "You'll find that with someone else I'm sure."

Jay comes out of the bathroom with his towel around his waist, his hair wet. He looks embarrassed seeing Xenia and Conrad lying side by side on the bed.

"Am I interrupting something?"

"No," Xenia says. "We were just breaking up."

Jay stands there uncertain, looking at the two of them. "Have you really thought it over?"

"Yes," they both say in unison.

Jay comes close to the bed. "You're my best friends," he says solemnly. "I wanted you to be happy."

"We will be," Xenia says, trying to be blithe, "only with other people." She goes into the bathroom and takes a shower herself.

Afterward, as she's standing there in the steamy bathroom, drying herself, the door opens. It's Jay, dressed as he was before.

"Be happy with *me*," he says, holding her at the waist.

Xenia kisses him, then half pushes him away. "You're impossible."

"Be unhappy with me," Jay says, "just *be* with me, Xen. Okay?"

Xenia feels dizzy from the hot shower, from Jay's body pressing up against her. "Okay," she says.

"I want to explain about my marriage," Pierson Beales says. He has gotten dressed and is sitting on the edge of Xenia's new couch, holding a sock.

Xenia holds up her hand. "You don't have to," she says.

"I want to," he insists. "I want you to know."

"It's *your* marriage," she says, equally insistently. She knows he thinks she means this differently than she does. He thinks she is being kindly, wanting to spare him the pain of reciting some long—he's been married over twenty-five years, three kids in college—agonized story. Whereas what she really means is, I know about your marriage. I've heard variations on your story a dozen times. It doesn't matter anymore. You're unhappy, she's unhappy, you want to leave her, you won't leave her. Xenia only wants to spare herself.

They flirted with each other at lunch a few times. He is a banker who belongs to a tennis club Xenia has joined in an attempt to lose a few pounds. Their lovemaking was awkward, intense but rushed, although no one was rushing them. When she makes love with a married man for the first time, Xenia always thinks of the Thurber cartoon of the first wife sitting on top of the cupboard. His wife is there with them in the man's mind, watching, criticizing, observing. For her it was awkward because she has firmly decided—in fact, this was one of her New Year's resolutions—never again to get involved with a married man. Not for moral reasons, just for the sake of her own peace of mind. Just before meeting Pierson Beales, she ended a longish off-and-on affair with a man who kept leaving his wife, returning to her, leaving again. The wife in *his* stories kept changing from the irascible bitch to the plaintive victim and back again.

"Whatever happens," Pierson Beales says, "you won't have destroyed my marriage. That's the main thing I want you to know. It's been moribund for quite some time."

And will be forever, Xenia amends in her head. Perhaps it's because her own marriage took place so long ago, a youthful marriage, no kids, that these middle-aged marriages in which people seem stuck like flies caught in jelly are incomprehensible to her. She and Jay fought, were cruel to each other, but it seems to her, unless she's deceiving herself, that their marriage, up to the final moment, was always alive. "You don't understand what it's like when children are involved," her former lover Morgan used to say with a sigh. "The indebtedness, the financial problems." "That's true, I don't," Xenia would reply, and add inwardly, Thank heaven.

What she is trying to do, at forty-two, is learn to cut her losses. Her friend Sally, who is just getting divorced herself, uses that term all the time. "Learn when to abandon the sinking ship," she tells Xenia. "Swim for shore." But when or how does one know the ship is sinking? Xenia jokingly tells everyone she is looking for a man whose wife is in an irreversible coma, someone who will not have to offer explanations or excuses.

Once, on jury duty, she met such a man, a very neat, dapper biologist with a handkerchief that matched his shirt. He said he had married a much younger woman and their only fear was that he would die first and she would be left alone. Then, one morning, she had a cerebral hemmorhage and lived on for six months in a coma, finally expiring. "Do you think I will ever recover?" he asked, once he heard Xenia was a psychiatrist. "She was so full of life and she died! How can you learn to take that kind of risk again?"

"I don't know," Xenia said.

She hates cynics, people who are living everything as though the end were spelled out before it even begins. Yet she can sense in herself some of that detachment. She can hear that in her voice as she says to Pierson Beales, "Aren't all marriages moribund?"

"No," he says. "I can't believe that. . . . What would one live for, then?"

"Work, friends . . . tennis." She just tosses in the latter since she is an indifferent athlete and he is excellent, prides himself on having stayed in shape, as she has not.

"Those are peripheral," he says. "Don't you think one needs a center?"

"One can be one's own center," Xenia says.

"I guess I haven't found that that works. It's so narcissistic. . . . When the children were young, they drew me out of myself. But that's long over."

"I never had children," Xenia says after a moment.

"Did you ever want them?"

He is asking in what seems a nonjudgmental way, so Xenia says, "I thought of it from time to time. But I've found my work satisfying and I'm not iconoclastic enough to have children on my own. Or maybe just too selfish. I like order and quiet."

Pierson Beales smiles. She likes his smile, quiet and wry. "Yes, that tends to go by the boards with children."

"Were your children very important to you?" She recalls how at their first lunch he took out photos of all of them: his daughter, the oldest, who is married; the son who is taking a leave of absence from college; his younger son, of whom he sounded the most fond.

"Important, but, as my wife would quickly point out, at a distance. She did all the work."

"Did she really?"

"Oh yes. . . . We had a very conventional marriage." He gazes away, then back. "We were—are—very conventional people. Our lives might have worked for many others. They just didn't for us."

"And you don't find having love affairs on the side solves that?" Xenia hates her voice when it gets its professionally smooth, unruffled quality.

"That's pretty sordid, don't you think?" Pierson Beales says. "Motels and all that. I mean, I've done it, but I hardly think it's a very satisfactory way of life . . . unless one is much more cynical than I find it enjoyable to be."

The way he puts it appeals to Xenia. "I'm afraid I'm becoming cynical," she admits. "And I do hate it. Forty-two seems too young to settle into that."

For some reason Xenia thinks of Susan. She no longer thinks of her all the time, as she did for a year or two after Susan died. But at times she is still pierced by a sense of loss that is dizzying. The soldiers walking down the beach, Susan looking through her camera, the quiet, their asking her how to get to the village . . .

She is not sure how long she has been sitting, half naked, in the chair.

He says gently, "I'm sorry if I've sounded pompous, or—"

"No," Xenia says, pulling herself together. "It's just my life, which may seem meager in some ways emotionally, is still all I've got and I rather like it. I don't want things changed irretrievably. I'm quite happy as I am."

"Are you?" He says this not in a snide way but just out of curiosity. Xenia feels he must know it's a lie.

She smiles. "I don't expect much of men . . . but I like them, I need them."

She expects a rejoinder, but he just says mildly, "Yes, I don't expect much of them either. I never know what to say to them, beyond the superficial things. Women try to break through, which can be exhilarating, or—"

"Infuriating?"

He laughs. "No, not at all. I like being shaken up."

Sally thinks men who claim to be feminists or who say they like women better than men are the ones to be wary of. "Ask their wives how feminist they are," she warns. Her soon–to–be–ex-husband is a lawyer for NOW, but never, she says, made a bed or washed a dish.

"I don't anymore," Xenia confesses. "It doesn't lead any-where, and it can be damn wrenching."

Sally says that the problem in all relationships is faulty timing, and Xenia thinks this may be true with Pierson Beales. Several years ago the prospect of "falling in love" with a married man who was urbane but had that slight awkwardness she likes in men might have been appealing. But Pierson Beales was somewhere else, doing, perhaps, the same thing with someone other than her or perhaps focusing all his attention on his work as, Xenia has found, many such men do once their children are grown. And she did fall in love with charming, crazy Morgan, whose wife, Alice, has started a second career as a female comic, telling ribald, hilarious stories about their sex life and how incompetent and infuriating he is.

Four months ago, fed up with Morgan, Xenia did what Sally suggested, what Sally claimed a friend had done, with wonderful results. She placed an ad in *The New York Review of Books*: "Dark, highly intelligent, almost zaftig, long-divorced female psychoana-lyst, 41, wants to be saved from cynicism by witty, observant, pas-sionate, single, divorced, or (even) married man." To her amaze-ment, she got forty letters; one from a philosophy professor in Vermont, one from a man who told about his real-estate holdings; one man sent a photo of himself with his Labrador retriever. An-other appeared at her apartment and announced he had been married and divorced five times and would only go out with her if she was "serious" about marriage. Xenia had thought her seriousness was proved by her abstaining, but this man, an oral surgeon from Westchester, took it exactly the opposite way.

"I think you're just toying with the idea," he said disapprovingly over coffee. "I'm an incurable romantic."

"I'm an incurable realist," Xenia said and watched his face fall. She wished that statement were as totally true as she made it sound.

These were not impossible men, not from their letters, as far as one could judge. Some sounded sensitive, some intelligent. But after meeting three for a drink or dinner, Xenia complained to Sally: "There's no divine spark."

"I thought you were the incurable realist," Sally pointed out.

"I am," Xenia countered. "And I realistically think that without a divine spark it's hopeless . . . unless one is looking for economic support or just companionship or someone to plant a seed. I'm earning enough, I can talk to you, I'm too old to have kids."

"That's probably why they like you," Sally said. "You're so undemanding." She thinks of Xenia as "popular with men," and no amount of evidence to the contrary seems to dispel this illusion. "My neediness scares them off. I'll have to settle for a dentist in checked trousers."

"My lack of neediness scares them off," Xenia said. "They want to tell me their problems, get a free analytic session. It's not romance."

When she was young and beginning her practice, she was afraid of looking too seductive and girlish and kept her long black hair pinned up, cultivated a dowdy appearance: chunky shoes, tailored blouses, tweed skirts. She thought of it as her uniform. Now it's as though she has mysteriously grown into the role. Her hair is turning gray, she's gained ten pounds, she truly does have an amiably matronly appearance that alternately horrifies and amuses her.

Pierson Beales enters the bathroom as she's pinning her hair up.

"It's so lovely long," he says, touching it. "Why not wear it loose?"

"It doesn't suit my image," Xenia explains, continuing to pin it. "I try to look like the kind of woman men feel at ease with, not intimidated by. Sexuality is threatening."

"Is it?" He looks at her in the mirror. "I think people appear as they really are, whether their intent is to conceal or reveal. To me you look, even in what you call your costume, provocatively dowdy . . . with the accent on provocative."

Xenia laughs, pleased.

They are so much more comfortable together this way, talking, exchanging views, that she wonders if it was a mistake to go to bed with him. In bed his urbanity vanished. He became anxious, as if he felt he shouldn't be there. Xenia wasn't even sure he had come; she knew men faked orgasms almost as often as women.

"I want very much to see you again," Pierson Beales says as they walk into the living room. He sounds somber, as though he were making an appointment for a stress test.

"We could go back to being friends . . . if you're more comfortable with that," Xenia says falteringly.

"No." He looks hurt. "Not that I don't have women friends or feel that men and women can't be friends, but I want . . . I think I want to marry you."

Xenia, unable to control herself, does the stupidest and cruelest thing imaginable. She laughs. "You don't know me," she says.

Partly she is angry with him. He doesn't know this, but Morgan said the same thing to her either on their second or third meeting. "In my book, married men who make remarks like that to women they scarcely know are irresponsible," she adds crisply.

"I didn't know we formed such a large group," he says, withdrawing.

"It proves seriousness of intent," Xenia tells him. "Please don't tell me you aren't aware of that."

He half smiles. "What if there *is* real seriousness of intent?"

"It doesn't exist. It's a purple cow."

"I thought you didn't consider yourself a cynic."

Xenia clarifies this. "A realist." She hesitates. She doesn't want to hurt him and regrets her laugh. "I think you're a very nice man, I really enjoy your company but—"

"Not a very competent lover?"

"It's always awkward the first time." That plays no part in her reasoning, in point of fact. She wants him to know this as well as to salvage his pride.

"Will there be no second time?" He is watching her anxiously, attentively.

"Of course," Xenia says, "but not ringed round with extravagant promises."

"Fair enough." He looks happy, relieved.

237

That evening Xenia is having dinner with Carol, with whom she's become friendly since Susan's and her own mother's death. When Susan died, Xenia, hearing about it, felt a flicker of horror, but no grief, as far as she was aware. She wondered at the time if it was because Susan lived so far away and they saw each other so infrequently. Part of her was half pretending Susan was still alive, though not pretending in any literal way. It was just that she often told Susan things in her mind that she never wrote down, and after Susan's death, she continued to. As with her patients, Xenia thinks illusions are allowable, if they help, and aren't serious distortions of reality.

A year after Susan's death, Mrs. Szengi was hit by a bus and died four hours later, never regaining consciousness. It was the same month in which Susan died, August, and the city was gripped in an oppressive, ugly heat wave. This time it was different. Xenia hadn't expected to be deeply affected by her mother's death. Mrs. Szengi was in her sixties and they had never been close. But perhaps in some way the two deaths joined, and together opened up some pit of darkness into which, for a year or more, Xenia stared, immobilized.

One of her colleagues had written a paper on "walking nervous breakdowns," in which the patient continues to function, goes through all the motions, but is mentally and spiritually dead. It was an extreme version of the kind of detachment she sometimes feels about her own life. But whereas the detachment is usually bearable and even a pleasant kind of protection, this was something harsher. After her last patient of the day, Xenia would sit in her analyst's chair and think: I don't care if any of these people get well, I have no idea if they will, and I have no idea if I'm helping them. Or if psychoanalysis ever helps anyone or is a total farce. Eagerly she read novels in which psychiatrists were stock figures of fun, caricatured, throwing tantrums, and she thought: Yes, that's me, that's everyone I know. It's all a farce. She went to analytic meetings and everyone struck her as absurd. There wasn't one person in the room, she used to think, who really believes a word of what they're saying or believes a word of what anyone else is saying. It's a charade. When she tried, tentatively, voicing this to a few colleagues, they all, with marvelous ease, agreed. Yes, it was a charade, a farce. But what else was there in life? If one was a dentist, one filled cavities. If one had spent infinite years training as an analyst, one "helped" or "tried to help."

But the mood receded. Either she simply digested this new version of herself, her profession, and the world or, in entering middle age, it didn't seem to matter that much. One has illusions, they vanish, but one goes on. So Xenia expressed it to herself. She wondered later if the immobilizing horror and grief that sprung out of these two deaths came from the fact that, in different ways, they were murders. Susan's an outright murder, her mother's an "accidental" murder in which it was never established if her mother had been crossing against the light or the driver of the bus had been careless. But for Xenia one day they were there, absolutely present, and the next day gone, inexplicably and totally, as though a big eraser had simply come down from the sky, eradicating them.

Her mother had always said she hoped to die suddenly, that she hated seeing friends disintegrate in painful or debilitating illnesses. "Shoot me if I get that way," she would say when a friend showed signs of senility or had to be moved to a nursing home. But when she died, she was in excellent mental shape, and active physically. Perhaps, for this reason, she seemed younger than she actually was.

At that time Xenia read an interview with Simone de Beauvoir in which she spoke of death losing its fearsomeness for her because so many of her friends were dying. The world becomes denuded, she said. Xenia never had deep regrets about not having children, but she wondered if it helped at times like this, seeing a new generation grow, produce. Single, she had no ties to the future, no human links, and, whether one retained any belief in immortality or not, the world seemed bleak. She toyed with the idea of adoption or even going to a sperm bank, as a woman friend had done. At her age, there would be minor risks but it would have been do-able. But she always preached to herself intelligent selfishness. There seemed to her no good reason to do anything other than that because, at some deep level, it would give her pleasure. She didn't see herself as a mother, despite having lost one. She was caught, at what seemed too early an age, without links to the past or present.

Was that why she became friendly with Carol, who, until that time, she had scarcely known—other than as "Susan's mother," someone she might say hi to if she met on the street? Xenia is forty-two, Carol is sixty. They are both women at different stages of middle age. Unlike Xenia, Carol has stayed slender and dyes her hair the same reddish blond it was twenty years earlier. Of course, she has lines on her face, but in certain ways it seems to Xenia they look of the same generation. Susan always made fun of her mother's girlish naïveté, the way she widens her eyes at something funny or surprising, her self-conscious laugh, the way she leans forward while listening, as though something profound or inspiring were about to be said. But Xenia finds it charming, so different from her own mother's world-weary, exhausted sophistication.

The same year Mrs. Szengi died, Winthrop Schuler had a heart attack and, after an attempt at open heart surgery, expired. Carol lives alone in the same apartment. She takes in boarders, as she did when Xenia and Susan were friends in high school and college. She still works as a commercial artist and even does volunteer work on weekends at the Museum of Modern Art. "I try not to think of things," is what she says when Xenia asks about her personal life. "It's the only way."

They go out to a small Italian restaurant near Carol's apartment.

"I eat here too much," Carol says. "It seems such a bother to cook. I was always a terrible cook. Poor Winthrop. He couldn't understand how anyone could be that bad. His first wife was wonderful—well, I ate at their house a lot. . . . But I think he liked me better just the same." She smiles her impish smile.

"I'm sure he liked you better," Xenia says. Everything on the menu looks ominously appealing. Should she be stern and order veal or self-indulgent and give in to fettucini Alfredo? Thinking of the pleasure Pierson Beales appeared to take in the rounded curves of her body, Xenia chooses, with only a small inner struggle, the fettucini.

Carol always orders chicken and then eats about a quarter of what's on her plate. Since Susan's and Winthrop's deaths she's lost weight. But she looks pretty and delicate in the dim light of the restaurant. The waiter, after taking their order, says to Carol, "Your sister?"

"No, I don't have a sister," Carol says. "This is my daughter's friend."

"Ah, your daughter's friend. . . . I thought there was some connection." He looks pleased and brings them a bottle of Soave.

"Do we look alike?" Xenia says. "I'm flattered."

"*I'm* flattered," Carol says. "I'm an old hag, an old bag. . . . You're still blooming."

240

"I'm forty-two. . . . Look at me." "Provocatively dowdy" is about the best that anyone could say, Xenia thinks, recalling Pierson Beales's attempt at a compliment.

"You look exotic," Carol says. She sips her wine. "I always wanted to look exotic, especially after I moved to New York. I look so American!"

Xenia smiles. The wine is cold and delicious. It's a Saturday, so she'll allow herself two or three glasses. No work tomorrow. "I got a sort of marriage proposal today," she says, eyeing a roll.

Carol raises her glass. "Mazel tov!"

"It doesn't mean anything," Xenia says. "Just another middle-aged married man trying to be persuasive . . . which was really unnecessary since we'd just gone to bed together."

"Maybe he meant it," Carol suggests.

"He's married."

"Yes, well, I agree. . . . One shouldn't because of the wife."

"But do you think that applies even if the wife is a bore or a scold or even if the marriage is dead, just two people clinging together out of anxiety or sheer inertia?" Xenia finds herself breathlessly reversing her usual position. "Even if they have no sex life? Are there no exceptions?"

Carol is picking sesame seeds off a breadstick and then eating them one by one. "Eating like a bird" flashes through Xenia's mind. "I suppose there are exceptions to everything," Carol says.

"Wasn't Winthrop married when you met him?" Xenia asks.

"When I met him, yes. But not when I started . . . not when we began to . . ." Carol falters when the conversation approaches sex. "We weren't drawn together because of sex. That wasn't the main thing. I'm not that interested in sex. Maybe I'm frigid." She says this perkily, as though the thought has just occurred to her.

"Even if you don't have orgasms, you aren't necessarily frigid," Xenia says, as she's said to hundreds of patients. "People express their sexuality in different ways."

With a little nip Carol bites into the breadstick. "I think it must have been a terrible trial to Winthrop. First my cooking. Then that . . . Yet he was so kind. He was a very sweet man. I just don't know if I ever loved him . . . properly."

Unable to resist, Xenia takes a roll and begins to butter it. "What's properly?"

"I don't know," Carol admits. "He tried so many different ways to get me to . . . I told him it didn't matter, but he felt . . . But then I think he finally gave up. Or maybe accepted it. It wasn't as though I turned him down," she adds quickly. "I don't believe a wife should ever do that."

"Maybe we expect too much of marriage in America," Xenia says. "Do you think it's that? Maybe in Europe they're more realistic. You marry to have a family, you seek 'pleasure on the side.' "

Carol frowns. "I don't think that sounds very appealing, though, do you?"

Xenia considers this. "I didn't have that kind of marriage, when I had one. I mean, we didn't marry to start a family and I wasn't looking for someone to take care of me financially."

The waiter brings their main courses and bends to grind pepper over the plates.

"It was for love," Carol says.

"Pardon?" says the waiter, thinking she is referring to what they have ordered.

"It's all delicious," she says, smiling at him. To Xenia she amends, "You married for love. With Jay."

"Love is a con game," says Xenia, sprinkling cheese on her fettucini.

"But isn't companionship nice?" Carol asks. "I liked that so much with Winthrop, all the little things, watching *Masterpiece Theatre* on Sunday night, taking walks in the park."

"Yes, I suppose," Xenia says. "But it's like the movies. I used to *hate* going to movies alone. I felt so self-conscious, laughing all by myself, not having anyone to discuss it with afterward. And now I've gotten so used to it that I hate *going* with someone. I don't want to discuss it, except with myself. If anyone asks me to see a movie with them, I say I've already seen it."

Carol is nibbling on her chicken, taking small bites. She stops, fork in midair. "You have your career," she says. "That makes you different. You're more independent."

"*You* have a career," Xenia points out.

"I got a job because I had to support Susan," Carol says. "And I like to work. Maybe it's that it's a career, but not a profession. I do it, I try to do it well. Then I go home and forget it. There's no big deal about it. I'm not changing people's lives if I design a different kind of container to store frozen peas in."

Xenia is already feeling annoyed with herself for eating so much. Her skirt feels tight. Why is food so good? She likes wine too. "I'm *not* changing people's lives," she says gloomily. "I'm giving them someone to talk to, to tell them what they already know."

"But that's something," Carol insists, as though this weren't a contradiction of what she said.

"Maybe they'd be better off taking a luxury cruise," Xenia says, her mouth set, "or talking to their dog or . . . What I mean is, if psychiatry was suddenly declared illegal or vanished as a thing to do, I wonder if people would be any worse off, I truly do."

Carol reaches over and pats Xenia's hand. "It's easy to be self-critical," she says. "You mustn't give in to that. Tell yourself what you're doing makes a difference. So it's a lie. I believe in lies. They keep one going."

"I agree," Xenia says. "But at times my life seems *all* lies and compromises." She laughs sadly. "I used to be so much more idealistic."

Carol pours herself another glass of wine. "Well, you adored your father. He was a psychiatrist, so you thought they were gods. Then you saw him as he really was."

This assessment is so bluntly, unsparingly accurate that Xenia is taken aback. *"You* should have been the analyst," she says. "That was really insightful."

Carol beams. "But I've known you since you were a girl," she says.

For dessert Xenia bravely resists rum cake and zuppa inglese. Provocatively dowdy. Oh no. Has it really come to the point where she is *pleased* at a remark like that? Xenia wonders if she should cut her hair, wear it loose again, perhaps slightly shorter, start buying dresses in brighter colors. The other image was necessary when she was in her twenties, but now, she realizes, it's redundant.

Her father's new "girl friend," Ilka Kornberg, dresses stylishly. She is in her sixties, tall and bosomy, but she wears bright blue dresses with slits up the side and pantsuits with expensive-looking boots peeking out. Xenia knows she should be pleased about Ilka. Of the many women who descended on her father in the year after her mother's death, Ilka is the most like her mother: European, maybe ten years younger than he is, formerly married to a psychiatrist. "I know the ropes," as she put it to Xenia one evening. And her father is impossible, Xenia now thinks, unable to figure out if he always was and she never noticed or whether age and becoming a widower have gone to his head.

"I am *inundated* with women," he said in that first year after her mother's death. "I tell you, Xenishka, women are coming out of my ears. Letters, casseroles! The world is composed entirely of lonely widows and they all want a part of me. I feel I should have myself cut into tiny pieces and give something to all of them."

"It must be nice to feel so popular," Xenia said dryly. Dr. Szengi was seventy-eight then and hardly an Adonis. It seemed absurd that Carol should have no one and her father be "inundated."

"I tell you, I thought I understood women, to the extent any man can," her father said. "But now I don't know. I feel I have to wipe the slate clean. Today a woman your age, in her forties, thirties, perhaps, made a pass at me. I said, 'My dear child, I am old enough to be your grandfather. Not just your father.' What can a woman like that want with an old geezer like me?"

"I have no idea," Xenia responded bluntly. It seems to her that her manner toward her father is very different than it once was. But he hardly seems to notice.

Her father still sees patients in the mornings, but he retired from the hospital ten years ago. He and Xenia's mother moved to a condominium in New Jersey. "A dangerous place," he says, "crammed with widows. One I had to turn away. She brought sweetbreads. 'My dear lady,' I had to tell her. 'I cannot eat offal.' She returned two hours later with chicken!" He laughed delightedly.

"Why do they have so much free time?" Xenia asked.

"Most of them never worked, they play cards, their grandchildren live far away. I have a nightmare that they will raffle me off in one of their card games and that, in the dead of night, I will awaken to find myself betrothed."

"Poor Poosh." Xenia can still put on her mock teasing tone with him.

"Do they want my body or my soul?" he went on. "That is what I ask myself. The pleasure of my witty conversation? Are they enamored of my achievements? Tell me, what is it?"

"Daddy, there just aren't very many men around at your age." Xenia feels she has to try to pierce his smug self-satisfaction.

"You mean that's all there is to it?" He looked mock dismayed. "It isn't me? It would happen to any man my age?"

"Pretty much."

He shook his head. "No, I have to differ. Daughterly disdain is operating here. I compared notes with Wilfred Hamm, whose wife died ten years ago. He has no casserole ladies. He sits at home and translates Goethe, poor fellow. I thought of handing out his number to some of those forlorn creatures, but then I wondered. Would I be doing Wilfred a service or not? Isn't he happier with his memories of Elizabeth?"

"Probably he is," Xenia said, annoyed. Does she feel if her father remarries he will be betraying her mother? Is it just Oedipal jealousy? But he's so absurdly vainglorious about it all. When she calls him to arrange a meeting, he says impishly, "Let me check my social calendar. I'm a busy man these days, you know."

What strikes Xenia is how startlingly like her mother Ilka is. If her parents had been divinely happy, she would find this comprehensible. But her father has found a woman who seems just as disdainful of psychiatry as her mother (her husband had affairs with patients, she told Xenia; she has "seen it all, and then some"). Like Mrs. Szengi, Ilka was a smoker, but has given it up and now eats mints that she always carries in her handbag. Xenia would not have been surprised if some mistress had turned up, some woman no one had known anything about with whom her father had had a long liaison. But evidently no such woman existed.

This evening Dr. Szengi announces that he and Ilka will be married in the fall. Ilka is sitting in an armchair, looking either smugly or radiantly happy, depending on how charitable you want to be.

"Aren't you going to congratulate us?" he asks, seeing Xenia's mixed feelings as clearly as if she had spoken.

"Why marriage?" she asks. "You both were miserable in your other marriages. Why get into that again?"

"Miserable?" Dr. Szengi looks astonished. "How can you say that? Magda and I had a complex, intricate relationship, but we—"

"You never *spoke* to each other," Xenia reminds him. "You didn't like any of the same things."

"This is your point of view," he says in that condescending voice it seems to her he uses all the time now. "I feel I got all that I bargained for. And now, at almost eighty, do you think I don't know my own mind?"

"It's nothing against *you*, Ilka," Xenia says apologetically. "I just think . . . why do it?"

"Why not?" Ilka says philosophically, popping a mint into her mouth. "It's not so much fun living alone. For you it's different, darling. You're another generation."

"She's miserable," Dr. Szengi puts in, derisively. "Look at her! *She* doesn't like living alone."

Xenia is furious. "I *do* like it," she says. "I'm perfectly content."

"No men," he goes on, mocking. "You allow yourself to gain weight, you've become grumpy. . . . Where is the charming young daughter I used to have? Gone, gone with the wind."

Xenia is stung. She is afraid he is right. But it seems cruel to make such remarks in front of Ilka, who is, after all, not even her stepmother yet. "I've joined Weight Watchers," she mutters. "I've lost five pounds."

"Bravo!" Dr. Szengi says.

"And I bought three new dresses today. Orange, red, and shocking pink."

"Wonderful," says Ilka. "You look so middle-aged. You need to—"

"She needs a man," Dr. Szengi says, shrugging. "It's unnatural, living alone."

"I *have* a man," Xenia snaps. "I just don't care either to live with him or marry him."

"Why not?" Ilka asks, surprised.

"He's married already," Xenia says, looking away. "Well, separated, actually."

Dr. Szengi comes over and takes Xenia's face between his palms. "My little puss, take him. He's yours. The poor man is miserable, caught between wife and mistress. Put him out of his misery."

"Daddy, it's not *like* that," Xenia says, flaring up again. "He's not caught. He's—"

"He *doesn't* want to marry you?" asks her father.

Xenia sighs. "Yes, he says he does, but the fact of the matter is he hardly knows me."

Dr. Szengi snorts. "The fact of the matter! What is all this with facts? Marry him! We'll have a joint wedding. You can't be outdone by your eighty-year-old father, can you?"

"I don't consider it 'outdone,' as you say," Xenia says, stiffly. "And my memories of marriage aren't as glowing as yours appear to be."

"But you were a child!" Dr. Szengi exclaims. "You married your childhood sweetheart. Such things never last."

"He wasn't my childhood sweetheart," Xenia says. Oh God, why is he being so impossible! "I met Jay in college, when I was *seventeen*."

"He was your first lover. What grounds for comparison did you have?"

Has her father forgotten everything they used to talk about in those days?

"I had many lovers," Xenia says haughtily. Hard as it may be to imagine now. "I didn't marry Jay for sex."

She returns home weary and disgruntled. Who has changed, she or her father? He used to seem so warm, so insightful, so wry. Now he seems condescending and interfering and even cruel. Who is he to say she should lose weight or dress differently or get married? What does *he* really know of her life?

But it's true, she was amazed when, a week after she had gone to bed with him, Pierson Beales called and said, his voice jubilant, "Xenia? I've left my wife. . . . I wanted you to know."

"But you've been married twenty-five years," Xenia said. "Please don't—not for me."

"For *me*," he said. "Can I do it for me?"

"I like you," Xenia explained. "I want us to be friends and even sleep together, but I'm not wife material. I'm a workaholic. I don't know how to cook. When I boil eggs, I leave them in so long they turn brown. Once they even hit the ceiling and splattered."

"I, on the other hand, am wonderful at boiling eggs," Pierson said. "You could search the world over and not find anyone better than I. I'm *not* a workaholic. Perhaps I should be, but I never was and I don't intend to start now. If I may say so myself, I think I was even a decent husband. B-minus, C-plus, anyway. Even Margaret might say so, if you asked her on the right day."

"You're deserting her," Xenia said. "After years of raising your kids, tending to your needs."

"She pitched me out," Pierson said. "She says she wishes she'd done it years ago."

Sally has a theory that men never leave their wives. They just become so impossible that their wives finally tell them to leave as an alternative to madness. Nonetheless, Xenia is startled, a day or two later, to receive a phone call from Pierson Beales's wife, Margaret.

"He says you're worried that you're a home wrecker," she says. "Forget it. I feel like I'm on my honeymoon, I've never been happier. Why didn't someone tell me about this twenty years ago? I never cook, I can watch TV instead of going to those ghastly early music concerts at the Met."

"I'm not as involved in this as you think," Xenia stammers. "We hardly know each other, actually."

Margaret snorts. "He was ready to fall from the tree," she says. "You just shook it and, plop, there he is at your feet."

"He's *not* at my feet," Xenia says, horrified at this analogy. "I'm like you. I love living alone. I've lived alone all my life. I don't want to change that."

"Then don't," Margaret advises. "Don't feel sorry for him either. He'll find someone else in a second. He's a nice guy, nothing hideously wrong with him."

"B-minus, C-plus?" Xenia suggests.

"Right. Compared with most of them out there, not bad at all. Just don't feel pressured."

"I don't," Xenia insists. Who said she did?

She has an awful feeling that maybe this is some game Pierson and Margaret play every five years to spice up their marriage. She pitches him, he proposes marriage to some new woman, then they make up. The "other woman" gets shafted, as always. She explains her theory to Pierson when they are in bed. This time, the second time, it's been good, which, as Xenia knows from years of experience, means nothing except that one will be in a state of mild dementia for several days and should not do anything even as risky as crossing the street against the light.

Pierson is lying naked, contented. He's a little plump himself, Xenia is glad to observe, but also muscular from years of squash and tennis. "You really think we would do this many times?" he asks, horrified. "Then your marriage must have ended extremely pleasantly. You obviously have no idea how painful it is."

"Of course I do!" Xenia says. "It's hideous. . . . But I thought Margaret was so happy now that you're gone."

"Only *because* we were miserable," Pierson says. "Twenty-five years, my dear! That's a long time to be at each other's throats."

"Then why—" Xenia begins.

"Children."

"Oh, I *hate* that," Xenia exclaims. "For the sake of the children! That's such a dodge. With parents screaming at each other every second. Do you really think your children didn't know?"

"First of all, we weren't screaming every second. It was more a cold, repressed kind of rage on both sides. And sure, they knew. It was for *us*. Don't you think parents want a family too? A lot of couples stay together because of the pleasure that gives them, not their children."

Xenia looks at him, trying to cling to detachment. "Well, I wouldn't know, never having had any."

He reaches out and strokes her shoulder. "You and your ex-husband never had any desire to have children?"

"We were just in our twenties," Xenia says evasively. "I was in medical school. It would've been . . ." She looks up at him. "I got pregnant and had an abortion without telling him. It was toward the end."

He looks at her without saying anything.

"Okay, well, give me your masculine diatribe on how unnatural and vicious that was to him, the poor old husband, not even knowing. Go on!"

"I wasn't going—" Pierson begins.

Suddenly Xenia is livid, way out of proportion to what they are talking about.

"I don't *want* children," she says. "I didn't then and I don't now. So if you're looking for some little broodmare to start a new nest, forget it, okay? I'd even be a rotten stepmother. I'm *awful* with kids. They cringe when they see me."

"I thought some of your patients were adolescents," Pierson points out calmly.

"Oh, I'm wonderful with my patients," Xenia says, sardonically. "That's the story of every shrink's life. That's the easy part. Give me a couch and a reclining chair and I become all-knowing."

He kisses her nipple. "Actually, I don't want another family," he whispers. "Do you believe me?"

"I don't know," Xenia says, already ashamed and a bit amazed at her outburst.

Although he makes love to her tenderly and forgivingly, she doesn't come. She doesn't want to, even. Good sex melts the brain. That has happened to her too often to be advisable again. She feels herself drawing close, then sinking back.

"Shall I caress you?" he asks when he has withdrawn.

"No, I'm fine," Xenia says, but quietly, disappointed and puzzled at her mixture of feelings.

She stares at the ceiling, thinking, for some reason, of Jay, of the day he proposed to her in front of the Cathedral Market, of their going back to his hotel room and eating peaches, making love. Nothing has ever been that silly and romantic and impulsive in her life since. She's done inadvisable things with inappropriate people, but not with that giddy sense of abandon. Should she be glad? "I wonder if Jay's happy," she says.

She isn't even sure she's spoken aloud, but Pierson says, "Who's Jay?"

249

"My ex-husband. . . . I haven't seen or heard from him in years."

"Would you like to?"

Xenia wonders. "Yes, I guess I . . ." What she thinks is that she would hate to see Jay happily married while she is still single. Why? Some old competition still between them, at least in her mind?

"We were babies," she says. "Only seventeen when we first . . ."

"My wife and I weren't that young," Pierson says. "I was twenty-five, she was twenty-three. We were both virgins, though."

Xenia is amazed. "At twenty-five?"

He looks abashed. "It was a different era."

"Yes, but that different?"

"I was extremely awkward with women. I gazed from afar, didn't know what to say. . . . Margaret's awkwardness appealed to me. We seemed well matched." He laughs dryly. "We were a little too well matched."

Xenia pursues the matter. "But you did it once you were engaged? Just to see—"

"No, we didn't. We fooled around a little, but . . . We were both from the Midwest. We didn't grow up the way you did, with sophisticated parents. My father would have shot me if I had—"

"I always thought in the country people did it at fourteen with sheep and half-wit sisters and that kind of thing," Xenia says, feeling sleepy and contented in the warm, dimly lit room.

"Have you ever been west of New Jersey?"

"Sure," Xenia says. "I've even milked a cow. Don't country people grow up in a terrible earthy, natural way, watching animals mate behind the barn?"

"Possibly on farms," Pierson says. "The Midwest has a few cities too. Were you aware of that?"

Xenia frowns. "Chicago?"

"That's one of them. There are several more, amazingly enough."

Suddenly Xenia feels depressed again. "But you're the one who turned out normally," she says. "What good did all that supposed European sophistication do if, at forty-two, I'm just a dumpy, provocatively dowdy, quote unquote, shrink, who hasn't even done her part in propagating the species?"

"Who turned out normal?" Pierson asks indignantly. "I protest! Margaret and I are as fucked-up as they come."

That doesn't impress Xenia. "But you did the right thing—married, hung in there, had kids you adore, and—"

"You mean, only New York Jews are allowed to be neurotic?"

"You were never in analysis, were you?"

"Sure, we both were. . . . Not that I think it did a huge amount of good, I'm sorry to say. I don't mean to malign your profession."

"Oh, feel free!" Xenia says cheerfully. "Malign away! . . . Didn't it really do any good at all?"

"Well, it gave us ammunition for fights. 'You're frigid because your mother was . . .' Or, 'You're a wimp because your father never . . .' We became a lot more deftly vicious. But was that worth fifty thousand?"

"Some might say it was," Xenia says. She isn't going to change jobs and she dreads becoming the kind of person who is always making fun not only of herself as a person, but of the profession to which she belongs.

Later, looking at her round, rosy face and plump, only slightly dropping breasts, in the mirror, Xenia thinks: It's spring. I'm allowed, at any rate, to fall in love.

In June there's a retrospective show of Susan's photos at the Museum of Modern Art. It's the third anniversary of her death. Pierson is out of town on a business trip; Xenia attends the opening with Carol. They separate almost at once. Carol is soon surrounded by friends. Xenia, looking around, realizes she knows no one here. It's strange seeing Susan's photos all around the room, beautifully enlarged. Xenia has seen most of the photos. She still has one framed above the couch in her office. But Susan's work, like Susan, was always private, and now there's this huge public display. It would have happened anyway, even without her death. What would that have been like? Xenia imagines Susan's confusion and embarrassment. She would hover in one corner with Xenia, making mocking remarks.

Xenia stands to one side, watching the people as well as the photos, pleased for Carol, who is radiant. She looks up when she hears a familiar voice.

"Xenia?"

"Con, my goodness! How wonderful that you're here. I don't know a soul." She is surprised at her excitement and delight in seeing him.

He looks different, his blond hair gray. He's grown a beard, neatly trimmed. He's still thin, still handsome, but—should she be surprised at this?—middle-aged. "Our gallery gave this same show two years ago," he says. "We've been working toward having it in New York."

"Do you think Susan would have been glad?"

"Yes, I think so. . . . Maybe not about all this"—he gestures toward the crowd—"but to be recognized, yes. I think she wanted that like anyone."

Xenia knows Conrad has a gallery in Paris and that he is living with another man: Susan told her. But, she realizes, that's about all she knows.

"Would you like to take a walk in the park," she suggests, "or do you feel you have to stay around? We can come back later, before it's over."

"I'd love to walk," Conrad says. "All this cigarette smoke. Let's try and push our way out."

She follows him through the crowd, and they walk to Fifth Avenue. It's overcast, but warm. Xenia is wearing a new dress and open-toed sandals. A month earlier she cut her hair, for the first time since she was twenty. It's shoulder-length, streaked with gray. Compared to the way she felt during the winter, it seems to her she looks sexy and attractive; but then she realizes Conrad hasn't seen her in years and must be as appalled as she was to see him changed.

"Do you ever paint?" she asks. "I would think, with running an art gallery—"

"No, not really. I know some people can convert a former passion to a hobby, but I wasn't one of them. . . . How about you? Still seeing patients?"

"I don't have much choice," Xenia says. "It's all I've ever done."

She hasn't meant to sound snappy, but he says, "Do you wish you *did* have a choice?"

"I feel a bit at a crossroads," she admits. "But I suppose I'll slog on. I don't think I'm doing harm to anyone."

He looks puzzled. "Why should you do harm?"

"I thought—" She hesitates. "I thought you felt psychiatrists were harmful." It was Susan who described the incident with Conrad at the hospital. Xenia feels it may have been tactless to refer to it, even indirectly.

But Conrad just brushes it aside. "I haven't had anything to do with them in years," he says.

Xenia looks up at him. Pierson is five feet nine; she's not used to gazing at someone six feet four. Though she feels perfectly natural with him, Conrad still has that slight aloofness that makes her reluctant to ask anything personal. "Do you hear from Jay, ever?"

Conrad smiles. "Yes, he's quite a family man now."

Xenia's heart starts thumping rapidly. "Really? What do you mean?"

"Well, Allegra's kids from her first marriage and then the twins . . . and a new addition as of a year ago, a kind of final shot, as it were."

Xenia is horrified. "My God. . . . All his?"

"Yes, father of five. Amazing, isn't it? I must say he seems to relish it."

Xenia tries to conceal her feeling of—what is it? envy? anger?

"I hope she—whatever her name is—is wealthy. How will they manage otherwise?"

"I gather her first husband was extremely well off," Conrad says calmly. "I admit I don't envy them, myself."

"I think it's terribly irresponsible," Xenia rushes on, "bringing such a horde of children into the world. Don't they have any sense of social responsibility?"

Conrad looks taken aback at this outburst. "I don't think they expected twins," he says. "And I think Jay wanted the experience of raising his own. Hers were teen-agers when they married."

"Is she older than he is?" Xenia asks, hoping she is.

"Our age, I think, roughly. . . . You never had any, then, I gather? I forget if you're married. I'm sorry. Susan may have mentioned it."

"No, I'm not," Xenia says, trying not to sound defensive. "I—well, I suppose I could have. People have asked me to marry them but—" Why is she doing this? Because she is afraid he will think of her as an old maid, alone because no one wanted her? Why does she care what Conrad thinks? He was never that judgmental.

They walk slowly through the park. People are jogging, strolling, walking their dogs. The magnolia trees have begun to open, the forsythia is in the past.

"I don't have any either," Conrad says. "I live with someone, but we don't especially want further complications in our lives."

Xenia wonders why he is so circumspect about referring to being gay, especially with her, whom he's known for years, even if not consecutively. "Yes, I totally agree," she says.

"Are you . . . with anyone?"

Two months earlier Pierson moved into her apartment, but Xenia still feels uncertain about announcing this to the world. "Yes, well, in a manner of speaking," she says.

"Which manner?" Conrad asks with a smile.

Suddenly it seems silly to Xenia to be so uptight with Conrad after so many years of friendship. They were even lovers once, unlikely as that now seems. "He's a fifty-year-old banker from Michigan," she says. "He's been married twenty-five years. I suppose to him it's all normal. Whereas I've lived alone for so long I can't quite get used to the presence of another person. I don't know if I like it, if I want it to be permanent. It's not a matter of children. I'm too old for that. I just don't know. . . . How long have you lived with your . . . friend?"

"About eight years." Conrad smiles his warm, appealing, but still slightly distant smile. He's carrying his jacket over one arm. "It doesn't sound like a long time when one thinks of our parents and their marriages."

"Are yours alive?"

"My father died in 1978 and my mother last year. How about yours?"

Xenia explains about her mother and her father's possible re-marriage. "He wants it to be a joint wedding! I thought that was rather obscene, actually. . . . Don't you think it's horribly tacky, remarrying at eighty? What's it for?"

"My mother did," Conrad says. "Why shouldn't old people have a love life? We'll want one when we're that age."

Xenia makes a face. "Will we? How scary! I was hoping I would drift into a kind of genial celibacy at around seventy."

"Sounds deadly."

She laughs. "Yes, I guess it does." She thinks of the night of the prom, Conrad going to sleep so early with her father's pills to knock him out, her making love to him in the middle of the night. I must have been so brave then, not being held back by Conrad's detachment. Or had she wanted to rescue him, to bring him to life? It's so long ago Xenia can't remember. She does remember being in the kitchen with her mother and Susan, washing up.

"I miss Susan," she finds herself saying suddenly.

"Yes," Conrad says. Meaning he does too or he understands her sense of loss?

"I don't have any friends that I feel close to in that way," Xenia says. "Colleagues and friends to talk to, but . . ."

"Maybe those early friendships are a trial run for what one has later, living with someone one loves," Conrad says. "What I mean is, maybe no one has both simultaneously."

"Is the person you live with . . . is it the way you used to feel about Jay?" Xenia asks, hoping he won't mind this intrusion.

"A little." Conrad laughs. "They both have that impetuous, more intense quality. I think they both regard me as an old stick."

Xenia looks out across the water, at the ducks settling on it. "I think Jay always admired you a great deal—your background, your polish, as it were. He was always so ashamed of his family."

"I don't see why," Conrad says. "What did my background give me, really, except a feeling of not belonging? When I visited Jay there was such warmth and liveliness, everyone yelling and rushing around. My parents were happy, but they were so stiff."

"He felt ashamed of his family's poverty, his father's failures," Xenia goes on. "That meant a lot to Jay. He was afraid he'd never escape somehow." She looks up at him. "Should I get married, do you think?"

Of course Conrad has no basis on which to make such a judgment, but he says, "Sure. Marry! How bad can it be?"

Xenia smiles grimly. "Pretty bad, as I recall."

"You were so young then." He hesitates. "I like being part of a permanent setup."

Xenia keeps staring at him, fusing the way he looks now with the way he used to look. "What makes you know it's permanent?"

"No one ever knows for sure. . . . But I think it is. We've been through a lot."

Wondering if this is going too far, she asks, "Is it monogamous?"

"Basically," Conrad says. "But, well, Dale's younger, and I suppose from time to time . . ."

"But you'd forgive him?"

"Yes,"

"I think Pierson would expect that I'd be faithful. I doubt if he'd be that forgiving. Not that I haven't done my share of fooling around. You just never know if you'll miss it once it suddenly becomes forbidden."

"So, you'll do it and not let him know," Conrad says easily.

"You don't feel that's very wrong, that kind of deception?"

"No. . . . But perhaps I'm different."

"I would want to try being faithful," Xenia says. "That isn't

255

what holds me back. I just haven't seen very many happy couples. The patients I've seen over the years—"

"Surely you can't judge by them," Conrad says. "They're disturbed or they wouldn't come to see you."

"I wish I thought that," Xenia says. "Actually, I don't think there's much difference between people who go into analysis and people who don't."

Conrad smiles. "I don't either. I thought you'd have to or the whole thing wouldn't make much sense."

"It doesn't always make much sense to me," Xenia admits.

Back at the museum, as Conrad is leaving, Xenia says, "Would you send me Jay's address? I haven't been in touch with him in such a long time."

"I'm sure he'd love to hear from you," Conrad says.

On the morning of the day on which they agreed to go to city hall and get married, Xenia wakes up with a headache. She takes a cold shower and dresses in black. When Pierson comments that she looks lovely, she snaps, "Do I look dowdily provocative enough for you?"

In the cab on the way down, she stares morosely out the window, beyond conversation or even inner debates about whether she is doing the right thing. Finally, Pierson reaches over and takes her hand.

"We don't have to do this," he says softly. "There's no law saying we have to get married."

"We can't turn back now," Xenia says, giving him a dark glance.

"Sure we can. . . . We can go back home and live happily in sin forever after."

"That's too easy," Xenia says. "That's a dodge. We're not kids. We have to go through with it. Then we can live unhappily ever after."

"I don't know about you," Pierson says, "but *I* intend to be happy."

"Good luck," Xenia says.

She knows this is absurd and disgraceful. She has acted badly before, but never, so far as she can recall, quite so childishly and spitefully. "You don't seem to have learned anything from past experience," she says.

"On the contrary," Pierson says. "I've learned enough to know that there's no need to make yourself miserable. Life takes care of that soon enough."

Xenia turns on him. "Please don't be cheerful or wise or urbane."

"I don't know," he replies. "I think two surly, disgruntled people on their way to get married might be a bit much."

He seems to be totally disregarding the fact that he's marrying *her*, that he's marrying an impossible person. He's acting as if he were any other middle-aged man who had found "new happiness" with a younger woman, and they were bouncing off to a fresh start. Xenia wishes there were hideous secrets about her past that she could spring on him now—family skeletons, breakdowns, other husbands. But unfortunately he knows just about everything.

Even the children have not been much of a problem—have, in fact, conspired to *not* put impediments in their path. His married daughter took Xenia aside and whispered, "I want to thank you. . . . I've never seen Dad so happy." His two sons seemed ill at ease at first, but then friendly. "Your children seem fine," Xenia said after she met them. "How *can* they be if you were so miserable?"

"There are inner scars," Pierson said. "You don't know them that well yet."

If they were young, preteens, Xenia feels, she would have backed off instantly. But there is something comforting about children who are, in fact, no longer children, whose hangups are firmly set in place. His son, Elton, who went to a psychiatrist once, asked, "Do you always try and figure people out when you meet them?"

"Sort of," Xenia admitted.

"What do you think of us?"

"You seem like pretty nice kids," Xenia said.

"I used to deal drugs," he boasted.

"I know," Xenia said. "Your father told me."

"Kitty's the smart one," he went on, "and Mickey is the well-balanced one. I'm the oddball. Like Dad."

"I like oddballs," Xenia said. But to her they didn't even seem that odd.

"Dad's very intellectual," Kitty informed her. "He needs someone who reads, someone to talk to about stuff like that."

"I don't read that much," Xenia said. "I don't have much free time."

"I think you're sort of like this woman he almost married," Kitty said. "Damaris Bates. Before he met Mom, I mean. . . . But he got scared. He thought he couldn't keep up with her."

Now, in the cab, Xenia says, "Maybe you should've married Damaris Bates."

Pierson looks at her. He's still holding her hand. "Despite her family money and her speech impediment and the fact that her mother told me she didn't even believe in sex after marriage?"

"Mere trifles," Xenia says.

"You could have stayed with Jay," he points out.

"No," Xenia says, "I couldn't. We drove each other crazy." Though she has said and thought otherwise at times.

"Damaris and I would've driven each other crazy," Pierson says, "*and* she wouldn't have been a good mother."

"Neither would I," Xenia says.

"You're too old to have children."

"Oh great. You mean if I wasn't too old, you wouldn't marry me? You know I'd be a lousy mother, but now that you've been married once to someone who threw her whole life away raising them, you can go on to someone who has a fine mind, quote unquote?"

Piersons kisses her gently on the nose. "Xen, let's take a vow of silence till the ceremony is over? Unless you truly want to go home and forget about it?"

"Okay," Xenia agrees.

Thus it is that her next words are "I do." Pierson takes her by the shoulders and kisses her firmly, his lips barely parted. "Hope springs eternal" goes through Xenia's mind. She touches the gold band on her left hand. Pierson is wearing an identical one. They go to a nearby bar and each orders a glass of champagne.

"Will this make my headache go away?" Xenia asks.

"Definitely."

She sighs. Some of her dark mood is fading, leaving her tired and uncertain. She looks down at her dress. "Wearing black to a wedding is tacky," she says.

"You look beautiful in black," Pierson says. "Limpid."

She has not told her father she was getting married. This is because she wasn't sure she mightn't, at the last minute, back down. But, returning home, after they make love and Pierson is in the shower, she calls him. It's four, he will have just emerged from seeing his last patient.

"Daddy, hi, it's Xenia," she says. "Guess what? I just got married."

"To who?" he asks.

Xenia is furious. "To Pierson, of course," she snaps. "Who else *could* it be?"

"Well, my darling girl, I don't know all the ins and outs of your private life. For all I know, Pierson could be just a foil for some secret lover you've been afraid to introduce to me."

"He's not a foil," she says, amazed. "I love him very much. . . . Are you pleased? You've been nagging me about it forever."

"I am half pleased," Dr. Szengi says, "*and* half despondent. He isn't good enough for you, no one is. But at eighty a father must accept that the man who deserves his daughter doesn't exist."

"You said I was fat and disagreeable," Xenia reminds him.

"Just gentle teasing," Dr. Szengi says. "Were you taken in by it?"

"Oh Daddy," Xenia says. "Why are you so impossible?"

"Impossible?" He sounds amazed. "But here Ilka has just been singing my praises in honeyed tones. You must be mixing me up with someone else."

"You mean I could have had two fathers and thought it was just one?" Xenia says. "That doesn't sound likely."

"You remember me as I was," Dr. Szengi says. "Perhaps when you were younger, I appeared formidable and distant, but surely now in old age, you see that I'm just an old pussycat, led hither and yon by all the women in my life."

Pierson has come out of the bathroom and is drying himself with a towel.

"Do you want to come over and celebrate?" Xenia asks her father, "or doesn't a second marriage seem like an event worth celebrating?"

"All marriages, even ninth and tenth marriages, are worth celebrating," her father says. "The triumph of hope over experience."

Xenia smiles up at Pierson, who has just sat down on the bed beside her. "I'm trying not to be that cynical," she says to her father, looking at her husband's body with detached appreciation.

"Cynical?"

She is allowing herself as much happiness as she can take, blithe in the assurance that it will fade. Without that assurance, Xenia would be nervous. Unfortunately, one side effect of happiness is that she and Pierson have both gained ten pounds, Xenia having regained what she lost in the preceding year.

259

"I suppose now that I have you, I'll let myself go to seed," she says, hugging him, after an especially delicious and fattening dinner that evening.

"This is temporary," Pierson says. "Anyway, you look voluptuous and enticing with a few extra pounds. I just look chunky, like a Toby jug."

"I'm afraid we both look like Toby jugs," Xenia says, patting his potbelly.

"I'll have to start chasing you around the bedroom," he says. "Put up more resistance."

Xenia sighs. "It's too late for that. Anyway, I was always a sucker for married men. You're just the only one I actually ended up marrying."

"I never felt that way about married women," Pierson confesses, "though I had a few who were extremely appealing. I always felt they were using me in relation to their husbands."

"Just what you were doing in relation to your wife," Xenia points out. "It's the classic male thing. You wanted someone's undivided attention but couldn't bear sharing."

"Am I that classic?" he says, aggrieved. He brings in the coffee and cream. "I thought I was a deviation from the norm. I read *Ms.* from time to time, I give money to female political candidates."

"Window dressing." Xenia says dismissively, pouring cream in her coffee. "I'm sure you know that's the easiest way to get someone in bed in the modern world."

He smiles. He is wearing a terry cloth robe and is barefoot. "You think I'm that calculating, do you? I thought I lured them with my impish charm and dry wit."

Xenia rolls her eyes. "Hey, we better get dressed. Daddy and Ilka'll be here in a second. We don't want them to catch us *in flagrante.*"

Dr. Szengi doesn't like champagne, so Xenia brings out slivovitz. He drinks from a tiny gold-rimmed glass, part of a set Xenia inherited from her mother.

"And next week you can drink to us," he says. "We wanted you to lead the way."

Ilka is sitting primly, her gorgeous legs crossed. She still wears high heels and shoes with delicate straps over the ankles.

Xenia says, "But Daddy, next week we'll be on our honeymoon. We're going to drive down the coast of northern California for ten days. It's the first real vacation I've had in years. Neither of us have seen California. Anyway, I never had a honeymoon the first time around."

"Of course you deserve a honeymoon," Dr. Szengi says. "Didn't you have one with that young fellow you were married to? What was his name?"

Xenia sighs.

"Jay. No, I didn't have one with Jay."

"Not in Europe?"

For some reason, Xenia blushes. "That was a pre-honeymoon."

Dr. Szengi smiles. "Those count too." He looks at Pierson, who is quietly contemplating the scene, as he tends to do in Dr. Szengi's presence.

Xenia wonders what her father thinks of Pierson. Jay, she knows, he regarded as a nothing, a nobody; and Jay, who was hypersensitive, sensed that and hated him. Pierson is infinitely less vulnerable to what Dr. Szengi thinks. Perhaps Dr. Szengi thinks nothing at all, is only concerned that, finally, Xenia is seemingly settled, will have financial security to some extent and companionship.

"I had a two-month honeymoon," Ilka says. "It was wonderful. We went to Paris, London, Vienna. . . ."

"But you were married during the war," Dr. Szengi says. "How could you do that?"

"We took our honeymoon at the five-year point," she says, looking dreamy. "By then we knew it would last."

"Such practical people," Dr. Szengi says.

Is he at all jealous, in retrospect, of Ilka's ex-husband, as she is of Margaret, with whom Pierson has occasional jocular-sounding conversations? Does any of that matter to him?

"Where did you and Mommy go," Xenia asks, "on your honeymoon?"

Her father looks at her. His eyes glaze. Xenia realizes he doesn't remember. He has these moments of forgetfulness, even about important things, which scare her, for fear of what they may lead to. "We had a very nice honeymoon," he says vaguely.

Does he even remember her mother that well? Once or twice he's referred to her by the wrong name. It's not as though he has negative memories, but it seems more frightening to Xenia that fifty years of marriage should just be wiped away by a gradual disintegration of the brain cells. Her parents' marriage is alive now mainly in her own mind, and even her memories are partial, incomplete. She never asked her mother anything about how she really felt about her life. Probably, if she were alive now, she wouldn't again, but she will always regret not asking.

Pierson's father died ten years earlier of a stroke, and his mother shortly thereafter. After their deaths, he said, more emotional attention was focused on his own marriage, and it couldn't stand the weight.

"Maybe if you had hung in there," Xenia says, "you would have gone on to a new stage." They are cleaning up after Ilka and her father have gone. "The way my parents seemed to."

"It's the 'seemed to,' " he says. "You only saw it from the outside. Many a marriage looks marvelous to the outsider. I take little account of that anymore."

Xenia doesn't think that's what she means. She doesn't think her parents' marriage ever looked marvelous from the outside, certainly not to her. But at the same time, the fact that they stayed together has affected her view of things, has made her have some nostalgic feeling about people who can ride through the bad times.

"I'd like to see Jay when we get to San Francisco," she says suddenly. "Would you mind?"

Pierson looks up with raised eyebrows. "Why should I mind?"

Later that evening Margaret calls. Xenia is in the bath, but she hears Pierson's end of the conversation. She knows Margaret is funny—but still, Xenia finds herself getting furious at Pierson's chuckles and once an outright hoot of laughter. He never laughs that much at anything *she* says. If they got along so well, why did they get divorced? Once she is out of the bath, he is off the phone and reclining on the bed, reading the paper.

"Who was that on the phone?" she demands.

"Margaret wondered if I could call her aunt in San Francisco as long as I was out there, just to tell her a few things."

"Why can't she pick up the phone and tell her herself?"

"Well, it seems more personal," he says, seeming unrepentant, "and I knew Sarah fairly well some years back. So why not, really? Do you mind?"

It seems petty to be jealous of an ex-wife's aunt. But Xenia knows it's not just that. She's jealous of his whole life, a kind of life she deliberately eschewed and probably would have hated if she'd had it, with family dinners and aunts and children. Is he really divorced when he and Margaret still have to consult about whether Elton should switch schools or Kitty name the baby this or that? She and Jay are *really* divorced. It was clean and bloody. They haven't been chatting on the phone for the past ten years about aunts and schools.

"I think you should make a clean break," Xenia says, pulling on her nightgown. She likes the sound of that phrase.

"We didn't have that kind of marriage," he says, looking up from his bifocals. "We don't hate each other in that emotional way people do when they split as kids. Besides, she's been a good mother. How can I hate her?"

"Then you should have stayed married," Xenia says, getting into bed. She turns away from him. "Or you should at least have the decency to have her call you at the office."

"The decency?" Pierson sounds amazed. "I thought it was more open having her call me here."

Xenia explodes. "I hate it! You sit there chuckling away, as though you were the best of friends. You may call that civilized. I think it's perverse."

Pierson sounds as if he is getting angry. "Then I'm civilized. I stand accused and plead guilty. . . . But I'm quite willing to let her call me at the office. I thought that would have overtones of, well, the other woman. And she *was* my wife, after all."

"Well, now we've changed places," Xenia says coldly. "I'm the wife and *she's* the other woman."

"Except Margaret and I aren't sleeping together," he points out.

"Oh, you probably will, in time," Xenia says. "You'll go over there and she'll be lonely and she'll ask you to help fix the drain or something and before you know it, nostalgia will lead to lust, and there you have it."

There is a pause.

"I'm hopeless at fixing drains," Pierson says.

Xenia doesn't reply.

"We both have pasts," he says quietly. "Different ones, but it's not *that* different. Why are we seeing Jay on our honeymoon, I might well ask?"

"I haven't seen him for ten years," Xenia says.

"Why see him at all? You don't have children in common. What's it for?"

She wants Jay to see her happy. She wants to flaunt her happiness. Maybe the weight of all those kids is dragging him down, maybe he's secretly miserable, maybe his wife is a ponderous nag and he thinks back warmly to the days with Xenia. Xenia turns around and kisses Pierson. "Well . . ." she says.

The trip down the coast of California is beautiful. They stop at small inns along the way, take hikes. Pierson gets up early to bird-watch. Xenia indulges in sleeping late and photographing especially dramatic views. She has the same camera she had in college, a Minolta autocord, the one with which Susan took those shots of Xenia, Conrad, and Jay in bed, mugging, which Xenia still has in an envelope in her desk. Susan will never meet Pierson, just as Xenia never met the professor Susan was in love with but wasn't certain if she should marry.

In her mind, walking alone on the shore, Xenia has an imaginary conversation with Susan, talks about what she hopes and fears about her marriage. She hears Susan saying, "Decide what you want, Xen. That's my trouble. I can't decide, or else I want irreconcilable things." "I wonder if when people get older they find these decisions easier," Xenia says. "It's so hard to imagine being middle-aged." Susan says, "Isn't it?" In Xenia's mind Susan isn't middle-aged. She's still slender, with boyish hips and those pale, almost translucent, blue eyes, the long eyelashes that she would never let Xenia coat with mascara. Maybe it's because Xenia knows she will see Jay that Susan is accompanying her on her honeymoon. Whatever it is, Xenia lets it happen and Pierson only occasionally asks why she is so dreamy and quiet. Actually, he confesses, it's a pleasant change.

When she calls Jay's number, a woman answers.

"Is Jay there?" Xenia asks. She and Pierson won't be in San Francisco for another week, but she wanted to call ahead.

"No, I'm sorry, he's out at the moment," the woman, who has a slight Southern accent, says. "Can I take a message?"

Xenia hesitates. "When will he be back?"

"I expect him back around dinnertime," the woman says. "Six or seven."

Southern. For some reason the knowledge or assumption that Jay has married a Southern woman pleases Xenia. At dinner, while Pierson is going over the wine list, she tries to imagine her. Didn't Conrad say they were the same age? A fading Southern belle, perhaps. Delicately pretty and blond when Jay met her, but already getting fine wrinkles around her eyes. Petite, possibly, but with that irritating baby-doll quality petite women often get in middle age. Gracious living. They eat by candlelight. Jay is bored. She nags him about not helping enough with the children. He's already cheating on her with one of his students, some idiot nubile blond. Stop! No! Why is she giving Jay an imaginary mistress, even if only to wreck his marriage? No, he's faithful, but only because he's too exhausted and harried with the financial problems of supporting five kids to think of cheating. They always do it in the same position. Southern Belle hates oral sex, she "allows" Jay to make love to her once a month and sighs with relief when it's over. . . .

". . . ought to be a good year?" Pierson is saying.

"What?"

"Why are you smiling?"

"I was having a lovely fantasy," Xenia says. "About how miserable Jay's marriage may be."

"Ten years seems a long time to bear a grudge," Pierson says. "Besides, I thought you pitched him."

"Women always pitch their husbands, because they make themselves so awful it's inevitable," Xenia says, mangling Sally's quotation.

"You weren't faithful."

"Neither was he." Xenia glares at him. "Why are you defending him? He made me miserable. He was a terrible, violent person. He made me cry all the time."

"Then why are we going to look him up?"

Xenia puts her head to one side. "Why are you so reasonable?"

Back at the hotel room, she calls Jay's number, while Pierson is in the bath. This time he answers.

"Jay? It's Xenia."

There is a pause. Surely he isn't about to say, "Xenia who?"

"Where are you?" he asks.

"In northern California . . . on my honeymoon." She is out of breath, appalled at the stab of pain that courses through her at the sound of his voice. "We thought we might visit you in San Francisco in a week."

"I never thought you'd marry again," Jay says.

"Why shouldn't I? *You* did. . . . I hear you have nine quadrillion children. I saw Conrad this past spring. He told me."

"They're marvelous," Jay says, sounding warm for the first time in the conversation. "Do you have any?"

"How could I?" Xenia says. "I'm on my honeymoon."

"Oh, that's right. . . . This is your first . . . You never married, remarried before this?"

"No, but Pierson has three grown children so I'm perfectly happy as a stepparent," Xenia retorts.

"I have two stepchildren," Jay says. "They're terrific, but it's not the same."

Why is he like this? Does he still feel he has to upstage her about everything? "Would you like to get together, then?" Xenia says, trying to sound cool and controlled.

"Yes, we'd love it. . . . How's Friday? You could come for lunch. Will you have a car?"

"Yes." Xenia takes down directions to their house. "We're having a very nice honeymoon," she says deliberately. "It's beautiful here."

"Yeah, I don't know how anyone can live in New York," Jay says. "I was back a few years ago and it seemed so incredibly filthy. To say nothing of—"

"To many people it's the most beautiful, exciting city in the world," Xenia exclaims, defensively. "Many people pity anyone who lives anywhere else."

"I guess there are more neurotics there than anywhere," Jay says. "Good for your practice. Or have you switched to another line of work?"

Another line of work? "Yes, I've run off and joined the circus," Xenia says. "That's how I met Pierson. He was a sword swallower." Not even if she is bound and gagged and sharp pins are shoved under her fingernails will she admit to Jay any dissatisfaction with her profession.

"Pierson?" Jay says, astonished.

"What about it?"

"What's his whole name?"

"Pierson Langley Beales."

"Just your average Jewish boy from the Lower East Side?"

"I thought it was time for a change. . . . I've decided Jews should never intermarry."

"Agreed. . . . Allegra isn't either."

Xenia isn't used to this kind of conversation, which, of course, in the past they had all the time—the quick repartee that switches from funny remarks to cruelty to put-downs with scarcely a pause for breath. She's relieved she can still keep her end up. "Pierson and I never had conversations like this," she says.

"Of course not," Jay says. "You make jokes and he laughs, right? He's a good listener."

"Is that so terrible?"

"Wait, let me imagine what he looks like. He's tall, six feet two, thin, graying hair, a distinguished air, older than you, family money, an excellent squash player, went to Princeton, drank too much in college, but is on the wagon now—"

"Stop!" Xenia cries, appalled at the accuracy of many of his guesses.

"Am I wrong?"

"He's five nine, not thin, no family money, and he went to the University of Michigan."

"What happened? Was he drinking in high school too? Lousy college boards?"

"He *comes* from Michigan," Xenia says, exasperated. Damn, this is what she didn't want to happen. Jay is setting the tone of the conversation. "That's where he *wanted* to go. How about Allegra? Shall I tell you what she's like?"

"Don't bother," Jays say blithely. "You'll see her in a week. You'll be wrong, anyway."

"I bet I'll be righter than you were about Pierson."

"Okay, write down what you expect on a piece of paper and show it to me after you come. You'll be dead wrong, I can assure you."

Xenia laughs. "You mean she's nice and actually loves you?"

Just as she is hanging up, still laughing, Pierson comes into the room, the same puzzled, aggrieved look on his face that she imagines she has when she hears him talking to Margaret.

"What was *that* all about?" he asks.

"Oh nothing. . . . Jay has a good sense of humor." Xenia apologizes. "But he can be a terrible pain. He's so competitive. With me, with you, even though he's never met you."

Pierson gets into his pale blue tailored pajamas. "What did you mean when you said, 'Pierson and I never have conversations like this'?"

"I just meant that kind of quick repartee, where each person keeps knocking the other person down verbally, and then tries to hold his own. It's exhausting, and it's stupid."

"I thought *I* had a good sense of humor."

"You do, sweetie. It's a different kind of humor, though. You don't try and annihilate people with it."

Pierson is gazing sadly out the window. "You haven't seen each other for ten years, and within five minutes you're relaxed and joking, even on the phone. I feel insanely jealous. . . . Is he handsome as well?"

Is Jay handsome? Of course Xenia can only think of him as he was in his twenties—wiry, scowling, intense black eyes, thick eyebrows, jutting lower lip. "It's more . . . If you're in love with him, he can *appear* handsome," she says cagily. "He's not intrinsically . . . Women like him, though. He can come on to them. I used to hate that, the way he did that at parties and God knows, while I wasn't there, I'm sure."

Pierson reaches over and takes her hand. "I can see why you hope he's not happily married," he says.

Xenia dresses carefully for the lunch at Jay's house, a high-necked, sleeveless red cotton dress, silver earrings. She's gotten a tan since they began traveling.

"I shouldn't have cut my hair," she says, suddenly despairing at the way she looks. Jay loved her long, thick, black hair. He used to play with it, stroke it, wash it for her. "Rapunzel, Rapunzel, let down thy hair," he would sing while he brushed it. But it's graying now and the thought of a mane of graying black hair didn't seem that appealing. You look intelligent, self-possessed, sophisticated, she tells herself. Oh, but why has she gained ten pounds? It seems to Xenia that if someone appeared and said that they would magically remove those ten pounds just for today on condition that she would have them for the rest of her life, she would agree in an instant, no questions asked.

And Pierson, whose looks she has come to love, suddenly appears plump and middle-aged and ordinary. She remembers how, when she first realized he would be her tennis partner, she had a pang of disappointment because she'd been hoping to meet a gorgeous tall man. "Ordinary" flashed dismissively through her mind as he asked if she preferred to play the backhand or forehand side. He has fair skin that hasn't tanned. He looks pink and lightly freckled, like a businessman on holiday. To make up for these unfair critical thoughts, Xenia hugs him, but continues thinking in the same vein as they drive up into the Berkeley Hills.

"What did you say his wife does?" Pierson asks while driving.

"Nothing, I imagine. . . . Five kids, after all."

"Five, goodness," is all Pierson says.

They park at the side of the house and are getting out of the car when Jay, with two small children tagging at his heels, emerges from the house. He's bald, totally bald! At this fact Xenia feels such an upsurge of delight that her self-confidence, which had seemed to ebb with every mile, rushes back. His body is still wiry, but he looks almost like a different person, his face longer and more severe. She goes over and hugs him.

"I look different, huh?" he says. "I gave all my hair away to charity. It was tax-deductible."

"This is Pierson," Xenia says, pleased beyond measure that Pierson has a full head of hair, gray though it is.

The two men shake hands.

"I'm delighted to meet you," Pierson says.

"Same here."

Jay glances up as a tall, slender black woman emerges from the house carrying a baby in her arms. "Allegra, these are . . . This is Xenia and . . . Pierson."

The same rush of delight Xenia felt a moment earlier recedes abruptly. Jay's wife is not only slender, but has that perfect posture Xenia has always observed with awe in other women. She's wearing white slacks and a white shirt, her dark, straight hair hasn't a streak of gray, she has beautiful, soft skin. Can she really be Jay's age? Her age? But it's not even her looks so much as her manner, which is so poised and even a little cool, despite the baby.

"You're on your honeymoon?" she asks.

"Yes, we're . . . Of course, it's our second honeymoon," Xenia babbles. "I mean, for us, as a couple, it's our first, but we both, we've both been married before."

Allegra smiles, a cool, self-possessed smile. "Yes, I know."

"Of course, we didn't have a honeymoon, did we?" Xenia asks Jay, trying to regain her self-esteem and composure. "I don't remember exactly."

Jay waggles a finger in the air. "Very significant. Ten days of mad, raving passion, and it's all blocked from her mind."

Despite herself, Xenia blushes.

The little girl who has been listening to the conversation says, "I went on a honeymoon with Daddy. We went to the beach."

Jay ruffles her hair. She looks very much like him—though, of course, she's not bald. "That wasn't a honeymoon, sweetie, that was a vacation."

The little girl frowns. "If you love someone and you go on a vacation with them, it's a honeymoon," she insists.

Her twin brother socks her. "Only if you're married!"

"So?" the little girl says. "He's married."

"That doesn't count."

Both Jay and Allegra are watching them with affection.

Allegra says, "Come on around to the back. I'll just set the baby in her carrier." Her Southern accent is soft, much gentler than it sounded on the phone.

They go around to the back of the house. There's a stone patio overshadowed by large trees, a small pond off to one side. Allegra sets the baby down in a screened carrier that is not much longer than the baby. Pierson leans down and peers into the carrier.

"What a lovely child," he says. "She's so quiet."

"Maybe by the fifth you get lucky," Allegra says, laughing.

"I only had three," he replies. After a second he adds, "From my first marriage."

Everyone here, Xenia thinks, has fathered or mothered a child, knows about babies, has secret connections the way people who grow up in the same family do. She feels barren, empty, unconnected to life except vicariously through her patients. "Are you glad you had five?" she asks in what she hopes is an ordinary voice. Does she sound petty, jealous?

"The fifth was a mistake," Allegra says, "but now that she's here, she seems to fit. I actually never thought I'd have children at all. I was the oldest of six and I spent so much time looking after my younger brothers and sisters that I didn't think I wanted to go through it all as an adult. But I guess my training as a dancer helped—I never had any trouble with the physical part, giving birth. It's the later part that gets to you, especially if you're trying to do something else."

"Do you still dance?" Pierson asks. Margaret and he loved ballet; their older daughter studied it for many years.

"No, I—I know this sounds like a rather abrupt switch, but I ended up getting a doctorate in analytic philosophy."

Xenia glances secretly at Jay. He looks proud, serene. What is this: rent-a-wife to impress your ex? He's ordered her from a catalogue. The minute they leave, she'll disappear into a box and the real wife, the faded, irascible Southern belle, will step out.

270

"You've developed your mind *and* your body," Pierson says. "A sensible combination."

Is he flirting? No, surely not, Xenia thinks. He's just being his sweet, decorous, urbane self. See? she thinks, darting a look at Jay again. I got a real man, a real grown-up. "Pierson and I met playing tennis," she says. "We try and keep in shape." Is everything she's saying a non sequitur or does it only seem that way because she's so self-conscious?

"You used to hate sports," Jay says, smiling.

"I'm still not very good," Xenia admits. Is she too plump to be wearing a red dress? In her mind she changes outfits rapidly.

"She has a remarkable backhand," Pierson says. "You never know where it's coming from."

He smiles at her so nicely that Xenia melts. Again she glances at Jay, hoping he appreciated this tribute to her skills. This time he catches her glance and smiles back, but wryly, as though to say he knows every thought that's in her head.

"Hon, why don't we have a drink?" he asks Allegra. "Some lemonade? Gin-and-tonic?"

"Why don't *you* get it?" Allegra says. "I want to keep an eye on the baby."

"*I* can keep an eye on her," Jay says.

Allegra gives him a long, cool glance. "Everything's all set up."

Reluctantly, Jay rises from his chair. Oh great, Xenia thinks. Family bickering. Mild, but still. . . . And good for Allegra, getting the upper hand.

"Men are so adept at being helpless," Allegra says.

"Tell me about it," Xenia says, liking her, forgetting her desire to hate her.

Pierson looks hurt. "I thought I helped a lot."

"Oh, I didn't mean you," Xenia says. "I mean men in general. Jay was always so—"

"I know!" Allegra says. "But compared to my first husband, he's marvelous, and that's about all the point of comparison I have, actually."

Meaning she's only slept with two men? Meaning she never fucked around or did idiotic things with married men who made her cry? Jay is carrying out the drinks on a tray.

"Xen has a lot of points of comparison," he says.

Xenia can't believe he would say anything that cruel in front of others. "Meaning?" she says, leaning forward.

271

At that point the baby wakes up and starts to scream. Allegra leans down and picks her up. She walks around, holding the baby against her. Jay fixes drinks for all of them. He raises his glass in the air. "To honeymoons!" he says.

"To second marriages," Pierson says.

"To Jay's book," Allegra says, waving a hand because she hasn't been able to sit down and get her drink.

"What book is that?" Xenia asks.

Jay looks disconcerted. "I just published a book of short stories with a university press," he says. "The first copy arrived yesterday."

"We'd love to see it," Pierson says.

Jay goes into the house and gets his book. He shows it to Xenia. *Coming of Age in Upper Manhattan and Other Stories.* She opens it and sees the dedication: "In memory of my father." Idly she glances down the table of contents. "I Want to Sleep." She looks up with a smile. " 'I Want to Sleep' is the one about me," she says, "isn't it?"

"Well, it wasn't really about you," Jay says sheepishly.

Xenia turns to Pierson. "When I was in med school, I was always falling asleep, often right while Jay was in the midst of some fascinating anecdote. So he got his revenge by writing this ghastly story about an awful woman who sleeps her whole life away and comes to a bad end."

"It isn't *that* bad," Jay says.

"Are you a writer?" Pierson asks. "I'm not that familiar with contemporary fiction, so excuse me if I don't know your name."

"Even if you were, you wouldn't," Jay says, looking down. He looks boyishly confused, more appealing than he's been so far. "I write occasionally, but to earn a living I teach journalism at SF State. That's where I met Allegra. She's in the philosophy department."

"I used to like your stories," Xenia says, looking through the book again. The print is too small, but the paper is good quality. "Are there any others from that bygone era?"

" 'Roaches,' " Jay says. "I don't think you ever read that one. It was after we—"

"Jay, people want fantasy in their fiction," Xenia says. "I don't think our apartment on a Hundred and Tenth quite fits the bill. By the way, it's all scaffolded up now. I passed it a few weeks ago."

Jay smiles at her for the first time with genuine warmth. "I wonder if the elevator is still so slow."

"You could practically marry and have a child just getting from one to ten, our floor," Xenia says to Pierson.

He is gazing at her carefully. Has she been talking too much? "One's youth is always so intense," he says.

How does he seem to Jay? Oh, why does she care? But she wants Jay to, if not approve, at least admire her choice. She wants Pierson not to sound stiff and boring, not to look like a banker.

But Jay is looking at Xenia when he replies. "Yes," he says wistfully.

After lunch Pierson sits down to read the twins a story, and Allegra goes in to nap. Jay glances at Xenia. "I could show you . . . There's a nice walk down the road, if you have the energy."

"Is that all right?" Xenia asks Pierson.

"Of course." He looks surprised that she should ask, and Xenia is not sure why she did. She and Jay are old friends who have things to catch up on that they might not want to bore the others with. Surely, one doesn't need permission for that.

Xenia thinks how comfortable and at ease Pierson looks reading to the twins, how both of them snuggle against him as he starts to read. He will make a wonderful grandfather, probably he was a wonderful father, but she didn't know him then and has to admit that, if she had, she wouldn't have given him a second glance.

Jay is walking ahead of her. He turns around and reaches for her hand. "It's a little steep here. Walk carefully."

It's not as though they were walking hand in hand, yet the physical connection stirs something in Xenia. It feels comfortable and right, just as sitting on the patio making idiotic chatter about their families seemed stiff and awkward.

"I like Allegra," she says, not even reluctantly.

Jay smiles. "Yeah, it's working. I guess we're more opposites. She doesn't explode the way I do. When she's mad, it's more the deep freeze."

"Same with us," Xenia says. "The first time I started screaming at him, Pierson thought it was all over. He actually turned pale gray. He and his wife were both the deep-freeze type."

"Sounds like a chilly marriage," Jay says. He is still holding her hand, though they've come out into a more open area.

"Now we each have a balance," Xenia says. "Maybe that's the key. We're both irascible, violent people, in our tempers anyway, so we need restraint." She hates the way she sounds, so phonily wise and mellow.

Jay is silent for a moment. Then he says, "Well, you never get everything."

Something in his tone catches at Xenia. "At times I hate being mature and settled," she says. "It all seems so dead. I even feel this crazy nostalgia for the time we spent together, yet at the same time it was so hideous. I felt that when I passed One Hundred and Tenth. Just a pang."

"Yes," Jay says.

"But we were horribly unsuited, and it's to both our credits that we . . . went on," she says, trying to return to her earlier detachment. "We didn't wreck each other's lives. I mean, I didn't turn you off women and you didn't, totally at least, turn me off men."

Jay drops Xenia's hand. "Listen, you did plenty," he says. "It took years. Maybe not for you. But a lot of women paid for the damage you did."

Xenia stares at him in amazement. "You just wanted to fuck around and now suddenly it's my fault? You broke the hearts of dozens of women, but it's all justified by: I was married to a bitch. That is absolutely the most hypocritical thing I've ever heard any-one say!"

Jay is staring at her, his eyes dilated. "I'm not talking about fucking around!" he yells. "I'm talking about horrible inner pain, torment, not believing anything would ever come right again. When I met Allegra, I was such a basket case, I was amazed she would even *look* at me."

"Why did she?" she asks scornfully.

"Because she saw through it to someone who had a lot to give, who could be terrific if someone believed in him, supported him, loved him, damn it, the way women are supposed to love men."

If Jay were half her height, Xenia thinks, she would knock him to the ground. "Are you writing pulp fiction now? 'The way women are supposed to love men'? I've never *heard* anything so idiotic. You don't want love. You want some groveling, blind animal who'll churn out babies. If that's what you call love, I really feel sorry for you."

"So, what's love, then?" Jay says, circling in front of her. "Making it with that poker-faced stiff who acts like he's been em-balmed? Is that fun? Is that sexy? Or is sex part of your scarlet past? Now you've settled for money and boredom and an occasional friendly fuck every few months."

"I've never *had* a better sex life," Xenia yells. "And believe me, I've looked."

"I believe you," Jay says with a smirk.

"Scarlet past!" she scoffs. "How about Betsy Myer? How about Christine Anderson? How about Maryanne Hoff?"

Jay looks rattled. "How did you know about Maryanne Hoff?"

"Because I read your stupid fucking journal," Xenia says. "Little checks for who was especially good in bed. What was the code? I forget. It was the most puerile, infantile misogynist thing I've read since Norman Mailer!"

"Hey, maybe I can use that as a blurb," Jay says with a grin. "I'm thinking of trying to publish it."

"Surely you jest," Xenia says, standing tall.

Jay looks right at her. "Yes, I jest," he says.

They walk on in silence.

"Why are we *doing* this?" Xenia says, more to herself than him. "I can't believe it. We're middle-aged, we have good marriages. . . . We're acting so childish and bitter."

"I guess because we still *are* childish and bitter," Jay says sadly, kicking a stone in the road.

"But I'm not normally," Xenia says. "It's only with you. I have to turn patients away. I get dozens of recommendations. Ask anyone."

"Should I ask Ralph Blumenthal?" Jay asks.

"He's dead, but otherwise, sure, ask him. . . . Look, ask Pierson. He says he's never been happier. He says his life began when he met me. How do you explain that? He says he knew the minute he saw me that he wanted to marry me."

She winds down breathlessly, waiting for his retort. But instead, Jay comes in front of her, takes her by the shoulders, and kisses her, a long, passionate kiss. Xenia's eyes widen.

"Is that an apology for everything you said?"

"No, it was just because I felt like it."

In her mind, she sees herself and Jay just walking on, he leaving behind five kids, she leaving Pierson ensconced on the couch reading *Where the Wild Things Are* to the twins. But the fantasy is just that: she and Jay walking endlessly into some never-reachable sunset, Allegra forever napping, Pierson never reaching the end of the story. No divorces or remarriages, no deserted husbands or wives or children. She tells Jay about her fantasy.

"I like it," he says. "It's nice, but—"

"It wouldn't work?" she finishes.

He nods.

They turn to go back to the house.

"Do you think we were naïve back then?" Xenia asks. "I know we didn't think we were, but when I look back, it all seems so fuzzy and idealistic."

"We graduated five months before Kennedy was assassinated," he says. "Another world."

Xenia thinks of Susan, her unfinished life. Susan hasn't been in her mind during this visit, but suddenly she's there, as she was so often when Jay and Xenia had their fights, watching them with incomprehension, but affection. She remembers one of Susan's photos, the donkey trotting through the desert, its mane illuminated by early sunlight.

"Maybe we better get back," she says. "They might begin to worry."

1·800·253·3360